Michael Della Penna, OFM, STD
with Preface by Murray Bodo, OFM

The Crucified Knight

The Spiritual Odyssey of St. Francis of Assisi
According to Henry of Avranches

TAU

The Crucified Knight

The Spiritual Odyssey of St. Francis of Assisi According to Henry of Avranches

Fr. Michael Della Penna, OFM, STD

Cover Photo: Stephen J. Binz
Cover and book design: Tau Publishing Design Department

For information regarding permission, write to:
Tau Publishing, LLC
Attention: Permissions Dept.
4727 North 12th Street
Phoenix, AZ 85014

ISBN 978-1-61956-288-2

First Edition April 2015
10 9 8 7 6 5 4 3 2 1

Published and printed in the United States of America by Tau Publishing, LLC, an imprint of Vesuvius Press Incorporated.

Text printed on 30% post-consumer waste recycled paper.

For additional inspirational books visit us at TauPublishing.com

TauPublishing.com
Words of Inspiration

Dedicated to my brother Mark
who inspired me to fight without fear.

Table of Contents

Preface

Crucified Knight. A knight crucified from within. What a stunning image that is! But such was Francis of Assisi whose whole life was that of a spiritual knight fighting his own demons, overcoming whatever would keep him from being a spiritual advocate and protector of those rejected or neglected by society, whatever would keep him from calling everything in creation his brother and sister. Such is the St. Francis who emerges in the pages of the second oldest hagiographical text about St. Francis, the so-called *Versified Life* of St. Francis by Henry of Avranches, renamed by Michael della Penna, *Crucified Knight, The Epic of St. Francis of Assisi.*

This epic poem, written in 1229/1220, was what I'd thought of as a mere versifying of Thomas of Celano's First Life of Francis. I thought that, not because I'd read it, but because that's what most scholars said it was. How wrong they and I were! What Della Penna has done for us, through his deep and extensive research, is to show how this early writing is an epic poem in its own right. And even though it follows the outline and original story written by Brother Thomas of Celano in 1227/1228, it has its own themes, its own hagiographical insights, and its own merits as a literary work.

I am amazed at how skillfully Della Penna has interwoven sources medieval and modern to open up this extraordinary poem. I have lived with his text for some time now, and for the first time, I see what Henry of Avranches was really about. His whole book is based on an early dream of Francis, the son of the merchant Bernardone, in which he saw a room whose walls were filled with shields, and when he wondered whose shields they were, he heard a voice saying that they were for Francis and his followers. And so Francis went to war twice in pursuit of that dream of knighthood, the first time ending up a prisoner of war in a Perugian prison, and the second time being told by God to return home to Assisi where it would be shown him what he was to do which, ultimately, was to repair God's house from within.

Even as Francis worked among the lepers and walked in the footsteps of the Crucified Christ, he never gave up his original dream of knighthood. He became a Knight of Christ, ending up in Della Penna's words, a "Crucified Knight." Everything in Henry's book-long poem advances that theme, as in Henry's icon of the stigmata of St. Francis:

> O soldier of Christ, you alone,
> Francis, bore the scars
> Of Life-triumph-in-death;
> hid in your soul when living,
> And displayed in your flesh when dying.

And again Henry writes,

> So does Jesus' passion remain implanted in his heart,
> So imprinted right though the marrow of his soul,
> That it cannot be hid, but must flood outwardly
> And mark its likeness on his partnered flesh,
> Becoming visible, as it were, through transparent limb.

It is as though Francis is already crucified from within, and so great is the love he has for Christ that what is within bursts forth in his flesh revealing that he is already a Crucified Knight.

I was amazed as I read parts of the poem at how brilliant is Della Penna's reading of the poem and how diligently he pursues his thesis by careful research of the aesthethics of the poem and of ancillary studies that contribute to a fuller understanding of how important such a study is.

Francis himself was a poet and wrote one of the great Italian poems in the Umbrian dialect, the "Canticle of the Creatures." That a long, epic poem should have been written in his honor and so early, three or four years after his passing in 1226, makes the poem in any case worthy of serious consideration as a poem and not simply as a versifying of the Legend of Thomas of Celano. And that is what Della Penna's book does: consider seriously this extraordinary epic of the Life of St. Francis.

What a delight it has been to read this book. For years I'd been looking for a text that would open up the world of the Troubadours and of Chivalry as they related to and determined the way St. Francis responded to God's call. He sang that call and he conducted himself like the ideal knight, a knight like St. George that the young Francis saw in a fresco at the school of San Giorgio where he attended school. All of this I suspected but could not find an early source that confirmed my vision of Francis.

And here it was along in the Versified Life of St. Francis by Henry of Avranches, which I had dismissed as a mere versifying of the First Life of St. Francis by Thomas of Celano, merely making Celano rhyme, dividing it into stanzas, prettifying and adorning Celano's already fine, rhetorical text.

I'm grateful to my confrere Fr. Michael Della Penna for all the deep and wide research he did and for writing this wonderful study of St. Francis, the Crucified Knight. This book adds another layer to all of the studies that have been done on St. Francis, and it reasserts and defends the place of poetry in the Franciscan story, beginning with Francis's own "Canticle of the Creatures." St. Francis himself called himself the Herald of the Great King, and he is certainly that. But he is also a Knight of the Great King, fighting those inner battles and righting those wrongs that contribute to repairing God's house, the Church itself.

This book opens up a whole new dimension of St. Francis for the reader who perseveres in reading this exciting story.

—Fr. Murray Bodo, OFM
Assisi, Italy

Abbreviations

AB	*Analecta Bollandiana*
AF	*Analecta Franciscana*
AFH	*Archivum Franciscanum Historicum*
FAED	*Francis of Assisi: Early Documents*
FS	*Franciscan Studies*
GR	*Greyfriars Review*
MF	*Miscellanea Francescana*
MHAIP	*Master Henry of Avranches as an International Poet*
MLPA	*Medieval Latin Poetic Anthologies*
MS	*Mediaeval Studies*
Ms.	Manuscript.

Sources

1C	*Life of St. Francis* by Thomas Celano
2C	*Remembrance of the Desire of a Soul* by Thomas Celano
3C	*The Treatise on the Miracles* by Thomas Celano
4C	*The Legend for Use in the Choir* by Thomas Celano
LV	*Legenda Versificata* by Henry of Avranches
AP	*Anonymous of Perugia*
L3C	*Legend of the Three Companions*
LJS	*Life of St. Francis* by Julien of Speyer
LM	*Major Legend* by Bonaventure
1MP	*Mirror of Perfection* (The Lemmens Edition)
2MP	*Mirror of Perfection*
AC	*Assisi Compilation*

Writings of St. Francis

Adm	*Admonitions*
RB	*Regula Bullata*
RNB	*Regula Non Bullata*

Introduction

> Put on the whole armor of God, that you may be able to stand against the wiles of the devil. For we are not contending against flesh and blood, but against the principalities, against the powers, against the world rulers of this present darkness, against the spiritual hosts of wickedness in the heavenly places. Therefore take the whole armor of God, that you may be able to withstand in the evil day, and having done all, to stand. Stand therefore, having girded your loins with truth, and having put on the breastplate of righteousness, and having shod your feet with the equipment of the gospel of peace; besides all these, taking the shield of faith, with which you can quench all the flaming darts of the evil one. And take the helmet of salvation, and the sword of the Spirit, which is the word of God.
>
> Ephesians 6:11-17

In the year 1205, Francis of Assisi had a dream in which he saw a vision of military arms and heard a voice say that these were for him and his soldiers.[1] Henry of Avranches, a thirteenth century Latin poet, believed this dream to be the key to understanding Francis, the pivotal event which not only revealed the nature of his conversion but also defined his entire life. Henry, therefore, in composing his *Legenda Sancti Francisci Versificata,*[2] a versification of Thomas of Celano's *Vita Prima,* used the dream as a hermeneutical lens to interpret Francis' spiritual odyssey. Could this eight hundred year old Latin manuscript, the second oldest existing account of the life of St. Francis really contain such an insightful but forgotten truth about him? If so, why has it been hidden for so long? Although the *LV* was once described as the "most popular and best loved version of Francis' '*gesta*', the life the friars preferred to hear,"[3] today, it is relatively unknown by modern audiences and is almost completely neglected by Franciscan scholars. There are several reasons for this. The initial decline in popularity may be attributed to a growing ecclesial critique against the secular ideals of knighthood;[4] not to mention the mandate of the General Chapter of the Order to destroy other earlier legends of Francis upon completion of Bonaventure's *Major Legend.* Moreover, many scholars concur with Paul Sabatier who is credited with initiating much of modern Franciscan scholarship, and assesses the *LV* in the following way:

> This work does not furnish a single new historic note. It is the Life by Celano in verse and nothing more; the author's desire was to figure as a poet. It is superfluous, therefore, to concern ourselves with it.[5]

This evaluation expresses two additional reasons why the *LV* may have been ignored for so long. The most obvious reason is the same one that Jean-Yves Tilliette postulates many verse biographies, like the *LV*, continue to be completely ignored by historians. He states they are simply marked by the fundamental flaw, that is, what he terms "the original sin," of being "reworkings of earlier prose texts"[6] and thus are not taken seriously but relegated as "mere" versifications. The other reason, the one especially perpetuated by scholars who use the historical critical method, contends that the *LV* does not contribute any "new" information or historic facts about Francis. Michael Bihl reiterates this position in the following way:

> It is clear that Henry of Avranches, in the Versified *Legend* of St. Francis, not only added no new facts to the *First Life*, but even if there were new additions to the facts, nowhere in his poem has he left a faithful and trustworthy record. He accounted these things not because he believed they were historical, but rather he added poetic flourishes and strove for harmony in his verses.[7]

Consequently, the *LV* has been consistently absent from most major critical studies and collections of sources for the life of Francis.[8] Despite either Raoul Manselli's appraisal that the *LV* is "a poem so far too under-valued"[9] and that it "has its own importance, much greater than commonly believed"[10] or Giuseppe Cremascoli's suggestion "to proceed in new and deeper studies"[11] which would interpret the *LV* within its literary context, most scholars continue to disregard it.[12] A good example of this can be seen in two critical studies of the sources of the life of Francis that epitomize general opinion of the *LV*. The first is Kenneth Baxter Wolf's *The Poverty of Riches*, one of the more recent Oxford studies in historical theology, which states Henry did not "add any information about the saint beyond what could be found in Thomas' official *Life of St. Francis*."[13] The second and more popular is Jacques Dalarun's *The Misadventures of Francis of Assisi*. After a brief consideration of the *LV*, Dalarun concludes that "the author knows nothing more than what is in the *First Life*" and "adds many useless details."[14]

On the contrary, this book specifically argues against both points. Firstly, as can be demonstrated from the corpus of his work, Henry certainly had knowledge of the Franciscans well before writing the *LV*, as will be seen later. Secondly, Henry's details, rather than being useless, are instead allegorical; they are pertinent artistic insertions, directly derived from his dream, that create a poetic icon of Francis as a new saintly hero. Henry in fact is the first to author a *Legenda* based completely on the dream that portrays Francis as a holy leader, a knight of Christ who leads his soldiers in the battle against the forces of evil.

Francis' dream itself has been the subject of several critical studies.[15] Few modern scholars affirm the importance of this episode more than Julio Micó, who assesses the impact of the dream on Francis in this way:

> His dream at Spoleto so changed his values and so broadened his horizons that it took him several years to realize the full implications of what had happened to him and to reorganize his life so that it was a coherent and sensible answer to the God who had transformed him with His presence.[16]

Medieval scholar Jacques Le Goff comments that Francis' nocturnal vision, which embodied his "chivalresque dream,"[17] not only "revealed how deeply this mode of feeling and self-expression had affected him"[18] but states that it "never completely vanished from his mind."[19]

Moreover, this heroic image of Francis is consonant with other contemporary authors and appears in subsequent *legendae* as well as in modern biographies by Hilarin Felder, Franco Cardini and Le Goff, who describes Francis as "a combination of knight of God, troubadour and jongleur."[20] Most impressively, Gilbert Keith Chesterton contends that of the three possible ways in which a sketch of Francis' life may be written, the best and most difficult of all is the one in which the writer places himself as an outsider and enquirer and recognizes:

> The first fact to realize about St. Francis is involved in the first fact with which his story starts; that when he said from the first that he was a Troubadour, and said later that he

> was a Troubadour of a newer and nobler romance, he was not using a mere metaphor, but understood himself much better than the scholars understand him.[21]

According to Chesterton's definition then, Henry as a non-Italian and a non-Franciscan is an "outsider and enquirer" who uses the "best approach" of telling the story of Francis, which seeks to understand his heroic life through his heroic dream.[22]

"Our truest life is when we are in dreams awake."
—Henry David Thoreau

According to Henry, Francis was a man who had a deep desire to become a knight and win worldly honor, riches, glory and fame. This desire, however, is redirected through his dream of arms, when Francis is shown weapons from heaven. While Henry uses his poetic license to color Francis and expand on different dimensions of his person, he substantially builds on the connection that Celano had already established between Francis' passion for military honor, glory and fame and his spiritual journey to God as *"miles Christi."* Henry does this by reworking the Celano material and extending the metaphor of the dream in such a way that it becomes a *leitmotif* of Francis' whole life. Henry, in other words, uses the dream as a paradigm to interpret Francis' spiritual experience.

Henry's icon of Francis as a crucified knight and new saintly hero not only represents an authentic image of Francis but also expresses a certain truth about his call. More specifically, Henry's interpretation of Francis emphasizes an important aspect about the saint's own self-understanding and the nature of his conversion. By focusing on the vision of arms, Henry portrays how Francis' inner desire for knighthood was transformed, purified and finally fulfilled in becoming a spiritual knight of Christ. In using the dream and its military motif as the controlling metaphor, Henry is able to develop other minor aspects of Francis that compliment and deepen the core icon.

Methodology

The choice of methodology for this study was guided by the conviction that hagiography, as its etymological roots indicate, is the study of "holy writings." As such, a valid interpretation of these "writings" must begin with a critical method of analysis, which uses scientific criteria to objectively assess the historical meaning. Following Cremascoli's observation that the *LV* "is above all the document of a literary experience and must be interpreted as such,"[23] this study addresses the various genres within the *LV*. The genre critique specifically studies the composition of the text in order to identify the historical development of different literary conventions and their influence on the *LV* within the actual social milieu in which it was written. This will not only include a form and source critique but also comparative inter-textual analysis. Since the purpose of hagiography however, does not lie in simply relating historical facts, one must recognize that they are not merely writings but "holy" writings and consequently must be understood as faith documents that present spiritual portraits of saints. A valid interpretation of these "holy writings" therefore must consider the spiritual sense or meaning.[24] Because hagiography was ultimately written to convey a spiritual message that edifies and inspires, it must be studied through the eyes of faith with the purpose of application or actualization for contemporary readers. This principle is well articulated by Duncan Robertson who writes:

> Saints Lives call imperatively for response in feeling and action, something more than reading as that activity is understood today. It follows that an adequate critical study of them should seek beyond the 'immanence' of the texts, into the domains of their transcendence: their reception by contemporary readers, their immersion in history and ultimately their outreach to readers today.[25]

The task of choosing a methodology that could derive a sound spiritual interpretation that is historically accurate was complicated by the fact that the poetic icon of Francis depicted in the *LV* is based on a dream. Since the field of investigation is precisely at the intersection of poetry and spirituality, many questions arise. Can an authentic, credible and historically accurate interpretation of Francis be extracted from a poem? What, if any, is the spiritual significance and meaning of the image of Francis presented in the *LV* for a modern reader today? Considering the complex nature of the task, I have chosen an interdisciplinary approach proposed by Italian scholar Réginald Grégoire in his *Manuale di agiologia: Introduzione alla letteratura agiografica*. This approach is necessitated by Henry's own definition of his image of Francis given in the closing chapters of the *LV*. Henry poignantly sums up the *LV* in the following way: "The verses above paint you a song of Francis."[26] Henry goes on to explain that these verses express the "Francis of my reflections or the image I have of him"[27] and "deposits in the mind ideas of a particular kind, even if not exactly the same."[28] Deciphering the mixed metaphor of ideas which Henry "deposits in the mind" and unlocking the deeper spiritual meaning contained in Henry's "painted song" of Francis can best be achieved by considering the image he presents as a hagiographic or verbal icon. Like any icon, the "painted" image of Francis is more than mere decoration and must be gazed upon and read with spiritual eyes as it speaks a symbolic language that is best understood through faith. The artist of an icon attempts to represent in paint the hidden spiritual reality contained within the soul of the person. Moreover, just as the goal of creating an icon is to allow the viewer an encounter or experience of God through the saint, Henry's icon can facilitate an experience of God in the spirit of Francis. Because the primary goal of this study is aimed at a spiritual interpretation of Henry's poetic image of Francis, the critical analysis of the words that "paint a song" of the icon of Francis necessarily dictate a methodology which incorporates an interdisciplinary approach that exceeds historical criticism.

Grégoire advocates a broader approach to hagiography, one that defines hagiography as a branch of hagiology, which, as an "expression of a religious culture," centers on the study of the transcendent holiness of the saint.[29] Because holiness is often conveyed through a "disconcertingly paradoxical"[30] play of signs and symbols, Grégoire contends hagiography can not be "limited to the critique of literary documents, but perceives the necessity of...the other auxiliary documentary sources."[31] A study of the expression of human holiness, therefore, calls for an interdisciplinary method that not only includes literary and historical studies, but also incorporates insights from various other fields including theological exegesis, spirituality, psychology, psycho-analysis, philology, iconographic analysis, liturgy, symbolism, etc.[32] This method is further justified by Grégoire's belief, "that the ultimate meaning of a hagiographical document lies below its surface, anterior to its particular historical details."[33] This interdisciplinary approach seeks a more holistic, informed and objective assessment of Henry's work; one which is better able to communicate the multi-valent nature of the icon. This study therefore, critically analyzes the constitutive elements of Henry's icon of Francis in order to offer a spiritual interpretation. This work would not be complete without reference to the other early *Legendae,* chronicles and documents, modern biographies as well as Francis' own writings, which are used to compliment and inform such a study. It is hoped that this methodology emphasizes a search not only of *scientia* (knowledge) but of *sapientia* (wisdom.)

Structure

This study is divided into four chapters in which, Henry, the *LV* and the icon of Francis are treated. In order to fully understand and appreciate the artistic icon of Francis in the *LV*, one must first know something about the artist and the context in which it was written. Chapter one, therefore, is a summary of my licentiate entitled *The Icon of Saint Francis of Assisi Depicted in Henry of Avranches' Legenda Versificata* and comprises a two-part study of the life and work of Henry of Avranches, and an introductory background to the *LV*. Part one examines Henry within the historical, social and political milieu in which he wrote. It begins with a brief survey of previous scholarship on his life and contains a sketch of Henry's career based on his poems. It includes an assessment of him in three categories: as "*vates*," "*magister*" and "*versificator*."[34] The second part is a study of the background necessary to understand the *LV* within its specific thirteenth century hagiographic context. This part begins with a brief introduction to the *LV* which relates the general characteristics and method of Henry's hagiography. The following section is a form critique which identifies the various literary genres within the *LV* and their socio-historical influence. A brief survey of Romance, chivalry and knighthood precede a critical discussion on the sources for the *LV*.

Chapter two considers the language of the central metaphor employed in the *LV* through a brief survey of the military motif. In order to determine the relevance and validity of Henry's icon, this section includes a historical-critical study of Francis, which investigates his relation to chivalry and knighthood through his writings and various documents, legends and biographies.

Chapter three begins by addressing the problems of interpretation and the limitations of understanding hagiography solely through the historical critical method. As stated, the methodology chosen represents a broader interdisciplinary approach that is better able to communicate the multi-dimensional aspects of the icon. A definition of the hagiographic aim is discussed and a hermeneutic tool to aid the reader in accessing the spiritual meaning of the text is offered. This is followed by a detailed analysis of the icon that Henry depicts in order to portray Francis as a new hero-saint. This study focuses on the dream of arms as the matrix of the icon. It begins with an in-depth investigation of Francis' conversion, and demonstrates in detail how Henry develops the Celano account.

Chapter four is a spiritual interpretation of the icon that begins with a brief survey of dream interpretation. This is followed by a study on how Francis lived the dream by focusing on the conversion of his deepest desire, which is the true nucleus of the icon. This section includes a study of the spiritual knighthood of Francis and his soldiers according to Henry's interpretation. This chapter considers the minor notes of the icon, in which Francis and myth, song and piety are analyzed. The conclusion includes a summary and articulation of the spiritual significance of the *LV* for the reader.

Chapter One: Background of Henry and the *Legenda Versificata*

Henry of Avranches

Henry of Avranches is the author of a thirteenth century Latin poem about the life of St. Francis called the *Legenda Sancti Francisci Versificata*. After Thomas of Celano's *Vita Prima Sancti Francisci*, which was approved in 1229, the *LV* is the oldest existing legend of Francis ever written. Henry probably composed the 2,585 Latin verses of the *LV* in 1229 or 1230, a year or two after Pope Gregory IX canonized Francis.[1] Because the *LV* is a versification based on Celano's prose model, it is often disregarded as a primary source for the life of Francis. Generally criticized for lacking any "new" historical facts about Francis, it has been given little attention by Franciscan scholars.[2]

Thus neither Henry nor his *LV* are well known today and remain somewhat enigmatic. In fact, persistent confusion about Henry's identity and a general neglect of the *LV* in Franciscan scholarship characterize much of the research since Antonio Cristofani published the first edition of the *LV* in 1882. At that time, Cristofani proposed John of Kent, an English Franciscan, to be the author of the only known manuscript of the *LV* contained in the Assisi Codex

(338).[3] A number of studies followed which attempted to verify authorship. Eduardo d'Alençon studied the text and published a collection of critical variations and additions,[4] producing a series of conjectures as to its author, which included John of Ceperano and Julian of Speyer. Then, in 1889, a second copy of the *LV* at Versailles was edited, revealing its author as a certain "Master Henry."[5] In 1908, Teofilo Dominicelli compiled the growing list of prospective authors, which now included Henry of Pisa, a friend of Salimbene, and an English Franciscan teacher in Paris, Henry of Burford, supporting Luke Wadding's supposition that the author was *Anglicus quidan*.[6]

It was not until the time of Andrew G. Little, through the Cambridge manuscript, that Henry of Avranches was positively identified as the author of the *LV* and the possible author of a score of other poems.[7] Because Little's information was contained in the supplement of a book, however, the author of the *LV* continued to be regarded as a Franciscan, at least until as late as 1959.[8] In 1926, Josiah Cox Russell's doctoral dissertation at Harvard, entitled *Master Henry of Avranches*, provided an abundance of new information about his life and work. Russell's comprehensive study and his subsequent articles and book remain the starting point of modern research.[9]

Once Henry of Avranches was identified as the author of the *LV*, the next task facing scholars was to determine who the real Henry of Avranches was. This process involved addressing at least two problems that are not unrelated. The first problem was sifting through the myriad of conflicting epitaphs he had acquired. Henry has been called everything from a thief to a poet laureate. The second problem was identifying the exact corpus of his work; this problem has not yet been resolved.[10]

These initial developments in the history of the scholarship on Henry of Avranches explain some of the confusion surrounding his person and work. On this point Russell is quoted as saying, "few other instances of mix-ups upon so grand a scale are known."[11] Inaccurate and sometimes conflicting information have distorted assessment of Henry and consequently obscured objective appraisal of the *LV*. Suffice to say these problems have contributed to the current neglect and relative obscurity of the *LV*.

Life

Henry was Norman and probably born in Avranches, sometime in the last decade of the twelfth century.[12] Little else is known of his birth except that his father's name seems to have been Troteman.[13] Henry was well educated and displays a substantial knowledge of classical literature, mythology, scripture, theology, philosophy, canon law and grammar (of which he regarded himself an authority).[14] He also had some understanding of medicine and at least a slight knowledge of Greek, English, French and German.[15]

Henry's earliest known work is a debate concerning

Innocent III and the Imperial claims of Otto IV and Frederick II.[16] The earliest poems that Henry may have written often contain appeals for money from patrons.[17] This supports the theory that Henry began his formative years as a poet by supporting himself as a courtier and later as a grammar master in England in the 1220's.[18] From about 1219 to 1227, Henry wrote for several ecclesial and courtier patrons in England, including an epitaph for William Marshal in 1219.[19] This was significant for two reasons. William Marshall, the Earl of Pembroke, who was considered the "greatest knight in the world" in tournaments, was King John's loyal general and councilor. When King John died, William helped govern and served as regent to the King's son, the young Henry III, whom Henry would later be employed by.[20]

While in England, Henry was commissioned to versify the Lives of leading English saints, (such as Birinus, Guthlac, Oswald and Hugh) which would comprise the bulk of his poetry. Henry was in Italy between 1227-1234.[21] From about 1228-1233, Henry was at the Papal Curia, where his knowledge of Canon Law allowed him to serve as a poet-advocate for a number of patrons, which probably included John Blund, Archbishop-elect of Canterbury,[22] a diocese in which the friars minor were already established.[23] During this time, he was commissioned by Pope Gregory IX to compose the *LV*. Upon completion of his work, Henry personally recited the 14 books of the *LV* before Gregory IX and the curia.[24]

On this occasion, Henry was criticized for his unconventional method of versifying such words as *"caritas," "unitas"* and *"trinitas."*[25] Henry's treatment of these words did not follow the proper rules of grammar.[26] In his defense, Henry is recorded to have argued his use of the word *"caritas"* by maintaining that "pagan poets, whose poetry had no place for that word, were quite ignorant of its inherent value."[27] Henry strongly believed divine words need not be constrained by human laws.[28] Thus Henry's motive behind the change was his conviction that "holy things may be expressed in holy verses," and "not subject to rules of pagan poets."[29] This impressed Pope Gregory IX so much that he "approved" the argument and "ordered it to be given his authority."[30] Because Henry received this special papal dispensation to write the word charity according to his scheme, some have called the *LV* the *Caritas*.[31] Here Henry's sincere intention to convey the spiritual value over poetic consideration or even convention, testifies to the seriousness in which Henry's theological interpretations can be measured.[32]

The entries in the Rolls also speak of his sacerdotal status. While Russell asserts that Henry was a clerk and probably studied canon law, his status as a canon has been disputed.[33] Henry is later referred to as "our clerk, Master Henry of Avranches."[34] The term *"clericus,"* which first referred to a member of the clergy, or someone in holy orders, later "was used for all kinds of officials who were professional readers and writers."[35] By the thirteenth century it referred to men of education, "who need not have identified strongly with the Church and it's teachings,"[36] but rather referred to anyone belonging to the university circle, student or teacher.[37] The broader meaning of the term also "applied to persons who were educated or who had the reputation of being learned,"[38] which included any literate official who transacted the legal business at courts.[39] Clerks enjoyed a certain type of diplomatic immunity and were sometimes the recipients of royal or ecclesial gifts.[40] Russell believes this entry suggests that Henry became one of the court chaplains, as he is documented as receiving the same three pence a day salary.[41] Russell supports this by pointing to Henry's reception of hospitality at various monasteries and the religious content of his poetry, especially his extended reflections on Christian doctrine.[42] Felice Accrocca, Giuseppe Cremascoli and Gregory Shanahan follow the Quaracchi editors and conclude that Henry was in fact a priest.[43] Henry's travel afforded him great access to the wealth of hagiography and literature which could be found at the various monasteries, not to mention the possible exchange of ideas, giving him ample opportunity to increase his learning and develop his skills as a poet and versifier. Henry is believed to have died in royal service sometime between January 1262 and April 1263.[44]

Hidden Life

Although Henry and his *LV* were quite popular in his day, both seem to have been quickly forgotten. One historical factor may have been the mandate of the General Chapter of the Order to destroy other earlier legends of Francis upon completion of Bonaventure's *Major Legend.* In reflecting on Henry's obscurity, Russell begins his chapter entitled, "The History of the Reputation of Master Henry of Avranches," by stating: "it might be said that his light was hidden not under one but under several bushels."[45] In addition to the historical accidents that prevented the discovery of the *LV* and its author and the subsequent scholarship that fostered anonymity, new research has revealed several other factors that help explain the esoteric character of Henry and his *LV.*

Henry was the subject of some invective poetry, which may have marred his reputation and diminished his appeal. Russell attributes at least some of the "unfavorable impression" of Henry on two things: the curious preservation of odd pieces of his work, such as his poem on beer and Michael Blaunpayn of Cornwall's caricature of him.[46] This caricature of Henry is taken from the debate poems that Henry participated in against his former students. One aspect of the poetic debate was using verse to insult and humiliate one another. In one such debate, Henry was paired with his former student, Michael of Cornwall, who according to Russell was one of the best-known poets of the middle of the thirteenth century.[47] Michael's abusive poetry, in addition to that from the Silas-Bordo debate, combine to portray Henry as a thief, a contemptuous, egotistical flatterer who drinks, visits prostitutes, and is preoccupied with himself.[48]

The notoriety of Michael's biting poem is particularly revealing, since it was copied in several manuscripts and read before prestigious audiences.[49] The damage done to his reputation and credibility is difficult to measure. It seems to have influenced the evaluation of Henry's poetry, since some scholars have described him as a "veritable Falstaff,"[50] and questioned his ability, or dismissed his work. Even Russell negatively assesses his early poetry as being pertinent to his day "but when patrons were dead, and the incidents forgotten, a large part of his poetry had little or no appeal."[51]

Henry's self-praise and boasting seems to have been at the root of some of the criticism. His self-praise and self-promotion, however, may be understood in light of the fact that in his early career, he was trying to sell his work and make a living.[52] Morton W. Bloom and Charles W. Dunn in *The Role of the Poet in Early Societies*, speak of such self-promotion as appropriate for poets within their social context.

> Boasting, comparison of merit and contests are often indulged in. These are demanded by a sense of public honor. One's activities are largely determined by status and tradition.[53]

Finally, the possibility that Henry can be seen as a Goliard, which will be taken up in the following section, also raises the question whether he was a social rebel or "whether this was merely a guise adopted for literary purposes."[54]

Another factor that continues to keep Henry and his work hidden is the nature of his poetry. A poem is a "composition written for performance by the human voice."[55] A thirteenth century audience was much better equipped to appreciate the performance of Henry's poetry than today's modern audience. In fact a modern audience would have difficulty understanding, let alone appreciating it. The Latin language in Henry's day was "a living spoken language and natural vehicle for verse, wit, story and song"[56] and thus helped to propagate Henry's poetry throughout Europe. Today Latin is a barrier for most readers who can access his poetry only through translation. A translation of the poetry of Henry's *LV,* like any translation, as Shanahan rightly points out, "is subservient to its original form."[57] Henry constructed his poetry not only to stir the visual imagination of the mind but also to delight the ear of his thirteenth century audience, an audience most likely in the upper class of society, or at least the well educated. While the literacy rate is believed to have been low during the Middle Ages, it was a "period of privileged orality."[58] Generally speaking, their oral capacity would have been greater than today's modern audience. Octavian Schmucki explains that "medieval man had a much better exercised memory than we do, and one which was attuned to mnemonics more finely than ours."[59] Their highly developed ear would have been entertained through all of the variation of metrical discourse that Henry employs. This variation consisted in highly structured patterns of sound that a poet could orchestrate in order to create specific auditory effects.[60] The importance of the oral effect of poetry is stressed by Bloom and Dunn, who equate the reading of poetry with its performance:

> Until poetry is spoken it is not performed because the eye does not give the effects that the ear demands, and the ear is primary in poetry. The performance of poetry, music, dance, in early societies is, at once, the creation, the text, and the circulation.[61]

Since Henry's poetry was designed to be read aloud, to be voiced by some performer, and received and perceived aurally,[62] some of its power and impact naturally rested on the eloquence of the speaker.[63]

There were many different literary techniques and poetic devices available to choose from in order for the poet to "color" or "decorate" ordinary language. Each of these devices, however, was governed by set rules for usage.[64] So structured were these rules, that an infraction against them was called a "vice."[65] While Henry's early poetry was experimental and varied, he followed a firm and fixed scheme as he matured.[66] Henry employs many classical rhetorical techniques; for example he uses apostrophe, a breaking off of the usual flow of the narrative to address a person or personified object, amplification, to expand his ideas and paranomasia on proper names, such as, "*honestatis et honoris*," with "*Honorius*" in *LV* X:3.[67]

Edith van den Goorbergh and Theodore Zweerman rightly observed that "In the unique interweaving of different elements (sound, rhythm, rhyme, double meaning, etc.) the genre of poetry evokes more than the mere sum of its linguistic parts."[68] Henry was surely in line with Horace's notion that "it isn't enough for poems to be things of beauty: Let them stun the hearer and lead his heart where they will."[69] As will be seen later, some of the literary devices that Henry incorporates into his poetry were far more than mere decoration or "poetic touches."[70] Suffice to say the transmission of Henry's poetry would have been an essential part of understanding and appreciating its deeper meaning.

Henry as *vates*

In the opening lines of the *LV*, Henry addressing Francis, refers to himself as "*vatis tibi*," which translated means "your poet."[71] In nearly half a century, Henry may have produced about one hundred and fifty poems across England, France, Italy, and Germany.[72] By any standard, Henry ranks as one of the foremost Anglo-Latin poets of the thirteenth century and holds the distinction of being one of the first professional Latin poets of the Middle Ages.[73] Manselli holds that Henry "ought to be considered one of the most important exponents of Anglo-Saxon culture."[74] The demand for Henry's poetry and the international patronage he received convincingly attests to his ability. Henry wrote for and maintained substantial dealings with the leaders of society, ecclesial and royal. This not only included the educated clergy, the abbots of monasteries, the bishops, archbishops, cardinals and at least one pope, but also the university masters and the royalty of his day, (particularly with Henry III).[75]

> Henry's service to Henry III is significant for several reasons.[76] As mentioned, Henry is the first poet on record to have received direct payment for his work. This distinction comes within a court rich in its literary heritage, at a time when the 'medieval renaissance' was blooming. It is of note that among all the learned poets, Provençals, Savoyards, and Poitevins that Henry III had access to, he chose Henry as his poet laureate.[77] In 1258, distinguished scholar-poet, John of Garland, praises Henry as one of the great courtiers of the English court, in a short list of what appears to be the King's most influential circle.[78] In a series of verse couplets, John praises him along with the Chancellor, the Treasurer, and the King's confessor and counselor, and refers to Henry as "the king of the poets."[79] This high acclaim becomes all the more significant, considering that John of Garland was master grammarian at Toulouse and Paris, and taught Roger Bacon.[80]

In this light, Henry of Avranches' poetic craft deserves greater attention, especially since his poetic output alone could prove as diverse as it was prolific. Henry's varying style and wide range of topics, which has often complicated efforts to determine the authorship of some of his poems, may prove to be the identifying characteristic of his work. Henry is believed to have composed poems praising almost everything from good beer, vacation time and widows, to the Fourth Lateran Council, the saints, the Blessed Virgin, and the Trinity.[81] His poems concern various topics from angels to canon law, philosophy to medicine and science to fables. Although Henry's versatile repertoire includes the profane and mundane, not all of his poetry can be relegated to the aesthetically entertaining category. Dutch historian Johan Huizinga goes as far as stating one must:

> Discard the idea that poetry has only aesthetic function or can only be explained in terms of aesthetics. In any flourishing, living civilization, above all in archaic cultures, poetry has a vital function that is both social and liturgical. All antique poetry is at one and the same time ritual, entertainment, artistry, riddle-making, doctrine, persuasion, sorcery, soothsaying, prophecy and competition.[82]

Henry in fact is a true "*vates*" in the classical sense, that is, an artist who possesses "extraordinary knowledge" and writes poetry with a deeper purpose.[83] He reveals the motivation behind his poetic endeavors in one of his debate poems where he defends his wanderings around Europe:

> You say that I am a lone wanderer and unsociable

> towards you, which I don't deny. I travel the world to learn poems to bring wisdom to men and for you to learn (which you don't).[84]

This is congruent with the roles of the poet that Bloom and Dunn articulate in their study of early poets:

> Teaching has always been recognized as an important function of poetry. Early poets were teachers, diviners, prophets, and preservers of tradition. Part of their sacred office was to admonish and warn rulers and subjects alike, and to hand on the accumulated wisdom of the past.[85]

Because poets, as Aquinas pointed out, were the first to explore the basic truths of our existence, and taught them through their art,[86] their wisdom was highly valued. While Henry's prominent teaching role will be taken up in the next section, Henry exercises his prophetic role in his poem to Emperor Frederick II, where he urges the emperor to codify civil law as Gregory IX had systematically organized canon law.[87] Later, in *Versus de corona spinea*, Henry urges Louis IX to undertake a six-year program to extinguish "the French habit of blasphemous swearing,"[88] suggesting that he impose fines that would be given to the poor.[89] In another poem Henry reveals his passion and love for the Church as he critiques the clergy, particularly the Cardinals and Bishops as he writes, "It drives me mad: I weep that the highest ranks of Rome are fallen into vice, vitiated by stains."[90]

One of the four poems which specifically concern the interpretation of prophetic or apocryphal visions is a versified prophecy of St. Hildegard of Bingen, which is entitled *Prophetia Sancte Hyldegardis de novis fratribus*. This poem is significant for several reasons and warrants special attention. According to Konrad Bund's study, this versification, probably written in 1222,[91] is evidence of Henry's prior knowledge of the Friars Minor, some seven or eight years before writing the *LV*. Henry's poem is a particular theological interpretation of Hildegard's prediction of an imminent chastisement to the clergy by a group of pseudo-prophets, who,

> feigning piety and extreme asceticism, living a life of poverty and mendicancy...will seduce the common people and incite them to rise up against the clergy, as just punishment for their laxity.[92]

The *Prophetia Sancte Hyldegardis de novis fratribus* can be counted among the various agents which severely frightened the local clergy of Cologne and may even have fostered anti-mendicant sentiments.[93] It thus shows Henry as a freelance poet who was not unwilling to versify anti-mendicant propaganda.[94]

In this light it may be possible to compare Henry to the group of poets known as the Goliards. The Goliards were wandering students and clerics scattered throughout twelfth and thirteenth century Europe, particularly England, France and Germany, who wrote satirical poems, which were often critical of the Church and clergy.[95] Frederick Brittain writes that Goliards were:

> Restless clerks who, living on the fringe of ecclesiastical society, moved from one monastery or episcopal palace to another, and later from one university to another, singing Latin songs in return for hospitality or alms.[96]

Some of these Goliards were renegade clerics with no fixed abode that had taken Orders and then reverted to their former state. Some gradually accustomed themselves to lay audiences, studying their tastes and abandoning their original intention of pursuing a clerical career.[97] This would shed light on some of the criticism levied against Henry and explain his Goliard-like poems in praise of drinking, since Goliards "were better known for their rioting, gambling and intemperance than for their scholarship."[98] The poetry of the Goliards in fact contained both spectrums of the pious and secular attitudes of twelfth century life.[99] While most of the evidence about Goliards cast them in a shadowy light, Paul Gerhard Schmidt portrays another type of Goliard, one that seems to be describing Henry. He states "they emerge not as *clerici vagantes,* but as holders of high ecclesiastical office, as officials in a royal Chancery, or as respected masters in schools."[100] In addition, the heavy influence of Goliard poets Peter Blois and Walter of Châtillon on Henry's work and the fact that some of Henry's poems have been found collected together with Goliard manuscripts contributes to this comparison.[101]

In short, the latest research of Henry's authentic poems convincingly attest to his technical expertise and creativity. While the longevity of his professional poetic career, his innovative verse and the breadth of its subject all speak of the level of his ability, his talent as a poet is certainly affirmed through the prestigious international patrons for whom he wrote and with whom he associated.

Henry as *magister*

An adequate assessment of Henry cannot be made without also understanding his place within the social and intellectual milieu in which he found himself. Since Henry is most frequently addressed as *magister,* the Latin term which means "teacher" or "master," it is important to understand the specific role of *magister* in his day.[102] *Magister* in fact had a very broad meaning in the context of medieval intellectual life, ranging from one who has earned a *licentia docendi,* the headmaster or principal of the university to "anyone whose authority is acknowledged and valued."[103] Sometime before 1243, Henry taught at Angers[104] and perhaps Oxford and Paris, which were some of the most important intellectual centers in Europe.[105] He also personally tutored the children of Baron Hamo de Pecche around this time.[106]

Beginning in the twelfth century and continuing well into the thirteenth century, a "scholastic revolution"[107] took place in most countries of the west. This great intellectual renewal produced an ever-growing demand for cultured men of letters.[108] The twelfth and first half of the thirteenth century, therefore, saw the birth of universities. The Church, as attested to in the documents of the Fourth Lateran Council,[109] sought a more educated clergy to preach against heresy and began to establish places of study to prepare canonists and preachers. According to M. Dominique Chenu, however, some of the *magistri* of these universities who were "counselors at times to princes both great and small...were open to every curiosity and adventure, anxious for every kind of physical and intellectual freedom."[110] Despite some opposition, the Church asserted an ever-increasing control of this education.[111] The Statutes for the University of Paris in 1215, for example, which demanded obedience under threat of excommunication, not only demanded that each student have a master but also dictated the minimum age of each master, what they could teach on which days, and even what they had to wear.[112]

The system that developed in Oxford, England consisted of an association called the *magister scolarum*.[113] Norbert Nguyên-Van-Khanh states that the role of the masters "was of paramount importance," since the "fame of the school depended upon its master."[114] These masters of the school were free from the authority of the ordinary bishop, who delegated his authority to a chancellor who, although a doctor of Theology, or Canon Law, was not from the Cathedral.

While the masters nominated this chancellor, it was ultimately the king himself who granted privileges rather than the pope.[115] It is to be noted that the universities normally "exercised complete control over recruitment of both their teachers and students," the majority of whom were clerics.[116] In order to teach it was first necessary to be solemnly received as a master or doctor by the university.[117] Gregory IX, himself a student of Paris, took an active part in insuring sound learning as a service to faith. In 1228, Gregory IX's *Ab Egyptiis* "firmly relegated" philosophy at the service of theology by warning against any "mental adultery" which mixed the teaching of philosophers with pure heavenly doctrine.[118] The *magister* was thus exhorted to teach theology without "the leaven of worldly knowledge, not adulterating the word of God with the construction of philosophers."[119] In 1231, Gregory IX revealed his enthusiasm and overwhelming support for this institution by extending special privileges to the university in his papal bull *parens scientarium*, which also sought to address specific problems.[120] These statutes exhorted the masters and students to be cautious of the dangerous errors of some natural philosophy and instead "strive to become God's learned."[121] Jacques de Vitry gives a picture of some of the problems involving the international conflicts at the schools as well as some of the doctors of theology, who "seated, in Moses' seat," were "swollen with learning, but their charity was not edifying."[122] He continues:

Teaching and not practicing, they have "become

> as sounding brass or a tinkling cymbal," or like a canal of stone, always dry, which ought to carry water to "the bed of spices." They not only hated one another, but by their flatteries they enticed away the students of others; each one seeking his own glory, but caring not a whit about the welfare of souls.[123]

Sometime after 1231, Henry III implemented a policy to personally protect these schools from rival schools.[124]

The university was an institution of superior teaching of pontifical or imperial foundation, and represented, in the "manner of the papacy itself, a kind of power at the heart of Christian society, an intellectual authority of a superior nature."[125] It is estimated that "one quarter of the Masters in Theology educated in Paris in the thirteenth century went on to become bishops or cardinals."[126] It is interesting to note that by 1230, the Friars Minor "had already established their convents and schools in Bologna, Paris, Oxford and Cambridge."[127] This situates Henry as a prestigious *magister* at the same time the Franciscans are beginning to settle into high academia, thus placing before them a proven and respected international poet who is expressing the charism of Francis for an educated audience.

Here a brief discussion of the philosophical and theological debates of the time will better situate Henry amidst the Franciscan intellectual tradition. A slew of translations in the twelfth century triggered a philosophical renaissance which gave accessibility to new sources from such authors as: Plato,[128] Aristotle,[129] Avicenna,[130] Galen and Hippocrates.[131] At this time, *Magister* Robert Grosseteste, a philosopher learned in Greek, Hebrew and Latin would have a profound effect on the Franciscans, especially in Oxford in the early years. Grosseteste was one of the first teachers of theology for the Friars from 1229-1235, and provided several influential commentaries.[132] While Aristotelian philosophy was suspect, especially in Paris,[133] Grosseteste translated the *Ethics*, and became the first Englishman to integrate these with Augustine and others.[134] Grosseteste's Metaphysics,[135] for example, although too elaborate to discuss in detail, would be taken up by his pupil, another Franciscan, named Roger Bacon, who would attempt to "save scholasticism by a return to Nature and Experience."[136] Henry's use of Aristotle's *Ethics* and other works as well as his references to Avicenna's philosophy, especially in terms of his view of nature will be taken up later.

Henry taught grammar and so it is not surprising that a number of his works were written in order to aid in the teaching of grammar.[137] For early medieval students, grammar, the first subject of the *trivium*,[138]

> included not only correctness in speaking and writing (*ars recte loquendi*) but also the further study of what we would today tend to call literature (*enarratio poetarum*), or the analysis and interpretation of existing literary works.[139]

The importance of the study of grammar can be measured by John of Salisbury's comment, "Grammar prepares the mind to understand everything that can be taught in words."[140] At this time, many educational institutions used Latin verse as a pedagogical tool for the study of Latin grammar and other subjects.[141] The *Aeneid,* for example, was in everyday reading use for the teaching of grammar. From 1175 to about 1280, several Latin works about verse writing were produced, including John of Garland's *De arte prosayca, metrica, et rithmica,* Matthieu de Vendôme's *Ars Versificatoria*[142] and Geoffrey of Vinsauf's *Poetria Nova,* which was dedicated to Pope Innocent III.[143] Most of these works use Virgil as an exemplar and follow Donatus' *Ars Minor,* (a work that Henry is thought to have versified), considered to be "probably the most successful single textbook in the history of western education."[144] These metrical Latin grammar textbooks were specifically written to provide a guide for writers of verse. They included all the rules and recipes for the art of metrical discourse: etymology, the role of tropes and figures, the nature of meaning, parts of speech, etc. These rules highlight the level of sophistication involved in versifying and explain why Henry would have to justify himself before the pope.

Because books were so scarce, students formed mnemonic verse in order to memorize information from every field of study from sacramental theology to law.[145] Henry's didactic innovation and piety are evident in his devising mnemonic poetry to aid students in learning canon law and pastorally exhorting a graduate of Canon Law to be a father to orphans, a bishop to the church and husband to widows.[146] His poems on the *Decretum* and the *Decretals*, composed for Gregory IX in 1234, display particular wit and invention.[147]

Students at this time would memorize the verses about the laws and practice the art of recitation and disputation in competitions.[148] This exercise fostered correct accentuation and pronunciation, and prepared the way for the understanding of scripture and for praying the Divine Office.[149] The universities, therefore, became "centers of debates of exceptional scope and extremely intellectual activity, practically without precedents in the west since Antiquity."[150] Verger concludes that a new social figure arose from the university, the medieval intellectual, who was neither truly secular, since the Church controlled academia under its authority, nor simply clerical.[151] This may explain some of the ambiguity in trying to distinguish the identity of Henry as a clerk, a goliard, or a priest.

The medieval intellectual's study of grammar went beyond poetics and into theology. Since William of Conches believed that grammar preceded every doctrine,[152] it is not surprising to find that John Wycliffe believed grammar was a necessary tool for theologians.[153] In fact, Alexander de Ville Dieu's *Doctrinale* (1199), "the standard medieval mnemonic of *grammatica*"[154] after 1200, defined grammar as:

> The gateway of all other sciences, the most apt purgatrix of stammering speech, the helper of logic, the master of rhetoric, the interpreter of theology, the refreshment of medicine, and the most praiseworthy foundation of all the quadrivium.[155]

Henry's love of grammar and his theology converge in a playful didactic rhyme written to help students memorize parts of speech.

> Chaste prelates go ahead like prepositions.
> I call those married to Christ adverbs.
> The penitent is an interjection.
>
> He who assembles and arranges holy sermons about Christ and Mary is called a conjunction.
>
> Every heretic, worthy of a Stigian prison, is the part that disagrees with the Incarnate: the irregular verbs.[156]

Henry, the author of a grammar book for children,[157] considered himself a master of grammar, a claim of proficiency which even his enemies admitted.[158] On one occasion Henry called himself *"poesis ego supremus in orbe professor,"* which translates "I am the topmost teacher of poetry in the world."[159] Henry's proficiency as a grammar master and its relationship to theology provides a new perspective in understanding him as a *versificator* of saints' lives. As will be seen, Henry utilizes his impressive linguistic skills and his vast knowledge of the classics to express his theological interpretation. This will be most evident in Henry's presentation of Francis' piety in chapter four.

Henry as *versificator*

Russell estimated that ninety percent of Henry's poetry was written for ecclesial patrons; the largest portion of which is specifically dedicated to versified saints' lives.[160] More than half of the Cambridge manuscript is hagiographic, comprising a total of 150 of the manuscripts 238 folios.[161] There are a total of eight full-length hagiographic works that have been positively attributed to Henry by internal and external evidence.[162] In addition, another hagiographic poem on the martyr saints, Crispin and Crispinian, has recently been determined to "strongly favour" coming from Henry's hand.[163]

These firmly established *Vitae* prompt a rethinking of Henry under Russell's main classification of poet. David Townsend categorizes Henry primarily as a hagiographer who versified older saints' lives. He proposes a reevaluation of Henry based on the "centrality of hagiography in the poet's oeuvre."[164] Regardless of the future attributions of his yet uncertain works, the majority of his undisputed work is versified hagiography. Henry, therefore, can be seen as a one of the master versifiers of hagiography from the thirteenth century. Henry seems to fit in well with Hans-Erich Keller's description of cleric-poets:

In the most refined circles, the clerics took over

> the role of the popular story-tellers, from whom they not only borrowed subject matter but style as well... The clerics transformed existing epic poems—as well as the stories that they themselves invented—into poems which exalted the virile virtues in the service of Christianity and at the same time censured excess and *démesure*.[165]

Although Henry was heir to a long tradition of Latin metrical *Vitae*, he was not bound by their convention and in fact, shows some originality in his technique. Townsend states:

> Henry exemplifies eleventh and twelfth century developments in the construction of the hexameter, although in the saints' lives he employs none of the rhyme-schemes which had profoundly influenced the metrical shape of the line of his day. His practice contrasts with the self-conscious metrical classicism of the twelfth-century epic poets Joseph of Exeter and Walter of Châtillon...At the same time, Henry also contrasts with the self-styled modernists. Such writers, following the dicta of the late twelfth and early thirteenth-century *artes poetriae*, not only avoided the fifth-foot caesura but renounced such "licenses" as elision found in the classical *auctores* themselves.[166]

Since medieval writers are usually characterized by their tendency to "combine original material with that derived from a variety of authoritative sources,"[167] Michael Idomir Allen categorizes Henry's skill as a metrician "according to medieval rather than classical standards."[168] His appraisal of the *Passio* sums up nicely Henry's method and style of versifying Saint's Lives: "By virtue of this variety of usage and inspiration, the verse of the *Passio* shares fully in the eclectic tradition of metrical prosody."[169]

Analyzing Henry's hagiography within its own literary context and convention reveals Henry's particular use of it. The overriding idea was to revitalize the antiquated saints' lives for modern audiences. This was done, according to Robertson, by revising "their source material with great freedom, using all the rhetoric at their command to clarify the meaning imparted and heighten its dramatic effect."[170] Henry, who was unique in using his talent to versify contemporary legal cases,[171] used that same skill to contemporize the Lives. In his *Life of Saint Oswald,* Henry describes himself by saying, "my spirit urges me to turn old prose to poems new."[172] Even Michael of Cornwall admitted, "When you treat what's faded, it shines."[173] Henry innovatively merges the old with the new. This motif was generally characteristic of twelfth century epic, which belonged to a wider genre called *historia*. *Historia* not only sought to interpret "historical events as part of a larger pattern of God's divine plan," but also "allowed its readers to come to an understanding of the events of their own time and to interpret otherwise mysterious omens and prophecies of the future."[174] Henry shows ample ability to adapt older material into contemporary contexts and thus offer a modern application to his audience. One such example of this is found in his treatment of the life of Thomas Becket. Henry personalizes this work by weaving the struggles of Becket together with those of his patron, Stephen Langton.[175]

Henry's skill at transforming old Vitae is remarkably varied and his style is creative. The creative diversity of his method is evident in Townsend's comment that Henry's "habits of adaptation" in his versified hagiography "elude easy summary."[176] Although Henry most often began with a prose model for his Saint's Lives,[177] he freely incorporated an assortment of material from various sources.[178] These additions, amplifications, and embellishments are often criticized or dismissed as being "useless details"[179] or merely entertaining diversions. New research, however, is beginning to surface, which is reevaluating Henry's use of rhetoric and his so-called digressions. A closer examination of both the content and the medium of these digressions reveal an unexpected depth. In referring to the use of metaphor, metonymy,[180] synecdoche[181] and irony as a means to communicate the saints' life, Thomas Heffernan states:

> These rhetorical tropes are not mere linguistic adumbrations superimposed on the life of this or that saintly man or woman; rather they create the type of life being narrated, since our comprehension of the life comes exclusively

through the filter of language.[182]

While the nature of hagiography and analogy will be taken up later, Heffernan's observations suggest that the very means by which the versified saints' life is communicated, namely the medium of poetry, is itself meaningful and able to express something of the mystery and paradox of the spiritual experience. This is in part a rediscovery of an ancient tradition. Geoffrey of Vinsauf's *Poetria nova* speaks of the function of such rhetorical figures as metonymy, synecdoche, and hyperbole. Geoffrey states that these expressions are used "in order to unlock the sealed spirit: they are, as it were, the keys of the spirit."[183]

Marie Anne Mayeski's research confirms that medieval authors of saints' lives "understood their narratives as fully theological works," and would not understand our modern distinction between hagiography and theology.[184] The real innovation of Henry's craft, then, is unveiled in his subtle and not so subtle theological hermeneutics. Claire Fanger's dissertation argues that Henry's strong interest in natural philosophy allowed him to reinterpret the miraculous in his *Life of Oswald* and in the *LV*.[185] In the *Life of Oswald*, Fanger shows how Henry's "rearrangement and ordering"[186] of the prose model subtlety redefines the divine operation of the miracle. Most surprisingly, rather than accentuate the supernatural or miraculous, Henry "economizes" it into a more natural process, highlighting how God works through the natural order of the ordinary.[187] Fanger's insight into Henry's use of the natural link between the body and soul in divine operation will be useful for understanding the icon Henry depicts of Francis.

Other pieces of Henry's work seem to be more explicitly theological and perhaps more Franciscan. Henry's theological discourses like those in the *Passio* are common in his works. Townsend holds that Henry's significant additions to his *Life of Saint Birinus* suggest an allusion to the new spirituality of the mendicants who combine an active and contemplative lifestyle.[188] In addition, Henry's poem on the relics of the crucifixion interprets the shape of the crown to symbolize the eternal heavenly Kingdom, and the cross itself as a complex geometrical symbol.[189] The affective language that Henry uses in these descriptions of the Incarnation, Virgin Birth and Passion has caused Townsend to inquire whether there was a "specifically Franciscan piety"[190] at work in his meditations. This affectivity however could also be reflective of the "intensely affective spirituality of the twelfth and thirteenth centuries," which was seen in the art of the day and sought to evoke an "emotional response."[191]

An example from the *LV* of Henry's ability to innovatively interpret Francis comes in his account of Francis and the possessed woman at San Gemini.[192] Henry, following Celano, relates that Francis instructed each of his three brothers to occupy a corner of the room, but then adds that Francis said "Let the cross we thus form be a sort of obstacle device, to prevent the evil spirit from thinking he can escape our hands."[193] Here

Henry interprets Celano's account as Francis having the friars form an X, or sign of the cross.[194]

In sum, Henry was an experienced *versificator* who not only had a mastery of the language, a facility for poetry, and a familiarity with the hagiographic genre, but also was well acquainted with the politics, goals and process of canonization. Therefore, Henry's reputation was well known and he was sought out for his work. Abbot Henry Longchamp, looking for quality, proudly had the *Life of Saint Guthlac* versified first by Peter of Blois, then by Henry.[195] Henry brings to the lives his own erudite philosophical and theological suppositions. A. G. Rigg observes that Henry "can find a central image, (such as…the etymology of a name) and build a poem around it."[196] The art of Henry's expansions serve not only to entertain but also have a specific theological and didactic dimension that will be more fully explored later. Henry's extraordinary facility to versify is at the service of his theological interpretation.

The *Legenda Versificata*

The *LV* was written in the form of a versified *legenda*,[197] a term translated as legend and derived from the Latin word *legere*, which means, "to read." These Legends were typically intended to be orally recited. The *LV* is contained in three manuscripts:

1. The Cambridge University Library ms. (Dd. 11.78)[198]

2. The Assisi Biblioteca Comunale ms. (338), (fols. 54r-71v)[199]

3. The Versailles Bibliothèque Municipale ms. 8, (fols. 73r-105v)[200]

Henry has versified at least eight saints' lives as well as the martyrs Crispin and Crispinian.[201] The *LV* holds the distinction of being one of only two hagiographic poems that Henry wrote about non-English saints.[202] The *LV* is also the longest of Henry's hagiographic legends about saints, and was written for one of his most influential patrons.[203] Although it has been called "the most striking of the poet's efforts,"[204] it should be noted, however, the *LV*, like Henry's other poetry, is somewhat removed from the modern reader, since a translation is often unable to convey the subtleties and nuances of meaning inherent in the original. Ironically, some of the reasons that have caused the *LV* to be overlooked and ignored are some of the very same reasons why it is so valuable and important. It is precisely because Henry follows Celano's *Vita Prima* so closely that Henry's unique contributions can easily be gleaned without the complications of other earlier Franciscan sources. Manselli noted the importance of this in what he referred to as the "essential critical principle," that is:

> The source that most slavishly follows another always has something in it to distinguish it, thus allowing historians to specify its character, and thus its meaning within the network of the

other sources.[205]

While the main structure and chronology of Francis' life is predetermined in Henry's versification of Celano, the major differences include the emphasis of certain events, the way in which the story is told (specifically the various genres and how they are used) as well as the stylistic variations of detail. Once these contributions have been isolated and analyzed, Henry's method of poetic interpretation and its impact on later authors can be better understood. Thus, its pride of place makes the *LV* one of the most important texts in terms of its potential influence on subsequent narratives of Francis.

Most of Henry's versified hagiographic poems of saints' lives bear resemblance. They usually begin with a similar introduction, which includes a prologue with a tripartite structure that states the theme, invokes the saint and asks for the indulgence of the patron.[206] The invocation of the saint follows in the epic tradition by a comparison of the saint with classic heroes.[207] Guthlac, Birin, Oswald, and Francis, for example, are all compared to Alexander, the world conqueror in Henry's writings.[208] Henry's prologues introduce his main themes. While the opening lines of *The Life of Oswald* are based on Ovid's *Metamorphoses*, the opening lines of *The Life of Saint Hugh*, and the *LV*, begin in imitation of Virgil.[209] Henry often employs patterned topoi in his hagiography such as mutually attested miracles, vivid and detailed medical descriptions, proverbs, psalms and onomastic wordplay.[210] Both Francis and Guthlac, for example, are shown to invoke Psalm 15:8 in their speeches.[211] Henry also uses similar conclusions in his works.[212]

The *LV* is divided into fourteen chapters, each of which begins with an introductory quatrain that summarizes the content of the chapter.[213] The *LV*'s first eleven chapters follow Celano's *Vita Prima* 1-87, while the last three chapters of the *LV* quickly condense the second half of Celano 88-151,[214] before concluding with a praising of patron, Gregory IX. Henry generally follows the sequence of Celano, although he frequently adapts, adds and freely transposes many passages using his own vocabulary and interpretation.

In the first chapter, the prologue (I:1-25) and the detailed description of Francis' illness (I:70-109) are original. Henry's other major original pieces are: II: 9-111, (a *psychomachia* between vice and virtue); III: 25-75, 87-126 (a speech by Francis to his father); IV: 92-105 (an admonition to monks); IV: 179-184, 218-225 (describing ruined churches); V: 46-78 (Francis' first sermon) and 180-330 (an exhortation on poverty); VII 151-75 (an ecclesial reflection and comment on Italy); VII: 176-181 and VIII: 15-74 (a classic description of storms at sea); VIII: 90-180 (Francis' sermon to the Sultan). Shanahan's summary captures the spirit of the *LV* succinctly:

> The poem sings from the outset of a great soldierly hero who, with spiritual weapons, wages a holy war on the powers of evil, and who

> musters his forces and trains them in the art of spiritual warfare. His successes are greater than those of Alexander the Great and Caesar. A whole inner world, as well as an outer world, is the scene of St. Francis's triumphs. The tone of military victory and knightly achievement is maintained throughout.[215]

As will be demonstrated in the chapter on the discussion of the icon, Henry's entire *LV* is basically an extension of Francis' dream, relating how he fulfilled it in living it out. For this reason, Henry saturates his poem in martial analogy and imagery from beginning to end. Francis is consistently described in martial language as he: "marches,"[216] "orders,"[217] "commands,"[218] "combats"[219] "battles"[220] and "fights"[221] his way through the world.

Form Critique: Literary and Socio-Historical Influences

The first task was to establish Henry within his historical, social and political milieu as an accomplished *vates*, a reputable *magister* and an experienced *versificator*. The following background study of the literary and hagiographic context of the *LV* will allow the prominent features of Henry's icon of Francis to stand out more clearly. The second part begins with a brief survey of the remote literary and historical influences on the *LV*. This background, necessary to understanding the icon, identifies the principal conventions of the different genres used in the *LV* as well as their socio-historical development. After a brief analysis of genre in the *LV*, a more detailed study of romance, chivalry and knighthood follows. This section ends with a critical study of the sources that Henry used to compose his *LV*.

The icon of Francis in the *LV* was created from a collage of different elements woven together from a medley of literary sources. This section seeks to identify and understand how Henry poetically harmonized the diverse literary genres in order to present Francis as a new saintly hero. Each of the genres will be analyzed within their own historical and social context in order to evaluate their influence on the *LV*. This study will provide more than a mere backdrop in which to appreciate Henry's *LV*, but can serve as an objective means to understand the wider socio-historical context in which it was written. Tatyana Ivanovna Shamkovich's brilliant study, *Saintly Hero: Mythological, Epic and Ecclesiastical Perspectives on the Image of the Saint in Medieval Hagiography*, describes the wide variety of influences on medieval hagiography:

> Throughout the centuries of human civilization, the nature of the saint has been shaped under the influences of different mythologies, folklores, popular beliefs, heroic epics, medieval romances, different philosophies, and theological teaching of the Church Fathers. The blending of all of these elements of orality and textuality with popular beliefs engendered the

> image of the saint and his *vita*, into the life of the ideal hero of Christianity, the saintly hero.[222]

Shamkovich's study of hagiography has led her to conclude that the middle ages "can be considered not only as the return of the heroic age, the age of heroes, but also the age of the saintly heroes," which she defines as a saintly soldier of the earthly *"militia Christi,"* who is on a quest or a journey towards God.[223] The hagiography of the *LV* is intespersed with a rich blend of literary allusions from a variety of genres, all of which combine to depict Francis as a saintly hero. The main genres include scripture, classic Latin poetry, epic, romance, mythology and philosophical discourse. While it is beyond the scope of this work to analyze every element appearing in each of the different genres, a general discussion of their respective literary conventions can serve to contextualize their influence in shaping the central image of Francis in the *LV.*

To begin, Henry uses a number of biblical allusions in which he compares Francis to Adam,[224] Job,[225] Peter,[226] Paul,[227] Ananias, Azarias and Mizael.[228] Henry alludes to about half of the books of the Bible, which, for the most part, follow and expand the scriptural references found in Celano, i.e. both compare Francis to Job (1C1 and *LV* I: 87). Henry also expands and develops Celano's passing reference to the three young men in the furnace in the Book of Daniel by individually naming them and paraphrasing their *Canticle*.[229] When Francis stands naked before the Bishop, however, Henry compares him to Adam and adds a theological reflection:

> But he differs from Adam in this: he suffers freely what Adam
> Was forced to endure; he suffers by merit what Adam endured for sin;
> And yet he is penalized as Adam was – though in a different way:
> Exposed was the shamefulness of Adam, while no shame
> Is discovered in him. Where is the shame in a naked body
> When the vesture of its soul is honor?[230]

Henry, unlike Celano, however, was not seeking evidence in order to proclaim a new saint, but rather in order to sing the praises of a new saintly hero. Henry therefore was not restricted to finding parallels in the Bible or using maxims from the Church Fathers but rather compares Francis to historic world leaders such as Caesar and Alexander.[231] Further, by dispersing his *LV* with allusions to historical leaders, legendary heroes and ancient mythology, Henry frees Francis from the conventions of the Christian hagiographic framework. In addition, Henry demonstrates his great learning by scattering the *LV* with a number of select quotes, aphorisms and maxims from classic secular authors such as Virgil, Ovid, Homer, Horace, and Juvenal, among others.[232] In this way, Henry skillfully weaves Francis into the fabric of the epic-mythic tradition of the ancient Greeks, comparing him to Aeneas,[233] Ulysses[234] and Antaeus.[235] Henry in fact will derive most of his material from the classical tradition, and specifically from the Latin poets Ovid, Virgil and Horace, the first two of which he usually quotes at the beginning of every chapter and throughout.[236] Because Henry relies so strongly on Virgil, one might say that he merges the *Vita Prima* with the *Aeneid* in order to create a hagiographic poem with an epic overtone that portrays Francis as another Aeneas. The fact that Henry begins the *LV* with the words: *"Gesta sacri cantabo ducis,"* which is quite reminiscent of Virgil's opening line of the Aeneid: *"Arma virumque cano,"* caused Shanahan to call Henry's poem the "Francisciad."[237] It should be noted that epic poets often began their works with a noun, which introduced their main theme. In this case the word *"gesta"* would have a particular nuance to medieval audiences as the *Gesta* was a medieval genre of historical prose, (e.g. *Gesta Innocentii PP. III,*) which provided "a contemporary background to the outstanding deeds of its principal character, usually portrayed as the hero of the piece."[238] In Francis' day, the gesta was at "the height of its development"[239] comprising a dramatic account that was sometimes written in verse.[240]

Henry's effort to portray a saint utilizing the classical tradition is hardly original, as the biblical epic tradition has a long history of "manipulating the classical tradition to subserve a deeply moral Christian purpose."[241] As early as the fifth and sixth centuries, biblical epicists who transformed scripture into epic poetry "served as a powerful evangelizing force in Western Europe."[242] These poets realized that "a Vergilian type epic is an excellent means for teaching the fundamental truths."[243] According to K. W. Grandsen, this lesson was heavily employed in the medieval ages when Virgil's popularity "reached its zenith" and he was revered as a '*magus*' and as '*anima naturaliter Christiana*,' a naturally Christian soul."[244] Henry specifically imitates Virgil's epic style in his elaborate variation (using several analogies), and concern for detail.[245] It is not surprising that the *LV* contains so many epic overtones, since the hagiographic genre is commonly acknowledged to have an intimate relationship with the epic.[246] Francis' long speeches in the *LV*, for example, are literary conventions used in the *Aeneid* to move the plot along and reveal the hero's motives.

The concept of the hero-saint or warrior-saint has been popular since antiquity, especially in the early Christian Mediterranean world and thus forms a distinct type in hagiography.[247] Some scholars, however, like Moses Hadas and Morton Smith contend that "the business of the saint and the business of the hero are so far removed from one another that each may be economically defined in terms of opposition to the other."[248] They hold that a saintly-hero is an "oxymoron" since the hero is "by nature self-assertive" and saints are "by nature self-effacing."[249] Lee Allison Crawford's study of hagiography however contends that the *LV* was written at a time that coincides with the flowering of the literary development of the warrior-saint, when the hero of the hagiographic epic and the saint "crystallize into one."[250] Le Goff and other scholars hold that "the saint of the thirteenth century was God's *knight*."[251] They relate that this period of the medieval ages "saw Christianity through heroic lens and heroes through Christian lens,"[252] and thus "medieval man thought of human greatness in terms of heroic combat."[253] Marco Bartoli writes, "Saints, like knights, were heroes who went into battle and triumphed for the faith and for the good of the weak."[254] Thus, much of the religious literature of this period, particularly the hagiography, sought to "provide ideologically suitable spiritual heroes for the faithful."[255] Henry, therefore, incorporates a number of the traditional conventions of epic into the *LV* in order to portray Francis as an epic hero: initial statement of theme, invocation to the muse, catalog, Epic simile, the arming of the hero, testing in battle against the enemy, frequent use of epithets, long formal speeches and a central unifying theme in which all other events relate in some way. In particular Henry uses the Virgilian concept of hero in order to establish Francis as a new icon of the hero-saint. Like Aeneas, Francis combines "military prowess and *pietas*"[256] as his journey too, leads him from "wanderer to that of *dux* (commander, leader), from exile and near despair...to a sense of mission and (moral) responsibility."[257] Francis, in his first speech to his Father states:

We are all in an exile, you surely must know,

> And from here is our journey as we seek our true homeland.
> The world is our exile, our roadway is time, our fatherland heaven.
> What a crime on your part to prefer exile to home and journey to goal![258]

Both Francis and Aeneas are legendary Italian heroes who as knights or soldiers are "called *pater* as often as *pius*."[259] Both love their fellow soldiers and make speeches that inspire, guide, and encourage their men. [260] Renown for their piety, devotion and compassion, both not only pray but are given heavenly armor[261] to "wage a great war in Italy."[262] In their overcoming storms and various evil monsters and personified vice, they are compared to the Morning star which scatters the darkness.[263] The ideal of knighthood, embodied in Aeneas, becomes Christianized in Francis as a knight of Christ.[264] Both heroes wander as exiles and carrying their God on a journey seeking a new home. Just as Aeneas founded a city that would become Rome, and have descendants without end, Francis too found a city of brothers and sisters that will have no end.[265] Francis then, like Aeneas, can be understood as a "cultural hero"[266] whose spiritual odyssey relates his struggle to discover who he is, what he thinks important and what he becomes.[267] This view of hero is different from the epic. Virgil had challenged the Homeric view of the epic hero by creating in Aeneas "a new type of hero, willing and ready to subordinate his individual will to that of destiny, the commonwealth and the future, reluctant to fight and not really interested in [military] victory."[268]

At the beginning of the thirteenth century, the epic and the romance genres were "mutual influences and rivals."[269] The narratives depicting the hero underwent certain developments in Francis' day that are reflected in the hagiography of the *LV.* of Francis' day. Charles F. Altman, in his article entitled *Two Types of Opposition and the Structure of Saints' Lives,* devised a simple but useful method of distinguishing the influence of epic and romance in hagiography. In analyzing the plot structures of medieval narratives, Altman has divided Saint *Lives* into two groups based on their style of contrast. He likens the first group to medieval epics, which commonly "operate according to the principles of diametric opposition," i.e. polemically contrasting vice and virtue.[270] This group is identified by the fact that "between the two sides there can be no middle ground, no mediation."[271] The epic convention perceives the world as a cosmic battle between good and evil, God vs. Satan. In this view Christians are seen as "*milites Christi,*" soldiers of Christ, who battle the external forces of evil. Christ's passion is seen as the ultimate royal victory that conquered Satan.

The second group, he states, "grew slowly away from the diametrical configuration...eventually adopting fully the gradational form of the romance" which contrasts the good with the better.[272] The Romance influence locates the struggle within the individual as one progresses in virtue. Applying this to the *LV,* it is easy to see both the epic and romantic influence. The epic motif of contrast, manifested in the myriad of polemics, beginning with the opening quatrain which contrasts Francis' "pursuit of the earthly" and "his love for the truly good." The polemics continue throughout the first chapter, introducing a theme that will permeates the entire work. This establishes a contrast between good and evil, light and darkness, interior and exterior: the flesh and the soul,[273] earthly and celestial,[274] mortal and durable,[275] love and hate,[276] fair and false,[277] pleasure and pain,[278] good and bad,[279] transient world and eternity,[280] measureless joys and insignificant things,[281] laurels mundane and true triumphs,[282] reason and sense or emotional feeling[283] and most extensively later in the virtues and vices of the second chapter. Finally, Henry even puts into Francis' mouth a radical speech contrasting the world and God:

> Flee the world and its fortunes before the day they fly away;
> While there is time, remember you can't have the world
> As well as God to enjoy. As you walk away from the world, trip it up,
> Or it'll trip you up.[284]

The romance elements of the *LV* are clearly seen in the emphasis on the adventure or journey motif motivated and elevated by faith or love, elements of the fantastic (monsters), the development of the interior or psychological realm, a more refined or sophisticated chivalrous speech and the attention to detail. For the romance hero, the enemy was within and according to Alison Goddard Elliott, the "symbolic nexus of the drama lies in images of interiority."[285] The "rhythmical and repetitive" motif is also used in romance to express the hero's journey or quest of withdrawal and spiritual martyrdom of *askesis*.[286] While the epic, like the early passion narratives and the martyrs, de-emphasizes personal identity, Henry used romance elements to draw the reader into Francis' inner psychological processes, adding detailed existential conflicts which raged within Francis' mind. In this regard, rather than using the traditional epic typology of the hero, who is usually weakly individualised,[287] Henry opts to flush out Francis' most personal thoughts as well as the deepest movements of his heart and soul.

While love is central to the hero of the romance, the goal of the epic hero, "*kleos aphthiton*" (undying glory), was defined in terms of the other.[288] In the *Chanson de Roland* for example, the hero motivates his knights into battle by warning them to fight bravely so that others will not make bad songs about them.[289] Francis before his conversion strove to be what can be considered as the epic notion of a hero, where a man's pursuit of honor leads him to choose one thing above all others, that is, immortal glory among mortals.[290] Francis sought to win worldly honor, glory, and fame in order to elevate himself above others. This conforms to the Epic heroes, who were men of action who sought the Aristotelian definition of honor, which not only understood honor as "the prize appointed for the noblest deeds" but as "the greatest of external goods."[291] Jupiter in the *Aeneid* defines the "task of the brave" in epic terms as enlarging "his fame by his actions"[292]

The romance and French heroic traditions, however, mark a shift in their depiction of the hero. Alois Wolf observes:

> Medieval Latin hagiography itself could not keep away from the influence of classical literature and Roman mannerism. The same seems to apply to French heroic traditions throughout their evolution. Their influence is manifest in the description of fights...in the insistence on the crude details of wounds, and in the handling of arms.[293]

In fact, *le Roman d'Eneas,* one of the earliest and most influential medieval French romances,[294] is a not merely a translation of Virgil's *Aeneid,* "but rather a rewriting into the cultural context of the twelfth century France."[295] It is arguably the most "Ovidian" of the old romances, depicting Eneas as wounded with desire in the cause of love.[296] It thus contains the classic Ovidian motifs: "love as a fever, a sweet pain or a welcome wound, the Beloved as a medicine or an enemy to be overcome" which are liberally scattered throughout the lyric poetry of the troubadours.[297] As will be pointed out later, this Ovidian theme of depicting love as a fever may have been particularly influential in Henry's interpretation of Francis' conversion. Like the author of *le Roman d'Eneas,* Henry uses methods that are constitutive of the Romance genre, such as monstrosity[298] and *descriptio*[299] in portraying his hero, Francis. Henry also furnishes Francis with a more cultured and refined manner of speaking typical of romance. Thus the *LV* not only contains epic elements but also elements of the Romance and the French heroic traditions.[300] This is further attested by Henry's extensive use of the classic Latin poets Ovid and Horace. The courtly love literature of Francis' day frequently drew heavily on Ovid, who "provided the manners and sentiments of chivalry."[301] Ovid wrote that love is war and thus "every lover is a soldier,"[302] and even defined "love" as a form of suffering.[303] Almost every chapter of the *LV* contains a quote from Ovid's *Metamorphoses* or *Fasti*.

A Comparative Analysis of Genre

Celano and Henry relate the story of Francis within the framework of the conventions of their respective genre. In traditional hagiographical style, Celano's opening lines reveal humility as one of his major themes, which will be developed throughout his entire work. Thus, the second sentence of his *Life* begins a reflection on the arrogance and vanity of the age, in which Francis' parents are accused of carelessness and indulgence in raising their children. Vanity, arrogance and pride, then, are advanced as the root cause of the present ills of society, affirming humility as a major lens through which he interprets Francis. Celano emphasizes vanity in Francis and his parents in the first chapter in order to sharpen the contrast of his humility schema.

Henry on the other hand is relating an epic-romance hybrid. The first chapter therefore introduces his hero and sets the tone of the entire poem. In his opening line, he introduces Francis as the "Godly captain," who masters monsters, overcomes a world, a foe and himself to be a "victor and victim in the same war." While Celano, true to his theme, portrays the young Francis as "advancing beyond all his peers in vanities," Henry's martial theme describes Francis' as a "crooked bow."[304] Henry also uses Francis' parents to strengthen his own schema of contrast between what is good and what is evil. The lines of this battle are clearly drawn, and reflected in his mother and father as well as within Francis himself. His mother represents what is "upright, unpretentious and kind."[305] She is the right path and embodies honor, courage, the celestial, and the durable, while his merchant father walks the left road, is violent, mighty and sly, embodying that which is earthy, mortal, wrong, and irresolute. Henry later weaves the mythic element into the narrative by comparing the "burning anger" and rage of Francis's father to the rage of Apollo's or "Pallas who tore asunder what victorious Arachne had wrought."

Romance, Chivalry, and Knighthood

A closer study of chivalry within the romance genre will shed more light on Franicis and knighthood as depicted in the *LV.* Romance,[306] the popular literature of Francis' day which developed in France in the twelfth century, was not only a departure from epic but owed much of its "spirit and ideas to troubadour poetry."[307] Romance itself was a modification of the *chanson de geste,*[308] which in turn had been derived from the ancient German epics like *Beowulf* and *Hildebrandslied*. The *chanson de geste*, most often orally transmitted,[309] was aimed at articulating the ideals of a warrior society, and its hero struggled against foreign or pagan foes. Thus the *chanson*, like the epic, placed great emphasis on fighting and military virtues such as physical strength, honor, loyalty and courage over and above any specific Christian virtue or doctrine.[310]

The Romance hero, however, was focused on the search for his individual identity within society. While the protagonist of the *chanson de geste* sought heroic glory on the battlefield, the hero of the Romance was more refined and is preoccupied with chivalry and the search for love at the court.[311] Naturally, in order to relate the feelings of love, the author of the Romance concentrated on the "psychological development of the hero."[312] The Romance took place at court of the feudal nobility and was usually dedicated to a royal patron. It was not merely read for pleasure, however, but expressed aristocratic society's most intimate ideals, namely that of chivalry. The word courtly even became synonymous with "refined" and "sophisticated."[313] In

Stephen Knight's study of the ideology of romance he points out that one of the central paradigms of romance follows a pattern in which the chivalric hero wins a Lady (more beautiful than all others) and thus establishes both a family and his honor while overcoming his enemies.[314] These ideals of chivalry in the romance found their way into the hagiography of the day. Shamkovich specifically points to:

> The Byzantine military legends, the crusades, the chivalric code of courtly society and the moral and political ideals of the medieval man as having significantly shaped the form of the saint's *Vita*.[315]

Although some authors such as Constance Bouchard warn against understanding the "knightly class" as living under a certain ethos,[316] many authors recognize that in the thirteenth century, the chivalric ideal of knighthood embodied the common cultural values of an ever-growing European society.[317] Chivalry even came to be looked upon as representing something sacred.[318] According to one source, the term knight can be traced to ancient Rome, when Romulus founded the city and selected "a thousand for war and called them knights."[319] Originally signifying soldier, *miles* or "one from a thousand" evolved to refer to a horseman in the middle ages.[320] Thus the word chivalry comes from *"chevalerie,"* which is derived from the French word *"cheval,"* which means a horse.[321]

The broader meaning of the term chivalry however is

"elusive of definition, tonal rather than precise in its implications."[322] Keen writes:

> Chivalry cannot be divorced from the martial world of the mounted warrior: it cannot be divorced from aristocracy, because knights were commonly men of high lineage: and from the middle of the twelfth century on it very frequently carries ethical or religious overtones.[323]

In the last decade of the twelfth century, the "*chevalerie*" became a distinctive social order "which bound together men of such otherwise disparate status in life"[324] and identified them with true *noblesse*: "loyalty, generosity, military prowess and courtly style."[325] Cardini, who has extensively researched the concept of knighthood holds that *miles*,

> was applied to all members of what ideally was supposed to have been a supernatural brotherhood in arms linked by the insignia and the tradition of knightly investiture.[326]

Chivalry, according to Thomas Bulfinch, framed "the ideal of the heroic character, combing invincible strength and valor, justice, modesty, loyalty to superiors, courtesy to equals, compassion to weakness, and devotedness to the Church."[327]

While the term chivalry is somewhat ambiguous, it expressed the shift of rough warrior customs to the mores of refined aristocratic gentility. The ideology of chivalry that arose during feudalism and the emergence of mercantilism allowed those of lower social standings to be associated with kings and princes.[328] Stacey reports, "in most Italian cities, mounted military service was compulsory for all male citizens above a set level of wealth."[329] Thus, knighthood was a means of entry into aristocratic society.

The sacralization of knighthood is often understood as having been developed as ecclesial authorities praised the Christian warriors who took part in the crusades wearing red crosses. Cardini however contends that "the *pugna spiritualis* lay at the base of the Christian legitimization of knighthood."[330] Another factor in bringing knights into the Church can be traced to the early "Peace of God" and "Truce of God" movements. In 978 at the Council of Charroux, the bishops of Aquitaine called all countries together for the purpose of reforming the peace. Warriors were asked to swear oaths to limit their violence, to not enter churches nor attack churchman, women, peasants or merchants. In 1027 the Council of Elne proposed a Truce of God which forbade attacks on unarmed clergy, men going to and from Church with their families, men with women or anyone on Sunday.[331] This resulted in the declaration that no Christian should kill another Christian. This was echoed in the Romance literature and emerging troubadour poetry of the day where these knights were promised indulgences and absolution from their sins for servicing and protecting the Church.[332] Chrétien de

Troyes' *Perceval,* the knight-errant, before beginning his journey, is instructed to go to church or chapel to hear mass regularly.[333] Francis Gies explains:

> Aside from its intrinsic literary value, and its influence on European thought and culture, chivalric literature played an important part in the history of knighthood. It contributed to fixing the self-image of the knight and to strengthening his *esprit de corps.* It helped define standards for knightly behavior, some of which were implicit in knightly life-style; some the religious and moral, set down in the codes of chivalry that began to appear late in the twelfth century. The rules of conduct that the poetry of the troubadours prescribed were mainly social: a knight should be courteous, generous, well-spoken, discreet, faithful in the service of love; he should have '*prez e valor,*' excellence and worth, as well as good sense.[334]

This development facilitated a greater integration of the warrior knight into the social sphere of church and society, not to mention an enhanced social status. A good example of this can be seen with the first of the military orders called the Knights Templar or the Chivalric Order of the Poor knights of the Temple of Solomon, who were also known as the Poor Fellow-soldiers of Jesus Christ.[335] These soldiers of Christ, founded and led by the French knight Hughes de Payens, the *Magister Militum Templi* (the Master of the Knights Templar) first "professed the wish to live in chastity, obedience and without property in perpetuity" in 1118.[336] In the words of Joshua Prawler, the Templars "fused two current ideals of Mediaeval society, knighthood and monasticism, into a code for a community of warrior monks."[337] It is interesting to note that these unordained knights: dressed simply, were often unwashed and uneducated, wore brown, followed a rule, prayed the office, were divided in provinces and under two classes: knights and serving brothers, held chapters, (where they confessed their sins and asked Christ for peace).[338] Upon entering the Templars the postulant was admonished in the following way:

> Good brother, you ask a very great thing, for of our Order you only see the surface which is the outside. For the surface is that you see we have beautiful horses and harness and eat and drink well and have beautiful clothes, and it seems to you as if you would be much to your ease there. But you do not know the harsh commandments which are within: for it is a hard thing that you, who are master of yourself, should make yourself serf to another.[339]

Several features of this "admonition" addressed to a "brother" are particularly striking as regards Francis and Henry's icon of him. The internal emphasis is reminiscent of Henry's opening paragraph: "The flesh he curbed with the soul's Commands, the foe brought down by orders derived within."[340] The mention of beautiful horses, Francis seeing saddles instead of beautiful clothes in the interior of his home, prepare for the greater irony of Francis' second dream which questions if it is better to serve the master or the servant. The Templars were officially recognized at the Council of Troyes in 1128 where Bernard of Clairvaux was commissioned to systematize their form of life.[341]

Another type of knight emerged called troubadours, knight-poets, or Provençal poets,[342] who, according to Séamus Mulholland "represented one of the great moments in European cultural and creative history."[343] While minstrels and jongleurs[344] were entertainers who merely sang the songs of others, these troubadours took their name from the French "*trobar*," which described their activity, that is, to find, discover, invent, and create.[345] The troubadour invented poetry by "finding new verse forms for his elaborate lyrics, and the melody for his songs."[346] Although these knightly poets could be princes or wandering adventurers, they were often from the middle class, "the son of a cloth merchant, of a tailor...or simply 'of bourgeois'."[347] The poetry that the troubadour created was considered his profession and vocation and was meant to be sung.[348] Their vernacular lyrics concerned knighthood and courtly love and thus were heavily influenced by Ovid, Boethius, and Venantius Fortunatus.[349] In the French lyrics of the troubadours, "the lover is always a knight," who idealized courtly perfection.[350] For the troubadour, love was a "means of man's self-realization"[351] manifested through his social duties which involved not only defending and maintaining the Church, the widows and the orphans, but also his earthly Lord.[352] The troubadours idealized Love and Woman, sacralized knighthood, and sang of the heroic deeds of Christian knights and kings.[353] Oktavian Schmucki points out that the troubadours "were a dominant force in molding the public opinion and tastes of the time."[354] Mulholland relates that the troubadours who "flooded into Northern Italy" following the Albigensian crusade, were welcomed by the "romantic openness" of the Italians.[355]

The replacement of epic by romance at this time was reflected in the troubadour's exultation of certain chivalric virtues. Traveling among the civilized courts, the troubadour sang of love and virtues that ensured a just and stable rule that defended the existing order and the observance of social form and rank.[356] Although A. R. Moncrieff cites that from as early as the tenth century, virtues of knighthood included "loyalty to Church and King, truth in speech and gentleness to women,"[357] Keller states:

> After 1150...the tastes of the audience now required that the poet praise not so much heroes with extraordinary physical force and endurance in the service of France and Christianity but heroes without ties with their own period, incorporating the virtues defined by the new type of knight of courtly society.[358]

Unlike the rough and "individually obscure Crusading warriors,"[359] the knight of courtly society was refined and well mannered. It was Chrétien de Troyes, who took the character of King Arthur from the secular cleric Geoffrey of Monmouth's *History of the Kings of Britain* written in 1136, and turned him into a true Christian hero to be emulated.[360] The ethical guidelines supplied by the Arthurian romances interwove knighthood with Christianity.[361] A good example of this is when the Lady of the Lake explains the origin and significance of knighthood to Lancelot. Gie summarizes the account:

> Once men were equal, but when envy and covetousness came into the world and might began to triumph over right, it became necessary to appoint defenders for the weak against the strong, and they were called knights.[362]

Gie accounts that the Lady of the Lake explained that God chose one man out of each thousand who was "most loyal, most strong, and most noble in spirit, and better educated and mannered than all the rest."[363] While Knighthood was united with Christianity, and "endowed with all the sanctity and religious awe that attended the priesthood,"[364] Margret Hurley cautions that this synthesis was less than perfect. She points out the distinction that whereas the saint leaves the world behind, to seek his reward in the next, the knight's reward "consists in a return and glorification by the secular society, which sent him forth."[365] Keen however, contends that the Church at least serves to give knighthood a vision:

> Church rites such as blessing of banners and swords, together with the cult of military saints did help to remind knights, through symbolism and ritual, that as Christians they should view their calling in Christian terms.[366]

Along side this movement, manuals of chivalry and chivalric biography were written in order to help "preserve the accumulated wisdom concerning the metier of the knight"[367] William T. Cotton's extensive study of chivalric biographies concluded that they focused "on the person as knight and not on the knight as person."[368]

Source Critique

This section on source criticism seeks to determine specifically what materials Henry had at his disposal in the process of producing his own literary creation. While the *Vita Prima,* completed on February 25, 1229, is considered the sole source for the *LV,*[369] there is strong evidence to suggest other sources. The entire dossier of Francis must be considered when discussing sources, some of which seem to have been overlooked.[370] As early as 1920, for example, Little postulated that the *LV* "contains some new statements based perhaps on oral tradition."[371] Before examining these sources, a discussion about the immediate context in which the *LV* was written and the author's perspective is warranted.

While Henry never states that he met Francis

personally, Manselli points out that Henry

> is a witness to the reality and reputation of Francis during that particular period when the saint was certainly well known, but not yet the center of controversy within the Order.[372]

Henry, however, had already written anti-mendicant propaganda against the Franciscans some seven or eight years earlier in his *Prophetia Sancte Hyldegardis de Novis Fratibus*. Although it is difficult to discern Henry's motivation, one can speculate. Henry's requests for patronage, especially early in his career, give evidence that Henry was a freelance *versificator*. In this light, Henry could be seen as merely earning his living by writing verse. Historically, however, his poem may have been a valid criticism of the early friars who were accused of heresy. It is also possible that Henry was criticizing the friars but not Francis himself or that his poem represents an older view that Henry held. In any case, in the *LV*, Henry addresses Francis himself in a prayer (*LV* I: 16-20) which endearingly asks him "Accept for yourself this work of your poet."[373] Later in chapter eleven, Henry justifies his reason for including a description of the features and temper of Francis by explaining that they contain "the Francis of my reflections or the image I have of him. Moreover, it deposits in the mind ideas of a partly similar kind, even if not exactly the same."[374] The detailed description of the city of Assisi in *LV* I: 29-31 suggests that Henry visited Assisi.[375] At the very least, Manselli concludes that Henry "no doubt had direct information about Italy, even if with our present knowledge we cannot say from whom."[376]

It is important at this time to recall to whom Henry presents his 'image' and to whom he dedicates the *LV.* Few men knew Francis better than Gregory IX, who, as Cardinal Bishop of Ostia, had been personally selected by Francis to be the first cardinal protector of the Order.[377] Gregory IX maintained, in his own words, a "great familiarity" with Francis.[378] Celano recounts their mutual admiration by relating that Gregory "felt great love for"[379] and "venerated the holy man of God with special affection"[380] while Francis "handed over and entrusted himself and his brothers wholeheartedly to the bishop"[381] and "clung to the bishop as a son does his father and an only child to its mother."[382] Celano goes as far as comparing their "close friendship" which was marked with "mutual and affectionate charity" to that of David and Jonathan's, writing that the bishop's "soul was joined to the soul of the holy man."[383] Another chronicler relates that for his part, the bishop supported Francis and his brothers "just as a mother hen cares for her chicks."[384] Henry writes that Francis "obtained first place in his heart as a father" so that he and Gregory IX "were joined in an unbreakable bond, a bond of friendship that had the strongest knot in the world; no two were ever more powerfully united."[385] Gregory IX would not only canonize Francis but as Henry's dedicatory acrostic implies, he commissioned Henry to write the *LV.* Although Anthony Mockler questions whether Gregory

IX actually commissioned the *LV*,[386] it is interesting to note that if the *LV* was commissioned, this would seem to make it an official legend, since according to Manselli's definition, it represents reworked material written upon request.[387] This gives rise to a number of questions. Why would Gregory IX request or accept another version of the official life in the first place and why would he ask an outsider and non-Franciscan to write it? While Thomas of Celano certainly was a student of rhetoric, Gregory looked outside the Order to enlist *magister* Henry. Was Gregory familiar with Henry's particular talents and ability to versify military saints? Was Gregory IX looking for a master versificator to interpret Francis in a deeper, poetic and spiritual way, or was he hired to merely entertain or to perpetuate Francis' legend throughout Europe and beyond? The fact that Henry wrote a poem in defense of Gregory IX's uncle, Innocent III, begs the question of how well Gregory IX knew Henry. Although it is not known just how they met, Gregory IX, as mentioned, studied at Paris and has been described as a "strong exponent of education, a patron of learned men, a reformer of curriculum and an advocate for serious students."[388] Henry's praise of Gregory IX can be seen several times in the *LV*. Henry calls Gregory IX: "Star of probity, flower of rectitude, splendor of clerics, Jewel among priests,"[389] "a gem amid crystals, a laurel in a grove of myrtles, like a true vine amid wild vine, a balsa-tree amid olives."[390] It should be noted however, that Henry, while praising Gregory IX in the *LV*, even calling him "greatest of mortals,"[391] was not uncritical of the Church as seen in his satirical poetry against the avarice of the curia written in his versification of the *Decretals*.[392] However, Gregory IX's approval of the *LV* is certain, for unlike later legends, the *LV* was read before the pope, and thus received at least implicit endorsement if not his full sanction. As mentioned, the only recorded critique of the *LV* by Gregory IX concerns not the content or image of Francis, but rather the poetic meter.

Several factors explain why Gregory IX certainly resonated with the poetic image of Francis presented in the *LV*. Firstly, before Gregory IX became pope, he had been commissioned to preach the Fifth Crusade and thus honed his rhetorical ability to motivate others to war.[393] Secondly, as pope, Gregory IX became the leader (*dux*) of the papal army, and thirdly, was himself a poet.[394] His propensity to use martial imagery can be demonstrated by analyzing his writings. In particular the letter of canonization issued for Francis as well as his own poetry, seem to have had significant influence on the *LV*. The letter of canonization, *Mira circa nos*, contains several themes that are extensively developed in the *LV*. The most predominant characteristic of the letter is its martial motif that portrays Francis as a heroic warrior. The 'slavery analogy' intertwined in this imagery which contrasts the flesh and the spirit, as well as the 'light imagery' will be examined more fully later. According to Emanuela Prinzivalli, the martial imagery and "warlike metaphors" which "recur insistently" in the letter reveal "how Gregory perceived Francis' activity."[395] *Mira Circa Nos* begins with a slavery reference and an allusion to Francis as another Shamgar, who has come in the "eleventh hour" to free Israel.[396] According to Origen's interpretation, Shamgar was a warrior who rescued Israel from the enemy through simple admonitions directed against vice.[397] Gregory then continues the military motif and 'liberator from slavery' theme by calling Francis "another Samson" who "broke the bonds that tied him to a seductive world."[398] With the "mighty strength of God," Francis' preaching is then depicted as slaying and subduing those enslaved to vice.[399] Henry calls Francis Christ's slave and a prisoner on several occasions.[400] Gregory's Francis, "uprooting his vices and courageously taking up the struggle against the world, the flesh, and the spiritual forces of evil,"[401] is also likened to Jacob, "the strong man" who rushes fearlessly into the enemy's camp, takes away their weapons. Gregory continues by stating "after many glorious combats in this life and triumphing over the world,"[402] Francis enters heaven by force. Note Henry even uses Gregory's same scriptural quote from Mathew 11:12, not found in Celano, which speaks of Francis taking heaven by force.[403] Gregory sums up his life by saying it was "so holy, so heroic."[404] Francis, holding a lamp in his hand, attracts others through his "shining deeds" which make him "like the Morning star."[405] As will be seen, these references are heavily developed throughout the *LV.*

More significantly, Gregory's poetry contains striking

connections to Henry's. In fact, if Gregory IX's poetry is any indication of how he viewed Francis, then Henry's legend stands as its greatest likeness and closest parallel. Gregory IX's poem about Francis called *Caput Draconis*[406] holds some striking similarities with the *LV.* Gregory IX's poem is about how Francis combats the "Last of the evil dragon's heads" in "The seventh of its savage wars." Both portray Francis as a "soldier"[407] and "chieftain of great renown,"[408] who "carried the regal banner forth"[409] and "upon whose holy body marked the ensign of the Cross."[410] Gregory IX also has Francis equipped with similar spiritual armor and weapons and the same "shield of faith."[411] As will be seen later in detail, Henry will use these and similar words to describe Francis. An example of Gregory IX's verse shows how he conceived of all three branches of the Franciscans in military terms.

> He marshaled three full battle lines
> Of soldiers ready for action,
> To put to flight and rout that force
> And that threefold demonic band
> The dragon ever kept at strength.[412]

In 1231 Gregory IX even employs martial imagery in his bull *parens scientarium,* which describes the University of Paris as a workshop where,

> Iron furnishes the armor of Christian warfare, the breastplate of faith and the sword of the Spirit; stony hearts are inflamed with the fervour of that Spirit in an academic forge

resonant with the preaching of Christ.[413]

It is interesting to note that Gregory IX granted an indulgence to those who prayed his poetry.[414] Gregory IX must have been delighted, therefore, in Henry's martial description of him as "Francis' Shield"[415] and his homily as a "penetrating swordlike sermon."[416]

It is likely that Gregory IX was not the only poet at the Curia before whom Henry was reciting his *LV*. Thomas of Capua, was "dictator"[417] at the Papal court and author of *ars dictamini,* the art of letter writing.[418] The poems of Thomas of Capua, like the poems of Gregory IX, also have a striking correlation with the *LV* in theme, tone and martial imagery.[419] The poetry of Thomas' *Hymn* of second vespers for example identifies Francis as "chief of the minors,"[420] exactly as Henry does in the *LV* IX: 83-84 and *LV* XIV: 83-84. Thomas also presents Francis as a "captain"[421] who is described as having "regal seals…imprinted on hand and side,"[422] under whom "the standards of the King draw nigh."[423] Additional references to Francis as *dux*, who conquers with heaven's weapons, can be found in the poetry of Gregory IX and Thomas of Capua. It is interesting to note that the poetry of Rainerius of Viterbo, also included in the Office in honor of Francis, contains martial imagery to describe Francis.[424]

Finally, two other poems entitled *Fregit Victor* and *Sanctitas Nova Signa,* both attributed to Thomas of Celano,[425] contain the same theme and image of Francis.[426] In *Sanctitas Nova Signa,* Francis, "bearing the marks of Christ the Lord"[427] triumphs over the world "by the signs of the Cross."[428] Francis is presented in the same way as he is in the *LV*, namely, as one whom, listening to the Kings commands, "curbed his flesh,"[429] and "quelled the carnal foe in a victory renowned."[430] In *Fregit Victor*, Francis is also depicted as the valiant victor who was "in spiritual battle, chief; peerless among those that love."[431]

These correlations and parallels, whether they reflect a source for Henry or an imitation of him, or neither,[432] are, nevertheless, a confirmation of a similar current of thought and interpretation of Francis by his contemporaries. In fact, this conception of Francis is documented as early as 1221 by Jacques de Vitry who, in his *Historia occidentalis*, describes the Franciscans as "valiant soldiers of Christ," who are armed with swords and go from gate to gate "slaughtering and devouring."[433] Roberto Paciocco also reports that in October of 1227, Gregory IX, in his pontifical letter *Licet sacrosancta Romana*, described the friars minor as "*milites Christi*."[434]

Taken together, these documents show that Francis was thought of in military terms as a spiritual "*dux*," "*princeps*," or "*miles*." He was considered a leader or chief, who, carrying the banner or standard of the king, conquered foes with heavenly weapons and led his army of friars to do likewise. This common image of Francis is significant not only because it is such an early conception of him, but also because it was independently conceived by those who intimately knew him.

Another consideration of source material for the *LV* was raised by Arnaldo Fortini, who proposed the possibility that Henry used "the process of canonization extant in the papal Curia" or testimony from eyewitnesses.[435] There is strong evidence to show that Henry used papal testimony from the canonization process when he wrote his *Life of Hugo*.[436] This raises the possibility that Henry had access to a larger dossier that included the witness testimony for Francis' canonization, which is now lost. Close textual analysis of some details inserted in the *LV* (see 3.5), reveal potential references to different sources. The presence of a heavenly intermediary during Francis' vision, which is not found in Celano, may also suggest another source. Francis' comparison to a slave, for example may be an allusion to Gregory IX's *Mira circa nos*.[437] Other details such as Henry describing Francis' tomb of pure stone at St. George could have come from first hand knowledge, eyewitnesses or possibly from the *Legend for Use in the Choir*.[438]

Another source that has been identified through recent scholarship is the Latin epic *Alexandreis* by Walter of Châtillon.[439] Walter, whom Raby referred to as "one of the most important figures among secular poets of the Middle Ages,"[440] was one of the most talented and prolific poets of the Goliards.[441] Walter produced his masterpiece, the *Alexandreis*, sometime between 1171-1189, and dedicated it to William, the Norman Archbishop of Sens and later Rheims.[442]

In this versification of Alexander's life, Walter made a "conscious effort to adapt traditional methods of Biblical paraphrase and commentary to a secular rather than biblical text."[443] Walter's style can best be understood within the context of the literary classicism of the twelfth century in France, which sought to revive ancient classics.[444] Thus, the 5,500 dactylic hexameters of the *Alexandreis* were crafted in the form of an ancient epic with classical vocabulary, themes and topoi, "for the purpose of presenting a comment relevant to his age and times."[445] Walter's heroic poetry, therefore, is full of allusions to Horace and "Virgilian simile," a device used to "dignify and diversify" heroic verse at this time.[446] Another device that Walter borrows from Virgil, and in turn is used by Henry, is the use of short verse summaries preceding each book, which imitate the verse *argumenta* accompanying the books of the *Aeneid*.[447] It is interesting to note that according to A. C. Dionisotti, these summaries used for the purpose of reference reveal Walter's work as "not mere aesthetic or literary entertainment" but as "serious prose."[448]

Walter's popular and much imitated *Alexandreis*[449] was an instant success, and before the end of the thirteenth century achieved the status of a classic, even becoming a schoolbook. Henry of Ghent, commenting on its success, observed, "it was held in such esteem in grammar schools that the study of the ancient poets is neglected in its favour."[450] Lafferty sums up its impact by stating:

> The *Alexandreis* rapidly rekindled the interest of

> Walter's contemporaries in the Latin epic form, a spate of full-length Latin epics soon appeared in response, like Joseph of Exeter's *Ylias,* on a classical subject to others like Guillaume le Breton's *Phillippidos* about Philip Augustus, based on contemporary events.[451]

The first letter of the first word of each of the ten chapters of the *Alexandreis* spells the name of Walter's patron, Guillermus. Henry borrows this acrostic device for his fourteen chapters to spell the name of GREGORIUS NONUS, for whom he dedicates the *LV.* In both works, each chapter begins with a synopsis of the upcoming narrative. Moreover, Henry's prologue contains some verbal echoes from Walter's that are verbatim. Neil Adkin's observations of Henry's imitation of Walter's *Alexandreis* in his proem of the *Life of Saint Guthlac* can be applied to the *LV.*[452] Both write in the style of Virgil, as Walter begins his proem "*Gesta ducis Macedum*" and Henry begins "Gesta sacri cantabo ducis." Walter's "*At tu*" (1.9) at the start of his line is also used by Henry (*LV* I: 21) to introduce his patron. As Walter compared Alexander as superior over "*caesareos...fama triumphos*" (1.7), Henry compares Francis as superior to "*Iulius*" and "*Alexander,*" since Francis has surpassed the "*fama triumphos*" of old (*LV* I:8).

Walter then uses a 'light' metaphor in comparing Alexander with Rome's rulers: "*Preradiaret...meriti fulgore*" (1.9), which Henry seems to echo when he compares Assisi with a similar 'light' metaphor:

"tantique refloret alumni illustrata novis fulgoribus urbs veterana Assisium" (*LV* I: 28-29).[453] Walter also heavily moralizes and personifies vice and her sisters in Book 10 just as Henry personifies vice in chapter two. Finally, Walter's so called "cosmological speculation of the natural poets," indicative of the naturalism of this time which sought to analyze and explain creation in human terms can also be seen in Henry as will be seen later.[454]

Some interesting parallels exist between Alexander and Francis if we consider how both of these men are fundamentally *dux* and *mile* who are seeking and desiring glory. Both then experience a prophetic vision of a military theme in which there is an unidentified figure.[455] Further, each initially misinterprets the message in both visions, an error which is compared to Aeneas' misreading the scenes depicted on Juno's temple in Carthage.[456] Most significantly, both are motivated by the vision throughout the entire action of the story. Both are stories of conquest, written in the epic style of Virgil, and have Christ as the real hero, at least implicitly.[457] While Alexander is an *exemplum* for the pride and "vanity of human achievement," Francis is the *exemplum* of humility and God's glory.[458]

The following description of Walter's style could also be used to depict Henry's overall style:

> The poet paraphrases into verse the material which is in prose, and by the processes of abbreviation, omission, literal paraphrase,

modal variation, periphrasis, synomic amplification and interpretatio he emphasizes those points he would like his readers to take to heart while enjoying the edifying material presented.[459]

Chapter Two: The *Legenda Versificata* and the Icon of Francis

Chapter two studies the historical relevance of the *LV* and its icon of Francis. Because the validity of Henry's icon is dependent upon Francis as a soldier, this section begins with a brief survey of the military motif and includes a critical historical analysis of Francis in relation to chivalry and knighthood. An examination of Francis' writings and other documents, legends and biographies provides a critical basis from which to assess the historical validity of Henry's icon.

Military Motif

Considering the central metaphor that Henry utilizes is the military motif, a deeper study of the development of this theme in Christian literature is appropriate. From the very earliest times, the Christian journey has been described in military terms.[1] M. L. Del Mastro explains that Paul was the first to use the military analogy as a metaphor for the Christian experience, particularly in his epistles Second Timothy 2:3 and Ephesians 6:10-17.[2] In these letters, Paul writes that every Christian be a "good soldier" and "put on the armor of God." Del Mastro states that military imagery, "while Pauline in origin, was Benedictine in development."[3] Benedict's Rule, in fact, begins with the definition of a monk as one who wages his war under a rule and abbot, learning to fight against the devil by preparing himself in the fraternal line of battle for the single combat of the hermit. Benedict states "you have seized the strongest and best weapons of obedience, in order to battle for Christ, the true King."[4] The Abbot leads this fight, "by deeds more than words" by first fighting against his own body and spiritual vices.[5] Thus the battle waged takes place in the soul, the real field of combat. This in fact represents the deepest aspect of asceticism, which can be seen as a personal battle, a constant spiritual exercise that trains the believer for spiritual combat, and the acquisition of virtue.[6] Louis Bouyer describes the interior struggle of the ascetic as the new man overcoming the old. He also points out that Scripture teaches this struggle is not merely interior combat but rather part of a war fought not against "enemies of blood and flesh" but against the "cosmic powers of this present darkness, against the spiritual forces of evil."[7] Francis' asceticism was perhaps the fruit of his aspiration to knighthood that is believed to have predisposed him to ascesis.[8] Bouyer states:

> [the ascetic] carries the struggle to a depth within himself which the layman knows nothing of, and which it is doubtless better that he should not know, for it would fill him with a vertigo against which he would have no effective defense.[9]

Bouyer further relates how the devil "uses all the weapons, or rather the intermediaries, which are familiar to him and by means of which he overcame man in the beginning."[10] Thus Ephesians 6:11 exhorts the Christian to put on the "whole" armor of God. Since the word 'armor' is a fusion of two Greek words meaning "all" and "weapons," it literally signifies the complete battle equipment of a soldier, and figuratively indicates all the resources that God makes available to those who enlist in spiritual warfare.

Through means of his poetic license, Henry's icon is able to reveal Francis' inner life, the place where the inward battle rages, and thus communicates the interior struggle within his soul. In this regard, there is an implicit allusion to a poem by Roman author Aurelius Prudentius Clemens entitled *Psychomachia,* "the first Western example of a purely allegorical poem."[11] The *Psychomachia,* literally the "war in the soul," is a poem about the battle of virtue and vice within the human soul. It is interesting to note, Stanislao Da Campagnola's study of Francis' writing compares his *Praises of the Virtues to the Psychomachia*.[12] Henry personifies vice and virtue in a similar fashion to the *Psychomachia* at a time (1200-1700) considered the beginning of "the great era of personification allegory in European literature."[13]

Henry's use of the virtues and vices will be taken up in greater detail in chapter four. The classification of virtues and vices and their personified warfare was developed in the twelfth century in the writing of Bernard of Clairvaux, Hildegard of Bingen, as well as Alanus Magnus de Insulis, as seen is his allegory

Anticlaudianus.[14] In this work, "Nature" calls together the celestial council of her sisters in order to band together to fight. Led by Concord, Peace, Plenty, Favour, Youth, Laughter (banisher of mental mists), Shame, Modesty, Reason (the measure of the good), Honesty, Dignity, Prudence, Piety, Faith, Virtue and Nobility join forces.[15]

Bouyer's caveat that "no war is waged except in view of peace,"[16] reminds the spiritual combatant that the goal of this war is interior peace, or "the perfect tranquility of the flesh and the spirit which the ancients called *hesychia.*"[17]

Historical Critique: Francis, Chivalry, and Knighthood

Julio Micó observed, "in order to understand Francis' religious experience we must see it in its immediate context, from which, as from fertile soil, it drew its existence and meaning."[18] Fortini eloquently articulates this truth:

> What is not so often said is that Assisi also made Francis...From his cradle, Assisi's legends, beliefs, traditions, and customs shaped the thinking of the unique man. Assisi schools, churches, and social institutions taught him. Assisi law set a standard for his conduct. The day to day happenings in Assisi—both small and large—in a turbulent period in its long history demanded his participation and inevitably left

> their mark upon him. Assisi social structures and economy defined him to himself and determined the channels in which his life as a youth moved, even the channels into which his life was directed once he rebelled against them. His Assisi friends and neighbors, along with his heroes and enemies, touched him and played their role in the life that he worked out as his own.[19]

The central metaphor of Henry's icon posits Francis as *"sacer dux"* and *"milites Christi."* Le Goff, who as mentioned once described Francis as "a combination of knight of God, troubadour and jongleur," has even suggested that Francis "introduced into Christianity the chivalrous ideal."[20] Since Mayeski warns that a solid and careful historical analysis must precede a theological reading, an important question must be addressed before proceeding, namely, the question of the historical validity of Henry's icon regarding Francis' life.[21] This survey of Francis' relationship to chivalry and knighthood, drawn from a variety of different sources, which include historical documents, chronicles, Francis' writings, legends, biographies and various studies,[22] demonstrates the relevance of Henry's icon in a critical way. Included in this inquiry is Francis' association to the troubadour and courtly romance tradition.

The complex matrix of Francis' spirituality includes the influence of cultural, socio-religious, socio-economic, and political factors.[23] According to Raphael Brown,

Francis' Etruscan, Umbrian and Roman ancestors bequeathed him a personality that could be described as a combination of "discipline with militancy and sanctity."[24] Whether or not this is true, Francis was certainly born at the dawn of chivalry into a world described as a "battlefield of danger and death."[25] The city of Assisi, as well as the wider peninsula of medieval Italy, had a long history of battles, crusades and wars. Noted Italian historian Marco Bartoli attests that in addition to the "perpetual war" of the domestic infighting between "the maiores or landowners and the minores or men of the people,"

> [the] continual state of belligerence within and without the city was kept alive and fed by the tensions between the Emperor Frederick II and the popes. Together they made central Italy, especially Umbria, their chosen battleground.[26]

He states that Francis was situated within a "warring society in which conflict was a condition of daily life,"[27] where kings and emperors led crusades and knightly battles were commonly fought in the name of God. Bartoli goes on to relate that the "culture of knighthood" was "at the very heart" of this warring.[28] Thus it can be concluded that the "cultural and social background of Francis was chivalry."[29] This is highlighted in Francis' first school, Saint George, a military saint who embodied the virtues of knighthood.[30] Fortini, for example, describes a fresco at the school depicting St. George, the protector of knights, in white armor.[31] He is riding a white horse and burying his lance into the neck of a dragon, while a princess looks on. The legend recounts how St. George, appearing as a great knight, rescued the fair princess from the dragon, preached a sermon, and then gave the horse and his armor to the poor for the love of Christ. St. George, one of the most universally popular saints since the fourth century, became a model of the virtues of courage and faith.[32] San Georgio is the site of several significant events in the life of Francis and Clare. It was the first church that Francis began to preach, where Clare may have heard him, the initial place of his burial, the location of his canonization as well as the place where Clare would later be buried.[33]

In 1187, when Francis was only five or six years old, Jerusalem fell into the hands of the Saracens, who defeated the knights of Outremer and the Grand Masters of the Military Orders at the Horn of Hattin.[34] Following this defeat, Pope Gregory VIII called for a new crusade and the "most emotive of rallying cries"[35] from Christendom arose for Christian knights to retake Jerusalem.[36] Among those who would heed the call of the Third Crusade were Richard the Lion Heart, King of England, Philippe Auguste, King of France, and even the Emporer himself, Frederick I, Barbarossa.[37]

As stated above, France produced many stories of romance and chivalry, both fiction and nonfiction, which were diffused within the culture of the day.[38] Le Goff relates that in general, society was heavily influenced by these courtly values of the aristocracy and knights.[39] Although it is impossible to know just how much these stories and the other Romance literature of France influenced Francis, it is certain Francis did have a connection to France, especially through his father Pietro, who named his son Francesco which translates "Frenchman."[40] Pietro is believed to have frequented France to attend the famous international fairs held in Champagne at Privons and Troyes.[41] It is debated whether Francis ever visited France himself or with his father, although one source holds that Pietro frequently sent his son to France for business purposes.[42] This opens the possibility that Francis visited Champagne, which would have placed him at the very center of what Mockler describes as an almost "new civilization, knightly but not militaristic, poetic not degenerate"[43] that produced an outpouring of new romance, epic literature and lyric poetry.[44] Mockler, a military historian, not only comments that the knights of Champagne were "the proudest and probably the richest in Europe," but that "the courts of Marie of Champagne at Troyes and her mother Eleanor of Aquitaine at Poiters became the most famous and renowned in Europe."[45] Whether Francis read any of the literature coming out of France or simply heard the stories, his knowledge of French is indisputable.[46] His mother Pica, who was perhaps from Picardy,[47] but most likely from France,[48] may have been responsible for Francis' ability to speak and sing "the songs of the French troubadours"[49] in the lyrical language of Provence.[50] It is not unreasonable to believe that Pietro himself may have known French and thus would have taught Francis the language of commerce as a matter of practical preparation for business. In either case, Schmucki observed that Francis' knowledge of French "gave him a window on the culture of the day," through which "he came into direct contact with the cult of chivalry."[51] There remains, however, some debate as to how much chivalric and romance literature Francis was actually exposed to in his life. Fortini holds that Francis would have read Andrea's *De Amore*, a lyrical poetic book of chivalry,[52] stating that it was "impossible that Francis, who knew French lyric inside out, did not know this book."[53] Manselli, on the other hand, refrains from hypothesizing whether Francis even knew the poems of Chrétian de Troyes.[54]

In addition to Francis' French connection, it is certain that the *Song of Roland*, whose protagonist has been considered 'the' ideal of Christian chivalry,[55] and the legends of King Arthur and the Knights of the Round Table, were already known throughout Italy.[56] Bartoli points out that courtly culture arose in Aquitaine and specifically relates that "many place names bear witness to the spread of various cycles of stories of knightly courtesy in Italy."[57] John Moorman relates, "Italy was resounding with songs of wandering minstrels who sang of love and chivalry or of their religious hopes and joys."[58] Lawrence S. Cunningham suspects that Francis would have had contact with this tradition "through the many French pilgrims who passed through Umbria on their way to Rome and the shrines of Christendom."[59] More specifically, Le

Goff relates that "even the urban society of the Italian communes" was heavily influenced by the courtly values of knighthood.[60] Fortini cites two records that attest to the existence of Carolingian epic poetry as being well known in Assisi.[61] He points to evidence which shows that the *chanson de geste* had spread into Assisi as early as 1121.[62]

Assisi was, in fact, no stranger to the pageantry and pomp of emperors, and the violence of soldiers and knights.[63] A consideration of the militaristic ambience of Assisi in which Francis was bred lends insight into the reality of Assisi at the turn of the thirteenth century and thus affirms the cultural and historical background pointing to the validity of Henry's icon. Built over Roman ruins and fortresses, Assisi contains several interesting landmarks that speak of its military history. The first and most obvious would be the walls surrounding the city, constructed in order to defend the city against attacking forces. These high defensive walls point to the reality that "all the citizens" of Assisi, a city no longer under the Roman peace, "had to be soldiers."[64] Another is an ancient Roman amphitheater, a reminder of the place where naval battles were recreated in all their violence. Hidden some six meters below the very heart of Assisi, directly under the Piazza Commune lies an altar dedicated to two famous mythological soldiers who were twin brothers, the heroes Castor and Pollux.[65] A walk through the older section of the city also reveals a visible testimony to the unrest that the Assisani endured. The doors of their homes were built about a meter above the street for defensive purposes. The devotional prayers of the Assisani even reflect this defensive attitude. Bartoli records a prayer to San Rufino, whose body was buried in the cathedral, built over the ruins of an ancient Roman fortress. "O San Rufino, always defend us, your servants...drive away the sorrows of war."[66]

A testimony from Brother Elemosina concerning the invasion of the Lombards in the fifth century speaks of Assisi's glorious but violent history:

> We found in the ancient writings that the city of Assisi, which was surrounded by the strongest walls and towers, adorned with palaces and strong structures, well populated with many gallant, high spirited people, defended by numerous brave warriors, was occupied by a terrible and ferocious people, who inflicted havoc on all the surrounding land.[67]

Another of the old legends, recorded in *Liber historiaum S. Ecclesiae,* tells of Charlemagne's siege of Assisi.[68] The story relates that Charlemagne conquered Assisi and established in it a new Christian and Catholic people. Assisi had also been host to Frederick Barbarossa in 1177 and hailed him a Caesar Augustus, Emperor of the Romans, who was invincible, great and glorious.[69] Frederick II would later be baptized in Assisi at the Church of San Rufino.[70]

The commune of Assisi had its own knightly pageantry as well, as the city required its citizens to be soldiers under the command of a leader called the *vessillifero*.[71] Fortini holds that Francis was a member of the *Compagnia dei Cavalieri*, the "strongest and most prestigious of all the commune's companies," which were comprised of *milites*, that is, noble knights and merchants, who could afford a horse and armor.[72] It is interesting to note that the first item that Celano relates in Francis' dream of arms is a saddle.[73]

Multiple attestation in the hagiography confirms that Francis was known as having been the leader of a band of youth.[74] In some small towns in Italy, it was common for certain troubadours known as the "Golden youth" to have a leader, *dux*, or master called a *podestâ*, who was often chosen from a wealthy family.[75] The generosity of the *podestâ* was relied upon in order to absorb the cost of their feasting.[76] Francis is even conjectured to have been the leader of Assisi's singing and dancing troupe known as the Tripudiante.[77]

The Church at this time was not only undergoing internal struggles but was confronted by grave challenges from the outside and therefore enlisted the aid of fighting men. As early as 1095, Pope Urban II had sounded a call to arms to Christians to recapture the city of Jerusalem. According to Christopher Arthur Ohan, Urban II "equated service in crusade with a love for God" and "convinced many that they were personally fighting on behalf of God."[78] While this call was directed to knights, Micó points out "it was the ordinary people who were the first to respond by setting out to conquer Jerusalem, unarmed and as penitents."[79] Innocent II issued three bulls that took the Knights Templar under greater papal control, and granting them such privileges as free disposal of the spoils of victory against infidels and indulgences to benefactors.[80] In 1184, Pope Lucius III issued the Bull, *Ad Abolendam*, giving Bishops indulgences as an incentive to use force against the Cathars. Micó relates that the Crusades fostered a spirituality that viewed the "Christian life as a battle to win heaven."[81] He continues by stating that at this time "the Church was seen as an organized structure" whose function seemed to be more political than sacramental.[82] The structure of Christian leadership in fact underwent a profound change with the death of Emperor Henry VI in 1197 and the election of Innocent III in 1198.

In 1198, when Francis was about sixteen years old, he may have seen the siege of the *Rocca Maggiore* fortress, from which Duke Conrad of Urslingen (Moscaincervello) had governed Assisi.[83] According to Julien Green, January of 1200 marked the beginning of the latest war between Perugia and Assisi,[84] who were intermittently battling against each other for over five centuries (between the eleventh and fifteenth century).[85] While it is not documented whether Francis participated in the siege of the *Rocca*, Francis did fight in the bloody battle against Perugia in November of the year 1202,[86] somewhere between Collestrada and Ponte San Giovanni.[87] Francis was taken captive and retained for about a year.[88] According to Fortini, however, because Francis was part of "the *societas militum,* made up of knights and of prosperous merchants," he was "imprisoned separately from the other soldiers."[89] The Fourth Crusade (1202-1204), once again led by the Champagne knights, also took place at this time.[90]

After Francis was released and recovered from his illness,[91] he decided to re-enter battle again. This, perhaps more than any other event in his life, shows his deep-rooted desire to fight as a knight and win glory, fame and wealth. It is generally agreed that Francis sought to join Count Gautier (Walter) de Brienne in Apulia, home of one of the original ten provinces of the Knights Templar.[92] Count Gautier was a famous French knight who had won Princess Albiria's hand in marriage by rescuing her mother the Queen Sibila from a dungeon.[93] Gautier, along with the Knights Templar made up a part of the personal pontifical army of Innocent III, and were considered the "militia of Christ by which the pope would enforce his will and attain his goals."[94] Innocent III, while not uncritical of the Templars, referred to them as "the beloved brothers of the militia of the Temple."[95] Backed by the King of France, Gautier had been recruiting knights in hopes of recovering Queen Sibila's former kingdom in Apulia. He had already sworn to fight Markward of Anweiler in the name of Pope Innocent III, who rewarded him by naming him Count of Lecce and Prince of Taranto.[96] Markward, who had served with Conrad,[97] is another example of the upward mobility open to knights. Markward in fact was a ministerial that had been Henry VI's tutor and served as regent during the minority of Frederick II. At this time in the Empire, many ministerials who were originally "household knights of servile status, rose to become members of the lesser nobility."[98] These ministerials were mainly responsible for the German literature of chivalry, which explained and justified the new social class they joined.[99] It is interesting to note that when Markward threatened to use force against the Cardinals after his siege of the Benedictine Abbey of Cassino in 1199, it was Hugolino himself who opposed him by supporting Innocent III's sentence of excommunication against him.[100]

Gautier and his soldiers wore a standard of the cross on their armor given to them by Pope Innocent III for this mission.[101] After their success against the army of Diopoldo di Vohburg when they were outnumbered 200 to 5000,[102] legends were told of Gautier bearing a flaming sword like the Angel of the Apocalypse.[103] At a critical moment in the following battle, it was said that Gautier flew upon his enemies when a "cross of gold appeared and led him to victory."[104]

The preaching of this period also echoed the chivalry of the day. An example of this can be found in the preaching of a priest named Fulk of Nevilly. Fulk, one of Pope Innocent III's chief instruments in the crusade during 1200-1204, demanded that King Richard give up his "daughters" of pride, greed and lust.[105] Williel R. Thomson mentions that Pope Innocent III's arsenal also included a large number of French knights, which he unleashed on the Albigensians in 1209.[106] He goes on to relate that at this particular time of crisis, Rome urgently required "a highly mobile and exemplary nucleus of faithful evangelical lieutenants" which was delivered through Cardinal John when he presented Francis and his followers to Pope Innocent III.[107]

The question, therefore, is not *whether* the historical and literary ambience of knightly chivalry or troubadour romance affected Francis but rather how did this specifically influence his life, personality and spirituality; that is, to what extent. While Manselli has pointed out that Francis' spirituality reflected the "'popular' psychology and culture" of his day,[108] Le Goff states Francis "felt the influence of this chivalresque culture," and also noted that "his cult of poverty had courtly overtones."[109] Schmucki goes further and states there is "no doubt that the ideals of chivalry had a decisive influence on the Saint's spirituality."[110] A study of Francis' writings give evidence of this influence.

The Writings of Francis

Francis identifies himself in chivalric terms as a "herald of the great king."[111] While a herald has certain biblical associations, its medieval context signified "an official of knightly birth who delivered the invitations or challenges at feasts...and had charge of the entire ceremonial at the court."[112] An examination of Francis' writings provide a critical basis from which to assess the historical validity of Henry's icon. Francis' thirty-eight writings vary in genre from letters, rules, admonitions, prayers and testaments. While Francis never explicitly speaks of knighthood, chivalry or soldiery in his writings, the motif of the battle between the flesh and the spirit is prominent and as Roberto Paciocco correctly points out,[113] his language has courtly connotations, especially regarding the concept of courtesy or sweetness. Francis in his *First Version of the Letter to the Faithful* revels in how "sweet" it is to have "such a Brother and such a Son: our Lord Jesus Christ."[114] In his *Parchment Given to Brother Leo,* Francis exalts God by proclaiming: "You are all our sweetness."[115] Finally Francis, at the end of his life, describes his conversion in the opening lines of his *Testament* by using the word sweet: "that which seemed bitter to me was changed into sweetness of soul and body."[116] In fact many of the biographers frequently use the word sweet or sweetness[117] when speaking of Francis' experience, for example, *A Mirror of Perfection* describes his spirit as in a state of "sweetness and consolation."[118] According to Adolf Holl, "the topos of sweetness appears so often and in so many different passages"[119] in the biographies of Francis, that it warrants attention. Holl points out that the word for sweetness in Florence, "*dolcezza,*" was "historically related to 'courtesy' which was modeled after the great courts, primarily those in South France."[120] In addition, Holl states that "*douceur*" the "corresponding (French) noun, means sweetness, mildness, smoothness, loveliness" and synchronizes with "the three sense perceptions–sight (lovely), taste (sweet), and touch (smooth)."[121] While the specific virtues of knighthood, besides prowess and loyalty, focused on largesse (generosity), "*courtoisie*,"[122] and "*franchise*,"[123] Sorrell holds that Francis' theological expression of "*cortesia*" seems to combine all three. According to Sorrell, the essential ideals of Francis' concept of courtesy combine several ideas. Sorrell states the result is that Francis is able to "'spiritualize' the chivalric value of largesse and noblesse oblige: beneficent magnanimity and special consideration or deference to others, especially those lower in station."[124] He goes on to define "*courtesia*" with God as involving a "magnanimous, self-denying effusion and bounty, a form of condescending love to those both just and unjust, chosen and unchosen."[125] In a similar way, Mulholland writes: "the largesse of God in the vision of Francis is the largesse of the perfect knight: kind, gentle, humble."[126]

The language Francis uses in his prayers also has specifically chivalric connotations. According to scholars Laurent Gallant and André Cirino, Francis' *Office of the Passion* is a type of medieval *geste*, which they define as "an extensive song or saga extolling the valor and the great deeds of a hero, such as King Arthur and his Knights of the Round Table."[127] In his *Office*, Francis composes an ensemble of poetic psalms, which contain the "essential components" of a *geste*: the hero, the mission, the enemies and the hero's victory.[128] Thus Francis daily sung of Christ as his 'King' and 'hero.'[129]

Francis' other poetry is also likened to that of the troubadours, especially the *Canticle of Creatures,* which venerates the natural order, a subject contained in some of the Provençal literature.[130] The *Canticle* is a song written in the vernacular in which Francis sings his praises to the Lord through creation, initially through "Sir brother sun."[131] Roger Sorrell explains that this "chivalric address" did not express affection but rather "it was part of Francis' unique way of showing his high regard for creatures by giving them the same type of chivalric honors he also gave to his human 'companions of the Round Table'."[132] Mulholland contends that the *Canticle* is a true "troubadour lyric and courtly novella"[133] because it "praises intimate Love," and has a "tremendous sense of *courtois,*" in which "Francis adopts the attitude of a courtly lover."[134] He states the "profound courtois" of the adjectives "gentle," "serene," "humble," "strong," "robust," "radiant," "precious," were the "attitudes and values that the knight was to hold."[135] Hilarin Felder states: "Francis made his whole life one great Christ-Epic"[136] and thus the *Canticle* can be seen as "one of the great events of his Christian knighthood."[137]

Perhaps the most striking examples however are the hymns and songs Francis composed: the *Salutation of the Blessed Virgin Mary,*[138] the hymn contained in the twenty third chapter of the *Earlier Rule* and the *Salutation to the Virtues,* which are reminiscent of medieval lyrics of the day.[139] Each of these, in fact, belongs to a genre of praises sung by troubadours called *laudi*,[140] a popular type of which originated in Umbria,[141] and according to Fortini, possibly from Assisi.[142] Stanislao da Campagnola wrote that these fragments alone would be enough to show the poetic soul of Francis.[143] During this time, religious devotion and chivalry seemed to converge in the cult of Our Lady, which involved a blending of the romantic and mystical idealization of womanhood.[144]

These courtly connotations are evident as Francis addresses the virtues of poverty and charity as Ladies, while calling wisdom a queen.[145] Francis refers to Mary, Jacoba and the Poor Clares as "ladies,"[146] just as the troubadours, who almost always spoke of their *domina* as the paragon of beauty and virtue. In addition, Francis also exhorted his brothers to "love and be faithful to our Lady Holy Poverty" in his *Testament* written in Siena.[147] Leonard Lehmann argued that the prayer hymn of praise and thanksgiving found in chapter twenty three of the *Earlier Rule* is closely linked with the *Canticle* in "ideas and context," and thus can be classified as a *laude* of the troubadours.[148] Moreover, in Regis J. Armstrong's study of the *Salutation* he writes, "Of all the writings of Francis, this is one that is perhaps the most clearly influenced by chivalry or the troubadour tradition."[149] Lehmann claims that the *Salutation*, "more than any other of Francis' writings, shows the influence of contemporary Latin rhythmical prose and the courtly lyrics of the Provençal poets." He states that Francis' use of the language of "courtly love" in the *Salutation* "embodies the spirit of the troubadours and minstrels, the lyric poets and the knights."[150] In turn, moreover, Sandro Sticca states that it was Francis and his movement which provided the *Lauda* "both its spirituality and its social and popular character."[151]

Francis, in his *Canticle of Exhortation to St. Clare and Her Sisters,* includes a royal image of each of the sisters being "crowned queen in heaven with the Virgin Mary."[152] This royal motif can be seen in his first admonition, which states how Jesus came "from his royal throne"[153] and appears again in a parable that Francis is believed to have received in a dream. The dream relates a woman who lives in the woods, is impregnated by the king, and later sends her son to court to be fed there. This event, recorded as early as 1219,[154] is significant because it is another example of how Francis conceives of God as king, and his followers as royal sons. Régine Pernoud notes:

> Throughout the entire Middle Ages...nobility had above all a *military character.*
>
> In fact, its duty of protection involved in the first place the military function, that of defending the domain against possible invaders.[155]

Franco Cardini's study of the writings of Francis emphasizes the feudal character of Francis's relationship with Mary and God. In particular, Cardini holds that the *Canticle of Creatures* is best understood within the context of a Lord-vassal relationship, along with the *Salutation* and the *Praises of the Virtues.*[156]

Christ as Lord in the medieval context would be defined as supreme suzerain of whom all would be considered vassals.[157] According to Nguyên-Van-Khanh, since "all lords in the Middle Ages were warriors, Christ the Lord was frequently represented with the features of a military king."[158]

Francis was also devoted to St. Michael the Archangel, the "great prince"[159] of the Angels, naming him four times in his writings, including a prayer to defend him in battle.[160] Francis had ordered that a chapter be held at St. Mary of the Angels twice a year, on Pentecost and the Dedication of St. Michael.[161] These references are particularly significant considering that in the Middle Ages, St. Michael was the "patron of every Christian Knight,"[162] especially venerated in his military capacity as a warrior angel and the leader and commander of the heavenly army.[163] The figure of St. Michael as a knight wearing armor, holding a sword or spear to vanquish Satan, under the banner of "Who is like God?" conveyed a clear message: "faith in the true God brings victory in battle."[164]

Francis' only autobiographical signature in his writing incorporates the Tau cross, which he favored over all others and "considered to be the coat of arms of his order."[165] The Tau is referred to in the Old Testament when God instructed the destroying angel to "mark" the foreheads of those that sigh and moan against the abominations of the times.[166] This cross was used in 1212 as a symbol for the crusade.[167] In his letter to the Patriarch of Armenia, Innocent III described the crusaders (cross-bearers) as signed on the forehead with a Tau like Ezechiel.[168] More significantly, Innocent III opened the Fourth Lateran Council in 1215 (which Francis may have attended)[169] by proclaiming that the Tau was exactly the same form as the cross on which our Lord was crucified.[170] He went on to warn that the only people who would obtain mercy were those who were marked with the 'sign' and had mortified their flesh and conformed their life to that of the Crucified Savior. He ended his speech with a dramatic exhortation to be champions of the Tau and of the cross.[171] It may be noted that in Christian leadership, Innocent III marked a shift from priest-like kings to king-like priests.[172] Innocent III claimed that as Vicar of Christ, he exercised spiritual authority that superseded temporal authority in the name of the 'King of Kings and Lord of Lords.'[173] He also claimed that no king could rule rightly unless he served the one universal Vicar of Christ who rules over the whole earth.[174] Thus for Francis, the Tau is "the sign of conquerors"[175] which Innocent III presented as an emblem of reform and symbol for conversion and renewal. It can be understood to have "colored his entire spirituality"[176] and seen as a type of banner or "coat of arms."[177]

In sum, after surveying Francis' writings, it is evident that some of his hymns like the *Saluation* utilize courtly troubadour language. Francis' devotion to Mary and St. Michael, as well as his autograph of the Tau, contain knightly overtones. Martha Rampton's study of Francis concludes by stating "the courtly and troubadour tradition" is "explicit in the writings of Francis."[178] Le Goff goes further in stating that "the courtly vocabulary of Francis" did not only reflect his culture but was an expression of the "exteriorization of the warrior heroism" that was characteristic of the spirituality of the day.[179]

Early Documents, Legends, and Biographies of Francis

In addition to the evidence already presented in the study on the sources for the *LV*, the link between Francis, the troubadour tradition, chivalry and knighthood is substantially reflected in the early documents and biographies.[180] A brief mention of some examples of these references is in order. One of the early legends, the anonymously authored work entitled *The Sacred Exchange between Saint Francis and Lady Poverty*,[181] is really a love story which shares some of the courtly romance clichés and techniques found in the *LV*: the personification of vice and virtue,[182] the military motif, and the royal imagery, especially of Christ as the King of Kings. In this poetic allegory, which has been compared to the *Queste del Saint-Graal*, and the *Romance of the Rose*, Francis is seen as a romance hero, a knight who is on a quest for his Lady Poverty.[183] Mulholland claims this work is a "courtly love novella" expressing a "sustained reflection" on the Troubadour idealization of women.[184] Manselli describes the *Sacred Exchange* as Francis' life experiences "transposed into terms taken from chivalry,"[185] claiming that it helps one understand "the sense and the importance of the saint's feelings."[186]

Celano's depiction of Francis has been criticized for downplaying both the romance and chivalrous elements in his life, which will be seen later in Little and Sorrell's study and for accentuating them. Rampton's study of the image of Francis in Celano demonstrates "the troubadour theme runs as a consistently discernable thread throughout the lives" in three ways: "Francis as the noble knight in quest of deeds, Francis as the poet and wandering minstrel, Francis as the Lover of lady Poverty and devotee of the Virgin Mary."[187] Both of Celano's *Lives* refer to Francis as a soldier—"the new soldier of Christ," "the bravest soldier of Christ."[188] Celano's *Vita Prima* describes Francis as one in search of *gestes*, that is, one who had "vowed, out of vainglory and vanity, to do great deeds."[189] Celano later relates the spousal imagery of how Francis, eager for "higher status," sought to "espouse" poverty and "became the lover of her beauty."[190] Francis is said to have "not only left his father and mother" but left everything "to cling to his wife," that the "two might be in one spirit" and to hold "her close in chaste embraces."[191] Most significantly Celano recognized that "even when meditating on sacred things, he maintained his courtly manners."[192]

Luke of Túy's treatise, dating from the early 1230's, calls Francis a "soldier of Christ," who "demonstrated his perfect victory over the struggle of the world" and through the "sign" of his stigmata, "was an imitator of his King."[193] Roger of Wendover's chronicle written sometime between 1225-1235 includes an excerpt which states that Francis "as a noble warrior, take up the spiritual battle against evil spirits and carnal vices."[194] The *Anonymous of Perugia* holds some interesting details that reveal Francis' earliest image of Christ and his knighthood. In the very first chapter, Francis, after sending away a poor man begging for arms in the Lord's name, scolds himself for his "great rudeness."[195] The phrase "*magna rusticitas*" translates as an "action contrary to the requirements of chivalry" or lacking in courtesy.[196] It not only shows Francis' conscious self-awareness of chivalrous duty but also presents it as the very first moment in Francis' process of conversion. He consequently reflects on this experience in terms that reveal his understanding of the cultural society and his royal image of God:

> If the poor man had asked in the name of a count or a powerful baron, you would have granted him his request. How much more should you have done this for the King of Kings and the Lord of all?[197]

Francis then resolves never to refuse alms to those invoking the Lord's name and begins by giving the poor man generous alms. This self-conscious act of chivalry is followed in the next chapter by a greater confirmation of his chivalrous aspirations in which Francis not only desires and arranges to be knighted in Apulia, but even obtains a squire.[198]

The *Legend of the Three Companions* also records that Francis wore precious goods so as to appear like a "troubadour,"[199] and wanted to be knighted, and even includes a prophesy in prison which manifests his deepest desire: "The day will come when I shall be honored by the whole world."[200] Even Francis' donation of his clothes to a poor knight is interpreted through his great desire for knighthood: "the promise of great chivalry and nobility was so strong in him, that it may be believed that the vision (of arms) may have provided the motive."[201] Francis is later described as "the very brave knight of Christ" who "was strengthened with Christ's armor of confidence."[202] The *Legend* also speaks of his knightly virtues, particularly, his "*courtoisie*," describing him as "naturally courteous in manner and speech."[203] Francis even reflects within himself:

> You are generous and courteous to those from whom you receive nothing except passing and worthless approval. Is it not right that, on account of God, who repays most generously, you should be courteous and generous to the poor?[204]

The first chapter of *A Mirror of Perfection* (The Lemmens Edition) begins by explaining why Francis held that begging was of "the greatest courtesy before God."[205] *A Mirror of Perfection* (Sabatier Edition) as well as *The Second Life* by Celano includes Francis exhorting brother fire to be courteous.[206] *The Little Flowers of Saint Francis* even has Francis give an exhortation on the "divine virtue" of courtesy:

> Dear Brother, know that courtesy is one of the attributes of God, who gives His sun and his rain to the just and unjust out of courtesy; and courtesy is the sister of charity, extinguishing hatred and preserving love.[207]

Bonaventure's *Legenda Maior* calls Francis "the new champion of Christ," and "the intrepid knight of Christ," exhorting him, "most vigorous knight of Christ, bear the arms of your invincible Leader."[208] Bonaventure also explains how God moved in him: "it was suggested to his spirit" that a "knight of Christ must begin with victory over one's self."[209] In the next scene, he records Francis himself remembering "he must first conquer himself if he wants to become a *knight of Christ*."[210] The *Assisi Compilation*, which represents material from Francis' earliest companions, records Francis as saying:

> The Emperor Charles, Roland and Oliver, and all the paladins and valiant knights who were mighty in battle, pursuing unbelievers with great toil and fatigue even to death, had a glorious and memorable victory for themselves, and, finally, died in battle fighting as holy martyrs for the faith in Christ.[211]

In *A Mirror of Perfection*, Francis compares his brothers to minstrels of the Lord, proclaiming: "We are minstrels of the Lord, and this is what we want as payment: that you live in true penance."[212] It also likens the brothers to the chivalrous knights of the Breton cycle:

> These brothers of mine are knights of the round table, who hide in deserted and remote places to devote themselves more fervently to prayer and meditation.[213]

According to Mockler, this comparison referred to the Knights of the Round Table, not in their glory but rather in the days following Arthur's death, when the king's body "had been taken to a hermitage where a solitary hermit, who had been the Archbishop of Canterbury, received and buried him."[214] Soon after the legend states that Sir Bedivere put upon himself poor clothes and remained there in prayer and fasting and great abstinence. Later, he was joined by Sir Lancelot, then by Sir Bors and within months by seven other knights who all renounced the riches of the world and shared a hut in order to live in great penance.[215]

Francis in fact did attract various nobles and knights.[216] Although Le Goff contends that Francis "did not conceive that his Order could include warriors," that is active military personal like St. Bernard's concept of "*milites Christi*," there is ample evidence to show that many knights were attracted to his lifestyle.[217] Although later legends speak of Br. Bernard of Quintavalle as a former knight,[218] Brother Angelo Tancredi, in *A Mirror of Perfection* is recorded to have been the first knight of the Order.[219] The historian Ludovicus Jacobili relates that Francis, having met Angelo while he was showing off his new knight clothes, said:

> Sir Angelo, you have been girding a sword for a long time, as well as similar weapons, now you had better gird on a rough rope instead of it, and you better have Christ's cross instead of the sword. You should go barefoot on dusty streets and squares...Follow me and I will knight you in the name of Christ.[220]

In addition, Brother Leonardo was a "prominent mature knight"[221] and Brother Masseo, a knight of Perugia.[222] From Assisi's feudal knightly families, Francis attracted St. Clare, who not only was expected to marry a knight, but whose father, as well as her relatives on both sides, were of the knightly class.[223] Lord Orlando, Count of Chiusi, was a "most valiant knight of the Emperor" who donated LaVerna to Francis and his brothers.[224]

Analysis

With so much evidence verifying the image of Francis as a courtly troubadour and chivalrous knight, the question emerges as to why this image is not as well known. If Russell is correct, Henry's work was unpopular a decade later.[225] One possible explanation for this can be found in the fact that while the military motif has always been a valid metaphor for the spiritual journey within the Christian tradition, the exercise of knighthood and chivalry have evoked both praise and criticism from the Church. David Carlson, in his study entitled *Religious Writers and Church Councils* observed that the attitudes of religious writers toward knighthood fluctuated and so were sometimes "openly hostile to chivalry."[226] As early as 1130, Church Councils such as the Council of Clermont condemned chivalry and placed a ban on tournaments.[227] Other religious writers such as Jacques de Vitry, who associate soldiers with *potentes*, "those who exercize any form of power," accuse them of abusing their position and raping and plundering their subjects.[228] De Vitry even details the seven deadly sins that were committed in tournaments.[229] Little expresses a similar sentiment when writing about Celano, who he believed had little understanding of the "romantic and chivalrous element" of Francis' spirituality. Little contends that Celano's allusions to it are "few and discreet" because as a conventional hagiographer, this material "was not quite proper for a saint."[230] Roger Sorrell goes further and believes there was an ecclesial bias against secular ideals of chivalry that caused both Celano and Bonaventure to diminish this aspect of Francis' character.[231] Sorrell cites that while Francis considered Br. Pacifico as a "noble and courtly master of song, whose status was worthy of comparison to the teachers of Paris,"[232] Celano describes him as "a man of the world who had forgotten himself and did not know God, and who had prostituted himself entirely to vanity...because he was prince of bawdy singers and creator of worldly ballads."[233] Another example of this can be seen when Celano places singing in his list of vain accomplishments in which the young

Francis tried to surpass everyone: "wit, curiosity, practical jokes and foolish talk, songs, and soft and flowing garments."[234] In addition, a cursory glance at the *Legend for Use in the Choir* reveals the omission of the dream vision of arms completely. This work also includes the comment that Francis "had not use for cringing courtesy."[235]

Rampton postulates another reason why there is "a real silence concerning this important element of the saint's persona" at least in the visual tradition in the first seventy-five years after his death.[236] She states that "the early artistic tradition avoided portraying Francis as a religious troubadour because this sort of image was inconsistent with the goals of the early order."[237] She believes that in the face of controversy (which included Paris and the novelty of the Stigmata) the order sought to "legitimize or standardize Francis" within the established religious tradition of the Church.[238] This position has considerable credibility given the fact that the love poetry of the troubadours had flirtatious and philandering connotations. Mulholland comments: "the Church did not take kindly" to the "highly charged erotic poems" which the Troubadours often wrote to married women.[239] Chesterton points out the "moral dangers" inherent in the troubadour culture.[240] The internal and external problems the Order faced in the rise of the Spirituals, the poverty controversies, rule interpretations, clericalism, may also be factors which lend credibility to a movement to depict Francis within the more traditional conventions of sanctity.

One of the most serious dangers surrounding the Franciscans was the interpretation of the Order within the spiritual framework of Joachinism. This can be seen as early as Celano, who spoke of Francis as a prophet announcing the "last time," and later appears in Bonaventure. Henry even has Francis preach:

> The day of reckoning's at hand, that will all of a sudden
>
> Grab and make off with all you have got. And you shall end up naked,
>
> And your fall will be all the lower, for having flown so high.[241]

In addition there was also fear of the Franciscans as fulfilling the prophecy of St. Hildegard through which some interpreted Francis an apocalyptic prophet. This is attested to in Caesar of Heisterbach's *Life of Saint Engelbert,* written between 1225-1235, which records the priors and priests of Cologne protesting against the presence of the friars in their territory.

> We are afraid that they are the ones that the Holy Spirit prophesied through the mouth of Saint Hildegard that would be a cause of grief for the clergy and danger for the city.[242]

Richer of Sens' chronicle, as mentioned earlier, written sometime between 1255-1264, also warns of the Franciscans as fulfilling St. Hildegard's prophecy. Christopher Ohan poses that these factors had "dangerous implications in the Church."[243]

A final consideration to explain the tendency to reject the image of Francis as a knight of Christ or at least the hesitancy to accept it, especially in the *LV*, is the argument that this image exaggerates, or at least distorts the full picture of the spiritual experience of Francis. This view holds that while Francis' dream may have been an important part of his conversion, Henry eclipses the other aspects of his spiritual development, failing to recognize any growth or deepening of his understanding of God and others through later experiences, reflection, and prayer. This depiction is said to reduce the breadth of Francis' spiritual maturation. In this case the dream is understood as being overemphasized, and limiting, especially in terms of the overall process of conversion. In the *Testament*, for example, Francis himself recalls at the end of his life, not the dream but the embrace of the leper as the most significant and pivotal moment of his life. While Henry's sustained military motif poignantly expresses the initial purgative stage of Francis' conversion, it overshadows all the developments of Francis' growth in his relationship with Christ and others, for example, his understanding of the forgiveness and mercy of God, etc.

Yet it should be noted that Francis himself continues to speak in these terms even later in his life, especially to the Poor Clares. The dating of Francis' *Canticle of Exhortation to St. Clare and Her Sisters* confirms that when he uses the royal motif to encourage the Poor

Clares to be "crowned queen in heaven with the Virgin Mary," that this motif continued to be operative in his consciousness and writing as late as 1225.[244] Francis also writes in *The Form of Life Given to Saint Clare and Her Sisters* that they made themselves "daughters and servants of the most high King."[245] Clare herself uses courtly language in her letters and receives a vision of God on her deathbed in which she states, "Do you see, O child, the King of glory Whom I see?"[246] This seems to suggest that while Vincent Kurusummootil's study entitled *The Religious Experience of St. Francis,* concludes that Francis' main image of God in his initial phase of conversion entailed a vision of God as his Master and King,[247] the image of God as king persists. This is substantiated by David Blowey's study of the writings of Francis who found that of the fifteen times Francis uses "king," most come from the *Office of the Passion,* written towards the end of Francis' life.[248] Blowey cautions against drawing strict conclusions that tie this regal symbolism to the chivalric literature of the day by reminding readers of the scriptural foundations of God as king in the both Testaments.[249] Felder, on the other hand, speaks of Francis' relationship with Christ in this way:

> The peculiar character of the relation between Francis and the God-Man lies in this, that he was a Knight of Christ, that he devoted himself with a truly chivalrous spirit and in a truly chivalrous manner to the service, the imitation, and the love of his Lord.[250]

The image of Francis as the military leader of soldiers did continue to be used in literature right through to Dante and beyond.[251] Jacopo de Voragine's *Golden Legend*, written sometime between 1255-1267 contains a description of Francis' preaching, comparing it to a battle-ax, which cuts down vice.[252] *The Annals of Santa Giustina*, for example, written sometime between 1260-1270, speaks of the Franciscans as doing "battle against the three-fold foe."[253] While other examples include Gerard de Frachet's *The Lives of the Brethren*,[254] the best imitation of Henry's style can be seen in Jacopone of Todi's *Lauds* number 61 and 62.[255]

In conclusion, Francis lived in an epoch considered the "apogee of knighthood."[256] Mulholland contends that Francis' "knowledge of and exposure to" the ideals and attitudes contained in the literature of his day "would have influenced the already present romanticism of his own heart and soul and strengthened his desire to be a knight."[257] This is confirmed by a certain strand of the hagiographic tradition and other documents that consistently image Francis as a jongleur, vagabond poet, minstrel or troubadour who had a deep desire of becoming a chivalrous knight.[258] Several scholars have commented on the intense desire of knighthood that Francis manifested; a subject that will be taken up further in chapter four. Felder writes, "Francis knew no greater ambition than to acquire the rank of knighthood," and that "his thirst for knightly fame and knightly deeds remained unabated."[259] Francis De Beer comments, "In his youthful dreams Francis was obsessed by chivalry and even the Crusade."[260] This desire is of fundamental importance in understanding Henry's Francis and can be seen as the true point of departure for his spiritual journey. David Bona, who studied Francis using a depth psychology approach, speaks of Francis' desire for knighthood in this way:

> Francis was not only determined but seemed consumed with being a knight. Knighthood was his aim, his direction, his target. It was the center to which all his thoughts and energies were directed. In his mind it was essential for his perceived happiness that he became a knight.[261]

Chapter Three: The Icon of the Crucified Knight

Chapter One began by establishing evidence of Henry's expertise as a *"vates," "magister"* and *"versificator"* of hagiography. It also provided an analysis of the *LV* in regard to the influence of other literature, which serves as a background to the icon, so that it could be critically evaluated within its literary context. Chapter Two studied the historical validity of the icon in terms of Francis, chivalry, and knighthood, especially as seen in his writings and other documents, legends, and biographies. This third chapter analyzes the genesis and heart of the icon through a comparative exegesis of the *Vita Prima's* 'vision of arms' and the dream sequence in the *LV*. Since hagiography can be difficult for the modern reader to comprehend, this chapter begins by considering some problems of interpretation. A tool is offered for understanding the spiritual significance of hagiographic texts.

Hermeneutics and Hagiography

Before analyzing the hagiographic icon of Francis that Henry used to express Francis as a crucified knight of Christ, one must first understand something of the hermeneutics of hagiography. Before beginning the task of theologically interpreting hagiography one must first address the problematic conception of hagiography as a fiction or false history. Mayeski, in her recent study of the history of hagiography, points out that recognition of the theological import of hagiographic texts has been restricted by the assumption that they merely reflect a "popular religiosity."[1] This bias results in a perception of hagiography as being uncritical and unrelated to the actual formulation of the tradition.[2] Contemporary scholars like Cynthia Hahn however, advocate the unique theological and spiritual significance of each version, finding that "each to some degree documents the religious experience and expression of its time."[3]

The more difficult challenge then seems to be a hermeneutic and methodological problem. One medieval scholar has pointed out that "over the past century 'hagiographical' materials have been approached from every conceivable perspective."[4] Le Goff cautions pure medievalists who "'scour' the sources for 'historical' information" which is only relevant to the subject matter of traditional history without considering that hagiographic legends were not produced as historical documents. Le Goff also warns that these legends "cannot be interpreted according to the same rules as the archival sources with which historians are accustomed to working, for their motivations and purposes are different."[5] Yet, Luigi Pelligrini, in his article, *A Century of Reading the Sources,* has shown that most study of Franciscan sources tends to rely on philological-literary analysis.[6] This is particularly true of the *LV,* whose heavy dependence on Celano's *Vita Prima* has sometimes limited study to narrow textual-historical reconstruction or negative critical comparisons. These comparative studies often describe the *LV* by what it is not or emphasize what it does not contain, i.e. any new biographical material, instead of serious consideration of what it is in itself. Thus the *LV* seems to be subject to a certain historical critical bias that can prevent one from accessing its real value and deeper meaning.

While the historical critical method used in the quest to unearth the factual truth of the 'real' Francis must be the starting point of all research, the spiritual meaning within hagiographic texts must also be considered. Although all Franciscan scholarly research seeks to reveal the truth about the real Francis, each utilizes a different means or method, which is comprised of vastly different criteria. Sabatier was well aware of the shortcomings of different historical methodologies in Franciscan research, citing that "objective history is then a utopia."[7] Regarding changing landscape, Sabatier states: "two persons who look at it at the same time do not find in it the same charm...and if you had it continually before your eyes, would never see twice alike."[8] The latest discussion on the method of reading Franciscan texts, according to Pelligrini, is centered around the question on the relationship between hagiographic interpretation and historical truth.[9] Issues of historical accuracy, improbable miracles, redundancy, repetition, topoi patterns as well as liberal 'borrowings' in the Lives is in fact an old problem which continues to call their truth into question. Duncan Robertson for example explains that Saint Jerome's *Saint's Lives,* which "model the extension of hagiographical 'truth' into edification and entertainment" is believed to have reoriented the genre by drawing upon a wide variety of pagan and Christian authors such as Virgil and Cicero.[10] One modern critique of St. Jerome's hagiography, (which could also be levied against Henry's *LV*), cogently argues:

> One need hardly note that these methods [the use of rhetorical ornamentation, etc.], far from embellishing the narrative, detract from its historical value. Indeed, once the possibility of non-historical additions is admitted, no narrative, especially one involving miracles, can claim unqualified truth. The fact that Jerome did not realize that shows that he lacked to a considerable degree the critical eye which is so necessary to the historian.[11]

While some scholars believe the historical truth of hagiographical legends seems to have "counted but little with the average reader" in the Middle Ages, who considered the legends "ethically rather than factually true,"[12] others hold that during the thirteenth century, the search for authenticity, "began an attack on the literature of imagination in general and verse in particular."[13]

The question of truth then is addressed by Prinzivalli,

who states the "truth, for the hagiographer, is not the same as our modern concept but rather a recognition that the divine project has been realized in the saint's life."[14] Père Hippolyte Delehaye affirms this by stating that while the literary historical questions are important, "the fundamental mistake would consist in interpreting them without taking account of the spirit that inspired them."[15] Delehaye highlights this point by classifying hagiography uniquely among other literary genres as religious documents, which aim not at historical truth but at increasing "spiritual devotion."[16] Likewise, Ludolf Müller defines hagiography as a "theological discipline," which "describes the continuous incarnation of the Holy Spirit in all believers, but especially in its 'chosen instruments'."[17] Müller emphasizes the importance of the spiritual meaning of hagiography by pointing to the etymology of the word hagiography; a term that is actually comprised of two Greek words ("*hagios*" and "*graphe*"), which taken together mean "holy writing."[18] Thus, the hagiographer, Hahn tells us, hopes to create a narrative that "will rise above mere words and deeds to reflect the grace of the saint."[19]

In order to better grasp this spiritual meaning, Grégoire advocates a broader approach to understanding human holiness through an interdisciplinary method which not only includes literary and historical studies, but also incorporates a consideration of the historical, literary, theological, philosophical and psychological perspectives.[20] The methodology, therefore, is at once historical-critical, descriptive, analytic, exegetical, and interpretative. This is specifically the approach adopted by this study which is grounded in Grégoire's conviction "that the ultimate meaning of a hagiographical document lies below its surface, anterior to its particular historical details."[21] Hahn clearly differentiates the nature of hagiographic Saint's Lives:

> A Saint's Life is not a biography in the modern sense, that is a recording of historical facts or the events of an individual life. Rather, it is a project that aims to match a collection of words to one central fact: ineffable holiness of a saint. Stephen Nichols describes the purpose of narrative in similar medieval stories as 'not to inform people more accurately about their world and neighbors, but to show how the world mirrored God's immanence, and therefore the subordination of the human to the divine.[22]

A greater understanding of the spiritual meaning of hagiographic texts may enable one to explore the richer "fuller sense" of sacred biographies. Heffernan states:

> The function of the text was not only to document thc wondrous appearance of the divine in a man or woman but also to interpret for the community what was only partially understood, mysteriously hidden in the well-known public record, buried in the very ideal of

sanctity itself.[23]

Leonid Ouspensky and Vladimir Lossky have claimed that "spiritual reality cannot be represented in any other way except through symbols."[24] A closer examination of Henry's use of symbol, allegory and myth in creating his icon, therefore, will help to reveal the truth behind Henry's interpretation of Francis' spiritual experience in its fullness. In order to appreciate the depth, richness, and potency of Henry's icon of Francis, a paradigm may be helpful. Müller offers an insightful analogy, which describes the nature of icon and hagiography. Müller believes there are three possible ways in which a saint may be depicted: "the photograph, the portrait, and the icon."[25]

> The photograph records the features exactly, but it may be a distortion of the person's nature. A kindly person may be photographed in a moment of anger; in this case, the exact record does not show his true nature. A successful portrait reproduces a person's features in a way that is true to life and recognizable; but at the same time it brings out his character and gives expression to his inner nature. An icon is not a photograph but a portrait. Yet it is more than a portrait. It aims at giving a true likeness of the person, and at the same time to portray him *sub specie aeternitatis*. An icon tries to bring out in a person what he has become through the power of the Holy Spirit.[26]

This analogy sheds light on the aim of hagiography, which is to present a community of believers with a model of holiness. The hagiographer can only succeed in achieving this goal by depicting a spiritual icon of a saint that expresses something about what God is doing within the soul of the person, that is, the deeper spiritual meaning, which Grégoire believes, lies hidden below the surface of the text.

A final consideration on Henry's specific purpose and the medium he used in order to portray his icon seems appropriate. As mentioned in the introduction, Henry wrote the verses of the *LV* in order "to paint" a song of Francis, which come from his "own reflections or the image" Henry has of him. Henry hopes his image of Francis "deposits in the mind ideas of a particular kind, even if not exactly the same." Sabatier once commented, "the more beautiful is the dawn, the less one can describe it."[27] Henry thus draws upon the symbolic language of poetry in order to express the true meaning of Francis' spiritual experience. Mulholland explains this process:

> The "poetic" dimension of Francis' life is not simply found in his writings in either prose or poetry but on a much deeper level. Poetry exists to present verbal ikons to the reader or listener. It is an art which uses imagination and concretization to present those images in its particular form i.e. words within rhythm, rhyme, stanza etc. The words themselves are subjugated to the imaginary content which in turn moves

> beyond the imaginary to become symbol. Here the symbol acts upon the unconscious psyche feeding it, sustaining and helping it to grow so that wholeness and integrity are brought about unconsciously.[28]

I.A. Richards, in a more systematic analysis of poetic expression, defines metaphor and analogy as having two parts: the vehicle, that is, the concrete image and the tenor, that is, the reality to which it points.[29] Richards believes that the vehicle and the tenor share a common "ground" and taken together express the meaning.[30] One of the advantages of using analogy and metaphor is their ability to convey the truth about an otherwise ineffable spiritual reality and express it in concrete terms. "The rhetorical device of metaphor elevates language to a higher level, and amplifies the significance of words from the flatness of literality to the depth of multiplicity of derived senses."[31] Most recently, Marilyn Hammond in *Francis of Assisi: History, Hagiography, and Hermeneutics in the Early Documents* has stressed the importance of metaphor and symbolic language in interpreting Franciscan texts.[32] In his comparison of history and poetry, Jean Francois Godet-Calogeras states while,

> Poetry is no less bound to the truth....(It) makes new links and connections between things to create new images that will encourage us to see reality differently. Poetry does not create another reality, it does not change reality, it reveals it better.[33]

Bloomfield and Dunn believe different "versions of a story or poem are held together by an underlying structure, which is the final test of its truth."[34] They share a simple example of how an ordinary everyday train ride can be seen on two different levels, each of which conveys two different meanings. They state, "The 8:40 train…fulfills the same function everyday in spite of the fact that no two journeys are exactly the same."[35] Analogously, the lives of the saints, despite their differences, are effective vehicles, or media to describe the ineffable reality of a soul's spiritual journey to God. In this way, each Saint's Life is able to articulate a common truth that unites them all. This is in harmony with Gregory of Tours who "reveals his understanding of the relationship between theological truth and language"[36] when he insisted upon using the "life" of the Saints, rather than the "lives" of the Saints. He writes, "although there is a diversity of merit and virtue in the world, one life nourishes all bodies."[37]

Analysis of Celano: Francis' Conversion-Part One

The following study examines the initial conversion of Francis as presented in the *Vita Prima*.[38] The *Vita Prima's* second chapter (1C 3-5) entitled "How God visited his heart through a bodily illness and a vision in the night"[39] relates the two-part process in which God works to effect Francis' conversion. The dream sequence in *Vita Prima* 5, is of particular importance because it constitutes the main font of Henry's icon of Francis the hero and spiritual knight. Celano's second chapter ends by explaining God's motivation for Francis' conversion:

> For the sake of his own name He removed His own anger far from him, and for His own glory He bridled Francis' mouth so that he would not perish completely. The hand of the Lord was upon him, a change of the right hand of the Most High, that through him the Lord might give sinners confidence in a new life of grace; and that of conversion to God he might be an example.[40]

Celano 3 relates how God visited Francis' heart, which was "still boiling in the sins of youthful heat," and "not knowing how to become tame."[41] This visitation comes through a bodily illness that brings "distress to his mind and affliction to his body,"[42] in order that he may recall the error of his judgment. This illness is referred to in multiple ways: "the divine vengeance or rather the divine anointing,"[43] "thorns,"[44] "a wall,"[45] a "punishment,"[46] "paternal chastisement,"[47] and later as "the rod of Justice."[48]

This illness changes Francis somewhat although "not completely or genuinely."[49] Thus Francis "reflected upon worldly matters" and "promised himself out of worldly glory and vanity to do great things."[50] Therefore, when Francis heard about a certain nobleman,[51] who was preparing a military campaign to Apulia in order to "enrich himself in money or distinction,"[52] he agreed to go with him. Celano emphasizes in the strongest terms that Francis "had devoted himself with all of his determination to accomplish these things and was eager, seething with desire, to make the journey."[53]

Analysis of Henry: Francis' Conversion-Part One

Henry's smoother and more dramatic account of Francis' conversion is contained in his first chapter (*LV* I: 70-240) entitled:

> Firstly, a description of francis in pursuit of the earthly, till the divine honor inflicts on him grave fever, then coaxing him with gleaming armor, converts him, and kindles his love for the truly good.[54]

This introduction contains several themes that Henry will later build upon. Note, the Latin word "*sequentem*," which appears in the first sentence (translated "in pursuit") is a particularly significant word to Francis who uses it in the first sentence of his RNB in order to encapsulate the heart of his way of life: "to follow the teaching and footprints of our Lord Jesus Christ."[55] The description of Francis' youth as in "pursuit of the earthly" serves to heighten the contrast of Francis' conversion by emphasizing the purpose Celano gives of why the Lord converted Francis: "that through him the Lord might give sinners confidence in a new life of grace; and that of conversion to God he might be an example."[56] Henry will deepen this contrast with a series of luminous imagery: "*radiantibus*," "*succendit*," "*lucens*," "*lucerna*," "*lumina*," "*enituere*,"[57] reminiscent of Gregory IX's *Mira Circa Nos*, which includes a "shining deeds" and "lamp" reference. Henry compliments these allusions with a martial image, "*vicit mundum*," taken from 1 John 5:4-5,[58] which relates "the one who believes in Jesus Christ conquers the world." The light motif continues throughout the work, that is, with his description of Assisi, thus emphasizing the overall theme of contrasting light vs. dark, good vs. evil. Note Henry's chivalric language in referring to God as the "divine honor" and his mentioning of armor.

In the account of Francis' conversion, Henry follows the two part scheme of Celano but juxtaposes "a change in the right hand of the Most High" which appears at the end of 1 Celano 2, with the deserved "whipping" that Francis receives.[59] God's action in the process of conversion (*LV* I: 70-181) is expressed in a series of colorful analogies, as a halting of an evil course, "a cutting down of him who would not surrender," reigning in the "unbridled one" and a taming of the "wild man."[60]

Henry also compares Francis' soul to a "long-lost coin that is found, with its surface buried in rust."[61] Henry extends the metaphor by having the divine image in Francis' soul, which "could scarce be seen,"[62] purged in the "forge's fire."[63] Henry playing on the words "*igne fabrilli*" and "*igne febrili*," identifies the "fever's fire"[64] as Francis' ailment. Henry then describes his illness using graphic details (*LV* I: 96-113) which reflect the medical knowledge of his day:[65]

> A burning strange to him
> Drives his natural heat through the body and it rages
> About the heart. In his small veins a fluid is produced
> By the burning heat of fever; while an inside warmth melts
> An exterior phlegm.[66]

While Celano does not indicate that Francis' sickness is a fever, Henry informs the reader it is in fact a fever. Although this may or may not reflect historical information, it is commensurate with the romantic sentiment inherent in Ovidian literature which portrays love as a fever. As mentioned earlier, the lyric poetry of the troubadours often depicted "love as a fever, a sweet pain or a welcome wound," and "the Beloved as a medicine or an enemy to be overcome."[67] The medical descriptions of the effects of the fever reveal a romantic influence as they contain an astute attention to anatomical detail, as well as various technical symptoms of tremors, numbness, thinning of the blood, urine tone, and pulse rate. Thus the "Doctor Above"[68] who "comes to cure the disease of the soul"[69]scourges "the patient" Francis until he finally repents of an ugly past life.[70] This process, which includes a psychological struggle against despair, ends with Francis praising God at his recovery, which is again graphically described.[71]

This additional material of Henry is a good example of Fanger's insight into the nature of Henry's reinterpretation of the role of the divinity. Fanger holds that because of Henry's interest in natural philosophy, he gives:

> a greater emphasis on natural causation in the total process of the miracle; and as a result of this, the sheer quantity of divine power needed to perform the miracle is greatly reduced.[72]

Fanger, in other words, believes that Henry's medical description of God's operation economizes the divine power. Fanger states that "Henry's marked tendency to minimize the role of divine power in his descriptions of miraculous phenomena"[73] in no way debunks the miraculous, but rather "does not require the continuous intervention of divinity in the natural order."[74] In Francis' conversion then, Henry explains how God works through natural means in turning Francis' heart to God.[75] Henry, for example, in the above excerpt explicitly adds the word "*naturalem*" to Celano's account of Francis' youthful heat. While Celano's account stresses the divine anointing as having caused distress to body and mind, Henry describes a more natural internal process. The effect of this allows Henry to provide a concrete picture of the mechanics in the process of Francis' inner conversion. Thus Henry offers a glimpse into a deeper dimension of Francis' initial "hardness of heart and the distress in his brain."[76] In comparison with what Celano tells us about Francis, Henry allows us to enter into Francis' inner world.

Henry effectively achieves this glimpse of the interior fiber of Francis by launching into a philosophically rich treatise concerning the inner dialogue of Francis where the "philosopher in him questions."[77] Henry is able to articulate the journey and struggle of a soul touched by God using such images as a ship in a head wind, being tossed by the winds of sense and reason. Francis metaphysically questions enjoyment, creation, possessions, and even himself as "his soul's simple nature is upset by various conflicts within him."[78] Henry records the inner debate and notes that in the battle between sense and reason, "One moment his mind is up in the air and again it is down on the ground; New suggestions he proffers, but falls back on what he's used to."[79] Francis is thus "carried in different directions; by a northerly blowing its pleasures, or a southerly breeze of good fortune."[80]

If Celano can be said to provide Henry with the skeletal framework for the character of Francis, Henry's artistry and imagination not only provides the flesh and muscle, but also the heart and soul. Henry breathes life into Francis, animating him so that we can better understand what he may have been experiencing during his conversion; to hear what he was thinking and sense what he was feeling. Henry brings this dynamism to the Celano account by skillfully filling in the inner psychological struggle of Francis. Henry will later develop this theme by revealing the inner battle that rages within Francis' soul.

Sabatier, who summarized Celano as a "soul-history, a sketch of the affecting drama of a man who attains to the conquest of himself"[81] speaks of this first part of Francis' conversion as a "holy violence" through which Francis "was to arrive at last at a pure and virile faith."[82] Sabatier continues:

> Those inner combats of the soul, such as St. Francis was waging, are indescribable, unspeakable: we know not how they commence, what first causes them, whither they are tending; one thing only we know, that since they take place in the individual, it is the individual who has to fight, to suffer; it is a night combat, mysterious, solitary–as at Bethel.[83]

By using his poetic license to sketch Francis' inner turmoil, Henry is able to give his work a psychological depth, which allows a glimpse into the inner life of the saint.

This inner battle with himself is a prelude to his battle against evil. Drawing upon the military analogy used in the early Anglo-Latin hagiographic tradition,[84] Henry is able to transform the physical battle to the spiritual battle, the exterior on to the interior. This military analogy, as will be demonstrated, is an important means through which Henry will articulate the inner struggle of Francis' spiritual experience. Del Mastro relates that,

> Those hagiographers who experienced the union of Christianity with political and military

> power seem to have seen things military not as an analogy for the Christian experience, but as the very stuff of that experience.[85]

The first part of the conversion ends when Francis, vacillating in his recovery between his old self and something new, hears of the "richest citizen in town"[86] planning to go to Apulia in hopes of "making plenty of money."[87]

Analysis of Celano: Francis' Conversion-Part Two

In the second part of Francis' conversion (1C 5), Celano relates that God visited him "in a vision during the night in the sweetness of grace."[88] According to Celano, God's strategy was to 'exalt and entice' Francis, who was "eager for glory" to achieve its "pinnacle."[89] After seeing a vision of his house filled with military arms,[90] Francis "though delighting for the most part"[91] also "silently wondered to himself about its meaning."[92] Then surprisingly, Francis, without vocalizing any question out loud, is "greatly bewildered" with the response, "that all these arms were to be for him and his soldiers."[93] Upon waking, Francis misinterprets the meaning of the vision and "did not at all understand the gift sent from Heaven."[94] Francis, in fact, considered the vision a prediction of success concerning Apulia. At this point Celano relates that Francis' spirit was not moved in its usual way and he had to force himself to continue on the journey he had desired. Celano concludes the second chapter:

> It is a fine thing that at the outset mention was made of arms, and very fitting that arms be handed over to a soldier about to do battle with one strong and fully armed. Thus like a second David in the name of the Lord God of hosts from the long-standing abuse of its enemies, he might liberate Israel.[95]

In the next chapter (1C 6-7), Francis, "changed in mind but not in body,"[96] abruptly refuses to go to Apulia. He then retires for a short time to direct his will to God's in prayer and seeks out a cave to speak with his special friend about the great treasure he found. Francis greatly suffers and is unable "to rest until he accomplished in action what he had conceived in his heart,"[97] that is, until the Lord shows him "what he must do."[98] "Burning inwardly with a divine fire," Francis is unable "to conceal outwardly the flame kindled in his soul." Celano then states that after the Lord showed Francis what he must do, Francis states he "will take a bride more beautiful than you have ever seen."[99]

Analysis of Henry: Francis' Conversion-Part Two

Francis, having his "habitual fire of cupidity fanned all the more" by the prospect of finding fortune in Apulia, begins his journey with the man. Henry then connects the second part of Francis' conversion process (*LV* I: 182-244) to the first:

> Celestial grace carries on the merciful work
> It began, healing his hardness of heart, the distress
> In his brain. Seeds spring up, left by that rooted-out
> Sickness, scars reappear in the wounds. But He who poured
> Wine in, now applies oil. So the one He tested with
> Violence, He might now tempt with sweetness, to move him
> By coaxing when He could not by scourging, and that he who
> Resisted when pressured, of his own will now might obey.[100]

Henry then prepares the following vision of arms by describing the conversion of Francis through God's perspective who first tests Francis by violence and scourging, and then tempts him by sweetness and coaxing, in order that "he who resisted when pressured, of his own will now might obey."

Henry writes, "as sleep dulls his feelings and his unhampered mind examines his venture" Francis, "is carried out of himself."[101] Henry's Pauline allusion (2 Cor. 12:2, 4) transforms Celano's "vision during the night"[102] into a rapture like that which Paul relates happened to someone who is carried into the third Heaven.[103] The designation of the vision as a rapture is in line with the biblical notion that a "real vision is always based upon ecstasy of one form or another."[104] It is interesting to note that although there is no explicit reference to Paul in the account of Francis' conversion in the *Vita Prima*, the *Vita Secunda* 6, includes a Pauline reference that relates Francis "became a Paul in place of a Saul."[105]

While in this state of rapture, Francis saw his own house filled with different weapons instead of cloth. Henry adds a detail about the type of cloth that Francis was used to seeing in his house, that is, cloth from Flanders and Britain, which was highly prized at the time.[106] The actual vision of arms is similar but more vivid in detail in Henry's account and includes a description of the arms: "axes glittering...polished swords...jeweled helmets, shields with golden sheen."[107] Another marked and significant difference is given in the response Francis hears from heaven, which is quoted directly: "God with these arms shall you and your comrades array."[108] While nothing in the Celano account suggests a third party, Henry's quote reveals that a heavenly intermediary is present and that God himself is not speaking to Francis. Later accounts like the *Anonymous of Perugia*,[109] the *Legend of the Three Companions*,[110] and the *Vita Secunda*,[111] will confirm the presence of another person. These examples point to the possibility of Henry having access to another source outside of Celano.

Henry's rendition of the vision contains several symbolic overtones. First, the added details and weapons that Henry includes bear resemblance to the *Labarum*[112]in Constantine's heavenly vision of arms.

Henry adds some "precious" objects like a spear and jewels, all with a "golden" sheen. Constantine saw a vision of a "spear overlaid with gold," which, with a traverse bar, formed the figure of a cross.[113] This cross was adorned with "a wreath of gold and precious jewels."[114] Henry's use of the verb "*insigniet*" also recalls the banner attached to Constantine's cross, which in Latin is rendered: "*In hoc signo vinces*," and which was later engraved on Constantine's soldiers' shields.[115] It is interesting to note that Bonaventure's *Legenda Maior* will also use this same word to describe the armor when he writes "…military arms emblazoned with the insignia of Christ's cross."[116]

Second, the use of the verb "*insigniet*" is key to Henry's icon. The verb, "*insigniet*," translated here as "array," holds a rich meaning. The Latin infinitive "*insignire*" can mean: "to mark with a characteristic feature, means of identity, to impress (such a mark), to adorn with marks of honor."[117] It is the same word Celano will use when he speaks of "the marks of the Crucified"[118] found on Francis. In addition, "*signa*," the root of the word, is not only used in Scripture to designate the seal of the Holy Spirit,[119] but is consistently used by Celano when referring to the "marks" of the stigmata.[120] By transposing the vocabulary of Celano, this reworking indicates that Henry is developing Celano's account of the stigmata in a very particular way, as will be seen.

Upon waking, Francis' keen "inner reflections"[121] begin to reinterpret these gifts as referring not to "laurels mundane, but rather triumphs that are true to their name."[122] Francis' decisive clarity about the meaning of the vision is emphasized as he, "with a different mind,"[123] immediately prepares himself from then on for "spiritual battles."[124] This discernment is considerably shorter as compared to Celano's account that lasts days. Francis, using force on himself, an allusion to 1 Celano 5, decides not to go to Apulia. Henry emphasizes this change by adding another Pauline allusion, which relates that Francis now "regards the goods to which he was used"[125] as "*stercora,*" the same word Paul uses for "dung" or "refuse."[126] At this point, Henry veers from Celano's account, and omits the extended prayer with a special friend, his time in the cave and the spousal imagery. Henry instead writes:

> With more than usual ardor and more prolonged [Francis] makes a prayer that the Lord convert him and not let his mind, clinging now to things above, fall back to things of earth. His plea goes up to heaven high, is inscribed by the finger of God's right hand, stamped with the seal of the holy and life-giving cross, so that he is enabled to manfully subdue his foe, and no longer crave for transient things.[127]

Henry connects the desire for conversion, the dream and the stigmata, by having his prayer "inscribed"[128] by "God's right hand stamped with the seal of the Holy and life giving cross." Once again, Henry is able to do this by importing, reworking and developing Celano's later material (I C 95:10; 114:1) where Celano speaks of the stigmata. First in 1C 95:

> Although the servant and friend of the Most High saw himself adorned with such magnificent pearls, like precious stones, and marvelously decorated beyond the glory and honor of all others, still his heart did not grow vain. Rather in every way possible he tried to hide these marks, so that human favor would not rob him of the grace given him.[129]

And again in 1C 114:

> This is a unique gift, a sign of special love: to decorate the soldier with the same arms of glory that in their great dignity belong to the King alone...Oh sublime splendor of the living cross, giving life to the dead.[130]

In these two excerpts, Celano describes Francis as "adorned" and "decorated" with the "marks" of the stigmata. Celano in the second excerpt (1C 114:1) alludes to a connection between the unique gift of the "sign" of the stigmata with the dream by referring to Francis as a soldier who is decorated with "arms of glory that belong to the King alone." Celano's brief allusion to the merging of these two events is extended and deepened by Henry.

Henry will interpret these arms of glory as referring to the arms that Francis received in the dream. According to Henry, then, Francis is decorated with the sign of the stigmata, interiorly, on his heart or soul at the time of the dream. Thus the weapons that Francis receives in the dream become the stigmata.

This can be demonstrated in several ways.

First, Henry prepares the way for the internalization of the stigmata in his opening introduction where he addresses Francis:

> O soldier of Christ, you alone, Francis, bore the scars
> Of Life-triumph-in-death; hid in your soul when living,
> And displayed in your flesh when dying.[131]

Francis is introduced from the very beginning as one who bears the scars the triumph of life in death, that is, the stigmata, inwardly hidden in his soul. Francis can then be understood as receiving the stigmata interiorly in his heart or soul at the time of the dream, before the La Verna event and the Seraph.

Second, Henry will later confirm this by explicitly speaking of the interior nature of the stigmata:

> On many, to be sure, was the Lord's death laden; in him
> It was bred in the bone. Many were forced to carry the cross;
> He bore it so in his soul, cherished it in his heart,
> So eagerly made it his own, that what was revealed
> And printed on his very flesh was a deep secret of soul.[132]

Again, Henry distinguishes and unites the hidden nature of the stigmata, which is buried interiorly within Francis' soul and cherished in his heart as later being revealed outwardly and printed on his flesh.

Finally, Henry reinforces this by explaining that the visible wounds of the stigmata is a natural outward manifestation of the internalized stigmata:

> So does Jesus' passion remain implanted in his heart,
> So imprinted right through the marrow of his soul,
> That it cannot be hid, but must flood outwardly
> And mark its likeness on his partnered flesh,
> Becoming visible, as it were, through transparent limbs.[133]

For Henry, therefore, Francis' stigmata are a natural result of Francis' deep love for the Passion of Jesus in his heart and soul. In Henry's account, the stigmata emerge from within and move outward. This interpretation emphasizes Francis' role in the stigmata, specifically through his great desire and love of the cross, which become the means to the miracle. Fanger holds that the stigmata are "most immediately caused by the strong impression of the image of the crucifixion on the saint's imaginative faculty."[134] This, Fanger claims, is an application of Avicenna's theory, that "the soul is the beginning or principle of that which occurs in matter."[135] Avicenna held that the body could be formed by what the soul imagined.[136]

In sum, this exegetical analysis highlights the subtle nuances of Henry's interpretation of Francis as a true knight, that is, a crucified knight, a new saintly hero and prepares a deeper understanding of how his inner desire is transformed in the following chapter.

Chapter Four: Living the Drean

This chapter interprets the spiritual significance of Henry's icon of Francis. Having analyzed the *LV*'s literary structure and having established the historical validity of the icon's military motif, this final chapter interprets how Henry uses the dream to intimately link Francis's own inward passion for military honor, glory and fame with his spiritual journey to God.[1] This chapter begins with a brief survey of dream interpretation before describing how the transformation of Francis' desire not only reorients him to a new goal, but also influences how Francis perceives God and all reality. This chapter also includes an analysis of the minor notes of Henry's icon, and some final considerations.

Dream Interpretation

Francis' dream of arms and Celano's account of it warrant special attention since Henry uses this experience as the major turning point and leitmotif of his entire legend. Because Franciscan scholars continue to debate the importance of the dream in the conversion and life of Francis,[2] the following study relies upon Thomas Fawcett's work entitled *The Symbolic Language of Religion*, and David Gerhard Condon's dissertation entitled *Christian Spiritual*

Dimensions of the Psychology of Carl Gustav Jung With Special reference to His Use of Dreams in order to provide a context for understanding the nature of religious dreams and visions. While some people believe dreams are meaningless, many faiths and cultures have long held dreams to be channels of communication from God: *"somnia a Deo missa."*[3] Condon states that divine revelation in dreams is understood in two ways by spiritual theology. Firstly, as a *"visio imaginitiva"* by which "God operates in human consciousness" through "an interior perception."[4] Secondly, "by means of the insight into the interior life which dreams bring, the believer becomes more attentive to God's indwelling presence."[5] According to Fawcett, traditionally, visions and dreams, especially those containing an angelic or divine being "consist of a moment of unusual perceptivity."[6] In these dreams and visions, "the ordinary has taken on a revelatory quality which is extraordinary," and is able to impart the subject with "supernormal sight."[7] The visionary is brought outside themselves and thus freed from the confines of time and space. This vantage point allows them to participate in some way in God's perception so that he or she is able to see events in their wholeness.[8] Otto Eissfeldt similarly describes this new way of seeing (through the eyes of faith) as providing "insight into the higher reality surrounding man in the present."[9]

Stephen F. Kruger, in *Dreaming in the Middle Ages,* relates that writers during this time "treated the experience of dreaming with simultaneous anxiety and fascination," believing them to be either dangerous or divinely inspired and able to foretell the events of the future.[10] While visions and dreams were linked in the medieval mind,[11] it is interesting to note that it was Hildegard of Bingen who, more than her "late-antique predecessors," assigned moral significance to dreams, even correlating "the individual dreamer's internal, moral state quite directly with the quality of her or his dreams."[12]

From a modern psychological and more scientific understanding, Calvin Hall, an expert in the field of experimental research on dream content, states he studies dreams "in order to enlarge our understanding of man."[13] According to Hall, a person's dream can yield information about the dreamer's self-concept that is not available from other sources as well as information on the relationship between self-concept and behavior.[14] In order to retrieve this information, most current theories of dream interpretation follow Sigmund Freud who believed dreams to be revelations of the depths of the human psyche. Freud called dream interpretation "the royal road to knowledge of the unconscious activities of the mind"[15] because he believed that the dream manifested a deep underlying desire or wish fulfillment. Dreams, then, are "the carriers of the repressed contents of the psyche" which "refer symbolically to those past experiences that the individual is unable to accept by the light of his conscious attitudes."[16]

Carl Gustav Jung, Freud's pupil, broadened this view by believing there to be a spiritual dimension to dreams which he saw as "a little hidden door in the innermost and most secret recesses of the soul."[17] Dreams consist of "a series of images, ideas, and emotions occurring in certain stages of sleep."[18] According to Jungian interpretation, these images from the dream "are accepted as facts presented by the dreamer's unconscious psyche."[19] The interpreter's role in the process is to seek the meaning of the phenomena in order to make a psychological statement that is relevant to the dreamer.[20]

Kelly Bulkeley's study of the religious meaning of dreams in modern Western culture incorporates Jungian analysis but does not limit interpretation to one school, but rather recommends "an interdisciplinary integration of the different fields of dream study with a theory of interpretation and a theory religious metaphor."[21] She holds that the religious meaning of dreams emerges out of "root metaphors" within the dreamer, which are defined as those metaphors that enable us to understand our ultimate questions of existence. People are believed to respond to these ultimate questions through "metaphors, images and symbols that shape our perceptions, inspire our ideals and motivate our behavior."[22]

Finally Ira Progoff, in *Waking Dream and Living Myth*, explains how Jung's analysis can be used to develop a more holistic understanding of dreams and myth through depth psychology. Progoff's approach is based on the concept of the Organic Psyche.[23] In this model, the psychological nature of man is likened to a seed which grows toward "a teleological goal that is inherent" within the person.[24] This movement from inner to outer is understood as a process in which the latent potentials of the person, expressed as images within the psyche, are actualized through their behavior. In this way a creative person, that is, one who is "able to draw upon the images within himself and then to embody them in outer works" can live the dream and thus help the seed to blossom.[25] This approach differs from the Freudian perspective which seeks to resolve issues of the past. Progoff contends this organic psychological process is "integrative," and thus able to "draw the entire personality into a progressively centered condition"[26] which guides one toward a sense of meaning.

In Freudian terms, Francis' dream can be understood as a wish fulfillment of his deepest desire to be a knight. Frank Chooi's psychobiographical study of Francis even postulates that initially war-time children "struggle psychologically with their aggressive and destructive impulses."[27] He claims the inner impulses of children who witness war at an early age receive external sanction and validation from warring societies, which reinforce their destructive wishes.[28] He then cites Anna Freud's *War and Children*, which states these conditions arouse fear in children that these impulses will be awakened in a destructive way. It is thus possible to conclude that Francis channeled this impulse into a healthy avenue which was made manifest in the dream.

In Professor Jean-Marc Charron's research into the psychological identity of Francis, he concluded the dream was "the imaginary realization of a desire not satisfied in reality...that of chivalrous glory to which Francis aspired."[29]

These psychological insights point to the fact that we shape our dreams but the following authors show how our dreams shape us. A Jungian perspective interprets the dream as having manifested a glimpse into Francis' soul. Using Bulkeley's insights and Progroff's model, Henry can be said to have understood Francis' dream as containing a "root metaphor" or seed of his future call and mission. It is interesting to note that this model is not unlike Avicenna's theory that "the soul is the beginning or principle of that which occurs in matter,"[30] as he held that the body could be formed by what the soul imagined.[31] According to Henry's interpretation of the dream, it is clear that "it carries an encompassing image of life" which served as a paradigm or "living myth" for Francis.[32] The "root metaphor" of Francis as a soldier who attracted other companions in arms to battle against sin is certainly depicted in the *LV* as having shaped his perceptions, inspired his ideals and motivated his behavior.[33] This comprehensive myth could enable Francis "to see the reality and keep perspective"[34] even against evidence to the contrary, that is, "when there is nothing visible on the outer level."[35]

This view of the dream vision, being shaped by Francis and subsequently shaping Francis, is congruent with Karl Rahner's theological insight on the nature of visions which recognizes that the "content of a vision is not only a "picture" of the actual divine contact but also of the person who receives it."[36] According to Rahner, a synthesis necessarily develops between "the divine influence and the seer's subjective limitations," so that the person and the vision are inexplicably bound together in such a way that it is impossible to separate the imaginative content of the vision from the inspiration of the Holy Spirit.[37] This affirms defining Francis' desire for knighthood as constitutive to his call and self understanding, which will be taken up in the next section.

The Transformation of the Desire of Francis' Heart

This section examines how Henry uses the dream and its fulfillment to interpret Francis' religious experience and the dream's relationship to his own self-understanding.[38] Henry's introductory quatrain to his first chapter reveals the key to Francis' conversion and the core of his icon. The opening words explain that what will follow is a description of how God converts Francis' "pursuit of the earthly."[39] God transforms Francis' desire for military honor and glory by "coaxing him with gleaming armor" from heaven and thus "kindles his love for the truly good."[40] Francis' desire is neither squelched nor diminished but rather purged and illumined so that it may be redirected and lured by something greater. Francis' desire, then, remains and becomes the impetus and the driving force that fuels his actions. Henry, unlike Celano, gives clear evidence that it is in fact these arms which now motivate him in the scene when Francis is hiding from his father in the second chapter. Celano relates that it is Francis' "indescribable happiness"[41] that impels him to emerge from hiding, and then adds that Francis rose "carrying the shield of faith for the Lord and strengthened with the armor of great confidence."[42] Henry, however, writes:

> But when he remembers those weapons divinely bestowed,
> He fears he'll have been unworthy by recoiling from
> Such great endowments, and recovers his scattered incentives.
> Shame on those who would do "mighty deeds" and had lain hid
> In such a hole for so long![43]

Thus the heavenly arms are explicitly cited as the motivation for Francis' actions. Moreover, this motivation, which Felder calls the spirit of chivalry, is precisely that which "predisposed the youthful Francis for that higher spiritual life" and can be said to be the key to understanding Francis' approach to life.[44] Several scholars propose similar conclusions. Little recognized that Francis' "early ambition was to be a soldier—a knight errant, such as he had heard tell of in the songs of chivalry—which he got by heart and sang in French."[45] Little further relates this desire was somehow internalized within Francis in such a way that it was transformed into "a kind of inverted chivalry."[46] Kurusummootil, in his study of the religious experience of St. Francis, states the spirit of chivalry was "sublimated to make him an excellent faithful knight of Christ."[47] Felder holds that Christ directed Francis' "inborn" spirit of chivalry and the "earthly ideal of the knight to a higher conception of spiritual knighthood."[48] Sorrell also explains that Francis did not "lose his respect for chivalric ideals when he underwent his conversion,"[49] but rather in the words of Nicholson, "as with all his natural gifts, he vitalized this, in his later life, by the force and intensity of his spiritual longings."[50] Le Goff, in the same way, writes "The chivalrous culture and sensibility that he acquired before his conversion became part and parcel of his new religious ideal."[51] All of these observations are variations of the original insight given by Celano, who identifies the convergence of these elements in Francis by observing, "even when meditating on sacred things, he maintained his courtly manners."[52]

The continuity with who Francis was and with who he becomes through this transformation can perhaps best be understood by comparing Francis' conversion to the conversion or call of Peter and the first disciples. According to all three of the synoptics, Jesus said to Peter and his brother who were fishermen: "Follow me and I will make you fish for people."[53] Jesus took them as they were and used a metaphor that redirected their abilities; he harnessed their gifts for the Kingdom. In the same way, God can be said to have transformed Francis, the soldier of Assisi, into Francis, the soldier of Christ. Francis, who once desired to be a knight of the world, became a knight of Christ. In this way, Jesus offered Francis and his followers, a vision of their mission.

John Navone's research offers insight into the nature and function of a defining vision for the believer. He begins with the assumption: "Every life story requires an initiating vision."[54] This vision is "essential" and "integral to human motivation and action; it shapes our lives" since "we cannot do what we cannot, at least in some way, imagine or envisage."[55] He continues: "Our lives bear witness to a basic vision; this vision includes images of ourselves, others, the world, human integrity and failure, God and so on."[56] Similar to Bulkeley's concept of the "root metaphor" and Progoff's paradigm of the Organic Psyche, Francis' dream vision, in Navone's model, reveals how Francis' own self-understanding and heroic vision fashioned how he conceived of God, Mary, his brothers and sisters, creation and his whole world. This follows Schleiermacher's insight that "imagination is the highest and most original element in us," and that it "creates the world for you" so that "everything besides it is merely reflection upon it."[57] This is another way of saying what Little observed, that the "ideals of chivalrous adventure remained with him and coloured all his life."[58] According to Navone, the defining vision of God we receive in scriptural icons serves as a matrix for Christian conversion by motivating faith.

> Inasmuch as we cannot do what we can in no way imagine, Jesus, as the perfect icon of God, motivates faith to a new way of being-in-the-world-together-with-others. Inasmuch as motivation is commensurate with concreteness and vividness and beauty of an image, the life story of the crucified and risen Jesus has proved a historically compelling image of God.[59]

Applying this to Francis, it is evident that, as seen in his *Office of the Passion*, one of his main images of Jesus became that of the hero of the passion. Thus Francis' worldly dream of knighthood is transformed into a desire to become a knight of Christ who seeks union with his crucified Hero, Christ the great King. Felder states:

> The peculiar character of the relation between Francis and the God-Man lies in this, that he was a *Knight of Christ*, that he devoted himself with a truly chivalrous spirit, and in a truly chivalrous manner, to the *service*, the *imitation*, and the *love* of his Lord.[60]

Mockler also states that:

> Francis saw himself as an Arthur; as a knight, and his company as a renewed fellowship of the Round Table, and his Order more as an Order

> of Knighthood than as an Order of Religious. Consciously or unconsciously he modeled the practices of this novel Order of his upon that of the knights of King Arthur.[61]

The earliest legend of King Arthur identifies Arthur as a "*dux bellorum*," who led his Knights of the Round Table in twelve battles.[62] According to Schmucki, "Francis used these chivalrous warriors as a metaphor when he spoke about the complex interrelationship between preaching, knowledge, and prayer."[63] He believed Francis drew a

> Parallel between the brothers' apostolate of charismatic exhortation to do penance and the 'joyous mission' of the wandering minstrels. That is to say, he saw the Friars Minor as itinerant singers of God's love.[64]

Schmucki thus concludes, "The spirit of chivalry expressed in the epics formed, as it were, the vehicle and leitmotif of his profound and deeply felt spirituality."[65] Just as Aquinas found that the use of metaphor in scripture was "both necessary and useful,"[66] Henry uses metaphor and symbol in order to show that Francis' passion for worldly glory and honor won through outward battles is now turned inward and directed toward heavenly glory won through inward battles. These deeds and battles are described in Henry's second chapter. Before analyzing this, it is worth noting that in later legends, (2 *Celano* 6, *Anonymous of Perugia* 5, and the *Major Life* 1:3) the dream takes on greater importance. In these legends, it is only after Francis has the dream that he decides to journey to Apulia in order to become a knight. After Henry, all of these later versions, as well as the *Three Companions*, expand the dream sequence to include a second dream, vision, or locution, which helps to explain the first. Thus, not only does the dream become the initial impetus which sparks or manifests Francis' desire to become a knight, but as seen in 2 *Celano* 6, it also explains that the dream will have a spiritual fulfillment: Francis "changes his carnal weapons into spiritual ones and in place of military glory he receives the knighthood of God."[67]

Spiritual Knighthood

The second chapter of the *LV*, which directly follows the dream sequence, is Henry's longest original addition to Celano's material. It serves to deepen and complete the dream sequence by having Francis metaphorically equipped with spiritual weapons from heaven and 'officially' made a knight of Christ. Shamkovich notes, "in accordance with the chivalric code, the knight, the hero, and, therefore, the saint, must fight with the monster, the dragon."[68] In Henry's hagiography, the vices are personified as monsters. This chapter, therefore, begins with a description of the seven vices and their counterparts personified as mythical monsters that stand against Francis.

The Spirit equips Francis with seven shields to protect him, that is, seven virtues, which battle and help him overcome the deadly vices (*LV* II: 10-130). The description of each vice holds a certain parallel with Homer's catalogue of ships in the second book of the Iliad, which lists the leading figures of the war. The medieval context, however, shows that Henry was doing more than adding classical allusion. Specifically, the years 1130-1275 represented a pivotal and formative period in the development of the definition of virtue and vice by philosophers and theologians.[69] According to Albrecht Diem's study, *Virtues and Vice in Early Texts,* there was "a true discursive explosion" of texts following the Fourth Lateran Council, which was aimed at implementing the pastoral concerns of the council through the catalogues of vice and virtue.[70] These catalogues "became the standard pieces of catechetical teaching" and were the "most widely used scheme according to which a priest was taught to ask about the sins of his penitent, or a Christian to examine his conscience."[71] Further, it was the Franciscans who played a key role in producing these texts.[72] Henry's work then can be seen as a forerunner of these Franciscan catalogues that became "important instruments of pastoral care and received a prominent position in popular notions of morality."[73] Robert Grosseteste's *Deus est and Templum Dei,* for example, attempted to systematize Christian morality using virtue and vice.[74] Henry, therefore, simultaneously creates an inspirational and heroic depiction of the battle within Francis' soul and provides a practical manual of vice and virtue. Moreover Henry's edification of virtue and suppression of vice not only responded to the "central objectives of pastoral care" mandated by Innocent III, but serves as a mini-dramatization of Francis' ninth chapter of the *Regula Bullata* and his 27th *Admonition* entitled "How virtue drives out vice."[75]

Henry paints a gruesome picture of vice and a heroic depiction of virtue. The mythical monsters Alecto, Megaera and Tisiphone, known as the Furies, lead the vices against the "holy army of divine sisters"[76] led by the graces, Aglaia, Pasithea and Euphrosyne, who help defend Francis. This chapter serves to heighten the epic momentum of the story by drawing the line of battle between heaven and hell, good and evil. The first line of battle begins within Francis himself. Henry, writing in the tradition of Prudentius' *Psychomachia*[77] describes how this spiritual battle is waged within the soul. Henry describes the inner struggle of human nature, and how one must master one's better self and bring the worse to heel, compelling not the spirit "to serve the flesh, but the flesh to render service to the spirit."[78] This inner struggle is an integral part of the icon of Francis and serves to describe what is happening within the soul of a saint, below the surface. Henry thus not only writes about Francis' interior, physically but also spiritually, giving us a glimpse of Francis from the inside out. The detailed description of the internal physical ailments is deepened to include a picture of Francis' psyche and relates the inner struggle, where the real battle of Francis' soul rages. This is where Francis' spiritual war is fought, from within. Henry writes that Francis mastered monsters and curbed the flesh with the commands of the soul so that the foe was "brought down by orders derived from within."[79] Henry thus can be said to articulate the inner turmoil of Francis' personal *aristeia* experience or the battle Francis the hero wages within. Once the "virtues gain mastery of the vices within him,"[80] Francis is officially 'armed' by Charity, the head of the virtues, who, "to her hero, hands heaven-made weapons."[81] Here, Francis is spiritually equipped with armor and definitively becomes a spiritual knight. The reception of this spiritual armor, reminiscent of Ephesians 6:11-17, fulfills Francis' dream and includes: two spurs, love and fear, a double greave of action and contemplation, a breastplate of justice, a shield of faith, and a helmet of hope strapped on with patience. His weapons include a spear, whose shaft is right judgment and whose point is fervent devotion, and a sword of the cross.[82] Henry completes the imagery by stating: "And from that time forward, nothing could he accomplish that did not bring him military honors and nothing stood in the way of his fierce courage."[83] Francis' christening as a "spiritual knight"[84] is later confirmed by Henry's inclusion: "Sacred was the inspiration that endowed him with this sacred office."[85]

While worldly leaders like Julius and Alexander conquered with "weapons physical,"[86] Francis is portrayed as a "Godly captain"[87] who conquers with spiritual weapons.[88] While Julius conquered a foe and Alexander a world, Francis bests them both by conquering not only "a world and a foe but also himself."[89] This emphasis on the deeper asceticism within the inner life was characteristic of the shift in the conception of spirituality and sanctity which was occurring in the thirteenth century.[90] André Vauchez describes the shift as being one from the contemplation of the infinite mystery of a totally other and inaccessible God to the imitation of Christ in whose footsteps one must follow.[91] Vauchez exaggerates this point in claiming Francis' "life was the fullest expression of the new conception of saintliness that sprang from inner experience."[92]

Soldiers of Francis

Francis having been established as a holy leader of men takes his rightful place upon the world stage of history and literature, becoming a legendary mythological-like figure in his own right. Francis, like Aeneas, is a model leader who musters his forces and trains his 'minors' in the art of spiritual warfare.[93] This fulfills the communal or fraternal dimension of the dream, which included a vision of armor for his soldiers. Francis, the "chief of the minors,"[94] orders them "to open their souls to heaven's will"[95] and "to join his war on sin."[96] Thus his knights:

> take up arms under the same commander;
> Rejecting the world with its destructive enticements,
> They wage war upon the malicious demons and impose
> Silence on the stupid ranting of the flesh.[97]

Francis' intentions are revealed in his touching defense of the lifestyle he and his brothers have chosen. In speaking to John of Saint Paul, who tries to persuade Francis to base his Order in a monastery, Francis states,

> "O man of great renown," replies Francis, "would you
> Advise to cling to cloister or hermitage men asked
> To heal a whole world? We feel obliged to carry weapons
> Not alone for ourselves but to guard all who are brethren to us."[98]

Henry's development of the theme of Francis' holy leadership deepens in the fifth chapter of the *LV*. Here, Celano's account of Francis' 'commissioning' his brothers becomes an opportunity for Henry to have Francis stir up the troops before battle and encouraging his soldiers about the war ahead. According to Henry, Francis passes on what he learned of the art of combat. Chapter Five of the *LV* then is the heart of Henry's military analogy, in which Francis "fulfills Christ's injunction,"[99] and embarks on his "new campaign."[100] Since a true hero is tested on the battleground, Henry brilliantly depicts Francis' true persona as the "holy captain,"[101] who teaches his "troops of friars."[102]

> Note well the situation you are in, and know that life here
> Is but a military campaign, and sides now eager

> for battle
> Have declared an unending war, each against the other.
> Souls belong to the side of heaven, bodies to the side of earth.[103]

Examining how subsequent biographers portray this same event can highlight Henry's particular emphasis. A good contrast to Henry's rendition is Julian of Speyer's *Life of St. Francis,* which has Francis kiss each of his followers "as affectionately as a mother embraces her sons,"[104] or Bonaventure's more paternal Francis who commissions as a "gentle father to his sons."[105] In keeping with the emphasis on fraternity, in *The Legend of the Three Companions,* we find Francis beginning his commission with the address "Dear brothers."[106]

According to Henry then, Francis' followers are decidedly his comrades in arms. Henry affirms this by once again emphasizing the importance of the dream, not only for him but also for his soldiers to come. Henry links the weapons from heaven with his followers, as they become the banner under which Francis' soldiers march and fight before. Henry does this by reworking Francis' prophecy of future friars in 1 Celano 27, adding that the "unnumbered friars that are to come from every race" were "bearing the arms of Francis" and carrying "his standard." Henry reiterates this several times: "These he enrolls under his banner;"[107] "Many of them he arms and enlists to follow his banner,"[108] "He shows the way to the trophy to all who will carry his banner,"[109] "Who follow his banner in the spiritual warfare."[110] Henry even ends the *LV* with a prayer that emphasizes Francis' leadership role: "May we to his company be led to Christ."[111] Little sums up Francis in this way:

> The imitation of Christ—"the poor Christ," to adopt a phrase often used in early Franciscan literature—became fused with service of Lady Poverty, the Gospel became the rule of life, and Francis no longer a solitary became again a leader of men, leading his knights on their great adventure of liberating the world from the wicked giants of avarice and hatred and pride... He made the glory and sacrifices of peace as compelling and romantic as the glory and sacrifices of war.[112]

And finally,

> He remained true to the principle he had always taught—that example and humility and love were the weapons of the true winner of souls.[113]

Minor Notes

While the major note of Henry's song of Francis is certainly the military march, it is not the only note. In iconography, the size of the figure is usually correlated to its significance, so that the largest figure is usually the most important and the smallest the least. Bona has pointed out that for Francis, chivalrous knighthood "was his aim, his direction, his target,"[114] in a word, his one passionate desire that formed "the center to which all his thoughts and energies were directed."[115] Henry's work uses the dream and its military motif as the controlling metaphor, which serves as the axis around which all of the other minor aspects of Francis gain meaning and can be understood. This is an epic convention which Henry builds into the *LV* that utilizes the central event of the dream as the nucleus of the story which all the other action revolves around, supports and relates back to, much like the spokes of a wheel that converge into a central axle. The literary function of this convention serves to give the *LV* an epic unity to which each of the minor aspects in the narrative converge and gain meaning only in reference to the major event.

This epic convention which enables all the other events and aspects of Francis' life to be understood through the metaphorical lens of the dream is very Franciscan. In fact this technique typifies one of the principle characteristics of medieval Franciscan literature which John V. Fleming's study, *An Introduction to the Franciscan Literature of the Middle Ages,* highlights. Fleming not only noted the "willingness" of Franciscan literature "to visualize concrete, verbal images"[116] but states, "In Franciscan imagery...there is a marked tendency to press metaphoric language as far as it can go and to advance significant claims for the letter of metaphor." These aspects will now be studied.

Francis and Myth

Because myth, like dreams, can be a rich source of psychological insight and is said to touch "the core of the nature of man," both have been seen as the "primary medium for intuitive insights into the ultimate nature of human existence."[117] Joseph Campbell even wrote that "myths are public dreams: dreams are private myths."[118] A more academic understanding of myth in hagiography was provided by Delehaye who defined myth as "the personification of a force or of an abstract idea."[119] In order to understand how Henry used mythical elements to construct his icon, one must understand something of mythological theory. There are two basic approaches to the interpretation of myth: one is the literal, and the other is the symbolic.[120] The literalists approach myth in the way that some scholars approach hagiography, that is, viewing it as an unscientific fable or fictional story that has no truth. The original meaning of the word myth, however, comes from "*mythos*," the ancient Greek word for "word," "tale," or "story,"[121] which has no connotation to truth or falsehood.[122] A closer study of myth can reveal a symbolic meaning, which understands these stories allegorically as "root stories," that hold "great power and perhaps even secret knowledge."[123] The Sophists of the Greek Enlightenment were among the first to interpret myths as "theogonic tales" which held moral truths.[124] David Bidney relates that like the Neo-Platonists, Stoics, and Epicurians who agreed that myths were not to be taken literally, the Emperor Julian and the philosopher Sallustius both regarded myths "as divine truths and mysteries hidden from the foolish crowd and apparent only to the wise."[125] This same view is articulated by the German philosopher Friedrich Wilhelm Joseph von Schelling, who defines myth as a "theogonic process" in which God is said "to reveal Himself historically through human consciousness."[126]

While science seeks causes to explain how the world works, myth and poetry seek meaning and try to explain the why.[127] According to Clinton Albertson, this is in line with the aim of hagiographers, who are "not interested in the historicity of facts but in their 'myth'—their meaning and significance."[128] Once referred to as "lies that tell the truth, unreal stories that signify the inner meaning of life,"[129] hagiographical stories and myths "give a sense of the movement of the soul's experience of the world."[130] Perhaps Henry's use of myth in the *LV* can best be understood in light of George Bradford Caird's thesis which contends that myth is used in scripture as a metaphor system for the theological interpretation of real historical events.[131] Caird draws from Rudolf Karl Bultmann who defined mythology as "the use of imagery to express the otherworldly in terms of this world and the divine in terms of human life, the other side in terms of this."[132] For Bultmann, mythology is fundamentally the theological use of metaphor.[133] He states:

> Above all it is a referential in the same fashion as metaphor is referential. It tells a story about the past, but only in order to say something

> about the present and the future. It has a literal referent in the characters and event of the vehicle story, but its tenor referent is the situation of the user and his audience. Like the user of other forms of metaphor, the user of myth says to his audience, "Here is a lens which has helped me to understand the world you and I live in: look through it yourselves and see what I have seen." To accept the vehicle in its literal aspect is the way of superstition: to accept its transcendental reference (the tenor) exclusively is the way of allegory.[134]

Two examples of Henry's use of myth will illustrate the point. The first is Henry's allusion to Antaeus, the mythical Libyan giant in the fourth chapter, which serves as an occasion for Henry to deepen his theological interpretation of Francis' conversion process. In speaking of Francis' regretful encounter with a beggar who asked him for alms "in the name of so great a King," Henry labels this a "*felix culpa*."[135] It is a happy fault because from that moment:

> he resolved in his heart and vowed
> That henceforth should he have anything, he would rebuff no one
> Who begged in the name of Christ.[136]

Henry then explains that a just man with "a divine call" learns from his misfortunes and "profits from his mistakes."[137] At this point, Francis is compared to Antaeus, who according to mythology was invincible because he was renewed in strength by his mother Gaea every time he fell to the ground.[138] Henry states:

> Daring to fall, contemptuously going to excess, he becomes a criminal:
> As soon as he is contrite, his rash daring becomes application,
> His lapse becomes rising, his contempt admission, his excess merit,
> His crime goodness. Thus did obstacles work in Francis, whose
> Double strength derived from falling—like that of Antaeus—
> Fought the better when it seemed it was already defeated.
> And by his own example Francis taught those whomsoever one mishap
> Confuted that they should throw every fault to the ground.[139]

The comparison of Francis to Antaeus accentuates the didactic element of Francis' soul; How Francis learns and grows from his mistakes and in turn, teaches others.

The second example of Henry's use of mythology is the allusion of Clare as Cynthia, whose brightness surpasses the stars, is laced with interpretative meaning.[140] It is very fitting that Henry would compare Clare to Cynthia, the virgin goddess of the moon. In this way Clare can be understood as another Cynthia, who humbly receives and absorbs the light of the sun, which in Christian terms could be interpreted as another Mary, clothed with the sun. Although Clare is an independent saint in her own right who contributes her own unique qualities to Franciscan spirituality, she can also be seen as one of Francis' greatest disciples, who, like the moon, best reflected the light of his spirit. Clare even referred to herself as his 'little plant.'

Finally, one may ask if Henry really believes Francis' soul literally passed Lethe[141] or even question whether he wants his readers to believe it. The obvious answer to these questions is certainly not. Henry's mythologizing is not to be taken literally, but it is meant to be taken seriously as it offers a symbolic discourse which, as a metaphor system for the theological interpretation of real historical events,[142] is in line with the *"officium poetae,"*[143] and aids in boosting Francis' epic heroism.

Francis and Song

Dante once wrote that Francis' life "could better be sung in the glory of Heaven" than written by human hands. Henry begins the *LV* by "singing" his poem of Francis in the tradition of the ancient epics. In the very first line of the *LV*, Henry introduces the "theme" of his "song" as the "great feats of a godly captain."[144] Like Homer and Virgil before him, Henry sings his tale in order to immortalize the great deeds of his hero Francis, who it has been said, "set the world singing."[145] Henry pleads with Francis to accept and hear Minerva, the Roman Goddess of the Arts, to "do the honors in song" to his princely campaign.[146]Henry, as noted, in his eleventh chapter states that the very image of Francis he depicts is a painted "song."[147] Henry the poet thus sings of Francis the poet, who loved to sing songs and listen to music throughout his entire life, beginning even before his conversion[148] and leading up to the very moment of his death.[149] Francis simply loved music and even enjoyed listening to the lute when he was sick.[150] Edouard Leclerc observed: "it is impossible to read the first biographies of Francis without being struck by the importance that song assumes in his life," and thus he regards song as "one of the characteristic themes of his walk towards God."[151] Although Francis was admired for singing vain and drunken songs in his youth,[152] Celano relates that after his conversion Francis was often "thinking and singing of Jesus...inviting all the elements to praise Jesus."[153] Even when Francis wasn't singing out loud, Celano tells us, "he sang in his heart."[154]

Celano relates that at Greccio Francis sang the Gospel in a "powerful voice, a pleasant voice, a clear voice, a musical voice."[155] Henry for his part uses the word 'sweet' three different times in the *LV* to describe Francis' voice: "dulcet voice"[156] "dulcet tones"[157] and "sweet-toned."[158] Before Francis sings at Greccio, Celano relates the brothers sing first, "giving God due praise."[159] This is very much in tune with Francis, who taught his brothers to be "minstrels of the lord" who "go around the world singing, and only after singing to preach a little."[160] This was natural for friars like Brother Pacifico, who, even before joining the friars, composed wanton songs, was known as a "courtly master of singers"[161] and was even crowned by the Emperor as *"Rex Versum."*[162] It is not surprising then to find that when Br. Pacifico was commissioned to France he took singers with him.[163] According to Homer G. Pfander, the sermons of the friars "often employed verse which they taught the common people."[164] Lawrence S. Cunningham states Francis' prayers and lauds were not written "to be read in prayer books but were to be sung either by the friars as part of their preaching exercises or as a part of their own devotions."[165] The twenty-first chapter of the *Earlier Rule* and the *Office of the Passion* which Francis composed from the psalms is a good example.[166]

Moorman relates that "the type of religion which St. Francis fostered naturally lent itself to song."[167] Francis not only wrote poetry and sang but also composed music in several languages including "Occitan, French, Latin and Italian."[168] Francis wrote a melody to the words of the *Canticle of Creatures*[169] and "certain sacred words and music" for the Clares.[170] Francis can be said to have turned his passion for secular music and poetry of the troubadours into God's service. One could conclude from Little's comment that the "songs and ideals of chivalrous adventure remained with him and coloured all his life"[171] that while the words changed, the tune of the music remained the same. In fact the Franciscans took a leading role in "adapting worldly literary forms to Godly ends."[172] A good example of this is when Francis used song to reconcile the Bishop and the *podestà* of Assisi.[173] Peter Loewen writes: "As minstrels sang secular songs in order to earn material wealth, so he sent his troupe of "*Joculatores Domini*" to win souls."[174] David L. Jeffrey even points to the Franciscans "as first and chief among clerical borrowers of the popular vernacular song."[175] An example of this comes from George Gordon Coulton, who relates that Francis,

> is recorded to have preached one of his most remarkable sermons from the text of a French love-song: and one of his early disciples, Brother Henry of Pisa, resolved that 'the Devil should not have all the best tunes,' and turned current love-songs into hymns.[176]

Loewen cites a version of the story about the sermon at Montelfeltro recorded in T*he Fioretti* from the *First Consideration of the Stigmata,* a text appended to the *Fioretti di Sancto Franciescho.*[177] The story narrates that Francis and his companions chanced upon noblemen gathered in a celebration for new knighting. As the friars approached the celebration, Francis heard a singer entertaining the crowd with a courtly love song. Francis is said to have jumped upon a wall and began preaching to the noblemen using the following song as his theme: *"Tanto è quello bene ch'io aspetto ch'ogni pena m' è diletto,"* meaning "So great is the good that I hope for, that all pain delights me."[178] This example, which led to the conversion of the knights, embodies one Franciscan historian's comment that "poetry and music were not only a prayer and a necessity for him, they were also a weapon for winning souls."[179]Cunningham writes of Francis' adaptation and transformation of the troubadour poetic tradition in this way:

> The peculiar gestalt that results from the blending of the jongleur singing of the courtly tradition that had come out of France into Italy (and which had influenced Francis so much) with a simple penetration of the truths of the Gospel is a blend characteristically Franciscan.[180]

Christopher Ohan, who studied the religious and artistic trends of the thirteenth century, wrote that Francis "emphasized a union with God through poetry and song."[181] Bradley Baker Dick, in his study of the poetics of Franciscan spirituality, speaks about the role of song, especially through the Lauds, in the spiritual life of the early friars:

> Singing opened up the friars' physical and mental being to a sensible prefiguration of the joy that they would experience in the spiritual consummation of their search for God's love. The subjects of the lauds—Christ, Mary, their virtues and their sacrifices, God's love—kept their attention focused on the objects of their spiritual quest.[182]

An example of the power and effectiveness of song in the early missionary experience of the friars can be seen in Loewen's study entitled *Francis the Musician and the Mission of the 'Joculatores Domini' in the Medieval German Lands*. Loewen writes that because the missionary friars "shared Francis' sense of piety and understanding of the rhetorical power of music,"[183] they "transmitted their spirituality to the German lands through music, as Francis himself had ordained,"[184] and "used music to communicate pious values to audiences."[185] Loewen points out that as early as 1228 the Franciscan Studium established in Magdeburg implemented musical ideas of Francis.[186] Dick explains in more detail how the recitation of the verses of the Lauds "not only provide a ritualistic vehicle to render praise to God" but how they provide a "mental vehicle to transcend the world's ills and 'find' God in an easy fashion."[187]

> Lauds express and actualize the individual's sense of immediate personal contact with God, substituting their imagery of a perfect, redeeming, and joyful psycho-spiritual world for the brutal ugly, violent experiences of the physical and social world.[188]

Loewen concludes his study by stating:

> The musical doctrine of Francis is unambiguous: The quintessential principles of Franciscan spirituality were to be transmitted to all people using the power of music and poetry.[189]

Henry thus presents his *LV* as the song of the life of Francis or the life of Francis in song. In doing so, Henry uses the medium of song as the message. The message of Francis' song is not only a marching hymn of the battle which raged in his warrior soul but also a ballad which expresses the joyful spirit of his troubadour heart. An eloquent example of this can be seen in the fourth chapter of the *LV* in which Henry adds seven more references to song not appearing in Celano, and refers to Francis as a "songster."[190] Only Henry's poetry is able to weave Francis and nature together so harmoniously that the reader is almost unaware that the two become one. Henry sets the stage by foreshadowing the event with a pair of questions which introduce an irony of opposites: "From fortune to misery, from riches to poverty; Or is it from misery to fortune and from poverty to riches?"[191] He then contrasts Francis' clothing of sackcloth, with his former clothes of soft wool which would "change with the season."[192] Henry continues to weave this theme of covering and revealing throughout the scene. While Celano only briefly alludes to the season with the presence of some snow, Henry elaborates on this scene by painting a beautifully rich and colorful landscape that echoes the interior movements of Francis.

Before Francis is stripped in the incident with the robbers, Henry describes Francis as "poor, needy, neglected and freezing."[193] As Francis walks along the road, however, something interesting happens: "the winter season"[194] and Francis are joined through Henry's poetry. He states: "as her bareness is swathed in the snow's woolen robe and adorned with crystals of ice."[195] As Francis continues, he rejoices and begins to sing, delighting in the freedom:

As Christ's slave and a free man himself; that being naked,
Makes the fierce cold almost soothing. For who is so rigid
He would not rejoice at the change from a worse to a better condition?
So many reasons for rejoicing transacting within his breast,
Francis opens up in song in the language of the French.[196]

The robbers encounter Francis and call him a "silly Herald"[197] and say, "For your song, these are the bed-clothes You're getting."[198] While Celano has the robbers throw Francis in a "ditch filled with deep snow,"[199] Henry writes that Francis is "covered" and thrown into a "snowy cave," and thus is "buried" in a "tomb."[200] This seems to imply a symbolic death that is paralleled in nature through the season of winter, which traditionally represents "the time of old age, barrenness."[201] For Henry, this reflects an allusion to St. Paul's 'old man' (Ephesians 4:2). After his encounter with the robbers, Henry has Francis take up his "unfinished song," and "with praise of the Creator, he pierces meandering hollows and trains the woods to re-echo the mysteries of Christ."[202] This is an allusion to Virgil's *Eclogue* in which Francis is likened to an exile or outcast singing to the Muse of the woodland. "We leave our native borders and pleasant fields; we fly our native land, while you, Tityrus, at ease in the shade teach the woods to echo fair Amaryllis."[203]

The next day, when Francis leaves the monks, external nature seems to coincide with Francis' internal awakening of life or rebirth as Henry prepares for the onset of spring in the following way.

> A humid and pore-opening wind exposing the ground's surface,
>
> And a south wind melts the snow and the ice
> The north wind piled up all around.
> Torrents are everywhere, and water from the mass
> Of snow and ice spreads over all the fields; crashing
> Stones are dragged along, and logs and uprooted oaks
> From the woods are afloat.[204]

Henry's connection between creation and Francis and how God transforms the forlorn Francis, wandering among the woods where "all pathways are foul, all roads obscure," culminates in a storm as the waters gush and flood, and the harsh wind blows.[205] While Celano states that Francis is left with a "cheap shirt" Henry states Francis is left with only a "shroud,"[206]which seems a reference to the shroud of Jesus and symbolizes the resurrection. Finally the sun melts the snow and Francis arrives at Gubbio where he receives a "new garment."[207] Henry concludes by adding:

> Through suffering so much destitution for Christ's name

> He always and constantly kept the same countenance;
> The poor outwardly, the more stalwart was he within.[208]

Henry continues this relationship, merging and contrasting Francis and nature, thus communicating his special link and attunement to all life around him. In a particular way it is a good example of how Henry is able to communicate what Loewen observed about Francis. He states Francis transformed the message in the song of the courtly poets which conveyed "that the pains of love are delightful, since they offer the hope of a lover's solace." Francis' song expressed that "the pains of pious suffering are delightful, since they offer a hope of redemption."[209] This theme, typical of the cansó, is taken from the secular Provencal poets and singers, who would sing songs of love in which the troubadour's mood would often be reflected by the seasons of the year.[210] Loewen states: "To sing people into spiritual joy was to evoke in them this same perception, and thus to lead them to redemption."[211] This poetic rendition of the symbiosis between Francis and nature seems to be the subject of Little's comment, "Art owed its rebirth to the union of nature and religion, which was embodied in this movement."[212]

Henry continues the theme of Francis and song right up until the end of his life, where he fittingly states that Francis "sings his own funeral rites, as his swan-song."[213] Francis' song does not end at his death however, as echoes can be found in later works. One of the friars from Francis' immediate circle is believed to have composed the *Canto dell'amore,* a meditative poem on the creative power and love of God expressed in nature.[214] The impact of the song of Francis' life, especially in the terms of Henry's depiction, can be seen in many ways. One example is in the work of the Franciscan poet Jacomino of Verona. Jacomino's poetry is modeled on the *chansons de geste* and uses the language of chivalry to depict knights fighting a battle. Moorman considered his work a direct forerunner of *The Divine Comedy.*[215] Another example is the influence that Henry's realistic and gruesome physical details had on the Franciscan movement. The motif of vividly depicting suffering in graphic details in order to evoke an emotional response is considered one of the hallmarks of Franciscan art and poetry.[216]

Francis and Piety

Piety is a highly polysemous word that is often misunderstood, especially in its contemporary usage.[217] Even a cursory glance at the word reveals such a wide breath of meaning which, in the words of John Dryden, "is more full than it can possibly be expressed in any modern language."[218] Considering "pietas" is translated in no less than four different ways in the *LV,* as pity, mercy, kindness and goodness, a thorough study of the history of the word piety is necessary. This study aims at understanding all of the nuances of Henry's creative and unique use of the word piety in his interpretation of Francis. According to the Oxford

Latin dictionary, the definition of the word *"pietas"* signifies "an attitude of dutiful respect towards those to whom one is bound by ties of religion," while *"pius"* means being "faithful to one's moral obligations, dutiful, conscientious, upright."[219] Piety, in fact, is one of three fundamental virtues on which Rome was founded and was considered essential to the security and stability of Rome's ideals.[220] The meaning of the word, however, is not simply Roman but "involves Greek precedents as well as subsequent Christian and medieval transformations."[221] Plato believed the essence of piety consisted "in being servants of the gods by doing good."[222] Piety, in classical antiquity signified "the application of all one's being to God's service," that is, "the profound religious sentiment of respect and love for the deity."[223]

Henry highlights Francis' piety by uniting God's piety to Francis throughout the *LV* but especially during his conversion. Francis' conversion is not only framed with references to piety but is laced with it throughout. In the very beginning of Francis' conversion, Henry reveals that God looks to Francis in his sickness "with fatherly piety"[224] and emphasizes "in piety...raises him up."[225] Henry then adds it is "celestial grace" which "carries on the work of piety," to transform him.[226] During this time, Henry also twice describes Pica as having piety for her son, by mercifully freeing him from prison.[227] This culminates in Francis' long speech in front of the bishop. There Francis tells his father that he cannot continue to "cheat" the faithful out of their money as an unjust merchant, but rather must prove his faith through works because he has "tasted the honey of divine piety."[228]

In each of these instances, piety connotes charity or active mercy, and echoes back to the Hebrew word from which piety is derived, namely "*hesed*," which is translated as "compassionate goodness" and describes "an attachment which implies efficacious and faithful help."[229] This definition emphasizes that piety is "shown through acts" or deeds, a theme running throughout the *LV* which speaks of Francis' understanding of the power of example and incarnating love in action. It is also connected to Paul's letter to Timothy, in which piety is named as the virtue that frees one from the love of money,[230] through a striving to acquire imperishable goods.[231]

When Henry describes Francis living with the lepers and beggars, he calls Francis "full of piety"[232] because he "saw no one go in want while he had plenty."[233] Henry then relates how Francis gave something of what he had to the hungry, thirsty, naked, etc.[234] This is in line with the New Testament interpretation of piety as "the filial love of God" which is proved "in effective love of neighbor."[235] This horizontal or social dimension which emphasizes brotherhood united under one father is a strong affirmation of the Franciscan value of fraternity.[236] This fraternal sense of piety and its option for the poor is also in line with Marco von Galli's "essentially Christian" interpretation of Francis' knightly "*cortesia*."[237] According to von Galli "everything we designate today as *solidarity* with the suffering and oppressed corresponds to the *cortesia* of Francis,"[238] which he states "contains much delicate reverence, but real involvement" and "concern for the person of one's fellow man."[239] It is worth noting that Francis' reverence, which one Franciscan commentator has defined as "an attitude of deep respect pervaded by wonder, admiration, awe and love," is believed to have "its roots in his upbringing by his mother and in his love of the ways of chivalry."[240] Francis is believed to have integrated this reverence with his devotion to God.[241] Henry's description of Francis as "full of piety" is all the more significant given the fact that the New Testament presents Christ as the "source and model"[242] of piety. In addition, Scripture reveals that it is through Christ that "the piety of God realizes His plan of salvation,"[243] and it is Christ's piety that is cited as the reason why God hears him.[244]

Henry begins his eleventh chapter by announcing that "Of virtues best, piety, is infused in his fair soul."[245] Henry thus saw piety as Francis' primary and greatest virtue. It is the very first virtue given to Francis by the Holy Spirit who arms him to battle against vice. Henry relates that the first virtue that Francis receives is Fear of the Lord, which renders him "knowledgeable in her piety."[246] This reflects Proverbs 1:7 which states: "Fear of the Lord is the beginning of wisdom," and that "Piety toward God is the beginning of perception."[247] Here Henry also grafts Francis into the heroic tradition of piety that associates it with persecution, battle and war. In fact the second meaning of piety given in the Oxford dictionary is "of wars justly waged."[248] This is an ancient tradition that goes back to the fourth book of Maccabees where the Hasidim fought to the death for their faith.[249] This book, "by far the most extensive treatment of piety,"[250] is a common text used in hagiography to depict heroic struggle. Here Eleazar, his wife and seven sons fight against oppressors by means of their piety, through which they "reverence highly the only living God."[251]Their commitment to "true piety" alone enables them to overcome even torture and death in order to remain faithful to the true religion.[252] After the sixth son refuses to obey the pagan king, and declares that he is suffering for the sake of piety,[253] the youngest son states the noble deaths of his brothers fulfilled their piety to God.[254] Most remarkably, a hymn in a work called 4 Maccabees sings of the exploits of these brothers, exhorting their common origins under one father, their love for one another, and their shared zeal for goodness, which unified them and allowed them to grow and gain strength from one another.[255] It is thus easy to see how piety is related to a knight or soldier's main virtue of loyalty and service to their king, since piety and fidelity are compenetrating in scripture.[256] It is interesting to note that Henry specifically points to "divine piety" as having kept Francis safe from any "hostile force."[257]

While the above insights shed light on the word piety in regard to its Hebrew, Greek and Latin roots as well as its biblical connotations, the following concentrates on the implications of piety within the medieval context in which the *LV* was written. Although piety represents a Roman ideal, it is an ideal that was "adapted to the cultural conditions of later times."[258] In order to understand Henry Tileman's comment: "The piety of Francis reveals the type of religious spirit of the Middle Ages in its perfection,"[259] and Adolf Harnack's remark that "in Francis medieval piety reaches its clearest and strongest expression,"[260] one must understand piety in its medieval context. The following section therefore, addresses the particular way in which Henry, in choosing to create a close association of Francis with Virgil's Aeneas, interprets the piety of Francis.

As mentioned earlier, Virgil's popularity "reached its zenith" in the Middle Ages where he was revered as "*anima naturaliter Christiana*," a naturally Christian soul."[261] Saverio Caramanica has even written that Virgil's "poetry is like the holiness of Francis,"[262] in regard to their "ideals of peace and of human solidarity, of love and of humility, and respect of nature and of God,"[263] which was "sung by them."[264] In fact, by identifying Francis so closely with Aeneas, Henry merges his icon of Francis with the well known icon of Aeneas, who was considered "*maximum pietatis exemplum*" in the Middle Ages.[265] Aeneas, who has even been regarded as "*pietatis* incarnate," epitomized right relationship between God and others as well as symbolized duty in family and public responsibility.[266]

Moreover, Henry accentuates Aeneas' numerous qualities in Francis: His loyal devotion to his God, religious spirit, zeal for his mission, attachment to his Father, goodness and wisdom, and faith in providence.[267]

It has been said a picture is worth a thousand words. Aeneas escaping Troy, carrying his father on his back, holding small statues of his gods, and leading his son by the hand is *the* classic medieval image of piety. It not only conveys the deep love and respect Aeneas had for his father and his gods but also his own paternal love for his son. Moreover, according to Gerald Malsbury, it "marks a great moment of conversion in the soul of the hero Aeneas."[268] Malsbury designates this moment as the pivotal moment that Aeneas chose to listen to the divine signs, and "instead of fighting to the death to defend Troy," leaves his homeland and sets out "on the adventure of destiny that would end in the founding of Rome."[269] In this way Virgil transforms the notion of piety by depicting Aeneas as saving civilization, since he "was more truly heroic" at this moment "than when fighting with his sword."[270] This is affirmed in the climactic moment of the first half of the Aeneid, when "the hero's voyage to the underworld which leads to reunion with his father," is depicted as a moment in which "*pietas* conquers the journey."[271] Aeneas is seen as being transformed by the journey to Rome, through which he "grows into an understanding of his characteristic virtue."[272] The impact of this interpretation of Aeneas' piety for Christians in the

Middle Ages was especially significant because of the rising cult of pilgrimage, which could be defined as "physical travel for a spiritual purpose."[273] John of Salisbury, for example, identified "the journey of Aeneas with the life of the human soul."[274] Dante will later describe the journey of the *Inferno* in terms of piety, stating: "*la guerra sì del cammino e sì de la pietate*."[275] Later, Erasmus, who saw Virgil's hero Aeneas as "a model for the militant Christian," not only referred to the Christian pilgrimage as "*pietatis via*,"[276] but saw *pietas* as the way.

Thomas Stearns Eliot demonstrates how piety is "the way" by explaining that Virgil's use of the word piety has "much wider associations of meaning" which he describes as "his attitude towards life."[277] According to Eliot, Aeneas' piety contains an "essential ingredient," which he states "is an analogue and foreshadow of Christian humility."[278] This he explains is because Aeneas' heroism stems from his being "a displaced person, the fugitive from a ruined city and obliterated society."[279] Thus he is described as "the prototype of a Christian hero, for he is humbly, a man with a mission; and the mission is everything."[280] This mission is begun when Aeneas escapes Troy and becomes an exile in search of his homeland. The journey itself transforms Aeneas.

This understanding of the '*pietas* of pilgrimage' has specific implications for Henry's interpretation of Francis and the manner in which the journey is turned inward. Because Henry depicts Francis' inner conversion as a battle, *pietas* can be seen in its Augustinian definition as "the power of penitence to conquer not nations or armies" but "*peccata*."[281] Here, the ascetic exercise of battling against one's sins can be seen as the interior process of Francis' journey of conversion. Just as the late Pope John Paul II had pointed out the reason why some biographers had failed to write the story of his life was because "they try to understand me from the outside. But I can only be understood from the inside."[282] Henry seeks to tell the story of the journey of Francis' soul into God through his inward pilgrimage of piety; it is an inner journey of God-inspired self-mastery in which Francis conquers his vices and gains virtues. Although the danger of reducing Francis to any one virtue, whether that be poverty, humility, simplicity, etc., detracts from the fact that Francis was a man who embraced the whole Gospel message, exalting piety as Francis' greatest virtue may be considered an exception, at least by Felder. Although the piety of Francis has been given little attention by Franciscan scholars, Felder dedicates a chapter to "The Piety of Francis" in *The Ideals of St. Francis of Assisi*. Felder holds that piety as the "sum, center, and substance of the ideals of St. Francis."[283] According to Felder, piety is defined as "the directing of the entire man to God."[284] In Francis, piety caused him to strive "to fulfill perfectly the entire Gospel in spirit and letter, to become like to the Saviour in every way."[285] Felder concludes by stating "To serve one's neighbor by works of charity and by the apostolate for love of Christ, constitutes the zenith of his piety."[286]

Henry's insistence on connecting Francis with the rich tradition of piety and naming it as his greatest virtue, invites the reader to consider this virtue anew. Francis in the *Legend of Saint Clare* is described as "a *new man*," who "was renewing with new virtues the way of perfection forgotten by the world."[287] Perhaps Henry's most important contribution to Franciscan spirituality can be found in his being the first to wed Francis and piety in such an intimate and intricate manner. According to Henry, Francis truly embodies piety; it is the virtue that best describes him. The theological significance of this assertion is most clearly demonstrated in how Francis epitomizes the modern definition of piety found in Jordan Aumann's *Spiritual Theology*. According to Aumann, the affective gift of piety is described as "the filial love for God as a Father, and a sentiment of universal love for all men and women as our brothers and sisters and as children of the same heavenly Father."[288] Piety "places in the soul a truly filial love for our heavenly Father,"[289] which consequently fosters "the sentiment of universal brotherhood with all others" that is manifested through an exquisite affection shown to others.[290] Aumann continues by stating for those who are imbued with piety,

> The world and all creation are considered as the house of the Father, and everything in the universe becomes testimony of his infinite goodness. Such persons are able to discover the religious meaning hidden in all things.[291]

Piety extends to include "the reverence we should have toward every creature as a product of God's goodness and generosity."[292] This description is particularly appropriate for Francis in light of his *Canticle of Creatures*.

According to Aumann, piety, quite remarkably, describes several other aspects of Francis' spirituality: It "perfects and intensifies the soul's filial love for the Blessed Virgin,...gives a "reverence for the Pope as Vicar of Christ on earth,...looks upon superiors as fathers and mothers and endeavors to obey them with filial joy,...has a deep veneration for Sacred Scripture and reads the revealed word of God as if it were a letter sent from heaven by the Heavenly Father,...has a respect for holy all holy things, and especially those articles as instruments in the service and worship of God," enables one to worship and adore God through silence, prayer and tears, and finally "is completely submissive to the will of God and seeks only to glorify God with all its powers, desiring that all beings should realize their adoptive divine filiation and live as true children of God."[293] Each of these speaks of Francis in a very particular way. Regarding the last point, it is interesting to note that according to German scholar Josef Pieper, the first step in re-establishing piety as "an integral part of the ideal image of man," in contemporary society is restoring familial order.[294] Francis, who offers a model of family order based on "God as a most loving Father,"[295] contributes greatly to this restoration by affirming the sacred bond between brotherhood and all creation.

Final Considerations

While the previous examples of Francis and myth, song, and piety are able to express a dimension of Francis which supports and points to the major controlling metaphor, the following considerations may best represent what Delehaye speaks of when he describes how some authors introduce "their own impressions, deductions and passions" into the text.[296] A critical analysis of Henry's *LV* must answer the question of how much Henry was seeing himself in Francis. Henry calls Francis a "wandering jester,"[297] "clown,"[298] and "a moneyless songster,"[299] each of which in a certain way, refers to how Henry had been perceived by some during his life.

While Francis' speeches in the epic tradition serve to further extend Henry's military motif as is seen in Francis exhorting his father to "fight like a man,"[300] Francis' rhetorical skills and ability as an orator obviously reflect more of Henry than Francis. Francis' first speech in chapter three (*LV* III: 24-57), for example, is an added discourse which begins by addressing his father in the following way: "What do you want of me, deceiving father."[301] This reflects an epic convention of heightening the contrast, in this case between earthly carnal paternity and the heavenly spiritual Father who gives true life. Henry then takes the occasion to weave some mythological allusion into the speech by having Francis ask his father if he wants him to return to the "Charybdim,"[302] the great whirlpool (of earthly life) that Aeneas avoided and Odysseus survived. This leads to Francis' second discourse, (*LV* III: 86-126) not found in Celano, which sets up Francis stripping before the bishop. The impact of this epic speech seems to influence later legends which, after Henry, include a speech given by Francis (*Three Companions* 20, 2 *Celano* 12, *The Major Life* 2:4). Each source has Francis denying his earthly father for his heavenly one. Another example occurs in the sixth chapter, when Francis defends his style of living the Gospel life to John of St. Paul. Here Henry gives voice to Francis the poet, who boldly proclaims his purpose and vision of living the Gospel to John:

> "O man of great renown," replies Francis, "would you
> Advise to cling to cloister or hermitage men asked
> To heal a whole world? We feel obliged to carry weapons
> Not alone for ourselves but to guard all who are brethren to us.
> Would you have us neglect to bring medicine
> To a plague-ridden world while merely wishing it well?
> Surely it is wicked to prefer our own saving to that of all men."[303]

Henry concludes Francis' speech by having him articulate his heroic mission in a rousing, inspiring and succinct manner.

> To bring back the guilty and stoop down to the fallen-
> That is my work. This is the cross that I shoulder.
> I earnestly yearn to follow Christ thus; and I think I can
> Follow him no otherwise; so do I learn from the very words of the Gospel.[304]

Francis' philosophizing and legalistic language, however, are most assuredly projection on Henry's part. A brief look at some examples will demonstrate this. Russell had earlier noted that Henry's frequent use of *sic* and *ergo* was in indication of his probable study of logic.[305] Henry describes Francis' initial conversion through philosophical inquiry, having Francis reflect upon whether more things exist in his mind than he perceives with his sense.[306] And using Aristotle's *De sensu et sensili,* Henry even describes a philosophical debate in Francis' soul:

> Sense looks to what may be done, reason to what soon
> May occur. Sense proceeds not to the end of reality; reason decides
> Things beforehand. Sense holds out feasts, allurements of love,
> Wealth and high honor and human approval–but cannot go on any further.
> Reason holds out life without end, delights in that City Above,
> Paradise joy, mysterious song, unspeakable light.[307]

Henry also has Francis ponder the natural sciences as Francis "gives some thought to this theory."[308]

> But by reason of the fact
> That the air on a height, being moist and having no force to withstand,
> Is moved away by all things opposing it, there is no doubt
> But that it transforms bodies that are naked, in accordance
> With the patterns by which it is itself transformed; nor does
> Our constitution suffer its continuous motions.[309]

Henry's account of Francis' meeting with the Sultan is another good example of Henry putting philosophical jargon into Francis' mouth, especially Aristotelian terms such as the "first cause,"[310] God's "existence,"[311] "first principle,"[312] "simple substance,"[313] and "essence."[314]

Henry's use of Aristotle, Plato, Boethius, and William of Conches is well documented.[315] Allen has recently drawn attention to the depth of Henry's philosophical discourses by stating there is ample evidence to show Henry's ability to interpret current philosophical thought and 'transform' it with his own thought.[316] Allen's research therefore calls for a broader perception of Henry as a thinker, and new appreciation of "his participation in the developing intellectual culture of his time."[317]

Finally, Henry, as Binkley has noted, "while perhaps no expert, was interested in and conversant with the scholastic legal culture of his day."[318] Henry's knowledge and creativity with the law is also at the service of constructing his icon as court language finds its way into the *LV*, where he uses legal terms to describe Francis. During his conversion for example, Henry describes Francis as an "unwise judge"[319] who "leans toward the unfavored party"[320] despite the fact that "clear evidence may be shown for the case."[321] He continues in relating "no cogent proof is advanced without quibbling,"[322] as he "makes no intervention for the right in the testimony's favor."[323] Later Henry even has Francis reflect within himself in legalistic terms.

> He himself is his own prosecution and defense!
> As witness and as plaintiff and as judge—no legal statute barring this—
> After he's gone through the case and weighed it he convicts himself!
> And his loins that have exposed themselves to seduction's fires
> Like robbers he dispatches them by hanging with his triple-knotted rope![324]

Conclusion

Henry of Avranches was not only an accomplished "*vates*", a prestigious "*magister,*" and an experienced "*versificator*" of some eight saint's lives, but his illustrious career was marked by his designation as "Archpoet Laureate" of Henry III. By any standard, Henry ranks as one of the foremost Anglo-Latin poets of the thirteenth century and holds the distinction of being one of the first professional Latin poets of the Middle Ages.[1] Henry's use of his extensive learning, as well as his own theological reflection on the meaning of the Franciscans, as seen in his *Prophetia Hildegard*, written seven or eight years before the *LV*, not only challenges any understanding of him as a mere poetic entertainer, but rather reveals Henry as a credible and gifted interpreter of Francis.

If Celano wrote his life in order to proclaim a new saint, Henry wrote his legend in order to proclaim a new saintly hero who could be imitated by all the faithful. Henry, one of the earliest poets to put Franciscan spirituality into verse, poetically depicts Francis as a true knight of Christ crucified and so offers him as a new paradigm for the crusader. The *LV* weaves the life of Francis with classical figures from history and literature and thus, universalizes Francis the hero. By packaging Francis using the Virgilian concept of the epic hero, that is, as a compassionate self-conquering hero, Henry helped export him beyond the borders of Italy. He also developed the story about the merchant-turned-pauper into a story about the soldier-turned-spiritual knight who was canonized a saint. In doing so, Henry helped propagate the legend of Francis and produced a poem that could not only be sung across Europe but across the ages. In poetically expressing the chivalrous spirit of Francis, Henry captures the heroic dimension of Francis' sanctity and provides a courageous example that can inspire others to fight spiritual battles against sin. This promoted new dignity to a type of Gospel chivalry that served as a model of 'noble' holiness in service to the true king, which was accessible to all levels of society. Thus as an artistic work of spiritual literature, the *LV* holds immeasurable value for what it has done in terms of promoting the story, sharing the adventure, and awakening the heroic dream of sainthood within.

Henry's entire *LV* is basically an extension of Francis' dream, relating how he fulfilled it in living it out. Henry extends the metaphor of the military motif in Francis' dream in order to accomplish different literary and theological ends. The *LV* is an adventure with a classic theme of Good triumphing over Evil, about an unlikely hero, who grows up in a small town, and has big dreams. It is a romance story about the hope of finding glory, honor and fame. It is a myth about a Godly captain who triumphs over monsters and the forces of evil. It is also a human story about a person who struggles against himself to overcome his own vice and then forms a small band of comrades to battle alongside. It is finally about not just finding one's dream, but living it out, fulfilling one's dreams.

It is through the vehicle of the dream that we are able to share in Francis' epic. Henry allows the reader to enter into the dream by transporting them into another world, a Christian-mythological realm where warriors, heroes, and monsters lurk. In this way the *LV* becomes a spiritual odyssey into the inner life of Francis. Henry opens a dream gateway into a mystical world in which Francis has blazed a path of glory for all to follow and so share in his spiritual experience: from the inner turmoil of his powerful conversion, to his consuming love of nature as seen through his open heart.

The *LV* is not simply a versification of Celano. More than an imaginative epic, it reveals how God transformed Francis into a spiritual knight, his own self understanding as a soldier, and the crucifixion he endured. Theologically, Henry does not interpret Francis as a failed knight but rather a converted knight who was directed to fight a different war. Francis realized he was fighting the wrong war and most importantly the wrong foe. Henry emphasizes how God coaxes Francis into a new mission, a new knighthood, and a greater glory by addressing and exhorting Francis precisely as a soldier who is going to fight a war. It is then a question of identity as God speaks to who Francis is, and in a language that he could understand. Henry simply holds that Francis not only received the vision as a soldier, heard the exhortation as a soldier but lived it out as one. God provides him the arms and empowers him with the cross as a means in which to battle the true enemy. It is worth noting that this divine mission included brothers-in-arms, companion-knights, which affirms the essential fraternal dimension of his call.

Some have dismissed the *LV* as nothing more than an attempt to poetically adorn the real Francis in martial garb, that is, as an exercise of coloring him with epic and romantic tones in order to entertain. Henry, however, uses this metaphor as a means to describe his interior journey. Henry's artistry and learning not only adds a color and richness to the Celano account and engages the senses, but also functions to add a psychological and spiritual depth. Vida Dutton Scudder once described the Franciscan movement as an 'adventure' which was responsible for the "restoration of inwardness to religion."[2] Henry accomplishes this by offering an inside view of Francis, a window into the inner workings of Francis' mind and heart. In articulating the inner struggle of the journey where the real war is fought, Henry is able to give voice to the hardest battle of all, the struggle the Muslims call the 'Greater Jihad', the spiritual warfare that rages in the soul. It is here, deep within the individual soul that the true battle between the principalities and powers are fought, and it is here that the real victory is won.

In particular, the use of military analogy and extended metaphor manifest Francis' deepest desires and make vivid the inner turmoil of his conversion experience. Francis' struggle against evil finds some of its most eloquent expression through Henry's poetry, which essentially is a song about Francis' dream; a song which is none other than the battle hymn of Francis' heart, the war cry of Francis' soul, sung in the tune of Virgil. This is very much in harmony with Francis and his early friars who wished "to go around the world singing, and only after singing to preach a little."[3] Godet-Calogeras once remarked that Franciscan poetry, like that of the *Sacrum Commercium*, "tells us more about Francis and his movement than many official documents."[4] This conviction was rooted in his belief that it "tells the truth about the identity of the Franciscan inspiration."[5] This insight seems particularly applicable to the *LV*, which reveals a certain insightful dimension about the truth of Francis. Henry saw that the key to understanding Francis was through his heroic dream of knighthood. Thus the *LV* may best convey Francis' own self-understanding and provide insight into the real passion and poetry of Francis' life. How else but through the medium of verse, with its rich use of figurative language, rhyme and meter, could the real meaning and poetry of Francis' experience be expressed?

According to Henry, Francis' *metanoia* teaches us that conversion does not mean suppressing violent impulses, but rather is a movement to redirect them through a new paradigm, that is, the "*militia caelestis*" which can transform our desire. God entices Francis to change his desire for worldly knighthood and his dream of military honor, glory and fame into something greater. God transforms Francis' worldly dream of glory into a divine and heroic dream of saintly glory. God *converts* his desire according to the root meaning of the word which can be defined as "something that is changed from one use, function or purpose to another."[6]

This manifests the natural inner desire outward, so that Francis' very desire for knighthood becomes a means to union with Christ. The conversion paradigm Henry advocates begins within and allows God's grace to first reconcile the inner warring forces. Asceticism and self-mastery can be seen as a means to integration and peace in which Francis conquers by being conquered by God's grace. Henry thus presents a valid paradigm for the conversion of Francis that expresses his conversion journey as a quest of faith, a daily battle with the world, flesh and the devil. By symbolically expressing Francis' interior response in martial language, Henry's icon forms a poetic crystallization of the Franciscan spirit of asceticism, depicting Francis as a crucified knight heroically fighting in spiritual combat. This metaphor, which serves as the nucleus of Henry's icon, contains several other minor aspects, perhaps the most theologically innovative and significant of these aspects being the unique interpretation of Francis' piety as his greatest virtue. Henry uniquely presents Francis as "full of piety," that is, the love for his God, his brothers and sisters, especially the poor, and for all creation.

Henry's icon depicts a Francis that is congruent with those who personally knew him, such as Gregory IX, and reflect a similar portrait found in the poems of Thomas of Capua and Thomas of Celano. Each in their own way reflect what is at the core of his dream; a manifestation of his inner desire for holiness, his longing for perfection and union with his Hero, Christ the great King.

According to Joseph Campbell, in *The Hero with a Thousand Faces*, this aspect of Francis' great quest defines him as a modern hero, whose struggle and conquest is over self. He explains: "Man is that alien presence with whom the forces of egoism must come to terms, through whom the ego must be crucified and resurrected, and in whose image society is to be reformed."[7] Thus the spiritual significance of the *LV*, in communicating the inner struggle of Francis' heart, the mystery within his soul and the heroic spirit that animated him, provides modern believers with a paradigm of conversion.

In this way, Francis becomes the model of a true Crusader, a real "*crucefanti*," that is "one signed by the cross." Unlike other medieval knights and crusaders, Francis is not content to merely adorn his clothes with the cross but internalizes the call and allows his heart and ultimately his very own body to bear the insignia of the crucified. Francis, the "want-to-be" crusader, radicalizes and reinterprets it, revealing the spirit behind the call to battle and so becomes the true "crusader" who teaches us how to "live spiritually."[8]

Rather than arguing against others, fighting and spilling blood, Henry depicts a Francis who conquered the "enemy" he had in his own body and so died to himself in order to be "reborn."[9] As Francis wrote in his tenth admonition, "each one has the [real] enemy in his power; that is the body through which he sins," and therefore must "always hold him captive and wisely guard himself against him, because as long as he does this, no other enemy, seen or unseen, will be able to harm him."[10] Could Francis have responded any more radically to Innocent III's challenge at the Fourth Lateran Council to take up the Tau, the exact form of the true cross and be "marked" by it, becoming one of those who have "mortified their flesh and conformed their life to that of the crucified Savior"? While many followed the war cry and went off to fight for the cross, Francis led others into a new way to fight; embracing it in such a way that he became a living icon of the crucifix. In this war, the only blood shed would prove to be his own. Francis as a *crucified knight* truly is an inspiring Christian hero who, as a soldier of Christ and a paragon of piety, won the victory of the good fight. In this way he became the immortal Seraphic knight; the knight closest to God, the knight who imitated Christ so fully and united with him so completely through the cross as to be deemed an *alter Christus*. He thus teaches us that the holy battle to sainthood is not an impossible dream. In the words of Henry who sought to immortalize Francis' spiritual battle:

"Victory over the world thus wrought is an

example spurring many to have a love for this spiritual war, and such virtue attracts others as followers of what was done in their sight."[11]

Endnotes

Introduction

1. Cfr. 1C 5. THOMAS of CELANO relates these items as *"militaribus armis"* which include "saddles, shields, spears and other equipment."
2. Hereafter referred to as the *LV.*
3. A. MOCKLER, *Francis of Assisi: The Wandering Years,* Oxford, 1976, p. 17.
4. Cfr. R. SORRELL., *Saint Francis of Assisi and Nature: Tradition and Innovation in Western Christian Attitudes Toward the Environment,* New York, 1988, pp.. 69-70.
5. P. SABATIER, *Life of St. Francis of Assisi,* trans. L. S. Houghton, New York, 1919, p. 390.
6. J. Y. TILLIETTE, *Les modèles du IXe au XIe siècle, d'après le témoignage des récits hagio-graphiques en vers métriques, in Settimane,* 36 (1988) pp. 387-388, quoted in F. LIFSHITZ, *Beyond Positivism and Genre,* in *Viator: Medieval and Renaissance Studies,* 25 (1994) p. 99.
7. M. BIHL, *De Legenda Versificata S. Francisci auctore Henrico Abrincensi,* in AFH, 22 (1929) p. 6.
8. Four notable examples are *Fonti Francescane,* Assisi, 1986, *Dizionario Franciscano,* a cura di E. Caroli, Padova, 1995, *St. Francis of Assisi: Writings and Early Biographies: English Omnibus of the Sources for the Life of St. Francis,* ed. M. A. Habig, Chicago, 1983, and the *Thesaurus Celanensis: Corpus Des Sources Franciscaines,* ed. G. Mailleux, vol. 1, Louvain, 1974. The *LV* is also conspicuously missing from the list of sources in Franciscan journals such as *Greyfriars Review.*
9. R. MANSELLI, *San Francesco e l'eresia, in In ricordo di Zelina Zafarana: Annali della Facoltà di Lettere eFilosofia dell'Università di Siena,* Roma, 1984, p. 65.
10. R. MANSELLI, *Francesco e i soui compagni,* Roma, 1995, p. 279.
11. G. CREMASCOLI, *Henrici Abrincensis Legenda Sancti Francisci Versificata,* in *Fontes Francescani,* a cura di E. Menesto – S. Brufani – G. Cremascoli – E. Paoli – L. Pelligrini – S. Da Campagnola, Assisi, 1995, p. 1130. (Translation mine)
12. It should be noted the *LV* is not cited in the Italian studies: G. B. MONTORSI, *Francesco D'Assisi: maestro di vita,* Padova, 1983; C. VAIANI, *La via di Francesco,* Milano, 2001; G. IAMMARONE, *La Spiritualità Francescana: Anima*

e contenuti fondamentali, Padova, 1993.

13. K. B. Wolf, *The Poverty of Riches*, Oxford, 2003, p. 95.
14. J. Dalarun, *The Misadventures of Francis of Assisi*, trans. E. Hagman, New York, 2002, p. 77.
15. Cfr. T. G. Zen, *I sogni di S. Francesco d'Assisi*, Ph. D. diss., Antonianum, Roma, 1975, includes a study of modern biographers from the last 75 years who comment on the dream. See pp. 67-127.
16. J. Micó, *The Spirituality of St. Francis: The Gospel Life*, in GR, 7 (1993) p. 271.
17. J. Le Goff, *Francis of Assisi between the Renewals and Restraints of Feudal Society*, in *Francis of Assisi Today*, ed. C. Duquoc – C. Floritan, New York, 1981, p. 7.
18. J. Le Goff, *Saint Francis of Assisi*, trans. C. Rhone, London, 2004, p. 120.
19. Le Goff, *Francis of Assisi between the Renewals and Restraints of Feudal Society*, 7.
20. J. Le Goff, *Saint Francis, Medieval or Modern?*, in *St. Francis of Assisi: Essays in Commemoration*, 1982, ed. M. W. Sheehan, St. Bonaventure, 1982, p. 20.
21. G. K. Chesterton, *Saint Francis of Assisi*, New York, 1990, p. 15.
22. Chesterton, *Saint Francis of Assisi*, 16.
23. Cremascoli, *Introduzione, Legenda Sancti Francisci Versificata*, 1128. (Translation mine)
24. Cfr. R. S. Martignetti, *Saint Bonaventure's Tree of Life: Theology of the Mystical Journey*, Roma, 2004, pp. 97-111 summarizes the three spiritual senses of scripture.
25. D. Robertson, *The Medieval Saints' Lives: Spiritual Renewal and Old French Literature*, Lexington, 1995, p. 17.
26. *LV* XI: 46. "*Supradicta tibi Franciscum carmina pingunt.*" All English translations (unless otherwise specified) for Henry's *LV* are taken from H. d'Avranches, *The Versified Life of Saint Francis*, in FAED: *The Saint*, vol. 1, 1999, pp. 428-520.
27. *LV* XI: 84-85.
28. *LV* IX: 85-86.
29. R. Grégoire, *Manuale di agiologia: Introduzione alla letteratura agiografica*, Fabriano, 1987, p. 11. (Translation mine)
30. Grégoire, *Manuale di agiologia*, 6. (Translation mine)
31. Grégoire, *Manuale di agiologia*,12. (Translation mine)
32. Cfr. J. Howe, *Hagiographic Handbooks*, in *Catholic Historical Review*, 80

(1994) p. 758. See also GRÉGOIRE, *Manuale di Agiologia*, 11.

33. HOWE, *Hagiographic Handbooks*, 758.

34. The *Oxford Latin Dictionary*, ed. P. G. W. Glare, Oxford, 1996, translates "*vates*" as poet (regarded as divinely inspired), prophet or bard, "*magister*" as a professional teacher or master, and "*versificator*" as versifier.

Chapter One

1. These dates are calculated between the completion of CELANO's *Prima Vita*, on February 25, 1229, and the translation of ST. FRANCIS' body from St. George to the Basilica of San Francis on May 25, 1230, which is not mentioned in the *LV*. The omission of mentioning the Basilica, the head and mother Church of the Franciscans, which Pope GREGORY IX heavily supported, is significant but not definitive. In addition, no after death miracle is included. A. CRISTOFANI, *Il più antico poema della vita di San Francesco d'Assisi, scritto innanzi all'anno 1230*, Prato, 1882, XIII, supports this early dating because BR. ELIAS is treated with more respect than he probably would have been later. A. FORTINI, *Francis of Assisi*, trans. H. Moak, New York, 1980, p. 101, holds that HENRY wrote the *LV* before 1230. J. C. RUSSELL, *Master Henry Avranches*, Ph. D. diss., Harvard University, 1926, p. 113, writes that 1232 "seems more probable because this is the first year after 1230 in which it is certain that the poet was in Italy." Other scholars, like G. SHANAHAN, *Henry of Avranches: Poem on the Life of Saint Francis (Legenda Sancti Francisci Versificata)*, in FS 48 (1988) p. 132, and F. URIBE, *Introduzione alle fonti agiographiche di san Francesco e santa Chiara d'Assisi*, Assisi, 2002, p. 156, believe a later date of 1232 or 1234. D. R. TOWNSEND, *An Edition of Saint's Lives attributed to Henry Avranches*, Ph. D. diss., University of Toronto, 1985, p. 25, however, holds 1234, on the basis that HENRY may be identified as the same Canon of Avranches who is known to have been at the curia in 1234.

2. J. MOORMAN, *A History of the Franciscan Order*, Oxford, 1998, p. 281, states the *LV* "had nothing new to offer." See also F. ACCROCCA, *Some Knotty Problems in the Franciscan Sources: Two Recent Editions*, in GR, 11 (1997) pp. 143-183 for a recent assessment of the general neglect of scholarship on the *LV*, stating how HENRY is "reduced by Bihl to the status of one who slavishly repeats the *First Life*," p. 161.

3. Cfr. CRISTOFANI, *Il più antico poema*, XIII-XV.

4. Cfr. E. D'ALENÇON, *Il più antico poema di vita S. Francesco*, in MF, 4 (1889) pp. 33-35; *Sul più antico poema di Vita S. Francesco*, in MF, 5 (1890) pp. 73-76; *Sul più antico poema di Vita S. Francesco*, in MF, 6 (1895) pp. 26-31.

5. J. P. HEIRONIMUS - J. C. RUSSELL, *The Shorter Latin Poems of Master Henry Avranches Relating to England*, Cambridge, Mass., 1935, p. 16.

6. Cfr. T. DOMENICELLI, *La "Legenda versificata" o il più antico poema di San*

Francesco, in AFH, I (1908) p. 209-216. LUKE WADDING's vague information on the author only suggested he was a certain Englishman.

7. Cfr. A. G. LITTLE, *A Guide to Franciscan Studies*, London-New York, 1920, pp. 12-13. The inscription on the Cambridge Ms. reads: *"Super vita beati Francisci versus magistri H. Abrincensis ad Gregorium papam nonum."*

8. Cfr. HEIRONIMUS – RUSSELL, *Shorter Latin Poems*, 16. See also FORTINI, *Francis of Assisi*, 218, who calls HENRY a Franciscan.

9. J. C. RUSSELL, MHAIP, in *Speculum*, 3 (1928) pp. 34-63. Appendix B, found on pp. 58-63 of this article includes a catalogue of the contents of the Mss. of HENRY's works.

10. Two critical studies published in MS contain a list of poems under consideration of HENRY's authorship. See D. R. TOWNSEND - A. G. RIGG, MLPA (V): *Matthew Paris' Anthology of Henry of Avranches* (Cambridge, University Library Ms. Dd. 11.78), in MS, 49 (1987) pp. 352-390, and P. BINKLEY, MLPA (VI): *The Cotton Anthology of Henry of Avranches* (B. L. Cotton Vespasian D.V., fols. 151-184), in MS, 52 (1990) pp. 221-254. For a list of the published works of HENRY see P. BINKLEY, *13th Century Latin Poetry Contests Associated With Henry of Avranches with appendix - new edited texts*, Ph. D. diss., University of Toronto, Toronto, 1991, I-X.

11. HEIRONIMUS - RUSSELL, *Shorter Latin Poems*, 17.

12. Cfr. BINKLEY, *13th Century Latin Poetry Contests*, 31, holds Avranches (Normandy) as the place of birth; RUSSELL, *Master Henry Avranches*, 145-146, states that HENRY was born in Germany, probably in 1190; Bund, *Die 'Prophetin'*, 220, states HENRY was born in Germany in 1191 or 1192. For additional information on HENRY's life see M. DELLA PENNA, *The Icon of Saint Francis of Assisi Depicted in Henry of Avranches' Legenda Versificata*, STL, Antonianum, Roma, 2003.

13. Cfr. BINKLEY, *13th Century Latin Poetry Contests*, 31.

14. Cfr. BUND, *Die 'Prophetin'*, 220, states that HENRY studied at Oxford and Paris.

15. Cfr. RUSSELL, MHAIP, 46. RUSSELL postulates his knowledge of English, German and French from his etymological puns. See also M. I. ALLEN, *The Metrical Passio Sanctorum Crispini et Crispiniani of Henry of Avranches*, in AB, 108 (1990) p. 383, which cites HENRY's use of Greek. In the *LV* I: 96-97, HENRY uses the words *"chymos"* (an excretion of the stomach, a juice), *"caumate"* (heat), and *"phlegma"* (pituitous slime) to describe a medical process.

16. Cfr. BINKLEY, *13th Century Latin Poetry Contests*, 102.

17. Cfr. RUSSELL, MHAIP, 38. See also E. SALTER, *English and International: Studies in the Literature, Art and Patronage of Medieval England*, Cambridge, 1988, p. 81. HENRY flatters a patron in the poem *To John* by writing: *"Ergo pauperis ferre teneris opem: Ergo michi, cum sim pauper,"* which translates,

"Therefore you are obliged to give help to the poor: and therefore to me, since I am poor."

18. Cfr. B. D'Angelo, *Poesia francescana inglese prima di Geoffrey Chaucer* (1340?-1400), in AFH, 75 (1982) p. 321, states that the "Franciscans exercised a notable influence in the civil and religious life" in England as early as 1224, and thus could have provided Henry contact with the Franciscans. (Translation mine)

19. Cfr. Russell, MHAIP, 35; Bund, *Die 'Prophetin'*, 221.

20. Cfr. F. Gies, *The Knight in History*, New York, 1984, p. 97. William Marshall (1144-1219) was a squire educated in Normandy who became the epitome of a knight-errant and then a baron of Normandy. He is said to have been the standard bearer and gateway through which chivalry returned at a time when it was dead. He later knighted the 'Young King' and became a Templar before he died. See also D. Carpenter, *The Minority of Henry III*, in *History Today*, 40 (1990) pp. 9-14. William would carry the young king on his shoulders and stated "I will never desert him even if I have to beg my bread." p. 11.

21. Cfr. Binkley, MLPA (VI), 254.

22. Cfr. Russell, MHAIP, 36.

23. Cfr. J. Moorman, *The Sources For the Life of St. Francis of Assisi*, Manchester, 1966, p. 72.

24. Cfr. Binkley, *13th Century Latin Poetry Contests*, 3.

25. Cfr. Binkley, MLPA (VI), 235, quotes the Latin in the prologue of the Versailles manuscript of the *LV* which contains an account of this.

26. Cfr. A. G. Rigg, *Henry of Avranches*, in *A History of Anglo-Latin Literature 1066-1422*, Cambridge, 1992, p. 193. Henry shortened the first syllable of the word *'caritas'* which scans as an amphimacer (long-short-long), turning it into an anapaest. Henry subsequently wrote a poem called *Petition Concerning Amphimacri*, which formally requested permission to change four *"nomina sacra"* from amphimacri to anapests. The fourth sacred name is believed to be *veritas*, found in *LV* III:106.

27. H. Avranches *The Versified Life of Saint Francis: Additions, Amplifications in Light of the "Major Legend,"* Prologue, in FAED: *The Prophet*, vol. III, ed. R. Armstrong – J. A. W. Hellmann – W. Short, New York, 1999, p. 78.

28. Cfr. Binkley, *13th Century Latin Poetry Contests*, 33.

29. Binkley, MLPA (VI), 234; translating H. Avranches *The Versified Life of Saint Francis: Additions, Amplifications in Light of the "Major Legend,"* p. 79. Prologue, vol. III. See also D. R. Townsend, *Henry Avranches: Vita Sancti Oswaldi*, in MS, 56 (1994) p. 31.

30. H. Avranches, *The Versified Life of Saint Francis: Additions, Amplifications in Light of the "Major Legend,"* 79.

31. Cfr. BINKLEY, *13th Century Latin Poetry Contests*, 33. Cfr. PRUDENTIUS, *Peristephanon*, in *Prundenti Carmina*, Internet (05.05.04): http://www.thelatinlibrary.com/prud.html, IV: 161-172. It should be noted that this incident is remarkably similar to what is recorded to have happened to PRUDENTIUS while writing his *Peristephanon*. When it was necessary for him to versify a proper name that would not scan correctly according to the standard laws of classical grammatical metrics, PRUDENTIUS too gloried and even boasted of breaking such pagan rules.

32. Another example of HENRY's hermeneutics can be found in his spiritual-poetic treatise entitled *Versus de corona spinea*, which he wrote for LOUIS IX about acquiring the relics of the crucifixion. See also D. R. TOWNSEND, *The 'Versus de corona spinea' of Henry of Avranches*, in *Mittellateinisches Jahrbuch*, 23 (1988) pp.154-170.

33. Cfr. RUSSELL, MHAIP, 37. Also see TOWNSEND, *An Edition of Saint's Lives*, 26, and BINKLEY, *13th Century Latin Poetry Contests*, 129-130 for a discussion of HENRY as a canon lawyer.

34. RUSSELL, MHAIP, 52, 55. This entry is taken from item 13 in the Rolls.

35. M. TEEUWEN, *The Vocabulary of the Intellectual Life in the Middle Ages*, in *Etudes Sur Le Vocabulaire Intellectuel Du Moyen Age*, Brepols, 2003, p. 53.

36. S. KAY, *Courts, Clerks and Courtly Love*, in *The Cambridge Companion to Medieval Romance*, ed. R. L. Krueger, Cambridge, 2000, p. 87.

37. Cfr. TEEUWEN, *The Vocabulary of the Intellectual Life in the Middle Ages*, 53-54.

38. TEEUWEN, *The Vocabulary of the Intellectual Life in the Middle Ages*, 53.

39. Cfr. T. BULFINCH, *The Age of Chivalry*, New York, 1965, p. 20.

40. Cfr. HEIRONIMUS - RUSSELL, *Shorter Latin Poems*, 21. See also BULFINCH, *The Age of Chivalry*, 20.

41. Cfr. RUSSELL, MHAIP, 52.

42. Cfr. RUSSELL, MHAIP, 37.

43. Cfr. R. PACIOCCO - F. ACCROCCA, *La leggenda di un santo di nome Francesco*, Milano, 1999, p. 54; CREMASCOLI, *Legenda Sancti Francisci Versificata*, 1126; SHANAHAN, *Poem on the Life of Saint Francis*, 125.

44. Cfr. BINKLEY, *13th Century Latin Poetry Contests*, 37. This date is calculated between his last gift of wine and "the first Issue roll from which HENRY's pension is absent." See also RUSSELL, MHAIP, 35.

45. HEIRONIMUS - RUSSELL, *Shorter Latin Poems*, 13.

46. HEIRONIMUS - RUSSELL, *Shorter Latin Poems*, 15.

47. Cfr. HEIRONIMUS - RUSSELL, *Shorter Latin Poems*, 15.

48. Cfr. RUSSELL, MHAIP, 39, 41.

49. Cfr. BINKLEY, *13th Century Latin Poetry Contests*, 9. These included the Abbott of Westminster, the Dean of St. Paul's, and later, the bishop of Ely and the chancellor of Cambridge, together with the university of masters. See. RUSSELL, MHAIP, 42. These poems were probably written between 1252 and 1255. See also BINKLEY, *13th Century Latin Poetry Contests*, 10, 11, 41. The second part of the debate was conducted at the highest court in England where HUGH MORTIMER, the official of BONIFACE of SAVOY, the Archbishop of Canterbury was in attendance. The third part of the debate was performed in front of the HENRY III's half brother, AYMER DE VALENCE.

50. BINKLEY, *13th Century Latin Poetry Contests*, 57.

51. RUSSELL, *Master Henry Avranches*, 217.

52. Cfr. RUSSELL, MHAIP, 49. At least two poems speak of accepting either 'temporal or spiritual' reward.

53. M. W. BLOOMFIELD - C. W. DUNN, *The Role of the Poet in Early Societies*, Cambridge, 1989, p. 7.

54. *"Goliard."* Encyclopædia Britannica. 2004. Encyclopædia Britannica Premium Service. Internet (20.03.04): http://www.britannica.com/eb/article?eu=38041.

55. *The Norton Anthology of Poetry*, 4th ed., ed. M. Ferguson – M. J. Salter – J. Stallworthy, New York, 1996, p. lxi.

56. J. STEVENS, *Words and Music In the Middle Ages: Song, Narrative, Dance 1050-1350*, in *Cambridge Studies in Music*, 1986, p. 4.

57. SHANAHAN, *Poem on the Life of Saint Francis*, 133.

58. A. WOLF, *Medieval Heroic Traditions and Their Transitions from Orality to Literacy*, in *Vox Intera: Orality and Textuality in the Middle Ages*, ed. A. N. Doane – C. B. Pasternack, Madison, 1991, p. 67.

59. O. SCHMUCKI, *The "Way of Life According to the Gospel" as It was Discovered by St. Francis of Assisi*, in GR, (1995) p. 3.

60. Cfr. J. J. MURPHY, *Rhetoric in the Middle Ages: A History of Rhetorical Theory From Augustine to the Renaissance*, California, 1974, p. 184.

61. BLOOMFIELD - DUNN, *The Role of the Poet in Early Societies*, 11.

62. Cfr. E. B. VITZ, *From the Oral to the Written in Medieval and Renaissance Saints Lives*, in *Images of Sainthood in Medieval Europe*, ed. R. Blumenfeld-Kosinski – T. Szell, Ithaca, New York, 1991, p. 101.

63. Cfr. BLOOMFIELD - DUNN, *The Role of the Poet in Early Societies*, 20.

64. Cfr. VITZ, *From the Oral to the Written*, 179, 186.

65. VITZ, *From the Oral to the Written*, 186.

66. Cfr. RUSSELL, MHAIP, 46. See also RIGG, *Henry of Avranches*, 193. HENRY usually wrote in unrhymed hexameters (six feet) and eligiacs; classical

Greek verse forms used in epic containing eight syllables to a line but with some variations.

67. Cfr. Townsend, *An Edition of Saint's Lives*, 33. All of the Latin citations of the *LV* are quoted from Cremascoli, *Legenda Sancti Francisci Versificata*, 1131-1242. Paronomasia is a rhetorical device which plays upon words that sound alike.

68. T. Zweerman - E. van den Goorbergh, *Respectfully Yours: Signed and Sealed, Francis of Assisi. Aspects of His Authorship and Focuses of His Spirituality*, New York, 2001, p. 290.

69. Horace, *Art of Poetry*, Internet (05.05.04): http://classicpersuasion.org/pw/horace/horacepo.htm 99-104.

70. Cremascoli, *Legenda Sancti Francisci Versificata*, 1128, claims that Henry added material not to "pay homage to history but to provide poetic touches."

71. *LV* I:19.

72. Cfr. Russell, *Master Henry Avranches*, 143.

73. Cfr. Townsend, *An Edition of Saint's Lives*, 352; See also Townsend - Rigg, MLPA (V), 179. From 1243-1260 Henry received payment from Henry III.

74. Manselli, *Francesco e i suoi compagni*, 279.

75. Cfr. Russell, MHAIP, 37. Henry's itinerant career from court to court and monastery to monastery was more apparent than actual, considering that he would write for a variety of patrons in each place.

76. Cfr. Salter, *English and International*, 78; Russell, MHAIP, 35. Henry was employed by Henry III from October of 1243 until Easter of 1260, for whom he composed versifications for the Lives of St. Edmund and St. George and may also have been employed on legal business for him at various European courtly centers.

77. Cfr. Russell, MHAIP, 52. See also P. Grosjean, *Magister Henricus de Abrincis Archipoeta*, in *Dublin Studies*, 17 (1928) p. 298, who states Henry was crowned "Archpoet Laureate" to Henry III in 1250.

78. Cfr. Salter, *English and International*, 81. One incident points to the high regard that Henry III held for Henry's art when in 1244, Henry III had a "certain poem '*quem faciet Magister Henricus versificator*' inscribed upon a ceremonial ring in honor of Thomas Becket."

79. Binkley, *13th Century Latin Poetry Contests*, 36. "*regius vates*." (Translation mine)

80. Cfr. F. J. E. Raby, *A History of Christian-Latin Poetry: From the Beginnings to the Close of the Middle Ages*, 2nd ed., Oxford, 1953, p. 386.

81. Cfr. Grosjean, *Magister Henricus de Abrincis Archipoeta*, 298. See also Binkley, *13th Century Latin Poetry Contests*, 34 and Russell, *Master Henry Avranches*, 178.

82. J. Huizinga, *Homo Ludens: A Study of the Play-Element in Culture*, Boston, 1955, p. 120.

83. Huizinga, *Homo Ludens*, 120.

84. A paraphrase of lines 167-177, taken from the Bordo-Silas poetic debate quoted in A. G. Rigg - P. Binkley, T*wo Poetic Debates By Henry of Avranches*, in MS, 62 (2000) p. 58. *"Ut meritus fame per secula lauder et a me discatis scioli michi nota poemata soli (Que minus attente didicistis), meque docente ut sapiant homines terram uisito fines."*

85. Bloomfield - Dunn, *The Role of the Poet in Early Societies*, 4.

86. Cfr. T. Aquinas' commentary on Aristotle's *Metaphysics*, XII I, 3; 55.

87. Cfr. Russell, MHAIP, 45.

88. Townsend, *The 'Versus de corona spinea'*, 155.

89. Cfr. Rigg, *Henry of Avranches*, 186. Cfr. Townsend, *The 'Versus de corona spinea'*, 154-170.

90. Henry of Avranches' *Versus de Decretalibus* quoted in Binkley, *13th Century Latin Poetry Contests*, 98.

91. Cfr. Bund, *Die 'Prophetin'*, 223.

92. Cfr. Kerby-Fulton K., *Hildegard of Bingen and Anti-Mendicant Propaganda*, in *Traditio*, 43 (1987) pp. 387-388.

93. Cfr. Caesarius of Heisterbach, *Life of Saint Englebert*, in FAED: *The Saint*, vol. 1, ed. R. Armstrong – J. A. W. Hellmann – W. Short, New York, 1999, pp. 594-595. Caesarius quotes the clergy reaction to the friars based on the fears of Hildegard's prophecy: "We fear these be those concerning whom the Holy Spirit prophesied through the mouth of the blessed Hildegard, through whom the clergy will be afflicted and the city endangered." For further reading on the anti-mendicant propaganda of Hildegard's poetry, see Kerby-Fulton, *Hildegard of Bingen and Anti-Mendicant Propaganda*, 386-399.

94. It is questionable whether it is Hildegard's prophecies or those of Joachim of Fiore, which Henry alludes to in the *LV* VI:33-35. "Some noised it abroad that at hand were the last days of the world of whose end an unknown Order would be herald." *"Rumor diffuditur, et sunt tempora a qui dicant instare novissima mundi, cuius inauditus finem praenuntiet Ordo."* Note *"Novissima"* is an allusion to *Jude* 18, which speak of the end times.

95. Cfr. N. F. Cantor, *The Civilization of the Middle Ages*, New York, 1994, pp. 344-345. See also *LoveToKnow Free Online Encyclopedia*, Internet (20.03.04): http://90.1911encyclopedia.org/G/ GO/ GOLIARD.htm.

96. F. Brittain, *The Medieval Latin and Romance Lyric to A.D. 1300*, Cambridge, 1937, p. 16.

97. Cfr. *LoveToKnow Free Online Encyclopedia*, Internet (20.03.04):

http://90.1911encyclopedia. org/G/GO/GOLIARD.htm.

98. *LoveToKnow Free Online Encyclopedia,* Internet (20.03.04): http://90.1911encyclopedia.org/G/ GO/ GOLIARD.htm.

99. Cfr. CANTOR, *The Civilization of the Middle Ages,* 345.

100. P. G. SCHMIDT, *The Quotation in Goliardic Poetry: The Feast of Fools and the Goliardic Strophe cum auctoritate,* in *Latin Poetry and the Classical Tradition: Essays in Medieval and Renaissance Literature,* ed. P. Godman – O. Murray, Oxford, 1990, p. 40.

101. BINKLEY, *13th Century Latin Poetry Contests,* 127. BINKLEY mentions that HENRY's verse summary of the *Decretum* appears in a Paris manuscript, BN lat. 118867, which contains Goliard hymns and satires.

102. Cfr. HEIRONIMUS - RUSSELL, *Shorter Latin Poems,* 19. HENRY'S poetic attributions are written *magister* as well as most of his entries in the English roles.

103. TEEUWEN, *The Vocabulary of the Intellectual Life in the Middle Ages,* 97.

104. Cfr. BINKLEY, *13th Century Latin Poetry Contests,* 14, places HENRY's teaching at Angers between 1240-1243 or 1245-1251.

105. Cfr. RIGG, *Henry of Avranches,* 179.

106. Cfr. BINKLEY, *13th Century Latin Poetry Contests,* 6, 35.

107. J. VERGER, *The Universities and Scholasticism,* in *The New Cambridge Medieval History V*: 1198-1300, Cambridge, 1999, p. 256.

108. Cfr. VERGER, *New Cambridge Medieval History V,* 264.

109. Cfr. M. GIBBS - J. LANG, *Bishops Reform 1215-1272: With Special Reference to the Lateran Council of 1215,* Oxford, 1962. Canon 10 called for schools to be opened.

110. M. D. CHENU, *La théologie au XII siècle,* Paris, 1957, p. 324.

111. Cfr. VERGER, *New Cambridge Medieval History V,* p. 256, 258. The *licentia docendi* of Pope ALEXANDER III reserved the founding of new schools to ecclesial authority.

112. Cfr. *Medieval Sourcebook:* Robert de Courçon: Statutes for the University of Paris, 1215, Internet (14.02.05): http://www.fordham.edu/halsall/source/courcon1.html." We decide concerning the theologians, that no one shall lecture at Paris before he is thirty-five years old, and not unless he has studied at least eight years, [later prolonged to fourteen years] and has heard the books faithfully and in the schools. He is to listen in theology for five years, be (sic) he reads his own lectures in public."

113. Cfr. VERGER, *New Cambridge Medieval History V,* 260.

114. N. NGUYÊN-VAN-KHANH, *The Teacher of His Heart: Jesus Christ in the Thought and Writings of St. Francis,* trans. E. Hagman, St. Bonaventure, 1994, p.

112.

115. Cfr. VERGER, *New Cambridge Medieval History V*, 260, 261.

116. VERGER, *New Cambridge Medieval History V*, 263, 266.

117. Cfr. VERGER, *New Cambridge Medieval History V*, 263.

118. P. O. LEWRY, *Papal Ideals and the University of Paris*, in *The Religious Role of the Papacy: Ideals and Realities 1150-1300*, ed. C. Ryan, Toronto, 1989, p. 369.

119. LEWRY, *Papal Ideals and the University of Paris*, 369.

120. Cfr. VERGER, *New Cambridge Medieval History V*, 259.

121. *Medieval Sourcebook:* Statutes of Gregory IX for the University of Paris 1231, Internet (14.02.05): http://www.fordham.edu/halsall/source/UParis-stats1231.html.

122. *Medieval Sourcebook:* Jacques de Vitry: Life of the Students at Paris, Internet (14.02.05): http://www.fordham.edu/halsall/source/vitry1.html.

123. *Medieval Sourcebook*: Jacques de Vitry: Life of the Students at Paris, Internet (14.02.05): http://www.fordham.edu/halsall/source/vitry1.html.

124. Cfr. VERGER, *New Cambridge Medieval History V*, 261.

125. VERGER, *New Cambridge Medieval History V*, 264.

126. VERGER, *New Cambridge Medieval History V*, 269.

127. VERGER, *New Cambridge Medieval History V*, 271.

128. Including the *Meno, Phaedo.*

129. Including the *Physics, De Generatione et Corruptione, Topics, Analytics, Meteorologica, Sophistic Elenchi.*

130. Including the *Sufficientia, De Anima, Canon, Metaphysica, De Caelo.*

131. Cfr. D. E. SHARP, *Franciscan Philosophy in the Thirteenth Century*, Oxford, 1930, pp. 3-4.

132. SHARP, *Franciscan Philosophy in the Thirteenth Century*, 12.

133. Cfr. SHARP, *Franciscan Philosophy in the Thirteenth Century*, 5.

134. SHARP, *Franciscan Philosophy in the Thirteenth Century*, 5,10.

135. Particularly interesting are his theory of becoming, theory of light and his natural theology.

136. E. HUTTON, *The Franciscans in England 1224-1538*, Boston, 1926, p. 135.

137. Cfr. VERGER, *New Cambridge Medieval History V*, 256, 258, 263. The universities at this time taught grammar and dialectics exclusively in Latin.

138. The trivium consists of grammar, rhetoric and logic.

139. MURPHY, *Rhetoric in the Middle Ages*, 136. Thus the term "grammar" corresponds more closely with our present day terms "philology" or "linguistics."

140. JOHN OF SALISBURY, *Metalogicon*, trans. D. D. McGarry, Berkley, 1955, p. 60. HENRY used parts of JOHN OF SALISBURY's prose life almost verbatim in his versification of the *Life of Becket*.

141. Cfr. BINKLEY, *13th Century Latin Poetry Contests*, 2.

142. Cfr. C. S. BALDWIN, *Medieval Rhetoric and Poetic*, Gloucester, 1959, p. 186, states this work was extensively influenced by HORACE's *Ars Poetica*, one of the poets HENRY quotes in the *LV*.

143. Cfr. MURPHY, *Rhetoric in the Middle Ages*, 135, 169.

144. MURPHY, *Rhetoric in the Middle Ages*, 139.

145. Cfr. BINKLEY, *13th Century Latin Poetry Contests*, 2.

146. Cfr. TOWNSEND - RIGG, MLPA (V), 373.

147. Cfr. RIGG, *Henry of Avranches*, 187-188.

148. Cfr. BINKLEY, *13th Century Latin Poetry Contests*, 2.

149. Cfr. BINKLEY, *13th Century Latin Poetry Contests*, 2.

150. VERGER, *New Cambridge Medieval History V*, 273.

151. Cfr. VERGER, *New Cambridge Medieval History V*, 275.

152. Cfr. ALLEN, *The Metrical Passio*, 382. HENRY's excursus on 'physics' in lines 59-68 closely follows that found in the *De Philosophia mundi* of WILLIAM OF CONCHES.

153. Cfr. MURPHY, *Rhetoric in the Middle Ages*, 137.

154. BALDWIN, *Medieval Rhetoric and Poetic*, 184.

155. ALEXANDER DE VILLE DIEU, *Doctrinale*, quoted in MURPHY, *Rhetoric in the Middle Ages*, 137-138. *"Grammatica est ostiaria omnium aliarum scientiarum, linguae balbutientis expurgatrix aptissima, logicae ministra, rhetoricae magistra, theologiae interpres, medicinae refrigerium et totius quadrivii laudabile fundamentum."* The *quadrivium* was the four essential medieval subjects: arithmetic, geometry, music, and astronomy.

156. HEIRONIMUS - RUSSELL, *Shorter Latin Poems*, 59. *"Casti prelati preeunt quasi prepositive. Coniugio Christi nexos adverbia dico. Peccatum plangens est interiectio. Fertur pars coniunctiva qui nectit et ordinat apte sacros de Christo sermones deque Maria. Pars incarnato discordat, anomala verba, quilibet hereticus Stigiali carcere dignus."*

157. Cfr. BINKLEY, *13th Century Latin Poetry Contests*, 12. This book is believed to have been written for the children of BARON HAMO DE PECCHE.

158. Cfr. RUSSELL, MHAIP, 39. See also MICHAEL OF CORNWALL's *Versus contra*

Henricum Abrincensem, lines 37-38, quoted in A. G. Rigg, *Michael of Cornwall*, in *History of Anglo-Latin Literature 1066-1422*, Cambridge, 1992, p. 194: "In verse you leave me far behind."

159. Rigg, *Henry of Avranches*, 192. In the poem *To Emperor Frederick II.* (Translation mine)

160. Cfr. Russell, MHAIP, 36.

161. Cfr. Townsend, *Vita Sancti Oswaldi*, 10.

162. Cfr. Russell, MHAIP, 40. Henry wrote Lives of Sts. Fremund, Hugh, Thomas, Edmund, Guthlac, Oswald, Birinus, and Francis.

163. Allen, *The Metrical Passio*, 358.

164. Townsend, *Vita Sancti Oswaldi*, 10.

165. H. Keller, *Changes in Old French Epic Poetry and Changes in the Tastes of its Audience*, in *The Epic in Medieval Society*, ed. H. Scholler, Tubingen, 1977, pp. 160-161.

166. Townsend, *Vita Sancti Oswaldi*, 20.

167. G. Meter, *Walter of Châtillon's Alexandreis Book 10- A Commentary*, Frankfurt, 1991, p. 8.

168. Allen, *The Metrical Passio*, 367.

169. Allen, *The Metrical Passio*, 367.

170. Robertson, *The Medieval Saints' Lives*, 12.

171. Cfr. Binkley, *13th Century Latin Poetry Contests*, 126. Binkley writes that "Henry and his opponents are, as far as I know, unique in using contemporary legal cases as the matter of verse competitions."

172. Quoted from the Prologue of Henry's *Vita Sancti Oswaldi* in Rigg, *Henry of Avranches*, 180. *"In nova fert animus antiquas uertere prosas carmina."*

173. Rigg, *Michael of Cornwall*, 194. *"Et quando recitas vetus incipit esse novellum."*

174. M. K. Lafferty, *Reading Latin Epic: Walter of Châtillon's Alexandreis*, Ph. D. diss., University of Toronto, Toronto, 1992, Abstract.

175. Cfr. Rigg, *Henry of Avranches*, 184. Stephen Langton was consecrated cardinal-deacon of S. Crisogono by Innocent III.

176. Townsend, *Vita Sancti Oswaldi*, 11.

177. Cfr. Townsend, *Vita Sancti Oswaldi*, 7. Henry's *Life of Oswald* cannot be shown to derive from any known prose source.

178. Cfr. Townsend, *Vita Sancti Oswaldi*, 12. In his *Life of Saint Guthlac*, for example, Henry adds original material, such as the recovery of a lost Psalter.

179. DALARUN, *The Misadventures of Francis of Assisi*, 77.

180. A metonymy involves the association of one thing with another which often occurs with or near it.

181. A synecdoche involves the substitution of a part for the whole, or the whole for a part.

182. T. J. HEFFERNAN, *Sacred Biography: Saints and their Biographies in the Middle Ages*, Oxford, 1988, p. 26.

183. HEFFERNAN, *Sacred Biography*, 26.

184. M. A. MAYESKI, *New Voices in the Tradition: Medieval Hagiography Revisited*, in *Theological Studies*, 63 (2002) p. 694.

185. Cfr. C. FANGER, *Signs of Power and the Power of Signs: Medieval Modes of Address to the Problem of Magical and Miraculous Signifiers*, Ph. D. diss., University of Toronto, 1993. FANGER analyzes HENRY's poetry on pp. 232-277.

186. FANGER, *Signs of Power*, 239.

187. FANGER, *Signs of Power*, 235.

188. Cfr. TOWNSEND, *Vita Sancti Oswaldi*, 12.

189. Cfr. RIGG, *Henry of Avranches*, 184, 185.

190. TOWNSEND, *The 'Versus de corona spinea'*, 156.

191. T. J. HERBST, *The Humanization of Christ in the Central Italian Panel Crucifixes of the Twelfth and Thirteenth-Centuries Reflected in the Development of Franciscan Christology*, MA. Thesis, Berkley, p. 148.

192. Cfr. 1C 69.

193. *LV* IX: 130-132.

194. BONAVENTURE will later develop the cross as a major motif in FRANCIS' life and use a similar interpretation to FRANCIS sending his friars out to the four parts of the world, which he understands as "forming a pattern of the cross." See LM 3:7.

195. Cfr. RUSSELL, MHAIP, 47.

196. RIGG, *Henry of Avranches*, 193.

197. Cfr. URIBE, *Introduzione alle fonti*, 36.

198. Cfr. TOWNSEND - RIGG, MLPA (V), 384. The Cambridge Ms., without attribution, is a revision of the oldest version in Assisi (338), and is believed to have been written after BR. ELIAS' defection in 1239 and after the death of GREGORY IX in 1241. See also RUSSELL, MHAIP, 35.

199. During the Middle Ages, public ceremony, art and architecture, were orchestrated in order to enhance a saint's popularity. HENRY's intricately decorated manuscript, like the Basilica, can be seen as an instrument used to promote the cult of FRANCIS and thus attract more pilgrims to Assisi.

See also B. ABOU-EL-HAJ, *The Medieval Cult of Saints: Formations and Transformations*, Cambridge, 1994, p. 3. This work studies the development of Saint's cults in the 11-13th century through illuminated manuscripts and architecture.

200. Cfr. TOWNSEND - RIGG, MLPA (V), 384. The Versailles Ms. has an attribution in the Prologue.

201. Cfr. RUSSELL, MHAIP, 40. HENRY is also believed to have versified the *Life of St. Martin*, another military saint, of whom CELANO compares FRANCIS. See also RIGG, *Henry of Avranches*, 180.

202. Cfr. RIGG, *Henry of Avranches*, 179. The other poem about non-English saints is on the life of CRISPIN and CRISPINIAN.

203. Cfr. RUSSELL, MHAIP, 40. HENRY wrote Lives of STS. FREMUND, HUGH, THOMAS, EDMUND, GUTHLAC, OSWALD, BIRINUS, and FRANCIS.

204. RUSSELL, MHAIP, 46.

205. MANSELLI, *Francesco e i suoi compagni*, 278.

206. Cfr. TOWNSEND, *An Edition of Saint's Lives*, 13. Cfr. *LV* I:13, fn. 5 in AF, p. 407.

207. Cfr. TOWNSEND, *An Edition of Saint's Lives*, 13.

208. Cfr. RUSSELL, MHAIP, 54.

209. Cfr. RIGG, *Henry of Avranches*, 180, 183.

210. Cfr. RIGG, *Henry of Avranches*, 180-181. E.g. "The blind can see the cripples run, The deaf can hear the dumb exchanging speech." Quoted from the *Life of St. Birinus* (lines 653-654). A similar couplet is found in the *Life of Edmund* (lines 566-567). RIGG includes an appendix of poetic terms on pp. 313-329.

211. Cfr. TOWNSEND, *An Edition of Saint's Lives*, 24. In *The Life of St. Guthlac*, when GUTHLAC is attacked by demons, II:769-770, *"est michi Christus a dextris ne commovear"* and when FRANCIS in the *LV* III:106-107 speaks to his father: *"Adstat namque mihi veritas via vitaque Christus a dextris, ne commovear."*

212. The Lives of GUTHLAC, FREMUND, BIRINUS, OSWALD, EDMUND, and FRANCIS, have similar endings.

213. Cfr. SHANAHAN, *Poem on the Life of Saint Francis*, 130.

214. Cfr. SHANAHAN, *Poem on the Life of Saint Francis*, 130.

215. SHANAHAN, *Poem on the Life of Saint Francis*, 131.

216. *LV* VI:6; IX:6; XIII:100.

217. *LV* V:119; VI:2; VII:113.

218. *LV* V:172; IX:169.

219. *LV* VI:6; XII:67.

220. *LV* XIII:72.

221. *LV* IV:161; V:85; VII:140; XI:88; XIII:98.

222. T. I. SHAMKOVICH, *Saintly Hero: Mythological, Epic and Ecclesiastical Perspectives on the Image of the Saint in Medieval Hagiography*, Ph. D. diss., New York State University, 1991, p. 7.

223. SHAMKOVICH, *Saintly Hero*, 28, iv.

224. *LV* III:146-151.

225. *LV* IV:2.

226. *LV* IV:109.

227. *LV* IV:108.

228. *LV* XI: 12.

229. 1C 80.

230. *LV* III: 147-152.

231. *LV* I:13.

232. For an in depth study of HENRY's use of the classics see G. CREMASCOLI, *I classici nella 'Legenda sancti Francisci versificata' di Enrico di Avranches*, in *Studi Medievali*, 40 (1999) pp. 523-534. In all, HENRY alludes to VIRGIL about a quarter as much as to OVID (almost 100 times), while HORACE is alluded to seven times and JUVENAL twice. Medieval hagiographers frequently enriched their work with quotes and allusions to Latin authors i.e. CELANO quotes SENECA and JUVENAL (1C and alludes to CICERO (1C 4). Both Pope INNOCENT III and GREGORY IX quote OVID in their writings.

233. The opening lines of the *LV* echo the *Aeneid* and FRANCIS' greatest virtue is identified as piety in *LV* XI:1.

234. *LV* IV:114.

235. *LV* IV:160. ANTAEUS was a giant who was son of EARTH. See also G. S. KIRK, *The Nature of Greek Myths*, Great Britain, 1974, p. 195.

236. All three were contemporaries who lived in the first century B.C. and were educated at Rome. OVID, born of a knightly family, wrote his most famous work, the great epic *Metamorphosis*, just before his exile from Rome. The *Metamorphosis* sought to link together into one harmonious whole, all the stories of classical mythology. VIRGIL, of course, wrote the greatest of the Roman epics, the *Aeneid*. HORACE, a friend of Virgil's, was born in Apulia, served as *tribunus militum* in Brutus's army, and was a master of the lyric form, unexcelled among Roman poets.

237. SHANAHAN, *Poem on the Life of Saint Francis*, 131.

238. B. BOLTON, *Too Important to Neglect: The Gesta Innocentii PP III*, in *Church and Chronicle in the Middle Ages: Essays Presented to John Taylor*, ed. I. Wood – G. A. Loud, London, 1991, p. 85.

239. Bolton, *Too Important to Neglect: The Gesta Innocentii PP III*, 85.

240. Cfr. Bolton, Too Important to Neglect: The Gesta Innocentii PP III, 86.

241. Meter, *Walter of Châtillon's Alexandreis*, 10. Juvencus, in the fourth century was the first writer of biblical epic to follow classic prosody.

242. Meter, *Walter of Châtillon's Alexandreis*, 11.

243. Meter, *Walter of Châtillon's Alexandreis*, 13.

244. K. W. Grandsen, *Virgil: The Aeneid*, Cambridge, 1990, p. 4.

245. Cfr. C. M. Bowra, *From Virgil to Milton*, London, 1945, pp. 4-5.

246. Keller, *Changes in Old French Epic Poetry*, 157.

247. Cfr. P. H. Delehaye, *Les légendes grecques des saints militaires*, New York, 1975.

248. M. Hadas - M. Smith, *Heroes and Gods: Spiritual Biographies in Antiquity*, New York, 1965, p. 12.

249. Hadas - Smith, *Heroes and Gods: Spiritual Biographies in Antiquity*, 12.

250. L. A. Crawford, *The Warrior-Saint and the Old French Hagiographic Epic, 1050-1250*, Ph. D. diss., Princeton University, 1991, p. 42.

251. Le Goff, *Saint Francis of Assisi*, 121.

252. Stevens, *Words and Music In the Middle Ages*, 236.

253. C. Albertson, *Anglo Saxon Saints and Heroes*, Fordham, 1967, p. 22. See also C. M. Bowra *Heroic Poetry*, London, 1952, p. 97, who writes in epic poetry, "the greatest heroes are primarily men of war."

254. M. Bartoli, *Clare of Assisi*, trans. F. Teresa, Quincy, 1993, p. 20.

255. H. Magennis, *Warrior Saints, Warfare, and the Hagiography of Aefric of Eynsham*, in *Traditio*, 56 (2000-2001) p. 27.

256. Grandsen, *Virgil*, 27.

257. Grandsen, *Virgil*, 31.

258. *LV* III: 29-32.

259. Grandsen, *Virgil*, 84.

260. Cfr. Virgil, *Aeneid*, trans. D. West, England, 2003, I:220.

261. Cfr. Virgil, *Aeneid*, VIII:441ff.

262. Virgil, *Aeneid*, I: 264. See also I:220; Aeneas prayed on several occasions.

263. Cfr. Virgil, *Aeneid*, VIII:590.

264. Cfr. C. S. Jaeger, *Courtliness and Social Change, in Cultures of Power: Lordship, Status, and Process in the Twelfth Century Europe*, ed. T. N. Bisson, Philadelphia, 1995, p. 293.

265. Cfr. VIRGIL, *Aeneid*, I:279. HENRY depicts FRANCIS as searching for his "true homeland," that is, Heaven in *LV* III:30.

266. GRANDSEN, *Virgil*, 7.

267. This can be seen most clearly in HENRY's added speeches he gives to FRANCIS.

268. GRANDSEN, *Virgil*, 94.

269. J. LE GOFF, *The Medieval Imagination*, trans. A. Goldhammer, Chicago and London, 1988, p. 126.

270. C. F. ALTMAN, *Two Types of Opposition and the Structure of Saints' Lives*, in *Medievalia Et Humanistica*, 6 (1975) p. 1.

271. A. G. ELLIOTT, *Roads to Paradise: Reading the Lives of the Early Saints*, Hanover and London, 1987, p. 17.

272. ALTMAN, *Two Types of Opposition and the Structure of Saints' Lives*, 1.

273. *LV* I: 6,17-18,50.

274. *LV* I: 40,110, 129, 132, 135, 162.

275. *LV* I: 40.

276. *LV* I: 58-59.

277. *LV* I: 136.

278. *LV* I: 136.

279. *LV* I: 137.

280. *LV* I: 141-142, 161.

281. *LV* I: 162.

282. *LV* I: 223.

283. *LV* I: 51, 152-159.

284. *LV* III: 40-43.

285. ELLIOTT, *Roads to Paradise: Reading the Lives of the Early Saints*, 42-43.

286. Cfr. ELLIOTT, *Roads to Paradise: Reading the Lives of the Early Saints*, 43.

287. R. BOYER, *An Attempt to Define the Typology of Medieval Hagiography*, in *Hagiography and Medieval Literature: A Symposium*, Odense, 1981, p. 29.

288. ELLIOTT, *Roads to Paradise: Reading the Lives of the Early Saints*, 23.

289. *The Song of Roland*, New York, 2002, 1014.

290. Cfr. BOWRA *Heroic Poetry*, 1-2.

291. ARISTOTLE, *Nicomachean Ethics*, Internet, (05.05.04): http://classics.mit.edu/Aristotle/nicomachaen.html, 1123a,20.

292. VIRGIL, *The Aeneid*, X: 469-470.

293. Wolf, *Medieval Heroic Traditions*, 78.

294. E. A. Hubble, *The Borrowed Knight: Representing the Masculine Hero in Twelfth-Century French Verse Romance*, Ph. D. diss., University of Michigan, 2002, p. 2.

295. Hubble, *The Borrowed Knight*, 2.

296. Kay, *Courts, Clerks and Courtly Love*, 88.

297. Kay, *Courts, Clerks and Courtly Love*, 87.

298. Hubble, *The Borrowed Knight*, 6. Monstrosity according to Hubble, "can be an integral part of what makes a knight a knight." Cfr. *LV* II:15 ff; IV:99; V:98,142, 147.

299. The set rules of the Latin art of *descriptio* (description) varied in authors like Matthew of Vendrome and Geoffrey of Vinsauf.

300. The *LV* follows in the French heroic tradition: by including description of fights (*LV* II:10-115), in the insistence on the crude details of wounds (and sickness), (*LV* I:96-108, XII:70-82, XIII:36-40) and in the handling of arms, (*LV* II:116-129).

301. W. P. Ker, *Epic and Romance, Essays on Medieval Literature*, New York, 1957, p. 346.

302. Ovid, *Elegy* IX.

303. Cfr. M. L. Colish, Medieval Foundations of the Western Intellectual Tradition 400-1400, New Haven and London, 2002, p. 181.

304. *LV* I:49.

305. *LV* I:32.

306. Cfr. D. Everett, *Essays on Middle English Literature*, Oxford, 1955, p. 2. The word *"Romanz"* originally meant the vernacular or spoken language, as opposed to Latin.

307. Gies, *The Knight in History*, 72.

308. Cfr. R. W. Kaeuper, *Chivalry and Violence in Medieval Europe*, Oxford, 1999, p. 45. The *chansons* had a single common subject: the exploits of Charlemagne and his followers.

309. Cfr. Gies, *The Knight in History*, 71.

310. Cfr. Everett, *Essays on Middle English Literature*, 19.

311. Cfr. Gies, *The Knight in History*, 71.

312. M. T. Bruckner, T*he Shape of Romance in Medieval France, in The Cambridge Companion to Medieval Romance*, ed. R. L. Krueger, Cambridge, 2000, p. 20.

313. Cantor, *The Civilization of the Middle Ages*, 348.

314. S. Knight, *The Social Function of the Middle English Romances*, in *Medieval Literature: Criticism, Idealogy and History*, ed. D. Aers, 1986, pp. 102-104, 106.

315. Shamkovich, *Saintly Hero*, 3.

316. C. Bouchard is quoted in E. B. Keiser - B. Wheeler, *Chivalry: From Footnote to Foreground*, in *The Study of Chivalry: Resources and Approaches*, ed. H. Chickering – T. H. Seiler, Kalamazoo, 1988, p. 136.

317. Cfr. R. Stacey, *Nobles and Knights*, in *The New Cambridge Medieval History V: 1198-1300*, Cambridge, 1999, p. 13.

318. Cfr. D. J. Leclerq - D. F. Vandenbroucke - L. Bouyer, *The Spirituality of the Middle Ages*, London, 1968, p. 277.

319. J. Bumke, *The Concept of Knighthood in the Middle Ages*, trans. W. T. H. – E. Jackson, New York, 1982, p. 22.

320. Bumke, *The Concept of Knighthood in the Middle Ages*, 22.

321. Cfr. M. Keen, *Chivalry*, New Haven and London, 1984, p. 2.

322. Keen, *Chivalry*, 2.

323. Keen, *Chivalry*, 22.

324. Stacey, *Nobles and Knights*, 13.

325. Stacey, *Nobles and Knights*, 13-15. Loyalty was a particularly valuable virtue considering vassalage was such an important political institution.

326. F. Cardini, *The Warrior and the Knight*, in *Medieval Callings*, ed. J. Le Goff, trans. L. G. Cochrane, Chicago, 1987, p. 104.

327. Bulfinch, *The Age of Chivalry*, 17.

328. Knight, *The Social Function of the Middle English Romances*, 99-100.

329. Stacey, *Nobles and Knights*, 22.

330. Cardini, *The Warrior and the Knight*, 101.

331. Cfr. D. Carlson, *Religious Writers and Church Councils*, in *The Study of Chivalry: Resources and Approaches*, ed. H. Chickering – T. H. Seiler, Kalamazoo, 1988, p. 143.

332. Cfr. Kaeuper, *Chivalry and Violence in Medieval Europe*, 232-233. See also T. Hunt, *The Emergence of the Knight in France and England 1000-1200*, in *Knighthood in Medieval Literature*, ed. W. H. Jackson, Suffolk, 1981, pp. 1-22. Hunt holds that chivalry was devoid of any strong connotation of value, moral, spiritual or social until 1180, when the knight is aligned with the Church.

333. Kaeuper, Chivalry and Violence in Medieval Europe, 45. Lancelot in *Mort Artu*, regularly hears mass and says the proper prayers 'as a Christian Knight should'. The fear of dying without confession often has the knight

confess before battle.

334. GIES, *The Knight in History*, 77-78.

335. The idea of "fighting monks" spread rapidly in the twelfth century and included new military orders such as the Order of the Hospital, the Orders of Calatrava, Santiago, Alcántara, as well as the Order of the Teutonic Knights confirmed by INNOCENT III in 1198. See M. BARBER, *The Trial of the Templars*, Cambridge, 1987, p. 6.

336. WILLIAM, Archbishop of Tyre, quoted in BARBER, *The Trial of the Templars*, 5. See also J. WASSERMAN, *The Templars and the Assassins: The Militia of Heaven*, Rochester, 2001. The Knights Templar were considered a knightly religious order of men who were organized by BERNARD OF CLAIRVAUX. The knights were tonsured, took vows, were devoted to Our Lady, fasted and wore secular clothing (with a cross on their chest) which was donated by the faithful.

337. J. PRAWLER, *The Latin Kingdom of Jerusalem: European Colonization in the Middle Ages*, London, 1972, p. 253.

338. A. H. HOOKER, *The Knights Templar: Fact and Fantasy*, Internet (06.12.04): http://www.hrshadows.com/library/misck-o/knightstemplar-factandfantasy.php. See also BARBER, *The Trial of the Templars*, 6-8,10.

339. BARBER, *The Trial of the Templars*, 11.

340. *LV* I:6-7.

341. BARBER, *The Trial of the Templars*, 6.

342. These knights wrote in Provençal or *langue d'oc*, a language closer to modern Portuguese or Spanish than French. Cfr. GIES, *The Knight in History*, 50.

343. S. MULHOLLAND, *The Canticle of Creatures: A Reflection on Creative and Artistic Influences*, in *The Cord*, 51 (2001) p. 229.

344. Cfr. R. MANSELLI, *St. Francis of Assisi*, Chicago, 1988, p. 138-146, argues that FRANCIS was a *"Ioculator Domini,"* the Lord's jester. See also BRITTAIN, *The Medieval Latin and Romance Lyric*, 16. The Goliards, who were contemporary with the troubadours and jongleurs, can be considered "in social standing as in other respects, the clerical counterparts of the latter rather than the former."

345. Cfr. GIES, *The Knight in History*, 50. The poet-composer was called in Latin, *"tropator."*

346. F. A. CHERIYAPATTAPARAMBIL, *The Troubadour Influence in the Life and Writings of the Man Saint of Assisi*, Ph. D. diss., Antonianum, 1985, p. 17.

347. GIES, *The Knight in History*, 51. Some troubadours were also clerics, monks, priests, or canons who had abandoned their vocations, having "fallen in love with the vain things of the world."

348. Cfr. M. Foss, *Chivalry*, Great Britain, 1975, p. 67.

349. Cfr. Gies, *The Knight in History*, 51, 53-54, 70. Some of the troubadour music was derived from Church hymns.

350. Mulholland, *The Canticle of Creatures*, 230.

351. Gies, *The Knight in History*, 59.

352. Cfr. Gies, *The Knight in History*, 79, 105.

353. Cfr. Mulholland, *The Canticle of Creatures*, 230.

354. O. Schmucki, *St. Francis' Level of Education* in GR, 10 (1996) p. 161. See also L. T. Topsfield, *Troubadours and Love*, Cambridge, 1975, p. 4. The first recorded troubadour was William IX (1071-1126), Duke of Aquitaine and the Count of Poitiers. Over the next 250 years, about 460 troubadours have been identified among the 2700 lyrics extent which contained in about fifty manuscripts.

355. Mulholland, *The Canticle of Creatures*, 230.

356. Cfr. Gies, *The Knight in History*, 48, 52. The virtues of the troubadour included courtliness, eloquence, excellence, worth, openhandedness, generosity or "larcs."

357. A. R. Moncrieff, *Romance and Legend of Chivalry: Myths and Legends*, London, 1994, p. 34.

358. Keller, *Changes in Old French Epic Poetry*, 173.

359. Gies, *The Knight in History*, 48.

360. Cfr. Cantor, *The Civilization of the Middle Ages*, 352.

361. Cfr. Gies, *The Knight in History*, 54-56; 78-79. Gies balanced presentation traces the historical development of the troubadours and sacralization of knighthood through Arthurian romance.

362. Gies, *The Knight in History*, 79.

363. Gies, *The Knight in History*, 105.

364. Bulfinch, *The Age of Chivalry*, 19.

365. M. Hurley, *Saints, Legends and Romance Again: Secularization of Structure and Motif*, in *Genre*, 8 (1975) pp. 69-70.

366. Keen, *Chivalry*, 50.

367. W. T. Cotton, *Teaching the Motifs of Chivalric Biography*, in *The Study of Chivalry: Resources and Approaches*, ed. H. Chickering – T. H. Seiler, Kalamazoo, 1988, p. 588.

368. Cotton, *Teaching the Motifs of Chivalric Biography*, 589.

369. Cfr. Townsend, *An Edition of Saint's Lives*, 25.

370. Cfr. Moorman, *The Sources For the Life of St. Francis*, 76-81. Moorman

argues for the existence of an early lost document containing the story of FRANCIS' conversion and the coming of his first companions which may have been used by CELANO, JULIEN of SPEYER and BONAVENTURE.

371. LITTLE, *A Guide to Franciscan Studies*, 12.

372. MANSELLI, *Francesco e i soui compagni*, 278.

373. *LV* I:19. *"Vatis opus tibi sume tui."* All English translations for THOMAS OF CELANO's *Vita Prima* are taken from FAED: *The Saint*, vol. 1, 1999.

374. *LV* XI:84-86. *"Franciscum recolam vel imaginer in se continet expressum mentique relinquit ideas partim consimiles, etsi non prorsus easdem."*

375. Cfr. AF, *LV* I: 28-31 p. 408, fn 12, which states HENRY must have visited Assisi. See also *LV* I: 234 which includes Henry's travel comment about an abandoned grotto directed to non-Italians: "you find them in Italy."

376. MANSELLI, *San Francesco e l'eresia*, 251.

377. L. K. COOK, *Francis of Assisi and the Thirteenth-Century Papacy*, MA. diss., Baylor University, Waco, 1978, p. 81.

378. GREGORY IX, *Mira circa nos*, 8, in FAED: *The Saint*, 569.

379. 1C 101. For an in-depth study on the relationship between FRANCIS and GREGORY IX see E. PÁSZTOR, *San Francesco e Il Cardinale Ugolino Nella "Questione Francescana,"* in *Collectanea Francescana*, (46) 1976, pp. 209-239.

380. 1C 73.

381. 1C 75.

382. 1C 74.

383. 1C 74 -75.

384. *Chronicle of Erfurt*, in FAED: *The Prophet*, 824.

385. *LV* X:38-39; 50-52.

386. Cfr. MOCKLER, *Francis of Assisi*, 17.

387. Cfr. E. GRAU, *Thomas of Celano: Life and Work*, in GR, 8 (1994) p. 177. GRAU discusses the criteria of official and unofficial legends.

388. COOK, *Francis of Assisi and the Thirteenth-Century Papacy*, 79. See also H. K. MANN, *The Lives of the Popes in the Middle Ages*, London, 1932, p. 172, fn. 3-5.

389. *LV* X:45-46.

390. *LV* XIV: 75-77.

391. *LV* I: 25.

392. Cfr. BINKLEY, *13th Century Latin Poetry Contests*, 97.

393. Cfr. Cook, *Francis of Assisi and the Thirteenth-Century Papacy*, 79-80.

394. Cfr. Arnald of Sarrant, *The Kinship of Saint Francis*, 10, in FAED: *The Prophet*, 689, which records that Gregory IX wrote "that first hymn *Proles de coelo prodiit*," the responsory *De paupertatis horreo*, as well as the sequence *Caput draconis*. In addition Salimbene de Adam also clearly identifies Gregory IX as author of these works. See *The Chronicle of Salimbene de Adam*, trans. J. L. Baird – J. Baglivi – J. R. Lane, New York, 1986, pp. 384-385.

395. E. Prinzivalli, *A Saint to be Read: Francis of Assisi in the Hagiographic Sources*, in GR, 15 (2001) p. 258.

396. Gregory IX, *Mira Circa Nos*, 1, in FAED: *The Saint*, 566.

397. Gregory IX, *Mira Circa Nos*, 1, 566.

398. Gregory IX, *Mira Circa Nos*, 3, 566.

399. Gregory IX, *Mira Circa Nos*, 3, 566.

400. *LV* I:85, 117; IV: 22; XIII:110.

401. Gregory IX, *Mira Circa Nos*, 4, 567.

402. Gregory IX, *Mira Circa Nos*, 5-6, 568.

403. See *LV* I:231 and *Mira Circa Nos*, 6, 568.

404. Gregory IX, *Mira Circa Nos*, 7, 569.

405. Gregory IX, *Mira Circa Nos*, 5, 568.

406. The Latin text for Gregory IX' s poem *Caput Draconis* is taken from *Sequentiae in Honorem S. Francisci* in AF, X, Quaracchi, 1936, pp. 401-404.

407. *Caput Draconis* VII: *"Militum."*

408. *Caput Draconis* V: *"princeps inclytus."*

409. *Caput Draconis* V: *"signum regale baiulat."*

410. *Caput Draconis* III: *"In cuius sacro corpore vexillum Crucis."*

411. *Caput Draconis* IV: *"fide clypeo."* Francis receives *"scutum Fedei"* in *LV* II:121.

412. *Caput Draconis* VI.

413. Lewry, *Papal Ideals and the University of Paris*, 371.

414. Arnald of Sarrant, *The Kinship of Saint Francis*, 10, in FAED: *The Prophet*, p. 698 vol. 3.

415. *LV* X:34.

416. *LV* XIV:55.

417. *Introduction to the Liturgical Texts*, in FAED: *The Saint*, 317.

418. Cfr. MURPHY, *Rhetoric in the Middle Ages*, 157.

419. The Latin text for the hymns of THOMAS OF CAPUA can be found in IULIANI DE SPIRA, *Officium Sancti Francisci*, in *Fontes Franciscani*, p. 1105-1121. THOMAS OF CAPUA's authorship is attested to by ARNALD OF SARRANT, *The Kinship of Saint Francis, 10*, in FAED: *The Prophet*, 689, who cites him as having written the hymns *In celesti collegio* and *Decus morum*. SALIMBENE also attests to this and adds *Carnis spicam*, SALIMBENE DE ADAM, *Chronicles*, 385.

420. *Ad Vesperas, 24 Hymnus*, I: *"dux minorum."*

421. *Ad Vesperas, 24 Hymnus*, VII: *"dux."*

422. *Ad Vesperas, 24 Hymnus*, VI: *"regis signum ducem dignum insignit manu, latere."*

423. *Ad Vesperas, 24 Hymnus*, V: *"Vexilla Regis prodeunt."*

424. The Latin text for the hymn *Plaude turba* by RAINERIUS OF VITERBO can be found in IULIANI DE SPIRA, *Officium Sancti Francisci* in *Fontes Franciscani*, p. 1116-1117. See II, and III in which FRANCIS is described as a champion who a crown of gold as victor for trampling the malignant foes.

425. GRAU, *Thomas of Celano: Life and Work*, 199. GRAU states that CELANO's authorship of *"Fregit victor"* is doubtful.

426. The Latin text for THOMAS OF CELANO's sequences *Sanctitas Nova Signa* and *Fregit Victor* are taken from *Sequentiae in Honorem S. Francisci* in AF, X, Quaracchi, 1936, p. 401-404.

427. *Sanctitas Nova Signa* XII: *"Defert ille signa Christi."*

428. *Sanctitas Nova Signa* XVII: *"Signis Crucis."*

429. *Sanctitas Nova Signa* XVII: *"Carnem frenat"*; *LV*I: 6, *"Carnem...frenavit."*

430. *Sanctitas Nova Signa* XVII: *"Carnem hostem superasti Incyta victoria."*

431. *Fregit Victor* II: *"princeps pugnae spiritalis, insignis amantium."*

432. Cfr. *The Liturgical Texts*, Introduction, in FAED: *The Saint*, 311-318. The dating for these liturgical texts is between 1230-1234.

433. JACQUES DE VITRY, *Historia Occidentalis*, in FAED: *The Saint*, 585.

434. PACIOCCO - ACCROCCA, *La leggenda di un santo di nome Francesco*, 126.

435. FORTINI, *Francis of Assisi*, 231.

436. Cfr. TOWNSEND, *Vita Sancti Oswaldi*, 13.

437. CELANO speaks of people being "slaves of sin" and FRANCIS as having been freed from bondage and the yoke of servitude.

438. Cfr. 4C 13.

439. Cfr. TOWNSEND, *Vita Sancti Oswaldi*, 11.

440. F. J. E. Raby, *A History of Secular Latin Poetry in the Middle Ages*, Oxford, 1957, p. 190.

441. Cfr. Brittain, *The Medieval Latin and Romance Lyric*, 17.

442. Cfr. N. Adkin, *The Proem of Henry of Avranches' Vita Sancti Guthlaci*, in AB, 108 (1990) p. 352. See also Meter, *Walter of Châtillon's Alexandreis Book 10-A Commentary*, 29, which states that Henry II's epitaph in 1189 is taken from book 10: 448-450.

443. Meter, *Walter of Châtillon's Alexandreis*, 1.

444. Meter, *Walter of Châtillon's Alexandreis*, 1.

445. Meter, *Walter of Châtillon's Alexandreis*, 1. Walter uses relatively pure prosody and diction, avoids rhyme and frequently quotes Virgil, Ovid and Lucan.

446. Salter, *English and International*, 64.

447. Cfr. A. C. Dionisotti, *Walter of Châtillon and the Greeks*, in *Latin Poetry and the Classical Tradition: Essays in Medieval and Renaissance Literature*, ed. P. Godman – O. Murray, Oxford, 1990, p. 74.

448. Dionisotti, *Walter of Châtillon and the Greeks*, 74.

449. Cfr. Adkin, *The Proem of Henry of Avranches' Vita Sancti Guthlaci*, 352-353. Other poets who have imitated Walter's proem are Albert of Stades' *Troilus*, William the Breton's *Philippeis*, Henry of Settimello's *Elegy*, Otto of Magdeburg's poem on Duke Ernest and Nicholas de Braye's poem on the deeds of Louis VIII.

450. Henry of Ghent in his index of authors of the *De scriptoribus ecclesiasticis*, quoted in M. K. Lafferty, *Walter of Châtillon's Alexandreis: Epic and the Problem of Historical Understanding*, Belgium, 1998, p. 11.

451. Lafferty, *Walter of Châtillon's Alexandreis*, 11. An example of this can be seen in Henri d'Andeli's *Bataille des Sept Arts*, written in the thirteenth century, where the *Alexandreis*, which had now become a classic, represents one of Grammar's knights in a battle against Logic.

452. Cfr. Adkin, *The Proem of Henry of Avranches' Vita Sancti Guthlaci*, 350-354.

453. Cfr. The Easter Exsultet "*tellus tantis irradiata fulgoribus*" found in *LV* 1:28 fn 10. See also Fortini, *Francis of Assisi*, 88, who states Henry's 'light' metaphor "very likely" inspired Dante's famous lines in the *Paradiso* XI:49-51. "*Di questa costa, là dov 'ella frange più sua ratteezza, nacque al mondo un sole,come fa questo tal volta di Gange*," quoted from Dante Alighieri, *La Divina Commedia*, Rome, 1972, p. 1044.

454. Meter, *Walter of Châtillon's Alexandreis*, 6.

455. Cfr. Lafferty, *Walter of Châtillon's Alexandreis*, 39.

456. Cfr. Lafferty, *Walter of Châtillon's Alexandreis*, 39, 48-49.

457. Cfr. Lafferty, *Walter of Châtillon's Alexandreis*, 60. The prophecy of the "New Man," in lines 150-63, which will bring forth a great novelty upon the earth, is an allusion to Christ, not Alexander.

458. Lafferty, *Walter of Châtillon's Alexandreis*, 13.

459. Meter, *Walter of Châtillon's Alexandreis*, 4.

Chapter Two

1. Jerome, Augustine and other Church Fathers used the term "soldiers of Christ." See "Militia" p. 559-560, in *Encyclopedia of the Early Church*, ed. A. Di Berardino, trans. A. Walford, Cambridge, 1992, where Tertullian, the son of a centurion, is cited as using the term *"miles"* to characterize the Christian vocation in regards the struggle for faith with the help of spiritual weapons against the adverse forces of the flesh and demons.

2. Cfr. M. L. del Mastro, *The Military Analogy in Early Anglo-Latin Hagiography*, Ph. D. diss., Fordham University, 1973, Abstract.

3. del Mastro, *The Military Analogy*, 290.

4. A. C. Meisel - M. L. del Mastro, *The Rule of St. Benedict*, New York, 1975, Prologue.

5. Meisel - del Mastro, *The Rule of St. Benedict*, 48.

6. Cfr. L. Bouyer, *Introduction to Spirituality*, trans. M. P. Ryan, New York, 1961, p. 200.

7. Ephesians 6:12.

8. Cfr. Robertson, *The Medieval Saints' Lives*, 152.

9. Bouyer, *Introduction to Spirituality*, 201.

10. Bouyer, *Introduction to Spirituality*, 201.

11. H. O. Taylor, *The Emergence of Christian Culture in the West: The Classical Heritage of the Middle Ages*, New York, 1958, p. 279.

12. S. Da Campagnola, *Francesco D'Assisi nei suoi scritti e nelle sue biografie dei secoli XIII-XIV*, Assisi, 1981, p. 55.

13. M. W. Bloomfield, *A Grammatical Approach to Personification Allegory*, in *Essays and Explorations*, New York, 1970, p. 246.

14. Cfr. *Alain de Lille*, Internet (22.02.05): http://historymedren.about.com/od/aentries /a/11_ alaindelille.htm.

15. Cfr. *Essays in Medieval Studies*, Internet (22.02.05): http://www.illinoismedievalorg/ems/VOL4/ sweeney.html.

16. Bouyer, *Introduction to Spirituality*, 202.

17. Bouyer, *Introduction to Spirituality*, 203. The peace of the "awakened" soul

in which Charity reigns.

18. J. Micó, *The Spirituality of St. Francis,* in GR, 7 (1993) pp. 1-26.
19. Fortini, *Francis of Assisi,* 1.
20. Le Goff, *Saint Francis, Medieval or Modern?,* 20.
21. Mayeski, *New Voices in the Tradition: Medieval Hagiography Revisited,* 709.
22. Cfr. F. Cardini, *L'avventura di un cavaliere di Cristo: Appunti per uno studio sulla cavalleria nella spiritualità di S. Francesco,* in *Studi Francescani,* 1-2 (1976) pp. 127-198.
23. Cfr. Micó, *The Spirituality of St. Francis,* 1-26.
24. R. Brown, *The Roots of St. Francis,* Chicago, 1982, p. 22.
25. I. J. Peterson, *Clare of Assisi: A Biographical Study,* Illinois, 1993, p. 60.
26. Bartoli, *Clare of Assisi,* 12.
27. Bartoli, *Clare of Assisi,* 18.
28. Bartoli, *Clare of Assisi,* 19.
29. R. Zavalloni, *La Personalità di Francesco D'Assisi: Studio psicologico,* Padova, 1991, p. 37. (Translation mine)
30. Cfr. 1C 23; LM 15.5. San Giorgio was a church, *schola minor,* and hospital for the poor.
31. Cfr. Fortini, *Francis of Assisi,* 95.
32. Cfr. D. Spoto, *Reluctant Saint: The Life of Francis of Assisi,* New York, 2003, pp. 19-21. The figure of St. George known in England, Palestine, Egypt, Sweden, Portugal, Russia and Ethiopia, presents a significant paradigm of a soldier who puts aside his weapons to serve the poor. The patron bishops of Assisi were also "presented at the school and in Church sermons as the models for knights brave enough to risk their own martyrdom in the Crusades."
33. Cfr. 1C 23; LM 15:5.
34. Cfr. Mockler, *Francis of Assisi,* 43.
35. Barber, *The Trial of the Templars,* 5.
36. Cfr. Spoto, *Reluctant Saint,* 11; Mockler, *Francis of Assisi,* 44. Because the capture of Jerusalem was seen as a divine punishment for Christian sin, the crusade included a call for fasting on every Friday for the next five years, with abstinence on Wednesdays and Saturdays, as well as the wearing of penitential garb.
37. Cfr. Mockler, *Francis of Assisi,* 44. Francis was a subject of Emperor Frederick I, a "model of knightly virtue," who was the "most legendary" and "most powerful" figure in Europe. He ruled Assisi indirectly at this time through Conrad of Lutzen.

38. One of the more romantic stories of the crusades comes from the French crusaders, led by HENRY II of Champagne, who conquered the Saracens and married the Queen of Jerusalem. Cfr. MOCKLER, *Francis of Assisi*, 45.

39. Cfr. LE GOFF, *Francis of Assisi between the Renewels and Restraints of Feudal Society*, 7.

40. Cfr. M. BIHL, *De Nomine S. Francisci*, in AFH, 19 (1919) p. 507, which notes the habit of naming infants after the land where the father traded. See also PETERSON, *Clare of Assisi*, 18, who notes that the main route traveled by pilgrims, traders and merchants from Assisi to France was called the *Via Francesco*. Another legend however claims that FRANCIS' name is derived from "*franciscae*," a term used for "the ax-shaped insignia which at Rome was carried before the consuls, and which generated terror and a sense of security and honor." See JACOPO DE VORAGINE, *Golden Legend*, quoted in FAED: *The Founder*, 791.

41. Cfr. FORTINI, *Francis of Assisi*, 39-40. Between 1150-1300, Champagne was the largest international fair in Europe. International fairs attracted merchants from France, Flanders, Germany, England as well as from Provence. FORTINI relates that PIETRO would have sought *panni franeschi*, the finest French and Flemish fabrics, which FRANCIS saw in his house in *LV* I:214. See also SPOTO, *Reluctant Saint*, 5, 22, who states PIETRO may have traveled two or three times a year to France on trips that lasted as long as two months.

42. RICHER OF SENS, *Gesta Senonensis Ecclesiae* 3, in FAED: *The Founder*, 809.

43. MOCKLER, *Francis of Assisi*, 35.

44. Cfr. H. NOLTHENIUS, *Un uomo dalla valle di Spoleto: Francesco tra i soui contemporanei*, Padova, 1991, p. 284, which holds that FRANCIS would have visited Troyes with his father, and may have likely encountered CHRÉTIEN's romances. See J. GIES, *Life in a Medieval City*, New York, 1981, p. 213 which states that the Knights Templar had a monopoly on wool weighing at the Fairs.

45. MOCKLER, *Francis of Assisi*, 35. MOCKLER relates that ELEANOR's grandfather, GUILLAUME IX OF AQUITAINE was the first troubadour.

46. Cfr. 1 C 16, which records that FRANCIS sang in French and 2C 13, 127 relates he spoke French. See also L. OLIGER, *S. Franciscus Cognovitne Pseudo-Turpinum, in Antonianum*, 2 (1927) p. 191. Based on a comparative linguistic study, he states FRANCIS was probably influenced by PSEUDO-JOHN TURPIN's *Life of Charlemagne* and *The Song of Roland*.

47. Cfr. G. ABATE, *La casa natale di S. Francesco*, Rome, 1966, pp. 77-84, who argues PICA was not from Picardy.

48. Cfr. H. FELDER, *The Knight-Errant of Assisi*, Youngstown, 1982, p. 17. According to FELDER, PICA's designation as *Donna, Domina, Madonna* or Lady in the documents of the notariate reveal her status as a noblewoman

and thus established the right for FRANCIS to seek knighthood.

49. T. MATURA, *The "Language" of Francis in His Writings*, in GF, 16 (2002) p. 30.

50. Cfr. FORTINI, *Francis of Assisi*, 232. Note, SCHMUCKI, *St. Francis' Level of Education*, 160, holds that FRANCIS would have learned French from his father. See also FELDER, *The Knight-Errant of Assisi*, 125, who cites examples of FRANCIS speaking French from the sources.

51. SCHMUCKI, *St. Francis' Level of Education*, 159, 169.

52. Cfr. FORTINI, *Francis of Assisi*, 180. ANDREA was chaplain to the king of France.

53. FORTINI, *Francis of Assisi*, 640.

54. Cfr. R. MANSELLI, *The Spirituality of St. Francis of Assisi*, in GR, 3 (1989) p. 51.

55. Cfr. S. MULHOLLAND, *St. Francis and the Themes of Medieval Literature*, in *The Cord*, 44 (1994) p. 110.

56. Cfr. NOLTHENIUS, *Un uomo dalla valle di Spoleto*, 282. Two examples of this are the famous door of the Cathedral of Modena and the mosaic of PANTALEONE in the Cathedral of Otranto. See also FELDER, *The Knight-Errant of Assisi*, 14.

57. BARTOLI, *Clare of Assisi*, 18.

58. MOORMAN, *A History of the Franciscan Order*, 271.

59. L. S. CUNNINGHAM, *St. Francis of Assisi*, Boston, 1976, p. 62.

60. LE GOFF, *Francis of Assisi between the Renewels and Restraints of Feudal Society*, 7.

61. Cfr. FORTINI, *Francis of Assisi*, 8.

62. Cfr. FORTINI, *Francis of Assisi*, 8, 72. He cites the names OLIVERO (OLIVER) DI MASCARELLO and ROLLANDO (ROLAND) DI GUALFREDO and others which indicate familiarity with the *Chanson de Roland* and give evidence for the participation of knights from Assisi in the Crusade. Other documents from 1151 speak of the same first names. It is interesting to note that FORTINI, *Francis of Assisi*, 288-291 relates that SR. BENEDETTA, who succeeded CLARE as Abbess, could also represent evidence of the popularity of the Arthurian legends as she was originally named GINEVRA (GUINEVERE).

63. P. RILEY, *Assisi's Political, Social History: 1175-1225*, in FS, 34 (1974) p. 398. Assisi was captured by Frederick's deputy, ARCHBISHOP CHRISTIAN OF MAINZ in 1174.

64. CHESTERTON, *Saint Francis of Assisi*, 32.

65. Cfr. *Mythology Guide*. Internet (25.1.05): http://www.online-mythology.com/castor_pollux/. After CASTOR was slain, POLLUX sacrificed his life to share it with his brother. They were called Dioscuri (sons of Zeus), wore

white armor, rode white steeds, and were believed to aid those in battle. Their story epitomizes the value Romans placed on fighting, fraternity and sacrifice.

66. Bartoli, *Clare of Assisi*, 21.

67. Fortini, *Francis of Assisi*, 3, 78.

68. Cfr. Brown, *The Roots of St. Francis*, 121-122. Other legends place Roland and Oliver in the Umbrian valley.

69. Riley, *Assisi's Political, Social History: 1175-1225*, 401. See also Brown, *The Roots of St. Francis*, 122 which notes that Barbarossa tried to have Charlemagne canonized in 1165 by the antipope Pascal III.

70. Cfr. Peterson, *Clare of Assisi*, 56, states that Frederick II was born on December 26, 1195 and baptized in Assisi. See also Fortini, *Francis of Assisi*, 81, 109, which indicates that records from the Cathedral of San Rufino confirm that Emperor Frederick visited Assisi in 1177, and that Frederick II was baptized in San Rufino when Francis was about 13.

71. Cfr. Fortini, Francis of Assisi, 65.

72. Fortini, *Francis of Assisi*, 65.

73. Cfr. 1C 5.

74. Cfr. 2C 7.

75. Cfr. F. A. Cheriyapattaparambil, *The Troubadour Influence in the Life and Writings of the Man Saint of Assisi*, Ph. D. diss., Antonianum 1985, p. 29.

76. Cfr. Cheriyapattaparambil, *The Troubadour Influence in the Life and Writings of the Man Saint of Assisi*, 29.

77. Cfr. Peterson, *Clare of Assisi*, 1.

78. C. A. Ohan, *The Poverello and the Franciscans: Religious and Artistic Transformations in Thirteenth-Century Italy*, Ph. D. diss., University of Texas, 1997, p. 13. The later crusades against the Cathars would offer indulgences and privileges to all nobles and warriors of France who fought to protect the Church. See M. Sandor, *The Popular Preaching of Jacques De Vitry*, Ph. D. diss., University of Toronto, 1993, p. 141.

79. Micó, *The Spirituality of St. Francis*, 19.

80. Cfr. Barber, *The Trial of the Templars*, 8.

81. Micó, *The Spirituality of St. Francis*, 20.

82. Micó, *The Spirituality of St. Francis*, 20.

83. Cfr. Riley, *Assisi's Political, Social History: 1175-1225*, 400. Conrad was Archbishop Christians' lieutenant whom Frederick made Duke of Spoleto and Count of Assisi from 1177 to 1198.

84. Cfr. J. Green, *God's Fool*, trans. P. Heinegg, New York, 1985, p. 40.

85. Cfr. Brown, *The Roots of St. Francis*, 143.
86. Cfr. Fortini, *Francis of Assisi*, 151.
87. Cfr. Felder, *The Knight-Errant of Assisi*, 29.
88. L3C 4, states Francis was released after a year.
89. Fortini, *Francis of Assisi*, 153. Cfr. L3C 4, which states that "because of his distinguished bearing, he was put among the nobles."
90. Cfr. Mockler, *Francis of Assisi*, 46.
91. L3C 5, states after a "few years."
92. Cfr. Moorman, *A History of the Franciscan Order*, 4-5; Fortini, *Francis of Assisi*, 179; Da Campagnola, *Francesco D'Assisi*,132. Note Apulia's port of Brindisi also offered the possibility of joining the many crusaders sailing to Constantinople and Jerusalem. See Spoto, *Reluctant Saint*, 39. See Barber, *The Trial of the Templars*, 10, who lists Apulia as the only province of the Knight Templars in Italy.
93. Cfr. A. House, *Francis of Assisi: A Revolutionary Life*, Mahwah, NJ, 2001, p. 45. O. Englebert, *Saint Francis of Assisi*, trans. E. Hutton, London, 1950, p. 55, states "the troubadours of Provence and Italy sang everywhere his exploits and throughout the peninsula soldiers rushed to enroll under the banners of the glorious knight."
94. Wasserman, *The Templars and the Assassins*, 192.
95. Innocent III, *Epistle XIII*, (1210), quoted in E. Burman, *The Templars: Knights of God*, Rochester, 1986, p. 118. Wasserman, *The Templars and the Assassins*,191 records that some of the Templars were upbraided by the Pope for their greed and their abuse of grants. The power and wealth of the Templars in Judaea was well known around the time of Francis' birth.
96. Cfr. Fortini, *Francis of Assisi*, 142. See also House, *Francis of Assisi: A Revolutionary Life*, 45.
97. Cfr. Riley, *Assisi's Political, Social History: 1175-1225*, 402.
98. Gies, *The Knight in History*, 98.
99. Cfr. Gies, *The Knight in History*, 98. Knights in France and England also rose to political positions (entering royal service or Parliament) and acquired the title of Sire.
100. Cfr. Bolton, *Too Important to Neglect: The Gesta Innocentii PP III*, 92.
101. Cfr. Mockler, *Francis of Assisi*, 72.
102. Cfr. Fortini, *Francis of Assisi*, 162. The battle took place on June 10, 1201.
103. Cfr. Fortini, *Francis of Assisi*, 162-163. The people of Apulia considered Gautier the last paladin of Charlamagne.
104. Fortini, *Francis of Assisi*, 163.

105. Cfr. J. J. Robinson, *Dungeon, Fire and Sword: The Knights Templar in the Crusades*, New York, 1991, p. 211.

106. Cfr. W. R. Thomson, *The Image of the Mendicants in the Chronicles of Matthew Paris*, in AFH, 70 (1977) p. 8.

107. Thomson, *The Image of the Mendicants in the Chronicles of Matthew Paris*, 8-9.

108. Manselli, *The Spirituality of St. Francis of Assisi*, 51.

109. Le Goff, *Francis of Assisi between the Renewels and Restraints of Feudal Society*, 7.

110. Schmucki, *St. Francis' Level of Education*, 160.

111. 1C 16.

112. Felder, *The Knight-Errant of Assisi*, 76.

113. Cfr. Paciocco - Accrocca, *La leggenda di un santo di nome Francesco*, 123.

114. Francis of Assisi, *First Version of the Letter to the Faithful*, 13, in *Francis and Clare: The Complete Works*, 63.

115. Francis of Assisi, *Parchment Given to Brother Leo, 6, in Francis and Clare: The Complete Works*, 100.

116. *Testament*, 3.

117. 1C 5 first speaks of the sweetness of grace which converts Francis. See *LV* I:206 in which God tempts Francis with sweetness.

118. 2MP 100. See also 2C 127.

119. A. Holl, *The Last Christian*, trans. P. Heinegg, New York, 1980, p. 35.

120. Holl, *The Last Christian*, 36.

121. Holl, *The Last Christian*, 36.

122. Cfr. Felder, *The Knight-Errant of Assisi*, 21-22. *Courtoisie* is defined as kindheartedness, generosity, or munificence.

123. Keen, *Chivalry*, 2. The classic virtues of good knighthood included franchise, "the free and frank bearing that is visible testimony to the combination of good birth with virtue."

124. Sorrell, *Saint Francis of Assisi and Nature*, 72.

125. Sorrell, *Saint Francis of Assisi and Nature*, 72. See also J. Micó, *The Spirituality of St. Francis: With Clean Hearts*, in GR, 8 (1994) 281-284, which has an in-depth study of the history of courtesy and its link to chivalry as well as a section on Francis' and God's courtesy.

126. Mulholland, *The Canticle of Creatures*, 233.

127. L. Gallant - A. Cirino, *The Geste of the Great King*, (Phoenix, AZ: Tau Publishing, 2012). p. 22.

128. Gallant - Cirino, *The Geste of the Great King*, 22.

129. Gallant - Cirino, *The Geste of the Great King*, 22.

130. Cfr. M. Rampton, *Francis as Troubadour*, in *The Cord*, 40 (1990) p. 300.

131. *Canticum fratis Solis* 3, in Esser, *Opuscula Sancti Patris Francisci Assisiensis*, 84. *"Messor lo frate sole."* See also LP 43 which records that Francis composed a melody to the words. Assisi Codex 338 in fact has blank spaces left for musical notation, which were never added.

132. Sorrell, *Saint Francis of Assisi and Nature*, 71.

133. Mulholland, *The Canticle of Creatures*, 233.

134. Mulholland, *The Canticle of Creatures*, 232.

135. Mulholland, *The Canticle of Creatures*, 232.

136. Felder, *The Knight-Errant of Assisi*, 122.

137. Felder, T*he Knight-Errant of Assisi*, 136.

138. Cfr. Rampton, *Francis as Troubadour*, 298 who relates some interpret "this period's deep devotion to the Virgin Mary as a precursor of the love motif in courtly literature." For further reference see P. S. Gold, *The Lady and the Virgin: Image, Attitude, and Experience in Twelfth-Century France*, Chicago, 1985, pp. 77-81; J. M. Erickson, *Saint Francis and His Four Ladies*, New York, 1970, pp. 101-109.

139. *Salutation of the Blessed Virgin Mary*, 1 and *Salutation to the Virtues*, 2, 3 in *Francis and Clare: The Complete Works*, ed. R. J. Armstrong - I. C. Brady, New York, 1982. See also 2C 55 in which Francis is depicted in Romance terms as espousing Lady poverty.

140. Cfr. L. Lehmann, *The Salutation of the Virtues*, in GR, 11 (1997) p. 230.

141. Cfr. Moorman, *A History of the Franciscan Order*, 271.

142. Cfr. A. Fortini, *La lauda in Assisi e le origini del teatro italiano*, Assisi, 1961, p. 480.

143. Cfr. Da Campagnola, *Francesco d'Assisi*, 54.

144. Cfr. E. A. Armstrong, *Saint Francis Nature Mystic: The Derivation and Significance of the Nature Stories in the Franciscan Legend*, Berkley, 1973, p. 21.

145. Francis refers to Lady Poverty in his *Testament written in Sienna*.

146. *Salutation to the Virgin Mary* 1; 3C 37; Epistola XIII, 1; *The Last Will Written for Saint Clare and Her Sisters*, 2.

147. *Testament Written in Sienna*, 4.

148. L. Lehmann, *"We Thank You": The Structure and Content of Chapter 23 of the Earlier Rule*, in GR, 5 (1991) p. 27.

149. R. J. Armstrong, *St Francis of Assisi: Writings for a Gospel Life*, New York, 1994, p. 191.

150. Lehmann, *The Salutation of the Virtues*, 230.

151. S. Sticca, *Drama and Spirituality in the Middle Ages*, in *Medievalia Et Humanistica*, 4 (1973) p. 78.

152. *Canticle of Exhortation to St. Clare and Her Sisters*, 6, in *Francis and Clare: The Complete Works*.

153. Adm. 1:16.

154. Cfr. G. Miccoli, *The Writings of Francis*, in GR, 15 (2001) pp. 143-144. The first appearance of this parable can be found in the sermons of the English priest Odo of Cheriton. See M. Bihl, *Sancti Francisci parabola in sermonibus Odonis de Ceritonia a. 1219 conscriptis*, in AFH, 20 (1927) pp. 584-586.

155. R. Pernoud, *Lumière du moyen-âge*, Paris, 1944, p. 36.

156. Cfr. Cardini, *L'Avventura di un cavaliere di Christo*, 135-136.

157. Cfr. Nguyên-Van-Khanh, *The Teacher of His Heart*, 28.

158. Nguyên-Van-Khanh, *The Teacher of His Heart*, 28.

159. 2C 197. Francis called St. Michael 'the great prince' and venerated the angels because they are "with us in battle." For a history of devotion to St. Michael in the Middle Ages see R. F. Johnson, *Archangel in the Margins: St. Michael in the Homilies of Cambridge Corpus Christi College*, in *Traditio*, 53 (1998) pp. 63-91.

160. Cfr. C. Esser, *Opuscula Sancti Patris Francisci Assisiensis*, Roma, 1978. *Exhortation to the Praises of God* 17, *Office of Passion* Antiphon 3, *Regula non bullata*, 18:1, on whose feast day the ministers were instructed to meet; 23:6. Francis' devotion to St. Michael brought him to La Verna on the day he received his stigmata for his annual fast.

161. L3C 57. During Francis' life, there were two feasts of St. Michael, May 8th and September 29th, a holy day of obligation commemorating the dedication of the Basilica of St. Michael, located near Rome.

162. Peterson, *Clare of Assisi*, 31.

163. Cfr. Johnson, *Archangel in the Margins*, 64, 68.

164. Peterson, *Clare of Assisi*, 31. Peterson, 37 notes the veneration of St. Michael by pregnant women like Ortalana, Clare's mother, who made a pilgrimage to Monte Gargano and received the prophetic words from the cross that "You will give birth to a light that will shine brilliantly in the world." Interestingly, Monte Gargano is located in Apulia, where Francis was heading on the night of his dream. It is also the place from which Bishop Guido was returning when he had a vision of Francis dying. See 2C 220; LM 14:6.

165. D. Lapsanski, *The Chartula of St. Francis of Assisi*, in AFH, 67 (1974) p. 36. See 3C3, 159.

166. Ezekiel 9:4.

167. D. Vorreaux, "Tau," in *Dizionario Franciscano*, a cura di E. Caroli, Padova, 1995, p. 2007.

168. D. Vorreaux, *A Franciscan Symbol: The Tau*, trans. M. Archer – P. Lachance, Chicago, 1979, p. 10.

169. Vorreaux, *A Franciscan Symbol: The Tau*, 7.

170. Englebert, *Saint Francis of Assisi*, 196-197.

171. Vorreaux, *A Franciscan Symbol: The Tau*, 10.

172. G. B. Ladner, *The Life of the Mind in the West Around 1200*, in *Images and Ideas in the Middle Ages: Selected Studies in History and Art*, Vol. II, Roma, 1983, p. 912.

173. R. W. Southern, *Western Society and the Church in the Middle Ages*, New York, 1990, p. 105.

174. Cfr. M. Deanesly, *A History of the Medieval Church: 590-1500*, Cambridge, 1989, p. 141.

175. Vorreaux, *A Franciscan Symbol: The Tau*, 12.

176. Vorreaux, *A Franciscan Symbol: The Tau*, 11.

177. Vorreaux, "Tau," in *Dizionario Franciscano*, 2007.

178. M. Rampton, *Francis as Troubadour*, in *The Cord*, 40 (1990) p. 300.

179. Le Goff, *Saint Francis of Assisi*, 121.

180. Cfr. Da Campagnola, *Francesco D'Assisi*, 132.

181. *The Sacred Exchange between Saint Francis and Lady Poverty*, in FAED: *The Saint*, 529-554. While some scholars believe the work to have been written as early as 1227, others date it between 1237-1239.

182. Rampton, *Francis as Troubadour*, 296.

183. Cfr. Cardini, *L'avventura di un cavaliere di Cristo*, 138-141. The *Romance of the Rose* presents the figures of Courtesy, Disdain, Fair-seeming, Shame and other qualities as ladies and gentlemen.

184. Mulholland, *The Canticle of Creatures*, 230.

185. Manselli, *The Spirituality of St. Francis of Assisi*, 51.

186. Manselli, *St. Francis of Assisi*, 142.

187. Rampton, *Francis as Troubadour*, 297. Note Rampton points to the "questing motif" of 1C 93.

188. 1C 9, 36, 93; 2C 6.

189. 1C 4.

190. 2C 55.

191. 2C 55.

192. 2C 7.

193. Luke of Túy, in FAED: *The Founder*, 596.

194. Roger of Wendover, 6, in FAED: *The Saint*, 599.

195. AP 4:3. "*magnae rusticitatis.*"

196. AP 4:3 fn a.

197. AP 4.

198. AP 5, 6.

199. L3C 2.7.

200. L3C 4, 5.

201. L3C 6.

202. L3C 12, 17.

203. L3C 3.

204. L3C 3.

205. 1MP 1.

206. 2MP 115; 2C 166.

207. *The Little Flowers of Saint Francis*, 37.

208. LM IX:7; XIII:9.

209. LM I:4.

210. LM I:5.

211. AC 103.

212. 2 MP 100.

213. 2MP 72, AC 103. See also Le Goff, *Saint Francis, Medieval or Modern?*, 20, who suggested that Francis' chapter meetings at the Porziuncula were patterned on the gatherings of the Knights of the Round Table.

214. Mockler, *Francis of Assisi*, 158. See also O. Schmucki, *Secretum solitudinis*, in *Collectanea Franciscana*, 39 (1969) pp. 5-58, which holds that the songs and poems of the Troubadours influenced Francis up till his last days.

215. Mockler, *Francis of Assisi*, 159.

216. *Norman Chronicle* (1269-1272), in FAED: *The Prophet*, 826, dated in the year 1216, there is an entry which states "many noblemen" were drawn to the Order.

217. Le Goff, *Saint Francis of Assisi*, 74.

218. Cfr. Chesterton, *Saint Francis of Assisi*, 61. Chesterton speaks of Bernard as occupying the place of Sir Bedivere, the "first made and latest left of Arthur's knights."

219. Cfr. 2MP 85; *The Kinship of Saint Francis*, 3c, 6h, in FAED: *The Prophet*, 690. Angelo is described as humane and courteous.

220. L. Jacobilli, Vite, vol. I, p. 243, quoted in *Brother Angelo Tancredi from Rieti*, Internet (05.05.04): http:// www. sanfrancescoassisi.org/index. php?dir=storia&subdir= compagni&lang= eng&url= angelo.htm.

221. Brown, *The Roots of St. Francis*, 145.

222. *The Tree of the Crucified Life*, 433, b17, in FAED: *The Prophet*, 183.

223. *Legend of Saint Clare* 1, For a complete study on Clare's family of origin see G. Fortini, *The Noble family of St. Clare*, in FS, 13 (1982) pp. 48-67. See also Peterson, *Clare of Assisi*, 56, which traces Clare's descendents to Charlemagne; *Process of Canonization*, 19.1 states there were seven knights in her household.

224. *Donation of LaVerna* (1274), in FAED: *The Prophet*, 802.

225. Russell, *Master Henry Avranches*, 217.

226. Carlson, *Religious Writers and Church Councils*, 142.

227. Cfr. Carlson, *Religious Writers and Church Councils*, 143.

228. Sandor, *The Popular Preaching of Jacques De Vitry*, 177. Caesarius of Heisterbach and Walter Map point out the extent of this criticism.

229. Cfr. Cardini, *The Warrior and the Knight*, 98. He lists pride, anger, acadia, envy, greed, gluttony and lust.

230. A. G. Little, *Franciscan Papers, Lists and Documents*, Manchester, 1943, p. 3.

231. Sorrell, *Saint Francis of Assisi and Nature*, pp. 69-70.

232. Sorrell, *Saint Francis of Assisi and Nature*, 70.

233. 2C 106.

234. 1C 2.

235. 4C 5.

236. Rampton, *Francis as Troubadour*, 295, 302.

237. Rampton, *Francis as Troubadour*, 302.

238. Rampton, *Francis as Troubadour*, 302.

239. Mulholland, *The Canticle of Creatures*, 229.

240. Chesterton, *St Francis of Assisi*, 67.

241. *LV* III:51-53.

242. Caesar of Heisterbach, *Life of Saint Engelbert*, in FAED: *The Saint*, 595.

243. Ohan, *The Poverello and the Franciscans*, 19.

244. *Canticle of Exhortation to St. Clare and Her Sisters*, 6, in *Francis and Clare: The Complete Works*.

245. *The Form of Life Given to Saint Clare and Her Sisters*, 1, in *Francis and Clare: The CompleteWorks*.

246. Clare of Assisi, *First Letter to Agnes of Prague*, exhorts Agnes to take a spouse "of more noble lineage." *The Legend of Saint Clare*, 46, in *Clare of Assisi Early Documents*, ed. and trans. R. J. Armstrong, New York, 1988.

247. V. Kurusummootil, *The Religious Experience of St. Francis*, in *Jeevadhara*, 37 (1977) p. 525.

248. Cfr. D. Blowey, *The Paternity of God in the 'Writings' of Francis of Assisi*, in MF, 98 (1998) pp. 312-313. Others also come from the RNB 23:1 and *The Praises of God* 2.

249. Cfr. Blowey, *The Paternity of God in the 'Writings' of Francis of Assisi*, 314.

250. H. Felder, *The Ideals Of St. Francis of Assisi*, trans. B. Bittle, Quincy, 1998, p. 19.

251. Dante Alighieri, *Divine Comedy*, canto XII, speaks of Francis as a leader of Christ's army who fights and defeats his enemies.

252. Jacopo de Voragine, *Golden legend*, quoted in FAED: *The Founder*, 791.

253. *Annals of Santa Giustina*, in FAED: *The Founder*, 811.

254. Gerard de Frachet, *The Lives of the Brethren*, in FAED: *The Founder*, 786-787.

255. Jacopone of Todi, *Laud* 61, 62 in FAED: *The Prophet*, 873-879.

256. Gies, *The Knight in History*, 103.

257. Mulholland, *St. Francis and the Themes of Medieval Literature*, 112.

258. Cfr. Fortini, *Francis of Assisi*, 231.

259. Felder, *The Ideals Of St. Francis of Assisi*, 20.

260. F. De Beer, *St. Francis and Islam*, in *Francis of Assisi Today*, ed. C. Duquoc – C. Floritan, New York, 1981, p. 15.

261. D. Bona, *The Dreams of St. Francis of Assisi: A Depth Psychology Study*, Ph. D. diss., Pacifica Graduate Institute, 1996, p. 158.

Chapter Three

1. Mayeski, *New Voices in the Tradition: Medieval Hagiography Revisited*, 691.

2. Cfr. Mayeski, *New Voices in the Tradition: Medieval Hagiography Revisited*, 691.
3. C. Hahn, *Portrayed on the Heart: Narrative Effect in Pictorial Lives of the Saints from the Tenth Through the Thirteenth Century*, California, 2001, p. 13.
4. Lifshitz, *Beyond Positivism and Genre*, 95.
5. Le Goff, *The Medieval Imagination*, 3.
6. Cfr. L. Pelligrini, *A Century of Reading the Sources*, in GR, 7 (1993) p. 327.
7. Sabatier, *Life of St. Francis of Assisi*, XXXII.
8. Sabatier, *Life of St. Francis of Assisi*, XXXI.
9. Cfr. Pelligrini, *A Century of Reading the Sources*, 343.
10. Robertson, *The Medieval Saints' Lives*, 88.
11. E. Coleiro, *St. Jerome's Lives of the Hermits*, in *Vigilia Christianae*, II (1957) p. 164. M. L. Laister, *Thoughts and Letters in Western Europe*, 2nd Edition, Ithaca, 1957, pp. 282-283. See also J. A. K. Thomson, *The Classical Background of English Literature*, London, 1962, p. 162, who also holds that readers in the middle ages sought to derive an "improving moral" from the story.
12. M. L. Laister, *Thoughts and Letters in Western Europe*, 2nd Edition, Ithaca, 1957, pp. 282-283. See also J. A. K. Thomson, *The Classical Background of English Literature*, London, 1962, p. 162, who also holds that readers in the middle ages sought to derive an "improving moral" from the story.
13. P. F. Dembowski, *Literary Problems of Hagiography in Old French*, in *Medievalia Et Humanistica*, 7 (1976) p. 127.
14. Prinzivalli, *A Saint to be Read*, 254.
15. P. H. Delehaye, *Cinq Leçons sur la méthode hagiographique*, in *Subsidia hagiographica*, 21 (1934) p. 8, quoted in Elliott, *Roads to Paradise: Reading the Lives of the Early Saints*, 2.
16. P. H. Delehaye, *The Legends of Saints*, trans. D. Attwater, Dublin, 1998, p. 3.
17. L. Müller, *The Theological Significance of a Critical Attitude in Hagiography*, in *Ecumenical Review*, 15 (1963) p. 279.
18. T. Noble - T. Head, *Soldiers of Christ: Saints and Saint's Lives from Late Antiquity and the Early Middle Ages*, University Park, 1995, p. XVII. For an extended definition of hagiography see P. H. Delehaye, *Les Légendes Hagiographiques*, 4th ed., Paris, 1955.
19. Hahn, *Portrayed on the Heart*, 30.
20. Cfr. Grégoire, *Manuale di Agiologia*, 11.
21. Howe, *Hagiographic Handbooks*, 758.

22. Hahn, *Portrayed on the Heart*, 30.
23. Heffernan, *Sacred Biography*, 21.
24. L. Ouspensky - V. Lossky, *The Meaning of Icons*, Crestwood, 1982, p. 27.
25. Müller, *Critical Attitude in Hagiography*, 279.
26. Müller, *Critical Attitude in Hagiography*, 279.
27. Sabatier, *Life of St. Francis of Assisi*, XXIX.
28. S. Mulholland, *St. Francis as Dramatist and Poet*, in *The Cord*, 38 (1988) p. 342.
29. Cfr. I. A. Richards, *The Philosophy of Rhetoric*, New York, 1965, pp. 96-101.
30. Cfr. Richards, *The Philosophy of Rhetoric*, 117-118.
31. A. Vettori, *Poets of God: The Rhetoric of Franciscan Prayerful Texts in the Middle Ages*, Ph. D. diss., University of Yale, 1995, p. 23.
32. Cfr. *Francis of Assisi: History, Hagiography and Hermeneutics in the Early Documents*, ed. J. M. Hammond, New York, 2004, p. 210-228.
33. J. F. Godet-Calogeras, *Don't Forget the Poet*, in *Haversack*, 21 (1998) p. 29. Parenthesis mine.
34. Bloomfield - Dunn, *The Role of the Poet in Early Societies*, 11.
35. Bloomfield - Dunn, *The Role of the Poet in Early Societies*, 11.
36. Heffernan, *Sacred Biography*, 7.
37. Gregory of Tours, *Liber Vitae Patrum*, in *Monumenta Germaniae Historica: Scriptores Rerum Merovingicarum*, ed. B. Krusch, Hanover, 1920, p. 662-663.
38. The Latin text is taken from *Vita Prima Sancti Francisci*, in *Fonte Franciscani*, 275-424 and the English translation from FAED: *The Saint*, 180-308 unless otherwise noted.
39. *"Qualiter Deus visitavit cor eius per corporis infirmitatem et nocturnam visionem."*
40. 1C 2.
41. 1C 3. "...iste iuvenile calore in peccatis fervesceret."; "*...mansuescere nesciens.*"
42. 1C 3. "*...animo angustiam et corpori molestiam inferendo.*"
43. 1C 3.
44. 1C 3. "*spinis.*"
45. 1C 3. "*maceria.*"
46. 1C 3.

47. 1C 4. *"paternae correctionis."* (Translation mine)

48. 1C 5.

49. 1C 4.

50. 1C 4. (Translation mine)

51. Cfr. FELDER, *The Knight-Errant of Assisi*, 27. Apulia was the site of a battle over the custody of FREDERICK II. It was fought between GAUTIER OF BRIENNE, head of INNOCENT III's papal militia and MARKWARD OF ANWEILER.

52. 1C 4.

53. 1C 5.

54. *LV* I: *Quatrain. "Primus Franciscum scribit terrena sequentem, Donec eum dignatio nunc divina flagelans Febre gravi nunc alliециens radiantibus armis, convertit verique boni succendit amore."* (Translation mine)

55. RNB 1. *"Domini nostri....doctrinam et vestigia sequi."*

56. 1C 2.

57. "gleaming," "kindles," "shining," "lamp," "torch," "out-shone." Note that the light imagery from Jn. 5:35 is in reference to JOHN THE BAPTIST.

58. 1 Jn. 5:4,5. "overcame a world."

59. Cfr. *LV* I:71. The Latin word used for whipping *"flagelli"* is the same word used for Jesus' whipping *"flagellatum"* in Mt. 27:26; Mk. 15:15.

60. *LV* I:74. Note the militant language of *"cedere"* and *"indomitum."* Cfr. *LV* I:85-90.

61. *LV* I:75-76.

62. *LV* I:81.

63. *LV* I:78. *"igne fabrilli."*

64. *LV* I:83. Cfr. *LV* I: 99. CELANO does not identify FRANCIS' bodily illness as a fever, nor does he give any symptoms. HENRY however, building on CELANO's use of the word *"fervesceret"* in reference to FRANCIS' "sins of youthful heat," diagnoses him with a fever and describes his symptoms.

65. Cfr. FANGER, *Signs of Power*, 245. See also *LV* I:98, fn. a, which states "Henri reveals himself as an expert in medicine."

66. *LV* I:96-100.

67. KAY, *Courts, Clerks and Courtly Love*, 87.

68. *LV* I:94.

69. *LV* I:94, 95.

70. Cfr. *LV* I:112.

71. Cfr. *LV* I:110-111.

72. Fanger, *Signs of Power*, 235.
73. Fanger, *Signs of Power*, 273.
74. Fanger, *Signs of Power*, 239.
75. Cfr. Fanger, *Signs of Power*, 246.
76. *LV* I:197, 198.
77. *LV* I:128-181.
78. *LV* I:150.
79. *LV* I:170-171.
80. *LV* I:175-177.
81. Sabatier, *Life of St. Francis of Assisi*, 397.
82. Sabatier, *Life of St. Francis of Assisi*, 17.
83. Sabatier, *Life of St. Francis of Assisi*, 23.
84. Cfr. del Mastro, *The Military Analogy*, 291. Henry uses the military analogy in a number of his saints lives i.e. *The Life of Saint Guthlac*, in which Guthlac fights visible devils with spiritual weapons.
85. del Mastro, *The Military Analogy*, 290.
86. *LV* I:182.
87. *LV* I:185.
88. 1C 5. Cfr. J. E. Miller, *Dreams and Prophetic Visions*, in *Biblica*, 71 (1990) p. 401. It should be noted that in Hebrew literature visions are usually ascribed to prophets, while dreams are not. Miller acknowledges that while dreams and night visions are usually equated in standard reference works, dreams are not ascribed to prophets except in denigration.
89. 1C 5.
90. Although absent in Henry's account, Celano curiously lists saddles as among the first items that Francis sees, indicating him as a cavalier.
91. 1C 5.
92. 1C 5.
93. 1C 5.
94. 1C 5.
95. 1C 5:9. *"Et quidem pulchre satis primo de armis fit mentio, et opportune multum arma traduntur contra fortem armatum militi pugnaturo, ut quasi alter David in nomine Domini Dei exercituum ab inveterato inimicorum opprobrio liberet Israelem."*
96. 1C 6.

97. 1C 6.

98. 1C 7.

99. 1C 7.

100. *LV* I:196-203.

101. *LV* I:204-206.

102. 1C 5.

103. 2 Cor. 12:2, 4 in *Biblia Sacra: Iuxta Vulgatam Versionem*, Stuttgart, ed. R. Weber, 1983. "...sive extra corpus nescio Deus scit raptum eiusmodi usque ad tertium caelum et scio huismodi hominem sive in corpore sive extra corpus nescio Deus scit quoniam ratus est in paradisum."

104. J. Lindblom, *Prophecy in Ancient Israel*, Oxford, 1962, p. 107.

105. 2C 6.

106. Cfr. *LV* I:214.

107. *LV* I:207-209.

108. *LV* I:217-218. *"Te sociosque tuos Deus his insigniet armis."*

109. AP 5. "...someone appeared to him calling him by name." The person is identified as a "guide."

110. L3C 5. "...someone appeared to him, a man calling him by name."

111. 2C 6. "...there he saw...a lovely bride."

112. *New Advent*. Internet (24.03.02): http://www.newadvent.org/cathen/08717c.htm. "The *Labarum* is the name by which the military standard adopted by Constantine...after the celebrated vision was known in antiquity."

113. *New Advent*. Internet (24.03.02): http://www.newadvent.org/cathen/08717c.htm.

114. *New Advent*. Internet (24.03.02): http://www.newadvent.org/cathen/08717c.htm.

115. *New Advent*. Internet (24.03.02): http://www.newadvent.org/cathen/08717c.htm.

116. LM I:3. *"...militaribus armis crucis signaculo insignitis."*

117. *Oxford Latin Dictionary*.

118. 2C 135. *"crucifixi insignia."*

119. Cfr. *Biblia Sacra Vulgata*, Jn. 6:27; Rom. 4:11; 2 Cor. 1:22.

120. 1C 94:7; 95:2, 3; 112; 113:2.

121. *LV* I:221.

122. *LV* I:223.

123. *LV* I:228.

124. *LV* I:224.

125. *LV* I:233.

126. *LV* I:233. See Phil. 3:8 in *Biblia Sacra: Iuxta Vulgatam Versionem.*

127. *LV* I:243-246. Brackets mine. *"Cuius in excelsis admissa petitio, dextrae Scripta Dei digito, bullata charactere anctae vivificaeque Crucis, superare viriliter hostem obtinet et rebus non plus inhiare caducis."*

128. *LV* I:242. *"scripta."*

129. 1C 95:10. *"Et licet tantis ac talibus margaritis tamquam pretiosissimis gemmis servus et amicus Altissimi se videret ornatum, atque supra omnium hominum gloriam et honorem mirifice decoratum, non evanuit tamen in corde suo, nec quaesivit inde alicui per appetitum vanae gloriae complacere."*

130. 1C 114:1. *"O singulare donum et praerogativae dilectionis indicium, iisdem gloriae armis militem adornari quae soli Regi excellentissima dignitate conveniunt!"*

131. *LV* I:16-18. *"O Cristi miles, qui solus stigmata Vitae Morte triumphantis vivens in mente latenter Et moriens in carne palam, Francisce, tuliste."*

132. *LV* XIV: 24-28. *"Mors equidem Domini multis illata, sed isiti Est innata; crucem multi subiere coacti: Iste crucem sic mente tulit, sic pectore fovit, Sic studiis coluit, ut et ipsa charactere carnis Se manifestarent animi secreta profundi."*

133. *LV* XII: 52-56. *"Passio namque Iesu sic permanet insita cordi Eius, sic animae totis impressa medullis, Ut minus abscondi queat, exteriusque redundet, Annexamque sui consignet imagine carnem, Et veluti per diaphanos transpareat artus."*

134. Fanger, *Signs of Power,* 253.

135. Fanger, *Signs of Power,* 253.

136. Cfr. Avicenna, *De Anima,* 4.4, quoted in Fanger, *Signs of Power,* 253-254.

Chapter Four

1. Shanahan, *Poem on the Life of Saint Francis,* 131.

2. Cfr. Zen, *I sogni di S. Francesco d'Assisi,* pp. 67-127.

3. The phrase "Dreams are sent by God" is attributed to the fifth century Roman author Macrobius. See C. A. Meier, *The Meaning and Significance of Dreams,* Boston, 1987, p. 55. See also B. Wollmering, *Dreams and Spirituality: An Historical Perspective,* in *Dream Time,* 14:2 (1997) pp. 6-7. Ancient peoples like the Babylonians and Egyptians, also believed dreams to be from supernatural beings.

4. D. G. Condon, *Christian Spiritual Dimensions of the Psychology of Carl Gustav Jung With Special reference to His Use of Dreams*, Excerpta ex Dissertatione ad Doctoratum, Gregorian University, Rome, 2001, p. 40.
5. Condon, *Christian Spiritual Dimensions of the Psychology of Carl Gustav Jung*, 42.
6. T. Fawcett, *The Symbolic Language of Religion*, Minneapolis, 1971, p. 181.
7. Fawcett, *The Symbolic Language of Religion*, 181.
8. Cfr. Fawcett, *The Symbolic Language of Religion*, 181.
9. O. Eissfeldt, *The Old Testament. An Introduction*, Oxford, 1966, p. 54.
10. S. F. Kruger, *Dreaming in the Middle Ages*, Cambridge, 1992, p. 7.
11. Cfr. F. Cardini, *S. Francesco e Il Sogno Delle Armi*, in *Studi Francescani*, 1-2 (1980) p. 15.
12. Kruger, *Dreaming in the Middle Ages*, 76.
13. C. S. Hall, *What People Dream About*, in *Scientific American*, 184 (1951) p. 63.
14. M. A. Mattoon, *Understanding Dreams*, Dallas, 1986, p. 3.
15. S. Freud, *The Complete Psychological Works of Sigmund Freud*, vol. 5, London, 1953, p. 608.
16. I. Progoff, *Waking Dream and Living Myth*, in *Myths, Dreams and Religion*, ed. J. Campbell, New York, 1970, p. 179.
17. C. Jung, *Civilization in Transition*, in *Collected Works*, ed. H. Read – M. Fordham – G. Adler – W. McGuire, trans. R. F. C. Hull, Princeton, 1964, pp. 304-305.
18. *The American Heritage Dictionary*, Boston, 1985.
19. Mattoon, *Understanding Dreams*, 2.
20. Cfr. Mattoon, *Understanding Dreams*, 2.
21. K. Bulkeley, *The Wilderness of Dreams: Exploring the Religious Meaning of Dreams in Modern Western Culture*, New York, 1994, p. 20.
22. Bulkeley, *The Wilderness of Dreams*, 21.
23. Progoff, *Waking Dream and Living Myth*, 181.
24. Progoff, *Waking Dream and Living Myth*, 181.
25. Progoff, *Waking Dream and Living Myth*, 184.
26. Progoff, *Waking Dream and Living Myth*, 191.
27. F. Chooi, *A Psychobiographical Approach to Interpreting Hagiography: An Exploratory Case Study of St. Francis of Assisi*, Ph. D. diss., University of California, Berkeley, 1984, p. 87.

28. Cfr. Chooi, *A Psychobiographical Approach to Interpreting Hagiography*, 87.
29. J. Charron, *Da Narciso a Gesù*, Padova, 1995, p. 63. (Translation mine)
30. Fanger, *Signs of Power*, 253.
31. Cfr. Avicenna, *De Anima*, 4.4, quoted in Fanger, *Signs of Power*, 253-254.
32. Progoff, *Waking Dream and Living Myth*, 195.
33. Cfr. Bulkeley, *The Wilderness of Dreams*, 21.
34. Progoff, *Waking Dream and Living Myth*, 195.
35. Progoff, *Waking Dream and Living Myth*, 195.
36. K. Rahner, *Visions and Prophecies*, Montreal, 1963, p. 62.
37. Cfr. Rahner, *Visions and Prophecies*, 62.
38. For a thorough comparative study of the dream in the other sources and biographies (excluding the *LV*) see Zen, *I Sogni di S. Francesco d'Assisi*.
39. *LV* I: Quatrain.
40. *LV* I: Quatrain.
41. 1C 10.
42. 1C 11.
43. *LV* II:198-202.
44. Felder, *The Ideals of St. Francis of Assisi*, 3.
45. Little, *Franciscan Papers, Lists and Documents*, 3.
46. Little, *Franciscan Papers, Lists and Documents*, 4.
47. Kurusummootil, *The Religious Experience of St. Francis*, 523-524.
48. Felder, *The Ideals of St. Francis of Assisi*, 3.
49. Sorrell, *Saint Francis of Assisi and Nature*, 69.
50. D. Nicholson, *The Mysticism of Saint Francis of Assisi*, London, 1923, p. 329.
51. Le Goff, *Saint Francis, Medieval or Modern?*, 20.
52. 2C 7.
53. Mt. 4:19, Mk. 1:17, Lk. 5:10.
54. J. Navone, *Enjoying God's Beauty*, Collegeville, 1999, p. 64.
55. Navone, *Enjoying God's Beauty*, 59-60.
56. Navone, *Enjoying God's Beauty*, 60.
57. F. Schleiermacher, *On Religion: Speeches to Its Cultured Despisers*, Cambridge, 1988, p.138.
58. Little, *Franciscan Papers, Lists and Documents*, 3.

59. Navone, *Enjoying God's Beauty*, 60.
60. Felder, *The Ideals of St. Francis of Assisi*, 19.
61. Mockler, *Francis of Assisi*, 159.
62. Cfr. Gies, *The Knight in History*, 72. Translated as " leader of wars or general."
63. Schmucki, *St. Francis' Level of Education*, 161.
64. Schmucki, *St. Francis' Level of Education*, 162.
65. Schmucki, *St. Francis' Level of Education*, 169.
66. T. Aquinas, *Introduction to St. Thomas Aquinas: Summa Theologica*, ed. A. C. Pegis, New York, 1948, p. 17, Ia,1,9.
67. 2C 6.
68. Shamkovich, *Saintly Hero*, 6.
69. Cfr. S. Wenzel, *The Seven Deadly Sins: Some Problems of Research*, in *Speculum*, 43 (1968) p. 3.
70. A. Diem, *Virtues and Vices in Early Texts on Pastoral Care*, in FS, 62 (2004) p. 193.
71. Wenzel, *The Seven Deadly Sins: Some Problems of Research*, 13.
72. Cfr. Diem, *Virtues and Vices in Early Texts on Pastoral Care*, 193.
73. Diem, *Virtues and Vices in Early Texts on Pastoral Care*, 195.
74. Cfr. Diem, *Virtues and Vices in Early Texts on Pastoral Care*, 197.
75. Diem, *Virtues and Vices in Early Texts on Pastoral Care*, 195.
76. *LV* II:114.
77. Cfr. Prudentius, *The Spiritual Combat: Psychomachia*, in *The Poems of Prudentius*, vol. 2 of *The Fathers of the Church*, ed. R. J. Deferrari, Washington, D.C., 1965, pp. 79-110.
78. *LV* V:187-188.
79. *LV* I: 6-7.
80. *LV* II:109.
81. *LV* II:127-128. *"caelestia tradit arma viro."*
82. Cfr. *LV* I:117-128.
83. *LV* I:129-130.
84. *LV* I:133.
85. *LV* I:132.
86. *LV* I:9-10.

87. *"sacer dux."*

88. *LV* I:1.

89. *LV* I:14-15. *"nec solum...mundum...et hostem, sed sese."*

90. Cfr. A. Vauchez, *The Saint, in Medieval Callings*, ed. J. Le Goff, trans. L. G. Cochrane, Chicago, 1987, p. 324.

91. Cfr. Vauchez, *The Saint*, 324.

92. Vauchez, *The Saint*, 327.

93. Shanahan, *Poem on the Life of Saint Francis*, 131.

94. *LV* XIV:83-84.

95. *LV* VI:2.

96. *LV* VI:36.

97. *LV* VI:27-30.

98. *LV* VI:85-88.

99. *LV* V: Title Quatrain. *"Quintus agit, Christi praeceptum quomodo complens."*

100. *LV* V:40. *"militiaeque novae."*

101. *LV* V.133. *"dux sacer."*

102. *LV* V:127. *"concio fratrum."*

103. *LV* V:180-183.

104. LJS 19.

105. LM 3:7.

106. L3C 36.

107. *LV* VI:159.

108. *LV* VIII:78.

109. *LV* VIII:89.

110. *LV* IX:123.

111. *LV* XIV:90-91.

112. Little, *Franciscan Papers, Lists and Documents*, 5.

113. Little, *Franciscan Papers, Lists and Documents*, 13.

114. Bona, *The Dreams of St. Francis of Assisi: A Depth Psychology Study*, 158.

115. Bona, *The Dreams of St. Francis of Assisi: A Depth Psychology Study*, 158.

116. J. V. Fleming, *An Introduction to the Franciscan Literature of the Middle Ages*, Chicago, 1977, p. 250.

117. PROGOFF, *Waking Dream and Living Myth*, 176.

118. J. CAMPBELL, quoted in P. COUSINEAU, *Once and Future Myths: The Power of Ancient Stories in Modern Times*, Berkley, 2001, p. 8.

119. DELEHAYE, *The Legends of the Saints*, 5.

120. Cfr. D. BIDNEY, *Myth, Symbolism, and Truth, in Myth: A Symposium*, ed. T. A. Sebeok, Bloomington and London, 1968, p. 21.

121. COUSINEAU, *Once and Future Myths*, 9.

122. Cfr. SHAMKOVICH, *Saintly Hero*, 79.

123. COUSINEAU, *Once and Future Myths*, 9.

124. BIDNEY, *Myth, Symbolism, and Truth*, 3.

125. BIDNEY, *Myth, Symbolism, and Truth*, 3.

126. F. W. J. VON SCHELLING quoted in BIDNEY, *Myth, Symbolism, and Truth*, 6.

127. Cfr. COUSINEAU, *Once and Future Myths*, 10. See also G. B. CAIRD, *The Language and Imagery of the Bible*, London, 1988, p. 221.

128. ALBERTSON, *Anglo-Saxon Saints and Heroes*, 26.

129. COUSINEAU, *Once and Future Myths*, 10.

130. COUSINEAU, *Once and Future Myths*, 10.

131. CAIRD, *The Language and Imagery of the Bible*, 219.

132. R. K. BULTMANN, quoted in CAIRD, *The Language and Imagery of the Bible*, 219.

133. Cfr. CAIRD, *The Language and Imagery of the Bible*, 219.

134. CAIRD, *The Language and Imagery of the Bible*, 224.

135. *LV* IV: 148.

136. *LV* IV: 149-151.

137. *LV* IV:154-155.

138. *LV* IV:160.

139. *LV* IV: 156-163.

140. *LV* IV:183.

141. *LV* XIV:3.

142. Cfr. CAIRD, *The Language and Imagery of the Bible*, 219.

143. Cfr. *Ovid Illustrated: The Renaissance Reception of Ovid in Image and Text*, Internet (22.05.05): http://etext.lib.virginia.edu/latin/ovid/notes.html. The "office of the poet" has been described as the allegorical veiling of the truth.

144. *LV* I:1.

145. E. Hutton, *Some Franciscan Poetry,* in *Dublin Review,* 442 (1948) p. 138.

146. *LV* I: 20. Minerva (Athena in Greek) is the Roman goddess of wisdom and the arts, (especially weaving and spinning) who leaped out of Jupiter's brain in complete armor.

147. *LV* XI: 46.

148. 1C2 *"in cantilenis."* Francis' first reading lessons were most likely the psalms.

149. On his deathbed, Francis summoned Br. Leo and Br. Angelo to sing in a loud voice and with joy, the *Canticle* to him: 1C 109, 2MP 123.

150. E. Leclerc, "Canto" in *Dizionario Franciscano,* a cura di E. Caroli, Padova, 1995, pp. 135.

151. (Translation mine).

152. 2C 7. Cfr. Peterson, *Clare of Assisi,* 1; Spoto, *Reluctant Saint: The Life of Francis of Assisi,* 29, which states that Francis was the leader (*signore*) of the *tripudianti,* a singing and dancing group from Umbria and Tuscany.

153. 1C 115.

154. 2C 7.

155. 1C 86.

156. *LV* VIII: 224.

157. *LV* IX: 14.

158. *LV* XI: 104.

159. 1C 85.

160. Mockler, *Francis of Assisi: The Wandering Years,* 250.

161. AC 65.

162. D. L. Jeffrey, *St. Francis and Medieval Theatre,* in FS, 43 (1983) p. 77.

163. Cfr. P. Loewen, *Francis the Musician and the Mission of the 'Joculatores Domini' in the Medieval German Lands,* in FS, 60 (2002) p. 260.

164. H. G. Pfander, *The Popular Sermon of the Medieval Friar in England,* New York, 1937, p. 6.

165. Cunningham, *St. Francis of Assisi,* 59.

166. RNB 21:1. Francis prefaces the praises he wrote with this instruction: "All my brothers can proclaim this or a like exhortation and praise."

167. Moorman, *History of the Franciscan Order,* 266.

168. Loewen, *Francis the Musician,* 253.

169. LP 43; 2MP 100.

170. 2MP 90. *"quaedam sancta verba cum cantu."*

171. Little, *Franciscan Papers, Lists and Documents*, 3.

172. M. H. C. Hodgart, *Medieval Lyrics and the Ballads*, in *The Pelican Guide to English Literature*, 1969, p. 158. See also B. Roest, *Franciscan Literature of Religious Instruction Before the Council of Trent*, Boston, 2004, p. 276, who states the Waldensians and Humiliati had already begun to exploit penitential songs around 1200.

173. 2MP 101.

174. Loewen, *Francis the Musician*, 260.

175. D. L. Jeffrey, T*he Early English Lyric and Franciscan Spirituality*, Lincoln, 1975, p. 27.

176. G. G. Coulton, *From Francis to Dante: Translations from the Chronicle of the Franciscan Salimben*e, 1221-1288, Philadelphia, 1972, p. 529.

177. Loewen, *Francis the Musician*, 253-254.

178. Cfr. Loewen, *Francis the Musician*, 254.

179. H. Holzapfel, *The History of the Franciscan Order*, trans. A. Tibesar – G. Brinkmann, Teutopolis, 1948, p. 13.

180. Cunningham, *St. Francis of Assisi*, 60.

181. Ohan *The Poverello and the Franciscans*, 31.

182. B. B. Dick, *Jacopone Da Todi and the Poetics of Franciscan Spirituality*, Ph. D. diss., New York University, 1994, p. 90.

183. Loewen, *Francis the Musician*, 253.

184. Loewen, *Francis the Musician*, 251.

185. Loewen, *Francis the Musician*, 253.

186. Cfr. Loewen, *Francis the Musician*, 264.

187. Dick, *Jacopone Da Todi and the Poetics of Franciscan Spirituality*, 91.

188. Dick, *Jacopone Da Todi and the Poetics of Franciscan Spirituality*, 90-91.

189. Loewen, *Francis the Musician*, 253.

190. *LV* IV: 35.

191. *LV* III: 183-184.

192. *LV* III: 187.

193. *LV* IV:5.

194. *LV* IV:11.

195. *LV* IV:13-14.

196. *LV* IV:22-26.

197. *LV* IV:38.

198. *LV* IV:39-40.

199. 1C 16.

200. *LV* IV:41-42.

201. D. L. Jeffrey, *Forms of Spirituality in the Middle English Lyric*, in *Imagination and the Spirit*, ed. C. Huttar, New York, 1971, p. 83. See also Ovid, *Metamorphoses*, XV, which develops the theme of the seasons of man and nature.

202. *LV* IV:47-50. *"Et Christi resonare docet mysteria silvas."*

203. Virgil, *Eclogue* I:5.

204. *LV* IV:55-61.

205. *LV* IV:62-63.

206. 1C 16; *LV* IV:62-63.

207. *LV* IV:117.

208. *LV* IV:120-122.

209. Loewen, *Francis the Musician*, 260.

210. Cheriyapattaparambil, *The Troubadour Influence*, 22.

211. Loewen, *Francis the Musician*, 259.

212. Little, *A Guide to Franciscan Studies*, 279.

213. *LV* XIII: Quatrain.

214. Cfr. Roest, *Franciscan Literature of Religious Instruction Before the Council of Trent*, 277.

215. Moorman, *History of the Franciscan Order*, 270-271.

216. Cfr. Jeffrey, *The Early English Lyric and Franciscan Spirituality*, 32.

217. Some of the meanings and connotations of piety include mercy, loving kindness, goodness, Godliness, faithfulness, holiness, reverence, respect, religion, loyalty, awe, fear of lord, meek, and clemency.

218. J. Dryden, *The Works of John Dryden*, ed. E. N. Hooker – H. T. Swedenberg, Berkeley, 1956, p. 286.

219. *Oxford Latin Dictionary*, pp. 1378, 1384.

220. Cfr. R. MacMullen, *Enemies of the Roman Order: Treason, Unrest and Alienation in the Empire*, Cambridge, 1966. See J. A. Kelly, *Piety*, in *The Cord*, 7 (1965) p. 192. The Romans had a Goddess called Pietas, and

a person was pius if they performed their duties with "reverence, loyalty, obedience and devotion."

221. G. Malsbary, *Pietas and the Origin of Western Culture, in Logos: A Journal of Catholic Thought and Culture,* 4:2 (2001) p. 93.

222. *Theological Dictionary of the New Testament,* ed. G. Kittel – G. Friedrich, Grand Rapids, 1976, p. 177.

223. *"Piety"* in *Encyclopedia of the Early Church,* ed. A. Di Berardino, trans. A. Walford, Cambridge, 1992, p. 687.

224. *LV* I:114. *"pietate paterna."* (Translation mine)

225. *LV* I: 146. (Translation mine)

226. *LV* I: 195. (Translation mine)

227. *LV* III: 77, 83.

228. *LV* III: 122-123. *"gustavi divinae mel pietatis"* (Translation mine)

229. *"Piety"* in *Dictionary of Biblical Theology,* 2nd edition, ed. X. Léon-Dufour, 1995, p. 429.

230. 2 Tm 3:10ff. See also *"Piety"* in *Dictionary of Biblical Theology,* 430.

231. 1 Tm 6:6-7.

232. *LV* IV: 134. *"pietate profusus."*

233. *LV* IV: 135-136.

234. *LV* IV :136-144.

235. *"Piety,"* in *Encyclopedia of the Early Church,* 687. See Js. 1:26-27.

236. 2 Pt. 1:6ff exhorts Christians to wed their endurance to godliness (piety) and their godliness (piety) to their brotherly affection.

237. M. von Galli, *Living our Future: Francis of Assisi and the Church Tomorrow,* trans. M. Sullivan – J. Drury, Chicago, 1972, p. 205.

238. von Galli, *Living our Future: Francis of Assisi and the Church Tomorrow,* 205.

239. von Galli, *Living our Future: Francis of Assisi and the Church Tomorrow,* 205.

240. M. Walsh, *Saint Francis and the Virtue of Reverence,* in *The Cord,* 31 (1981) p. 18

241. Walsh, *Saint Francis and the Virtue of Reverence,* 18.

242. *"Piety,"* in *Dictionary of Biblical Theology,* 430.

243. *"Piety,"* in *Dictionary of Biblical Theology,* 430.

244. Jn. 8:29; 9:31; Hb. 5:7.

245. *LV* IX:1.

246. *LV* II:12.

247. Cfr. *Dictionary of Judaism in the Biblical Period 450 B.C.E. to 600 C.E.*, ed. J. Neusner, Peabody, 1996, p. 485.

248. *Oxford Latin Dictionary*, p. 1378.

249. Cfr. *"Piety,"* in *Dictionary of Biblical Theology,* 430, which defines the Hasidim from the Hebrew for "pious."

250. *Dictionary of Judaism in the Biblical Period 450 B.C.E. to 600 C.E.*, 486.

251. 4 Mac. 5:24.

252. Cfr. *Dictionary of Judaism in the Biblical Period 450 B.C.E. to 600 C.E.*, 486. See 4 Mac. 9:6-7, 24.

253. 4 Mac. 10:20-21.

254. 4 Mac. 12:14.

255. Cfr. *Dictionary of Judaism in the Biblical Period 450 B.C.E. to 600 C.E.*, 487.

256. Cfr. *"Piety,"* in *Dictionary of Biblical Theology*, 429. See Gn. 24:49; Pr. 20:28; Ps. 25:10.

257. *LV* IV: 43-44. (Translation mine)

258. J. D. Garrison, *Piety from Vergil to Dryden*, Pennsylvania, 1992, Preface.

259. H. Tilemann, *Studein zur Individualität des Franziskus von Assisi*, Leipzig-Berlin, 1914, p. 213.

260. A. Harnack, quoted in Felder, *The Ideals of St. Francis of Assisi*, 380.

261. Grandsen, *Virgil*, 4.

262. S. Caramanica, *Pax, Pietas, Humanitas in S. Francesco e Virgilio,* in *Studi Francescani*, 3-4 (1982) p. 351. (Translation mine)

263. Caramanica, *Pax, Pietas, Humanitas in S. Francesco e Virgilio*, 345. (Translation mine)

264. Caramanica, *Pax, Pietas, Humanitas in S. Francesco e Virgilio*, 345. (Translation mine)

265. Garrison, *Piety from Vergil to Dryden*, 11.

266. F. Cairns, *Virgil's Augustan Epic*, Cambridge, 1989, p. 22.

267. *The Oxford Dictionary of the Christian Church*, ed. F. L. Cross – E. A. Livingstone, Oxford, 1997, p. 1702.

268. Malsbary, *Pietas and the Origin of Western Culture*, 94.

269. Malsbary, *Pietas and the Origin of Western Culture*, 95.

270. Malsbary, *Pietas and the Origin of Western Culture*, 95.

271. Garrison, *Piety from Vergil to Dryden*, 2.

272. Garrison, *Piety from Vergil to Dryden*, 2.

273. Malsbary, *Pietas and the Origin of Western Culture*, 109.

274. John of Salisbury, *Polycraticus*, 8:24, quoted in Garrison, *Piety from Vergil to Dryden*, 25.

275. Dante, *Inferno*, 2:4-5, quoted in Garrison, *Piety from Vergil to Dryden*, 2. "The war, both of the journey and the piety." (Translation mine)

276. Garrison, *Piety from Vergil to Dryden*, 2-3.

277. T. S. Eliot, *On Poetry and Poets*, Boston, 1957, p. 127.

278. Eliot, *On Poetry and Poets*, 127.

279. Eliot, *On Poetry and Poets*, 127.

280. Eliot, *On Poetry and Poets*, 128.

281. Garrison, *Piety from Vergil to Dryden*, 91.

282. G. Weigel, *Witness to Hope: The Biography of Pope John Paul II*, New York, 1999, p. 7.

283. Felder, *The Ideals of St. Francis of Assisi*, 380.

284. Felder, *The Ideals of St. Francis of Assisi*, 380.

285. Felder, *The Ideals of St. Francis of Assisi*, 380.

286. Felder, *The Ideals of St. Francis of Assisi*, 380.

287. *Clare of Assisi: Early Documents*, 1:5.

288. J. Aumann, *Spiritual Theology*, London, 1988, p. 293.

289. Aumann, *Spiritual Theology*, 294.

290. Aumann, *Spiritual Theology*, 293.

291. Aumann, *Spiritual Theology*, 293-294.

292. Kelly, *Piety*, 192.

293. Aumann, *Spiritual Theology*, 294-295.

294. J. Pieper, *The Four Cardinal Virtues*, Notre Dame, 1966, p. 108.

295. Aumann, *Spiritual Theology*, 293.

296. Delehaye, *The Legends of the Saints*, 15.

297. *LV* IV: 4.

298. *LV* IV: 80.

299. *LV* IV: 35.

300. *LV* III: 95.

301. *LV* III: 23. (Translation mine)

302. *LV* III: 24. (Translation mine)

303. *LV* VI: 85-91.

304. *LV* VI: 92-95.

305. Cfr. Russell, *Master Henry Avranches*,152. See also Russell, MHAIP, 39.

306. Cfr. *LV* I:151-152.

307. *LV* I: 155-159.

308. *LV* III: 177.

309. *LV* III: 171-176.

310. *LV* VIII: 153.

311. *LV* VIII: 155.

312. *LV* VIII: 157.

313. *LV* VIII: 157.

314. *LV* VIII: 159.

315. Cfr. Allen, *The Metrical Passio*, 382. Lines 59-68.

316. Cfr. Allen, *The Metrical Passio*, 383. Henry transforms Anselm's debates on redemption.

317. Allen, *The Metrical Passio*, 364.

318. Binkley, *13th Century Latin Poetry Contests*, 130.

319. *LV* I: 165.

320. *LV* I: 167.

321. *LV* I: 162.

322. *LV* I: 164.

323. *LV* I: 166.

324. *LV* V: 32-36.

Conclusion

1. Cfr. Townsend, *An Edition of Saint's Lives*, 352; See also Townsend - Rigg, MLPA (V), 179. From 1243-1260, Henry received payment from Henry III.

2. V. D. Scudder, *The Franciscan Adventure: A Study of the First Hundred Years of the Order of St. Francis of Assisi*, London and Toronto, 1931, p. 29.

3. Mockler, *Francis of Assisi*, 250. Before joining the friars, Br. Pacifico

composed wanton songs and was crowned by the Emperor as *"Rex Versum."* See also D. JEFFEREY, *Forms of Spirituality in the Middle English Lyric,* in *Imagination and the Spirit,* ed. C. Huttar, New York, 1971, p. 77.

4. GODET-CALOGERAS, *Don't Forget the Poet,* 29.
5. GODET-CALOGERAS, *Don't Forget the Poet,* 29.
6. *American Heritage Dictionary.*
7. J. CAMPBELL, *The Hero with a Thousand Faces,* 2nd ed. Princeton, 1968, pp. 390-391.
8. ER XVI: 5.
9. ER XVI: 7.
10. Adm. 10:2-3.
11. *LV* V:99-102.

Bibliography

Primary Latin Sources and Editions

ABRINCENSIS H., *Legenda Versificata: S. Francisci Assisiensis,* in AF, X, Quaracchi, 1936, pp. 405-521.

CREMASCOLI G., *Henrici Abrincensis Legenda Sancti Francisci Versificata,* in *Fontes Franciscani,* Assisi, 1995, pp. 1131-1206.

Fontes Francescani, a cura di E. Menesto' – S. Brufani – G. Cremascoli – E. Paoli – L. Pelligrini – S. Da Campagnola, S. Maria degli Angeli-Assisi, 1995.

CRISTOFANI A., *Il più antico poema della vita di San Francesco d'Assisi, scritto innanzi all'anno 1230,* Prato, 1882.

D'ALENÇON E., *Il più antico poema di vita S. Francesco,* in MF, 4 (1889) pp. 33-35.

__________, *Sul più antico poema di Vita S. Francesco,* in MF, 5 (1890) pp. 73-76.

__________, *Sul più antico poema di Vita S. Francesco,* in MF, 6 (1895) pp. 26-31.

FRANCIS OF ASSISI, *Opuscula Sancti Patris Francisci Assisiensis,* ed. C. Esser, Roma, 1978.

GREGORY IX, *Caput Draconis,* in *Sequentiae in Honorem S. Francisci,* in AF, X, Quaracchi, 1936, pp. 401-404.

THOMAS OF CELANO, *Sanctitas Nova Signa,* in *Sequentiae in Honorem S. Francisci,* Quaracchi, in AF, X (1936) pp. 402-403.

__________, *Fregit Victor,* in *Sequentiae in Honorem S. Francisci,* in AF, X, Quaracchi, 1936, pp. 403-404.

Modern Biographies

CHESTERTON G. K., *Saint Francis of Assisi,* New York, 1990.

CUNNINGHAM, L. S., *St. Francis of Assisi,* Boston, 1976.

ENGLEBERT O., *Saint Francis of Assisi,* trans. E. Hutton, London, 1950.

FELDER, H., *The Knight-Errant of Assisi,* Youngstown, 1982.

FORTINI A., *Francis of Assisi,* trans. H. Moak, New York, 1980.

GREEN J., *God's Fool,* trans. P. Heinegg, New York, 1985.

HOLL A., *The Last Christian,* trans. P. Heinegg, New York, 1980.

HOUSE A., *Francis of Assisi: A Revolutionary Life,* Mahwah, 2001.

LE GOFF J., *Saint Francis of Assisi,* trans. C. Rhone, London, 2004.

MANSELLI R., *St. Francis of Assisi,* Chicago, 1988.

MOCKLER A., *Francis of Assisi: The Wandering Years,* Oxford, 1976.

SABATIER P., *Life of St. Francis,* trans. L. S. Houghton, New York, 1920.

SPOTO D., *Reluctant Saint: The Life of Francis of Assisi,* New York, 2003.

Primary Translations:

D'AVRANCHES H., *The Versified Life of Saint Francis,* in FAED: *The Saint,* vol. 1, 1999, p. 428-520.

Fonti Francescane, Assisi, 1986.

Francis of Assisi, *Francis and Clare: The Complete Works,* ed. R. J. Armstrong – I. C. Brady, New York, 1982.

Francis of Assisi: Early Documents, 3 vols., ed. R. J. Armstrong – J. A. W. Hellmann – W. Short, New York, 1999-2001.

St. Francis of Assisi: Writings and Early Biographies: English Omnibus of the Sources for the Life of St. Francis, ed. M. A. Habig, Chicago, 1983.

Shanahan G., *Henry of Avranches: Poem on the Life of Saint Francis (Legenda Sancti Francisci Versificata),* in FS, 48 (1988) pp.125-212.

Townsend D. R., *An Edition of Saint's Lives attributed to Henry Avranches,* Ph. D. diss., University of Toronto, 1985.

__________, *The 'Versus de corona spinea' of Henry of Avranches, in Mittellateinisches Jahrbuch,* 23 (1988) pp. 154-170.

__________, *Henry Avranches: Vita Sancti Oswaldi,* in MS, 56 (1994) pp. 1-65.

__________, *From Henry of Avranches's 'Vita beati Francisci': A likeness in Verse, in Anglo-Latin and its Heritage: Essays in Honor of A. G. Rigg on His 64th Birthday,* Publications of the Journal of Medieval Latin, ed. S. Echard – G. Wieland, 2001, pp. 149-162.

Other Sources and Translations:

Bund K., *Die 'Prophetin', ein Dichter und die Niederlassung der Bettelorden in Köln,* in *Mittellateinisches Jahrbuch,* 23 (1988) pp. 171-260.

Clare of Assisi Early Documents, ed. and trans. R. J. Armstrong, New York, 1988.

The Chronicle of Salimbene de Adam, trans. J. L. Baird – J. Baglivi – J. R. Lane, New York, 1986.

Dante Alighieri, *La Divina Commedia*, Roma, 1972.

Gregory of Tours, *Liber Vitae Patrum*, in *Monumenta Germaniae Historica: Scriptores Rerum Merovingicarum*, ed. B. Krusch, Hanover, 1920.

John of Salisbury, *Metalogicon*, trans. D. D. McGarry, Berkley, 1955.

Prudentius, *The Spiritual Combat: Psychomachia*, in *The Poems of Prudentius*, vol. 2 of *The Fathers of the Church*, ed. R. J. Deferrari, Washington, D.C., 1965, pp. 79-110.

The Song of Roland, New York, 2002.

Virgil, *Aeneid*, trans. D. West, England, 2003.

Weigel G., *Witness to Hope: The Biography of Pope John Paul II*, New York, 1999.

Reference Works:

Aquinas T., *Introduction to St. Thomas Aquinas: Summa Theologica*, ed. A. C. Pegis, New York, 1948.

Biblia Sacra: Iuxta Vulgatam Versionem, Stuttgart, ed. R. Weber, 1983.

Dictionary of Biblical Theology, 2nd edition, ed. X. Léon-Dufour, 1995.

Dictionary of Judaism in the Biblical Period 450 B.C.E. to 600 C.E, ed. J. Neusner, Peabody, 1996.

Dizionario Franciscano, a cura di E. Caroli, Padova, 1995.

Encyclopedia of the Early Church, ed. A. Di Berardino, trans. A.

Walford, Cambridge, 1992.

The Norton Anthology of Poetry, 4th ed., ed. M. Ferguson – M. J. Salter – J. Stallworthy, New York, 1996.

Oxford Latin Dictionary, ed. P. G. W. Glare, Oxford, 1996.

The Oxford Dictionary of the Christian Church, ed. F. L. Cross – E. A. Livingstone, Oxford, 1997.

Theological Dictionary of the New Testament, ed. G. Kittel – G. Friedrich, 10 vols., Grand Rapids, 1976.

Thesaurus Celanensis: Corpus Des Sources Franciscaines, ed. G. Mailleux, vol. 1 Louvain, 1974.

Studies:

ABATE G., *La casa natale di S. Francesco*, Rome, 1966.

ABOU-EL-HAJ B., *The Medieval Cult of Saints: Formations and Transformations*, Cambridge, 1994.

ACCROCCA F., *Some Knotty Problems in the Franciscan Sources: Two Recent Editions*, in GR, 11 (1997) pp. 143-183.

ADKIN N., *The Proem of Henry of Avranches' Vita Sancti Guthlaci*, in AB, 108 (1990) pp. 349-355.

ALBERTSON C., *Anglo Saxon Saints and Heroes*, Fordham, 1967.

ALLEN M. I., *The Metrical Passio Sanctorum Crispini Et Crispiniani of Henry of Avranches*, in AB, 108 (1990) pp. 357-386.

ALTMAN C. F., *Two Types of Opposition and the Structure of Saints' Lives*, in *Medievalia Et Humanistica*, 6 (1975) pp. 1-11.

ARMSTRONG E. A., *Saint Francis Nature Mystic: The Derivation and Significance of the Nature Stories in the Franciscan Legend*, Berkley, 1973.

ARNOLD P., *Wildmen, Warriors and Kings: Masculine Spirituality and the Bible*, New York, 1991.

ARMSTRONG R. J., *St Francis of Assisi: Writings for a Gospel Life*, New York, 1994.

AUMANN J., *Spiritual Theology*, London, 1988.

BALDWIN C. S., *Medieval Rhetoric and Poetic*, Gloucester, 1959.

BARBER M., *The Trial of the Templars*, Cambridge, 1987.

BARTOLI M., *Clare of Assisi*, trans. F. Teresa, Quincy, 1993.

BEQUETTE J. P. A., *Constructing an Image of St. Francis: A Rhetorical Investigation of Thomas of Celano's Vita Prima Sancti Francisci*, Ph. D. diss., Saint Louis University, St. Louis, 2001.

BIDNEY D., *Myth, Symbolism, and Truth, in Myth: A Symposium*, ed. T. A. Sebeok, Bloomington and London, 1968, pp. 3-24.

BIHL M., *De Legenda Versificata S. Francisci auctore Henrico Abrincensi*, in AFH, 22 (1929) pp. 3-53.

__________, *Sancti Francisci parabola in sermonibus Odonis de Ceritonia a. 1219 conscriptis*, in AFH, 20 (1927) pp. 584-586.

__________, *De Nomine S. Francisci*, in AFH, 19 (1919) pp. 469-529.

BINKLEY P., MLPA (VI): *The Cotton Anthology of Henry of Avranches (B. L. Cotton Vespasian D.V., fols. 151-184)*, in MS, 52 (1990) pp. 221-254.

__________, *13th Century Latin Poetry Contests Associated With Henry of Avranches with appendix - new edited texts*, Ph. D. diss., University of Toronto, Toronto, 1991.

BLOOMFIELD M. W., *A Grammatical Approach to Personification*

Allegory, in *Essays and Explorations*, New York, 1970, pp. 243-260.

BLOOMFIELD M. W. - DUNN C. W., *The Role of the Poet in Early Societies*, Cambridge, 1989.

BLOWEY D., *The Paternity of God in the 'Writings' of Francis of Assisi*, in MF, 98 (1998) pp. 289-347.

BOLTON B., *Too Important to Neglect: The Gesta Innocentii PP III, in Church and Chronicle in the Middle Ages: Essays Presented to John Taylor*, ed. I. Wood – G. A. Loud, London, 1991, pp. 85-99.

BONA D., *The Dreams of St. Francis of Assisi: A Depth Psychology Study*, Ph. D. diss., Pacifica Graduate Institute, 1996.

BOUYER L., *Introduction to Spirituality*, trans. M. P. Ryan, New York, 1961.

BOWRA C. M., *Heroic Poetry*, London, 1952.

__________, *From Virgil to Milton*, London, 1945.

BOYER R., *An Attempt to Define the Typology of Medieval Hagiography*, in *Hagiography and Medieval Literature: A Symposium*, Odense, 1981, pp. 27-36.

BRITTAIN F., *The Medieval Latin and Romance Lyric to A.D. 1300*, Cambridge, 1937.

BROWN R., *The Roots of St. Francis*, Chicago, 1982.

BRUCKNER M. T., *The Shape of Romance in Medieval France*, in *The Cambridge Companion to Medieval Romance*, ed. R. L. Krueger, Cambridge, 2000, pp. 13-28.

BULFINCH T., *The Age of Chivalry*, New York, 1965.

BULKELEY K., *The Wilderness of Dreams: Exploring the Religious*

Meaning of Dreams in Modern Western Culture, New York, 1994.

Bumke J., *The Concept of Knighthood in the Middle Ages,* trans. W. T. H. – E. Jackson, New York, 1982.

Burman E., *The Templars: Knights of God,* Rochester, 1986.

Caird G. B., *The Language and Imagery of the Bible,* London, 1988.

Cairns F., *Virgil's Augustan Epic,* Cambridge, 1989.

Campbell J., *The Hero with a Thousand Faces,* 2nd ed. Princeton, 1968.

Cantor N. F., *The Civilization of the Middle Ages,* New York, 1994.

Caramanica S., *Pax, Pietas, Humanitas in S. Francesco e Virgilio,* in *Studi Francescani,* 3-4 (1982) pp. 343-356.

Cardini F., *The Warrior and the Knight,* in *Medieval Callings,* ed. J. Le Goff, trans. L. G. Cochrane, Chicago, 1987, pp. 75-111.

__________, *S. Francesco e Il Sogno Delle Armi,* in *Studi Francescani,* 1-2 (1980) pp. 15-28.

__________, *L'avventura di un cavaliere di Cristo: Appunti per uno studio sulla cavalleria nella spiritualità di S. Francesco, in Studi Francescani,* 1-2 (1976) pp. 127-198.

Carlson D., *Religious Writers and Church Councils,* in *The Study of Chivalry: Resources and Approaches,* ed. H. Chickering – T. H. Seiler, Kalamazoo, 1988, pp. 141-171.

Carpenter D., *The Minority of Henry III,* in *History Today,* 40 (1990) pp. 9-14.

Charron J., *Da Narciso a Gesù,* Padova, 1995.

Chenu M. D., *La théologie au XII siècle,* Paris, 1957.

CHERIYAPATTAPARAMBIL F. A., *The Troubadour Influence in the Life and Writings of the Man Saint of Assisi*, Ph. D. diss., Antonianum, Roma, 1985.

CHOOI F., *A Psychobiographical Approach to Interpreting Hagiography: An Exploratory Case Study of St. Francis of Assisi*, Ph. D. diss., University of California, Berkeley, 1984.

COLEIRO E., *St. Jerome's Lives of the Hermits*, in *Vigilia Christianae*, II (1957) pp. 161-178.

COLISH M. L., *Medieval Foundations of the Western Intellectual Tradition 400-1400*, New Haven and London, 2002.

CONDON D. G., *Christian Spiritual Dimensions of the Psychology of Carl Gustav Jung With Special reference to His Use of Dreams*, Excerpta ex Dissertatione ad Doctoratum, Gregorian University, Rome, 2001.

COOK L. K., *Francis of Assisi and the Thirteenth-Century Papacy*, MA. diss., Baylor University, Waco, 1978.

COTTON W. T., *Teaching the Motifs of Chivalric Biography*, in *The Study of Chivalry: Resources and Approaches*, ed. H. Chickering – T. H. Seiler, Kalamazoo, 1988, pp. 583-609.

COULTON G. G., *From Francis to Dante: Translations from the Chronicle of the Franciscan Salimbene, 1221-1288*, Philadelphia, 1972.

COUSINEAU P., *Once and Future Myths: The Power of Ancient Stories in Modern Times*, Berkley, 2001.

CRAWFORD L. A., *The Warrior-Saint and the Old French Hagiographic Epic*, 1050-1250, Ph. D. diss., Princeton University, 1991.

CREMASCOLI G., *I classici nella 'Legenda sancti Francisci versificata' di Enrico di Avranches, in Studi Medievali*, 40 (1999) pp. 523-534.

Da Campagnola S., *Francesco D'Assisi nei suoi scritti e nelle sue biografie dei secoli XIII-XIV,* Assisi, 1981.

D'Angelo B., *Poesia francescana inglese prima di Geoffrey Chaucer (1340?-1400),* in AFH, 75 (1982) pp. 320-361.

Dalarun J., *The Misadventures of Francis of Assisi,* trans. E. Hagman, New York, 2002.

Deanesly M., *A History of the Medieval Church: 590-1500,* Cambridge, 1989.

De Beer F., *St. Francis and Islam,* in *Francis of Assisi Today,* ed. C. Duquoc – C. Floritan, New York, 1981, pp. 11-20.

Delehaye P. H., *The Legends of Saints: An Introduction to Hagiography,* trans. D. Attwater, Dublin, 1983.

__________, *Les légendes grecques des saints militaires,* New York, 1975.

__________, *Les légendes Hagiogaphiques,* 4th ed., Paris, 1955.

Della Penna M., *The Icon of Saint Francis Depicted in Henry of Avranches' Legenda Versificata,* STL, Antonianum, 2003.

del Mastro M. L., *The Military Analogy in Early Anglo-Latin Hagiography,* Ph. D. diss., Fordham University, 1973.

Dembowski P. F., *Literary Problems of Hagiography in Old French, in Medievalia Et Humanistica,* 7 (1976) pp. 117-130.

Dick B. B., *Jacopone Da Todi and the Poetics of Franciscan Spirituality,* New York University, Ph. D. diss., New York University, 1994.

Diem A., *Virtues and Vices in Early Texts on Pastoral Care,* in FS, 62 (2004) pp. 193-223.

Di Fronzo L., *Lodi e Canto di S. Francesco al "Bon Signore" per la fraternità e nella vita*, in MF, 102 (2002) pp. 473-491.

Dionisotti A. C., *Walter of Châtillon and the Greeks*, in *Latin Poetry and the Classical Tradition: Essays in Medieval and Renaissance Literature*, ed. P. Godman – O. Murray, Oxford, 1990, pp. 73-96.

Domenichelli T., *La 'Leggenda versificata' o il più antico poema di San Francesco*, in AFH, I (1908) pp. 209-216.

Dryden J., *The Works of John Dryden*, ed. E. N. Hooker – H. T. Swedenberg, Berkeley, 1956.

Duby G., *Le temps des cathédrales. L'art et la société 980-1420*, Paris, 1976.

Eissfeldt O., *The Old Testament: An Introduction*, Oxford, 1966.

Eliade M., *Myths, Dreams and Mysteries: The Encounter Between Contemporary Faiths and Archaic Realities*, trans. P. Mairet, New York, 1960.

__________, *Traite d'histoire des religions*, Paris, 1949.

Eliot T. S., *On Poetry and Poets*, Boston, 1957.

Elliott A. G., *Roads to Paradise: Reading the Lives of the Early Saints*, Hanover and London, 1987.

Erickson J. M., *Saint Francis and His Four Ladies*, New York, 1970.

Everett D., *Essays on Middle English Literature*, Oxford, 1955.

Fanger C., *Signs of Power and the Power of Signs: Medieval Modes of Address to the Problem of Magical and Miraculous Signifiers*, Ph. D. diss., University of Toronto, 1993.

Fawcett T., *The Symbolic Language of Religion*, Minneapolis, 1971.

FELDER H., *The Ideals of St. Francis of Assisi*, trans. B. Bittle, Quincy, Illinois, 1998.

FLEMING J. V., *An Introduction to the Franciscan Literature of the Middle Ages*, Chicago, 1977.

FORTINI A., *La lauda in Assisi e le origini del teatro italiano*, Assisi, 1961.

FORTINI G., *The Noble family of St. Clare*, in FS, 13 (1982) pp. 48-67.

FOSS M., *Chivalry*, Great Britain, 1975.

Francis of Assisi: History, Hagiography and Hermeneutics in the Early Documents, ed. J. M. Hammond, New York, 2004.

FREUD S., *The Complete Psychological Works of Sigmund Freud*, vol. 5, London, 1953.

GALLANT L. - CIRINO A., *The Office of the Passion of St. Francis of Assisi: The Geste of the Great King*, Phoenix, 2012.

GARRISON J. D., *Piety from Vergil to Dryden*, Pennsylvania, 1992.

GELBER H. G., *Revisiting the Theater of Virtue*, in FS, 58 (2000) pp. 19-36.

GEROULD G. H., *Saint's Legend's*, Boston, 1916.

GIBBS M. - LANG J., *Bishops Reform 1215-1272: With Special Reference to the Lateran Council of 1215*, Oxford, 1962.

GIES F., *The Knight in History*, New York, 1984.

GIES J., *Life in a Medieval City*, New York, 1981.

GODET-CALOGERAS J. F., *Don't Forget the Poet*, in *Haversack*, 21 (1998) pp. 29-37.

GOLD P. S., *The Lady and the Virgin: Image, Attitude, and*

Experience in Twelfth-Century France, Chicago, 1985.

GRANDSEN K. W., *Virgil: The Aeneid*, Cambridge, 1990.

GRAU E., *Thomas of Celano: Life and Work*, in GR, 8 (1994) pp. 177-200.

GRÉGOIRE R., *Manuale di Agiologia: Introduzione alla Letteratura Agiografica*, Fabriano, 1987.

GROSJEAN P., *Magister Henricus de Abrincis Archipoeta, in Dublin Studies*, 17 (1928) pp. 295-308.

HADAS M. - SMITH M., *Heroes and Gods: Spiritual Biographies in Antiquity*, New York, 1965.

HAHN C., *Portrayed on the Heart: Narrative Effect in Pictorial Lives of the Saints from the Tenth through the Thirteenth Century*, California, 2001.

HALL C. S., *What People Dream About, in Scientific American*, 184 (1951) pp. 60-63.

HEFFERNAN T. J., *Sacred Biography: Saints and their Biographies in the Middle Ages*, Oxford, 1988.

HEIRONIMUS J. P. - RUSSELL J. C., *The Shorter Latin Poems of Master Henry Avranches Relating to England*, Cambridge, Mass., 1935.

__________, *The Grammatical Works of Master Henry of Avranches*, in *Philological Quarterly*, 8 (1929) pp. 21-38.

HERBST T. J., The *Humanization of Christ in the Central Italian Panel Crucifixes of the Twelfth and Thirteenth-Centuries Reflected in the Development of Franciscan Christology*, MA. Thesis, Berkley, 1989.

HIGHET G., *The Classical Tradition: Greek and Roman Influences on Western Literature*, Oxford, 1967.

HODGART M. H. C., *Medieval Lyrics and the Ballads*, in *The Pelican Guide to English Literature*, 1969.

HOLZAPFEL H., *The History of the Franciscan Order*, trans. A. Tibesar – G. Brinkmann, Teutopolis, 1948.

HOWE J., *Hagiographic Handbooks*, in *Catholic Historical Review*, 80 (1994) pp. 757-761.

HUBBLE E. A., T*he Borrowed Knight. Representing the Masculine Hero in Twelfth-Century French Verse Romance*, Ph. D. diss., University of Michigan, 2002.

HUIZINGA J., *Homo Ludens: A Study of the Play-Element in Culture*, Boston, 1955.

HUNT T., *The Emergence of the Knight in France and England 1000-1200*, in *Knighthood in Medieval Literature*, ed. W. H. Jackson, Suffolk, 1981, pp. 1-22.

HURLEY M., *Saints, Legends and Romance Again: Secularization of Structure and Motif*, in *Genre*, 8 (1975) pp. 60-73.

HUTTON E., *Some Franciscan Poetry*, in *Dublin Review*, 442 (1948) pp. 138-142.

__________, *The Franciscans in England 1224-1538*, Boston, 1926.

IAMMARONE G., *La Spiritualità Francescana: Anima e contenuti fondamentali*, Padova, 1993.

JAEGER C. S., *Courtliness and Social Change*, in *Cultures of Power: Lordship, Status, and Process in the Twelfth Century Europe*, ed. T. N. Bisson, Philadelphia, 1995, pp. 287-309.

JEFFREY D. L., *St. Francis and Medieval Theatre*, in FS, 43 (1983) pp. 321-346.

__________, *The Early English Lyric and Franciscan Spirituality*,

Lincoln, 1975.

__________, *Forms of Spirituality in the Middle English Lyric*, in *Imagination and the Spirit*, ed. C. Huttar, New York, 1971.

JOHNSON R. F., *Archangel in the Margins: St. Michael in the Homilies of Cambridge Corpus Christi College*, in *Traditio*, 53 (1998) pp. 63-91.

JUNG C., *Civilization in Transition* in *Collected Works*, ed. H. Read – M. Fordham – G. Adler – W. McGuire, trans. R. F. C. Hull, Princeton, 1964, pp. 304-305.

KAEUPER R. W., *Chivalry and Violence in Medieval Europe*, Oxford, 1999.

KAY S., *Courts, Clerks and Courtly Love*, in *The Cambridge Companion to Medieval Romance*, ed. R. L. Krueger, Cambridge, 2000, pp. 81-86.

KEEN M., *Chivalry*, New Haven and London, 1984.

KEISER E. B. - WHEELER B., *Chivalry: From Footnote to Foreground, in The Study of Chivalry: Resources and Approaches*, ed. H. Chickering – T. H. Seiler, Kalamazoo, 1988, pp. 115-138.

KELLER H., *Changes in Old French Epic Poetry and Changes in the Tastes of its Audience*, in *The Epic in Medieval Society*, ed. H. Scholler, Tubingen, 1977.

KELLY J. A., *Piety*, in *The Cord*, 7 (1965) pp. 189-194.

KER W. P., *Epic and Romance, Essays on Medieval Literature*, New York, 1957.

KERBY-FULTON K., *Hildegard of Bingen and Anti-Mendicant Propaganda*, in *Traditio*, 43 (1987) pp. 386-399.

KIRK G. S., *The Nature of Greek Myths*, Great Britain, 1974.

KNIGHT S., *The Social Function of the Middle English Romances*, in *Medieval Literature: Criticism, Idealogy and History*, ed. D. Aers, 1986, pp. 99-121.

KRUGER S. F., *Dreaming in the Middle Ages*, Cambridge, 1992.

KURUSUMMOOTIL V., *The Religious Experience of St. Francis*, in *Jeevadhara*, 37 (1977) pp. 514-535.

LADNER G. B., *The Life of the Mind in the West Around 1200*, in *Images and Ideas in the Middle Ages: Selected Studies in History and Art*, Vol. II, Roma, 1983, pp. 903-929.

LAFFERTY M. K., *Walter of Châtillon's Alexandreis: Epic and the Problem of Historical Understanding*, Belgium, 1998.

__________, *Reading Latin Epic: Walter of Châtillon's Alexandreis*, Ph. D. diss., University of Toronto, Toronto, 1992.

LAISTER M. L., *Thoughts and Letters in Western Europe*, 2nd ed., Ithaca, 1957.

LAPSANSKI D., The *Chartula of St. Francis of Assisi*, in AFH, 67 (1974) pp. 18-37.

LECLERC E., "Canto" in *Dizionario Franciscano*, a cura di E. Caroli, Padova, 1995, pp. 135-136.

LECLERQ D. J. - VANDENBROUCKE D. F. - BOUYER L., *The Spirituality of the Middle Ages*, London, 1968.

LE GOFF J., *The Medieval Imagination*, trans. A. Goldhammer, Chicago and London, 1988.

__________, *Saint Francis, Medieval or Modern?*, in *St. Francis of Assisi: Essays in Commemoration, 1982*, ed. M. W. Sheehan, St. Bonaventure, 1982, pp. 13-24.

__________, *Francis of Assisi between the Renewals and Restraints of Feudal Society*, in *Francis of Assisi Today*, ed. C. Duquoc –

C. Floritan, New York, 1981, pp. 3-10.

LEHMANN L., *The Salutation of the Virtues,* in GR, 11 (1997) pp. 229-241.

__________, *"We Thank You": The Structure and Content of Chapter 23 of the Earlier Rule,* in GR, 5 (1991) pp. 1-54.

LEWRY P. O., *Papal Ideals and the University of Paris,* in *The Religious Role of the Papacy: Ideals and Realities 1150-1300,* ed. C. Ryan, Toronto, 1989, pp. 363-388.

LIFSHITZ F., *Beyond Positivism and Genre,* in *Viator: Medieval and Renaissance Studies,* 25 (1994) pp. 95-113.

LINDBLOM J., *Prophecy in Ancient Israel,* Oxford, 1962.

LITTLE A. G., *Franciscan Papers, Lists and Documents,* Manchester, 1943.

__________, *A Guide to Franciscan Studies,* London-New York, 1920.

LOEWEN P., *Francis the Musician and the Mission of the 'Joculatores Domini' in the Medieval German Lands,* in FS, 60 (2002) pp. 251-290.

MACMULLEN R., *Enemies of the Roman Order: Treason, Unrest and Alienation in the Empire,* Cambridge, 1966.

MAGENNIS H., *Warrior Saints, Warfare, and the Hagiography of Aelfric of Eynsham,* in *Traditio,* 56 (2000-2001) pp. 27-51.

MALSBARY G., *Pietas and the Origin of Western Culture,* in *Logos: A Journal of Catholic Thought and Culture,* 4:2 (2001) pp. 93-116.

MANN H. K., *The Lives of the Popes in the Middle Ages,* London, 1932.

MANSELLI R., *Francesco e i suoi compagni*, Roma, 1995.

__________, *The Spirituality of St. Francis of Assisi*, in GR, 3 (1989) pp. 43-54.

__________, *San Francesco e l'eresia*, in *In ricordo di Zelina Zafarana: Annali della Facoltà di Lettere e Filosofia dell'Università di Siena*, Roma, 1984.

MARTIGNETTI R. S., *Saint Bonaventure's Tree of Life: Theology of the Mystical Journey*, Roma, 2004.

MATTOON M. A., *Understanding Dreams*, Dallas, 1986.

MAYESKI M. A., *New Voices in the Tradition: Medieval Hagiography Revisited*, in *Theological Studies*, 63 (2002) pp. 690-710.

MEIER C. A., *The Meaning and Significance of Dreams*, Boston, 1987.

MEISEL A. C. - DEL MASTRO M. L., *The Rule of St. Benedict*, New York, 1975.

METER G., *Walter of Châtillon's Alexandreis Book 10- A Commentary*, Frankfurt, 1991.

MICCOLI G., *The Writings of St. Francis*, in GR, 15 (2001) pp. 135-170.

MICÓ J., *The Spirituality of St. Francis: With Clean Hearts*, in GR, 8 (1994) pp. 267-301.

__________, *The Spirituality of St. Francis: The Gospel Life*, in GR, 7 (1993) pp. 271-297.

__________, *The Spirituality of St. Francis*, in GR, 7 (1993) pp. 1-26.

MILLER J. E., *Dreams and Prophetic Visions*, in *Biblica*, 71 (1990) pp. 401-404.

MONCRIEFF A. R., *Romance and Legend of Chivalry: Myths and Legends*, London, 1994.

MONTORSI G. B., *Francesco D'Assisi: maestro di vita*, Padova, 1983.

MOORMAN J., *A History of the Franciscan Order*, Oxford, 1998.

__________, *The Sources For the Life of St. Francis of Assisi*, Manchester, 1966.

MULHOLLAND S., *The Canticle of Creatures: A Reflection on Creative and Artistic Influences*, in *The Cord*, 51 (2001) pp. 228-233.

__________, *St. Francis and the Themes of Medieval Literature*, in *The Cord*, 44 (1994) pp. 109-117.

__________, *St. Francis as Dramatist and Poet*, in *The Cord*, 38 (1988) pp. 339-343.

MÜLLER L., *The Theological Significance of a Critical Attitude in Hagiography*, in *Ecumenical Review*, 15 (1963) pp. 279-282.

MURPHY J. J., *Rhetoric in the Middle Ages: A History of Rhetorical Theory From Augustine to the Renaissance*, California, 1974.

NAVONE J., *Enjoying God's Beauty*, Collegeville, 1999.

NGUYÊN-VAN-KHANH N., *The Teacher of His Heart: Jesus Christ in the Thought and Writings of St. Francis*, trans. E. Hagman, St. Bonaventure, 1994.

NICHOLSON D., The *Mysticism of Saint Francis of Assisi*, London, 1923.

NOBLE T. - HEAD T., *Soldiers of Christ: Saints and Saint's Lives from Late Antiquity and the Early Middle Ages*, University Park, 1995.

NOLTHENIUS H., *Un uomo dalla valle di Spoleto: Francesco tra i suoi contemporanei*, Padova, 1991.

OHAN C. A., *The Poverello and the Franciscans: Religious and Artistic Transformations in Thirteenth-Century Italy,* Ph. D. diss., University of Texas, 1997.

OLIGER L., *S. Franciscus Cognovitne Pseudo-Turpinum,* in *Antonianum,* 2 (1927) pp. 277-280.

OUSPENSKY L. - LOSSKY V., *The Meaning of Icons,* Crestwood, 1982.

PACIOCCO R. - ACCROCCA F., *La Leggenda di un Santo di Nome Francisco,* Milano, 1999.

PÁSZTOR E., *San Francesco e Il Cardinale Ugolino Nella "Questione Francescana,"* in *Collectanea Francescana,* 46 (1976) pp. 209-239.

PELLIGRINI L., *A Century of Reading the Sources,* in GR, 7 (1993) pp. 323-346.

PERNOUD R., *Lumière du moyen-âge,* Paris, 1944.

PETERSON I. J., *Clare of Assisi: A Biographical Study,* Illinois, 1993.

PFANDER H. G., *The Popular Sermon of the Medieval Friar in England,* New York, 1937.

PIEPER, J., *The Four Cardinal Virtues,* Notre Dame, 1966.

PRAWLER J., T*he Latin Kingdom of Jerusalem: European Colonization in the Middle Ages,* London, 1972.

PRINZIVALLI E., *A Saint to be Read: Francis of Assisi in the Hagiographic Sources,* in GR, 15 (2001) pp. 253-298.

PROGOFF I., *Waking Dream and Living Myth,* in *Myths, Dreams and Religion,* ed. J. Campbell, New York, 1970, pp. 176-195.

RABY F. J. E., *A History of Secular Latin Poetry in the Middle Ages,* Oxford, 1957.

__________, *A History of Christian-Latin Poetry: From the Beginnings to the Close of the Middle Ages*, 2nd ed., Oxford, 1953.

RAHNER K., *Visions and Prophecies*, Montreal, 1963.

RAMPTON M., *Francis as Troubadour*, in *The Cord*, 40 (1990) pp. 295-303.

RICHARDS I. A., *The Philosophy of Rhetoric*, New York, 1965.

RIGG A. G., *Henry of Avranches*, in *A History of Anglo-Latin Literature 1066-1422*, Cambridge, 1992, pp. 179-193.

__________, *Michael of Cornwall*, in *A History of Anglo-Latin Literature 1066-1422*, Cambridge, 1992, pp. 193-197.

RIGG A. G. - BINKLEY P., *Two Poetic Debates By Henry of Avranches*, in MS, 62 (2000) pp. 29-67.

RILEY P., *Assisi's Political, Social History: 1175-1225*, in FS, 34 (1974) pp. 393-424.

ROBERTSON D., *The Medieval Saints' Lives: Spiritual Renewal and Old French Literature*, Lexington, 1995.

ROBINSON J. J., *Dungeon, Fire and Sword: The Knights Templar in the Crusades*, New York, 1991.

ROEST, B., *Franciscan Literature of Religious Instruction Before the Council of Trent*, Boston, 2004.

RUSSELL J. C., *Master Henry Avranches*, Ph. D. diss., Harvard University, 1926.

__________, *Master Henry of Avranches as an International Poet*, in *Speculum*, 3 (1928) pp. 34-63.

SANDOR M., *The Popular Preaching of Jacques De Vitry*, Ph. D. diss., University of Toronto, 1993.

SALTER E., *English and International: Studies in the Literature, Art and Patronage of Medieval England*, Cambridge, 1988.

SCHLEIERMACHER F., *On Religion: Speeches to Its Cultured Despisers*, Cambridge, 1988.

SCHMIDT P. G., *The Quotation in Goliardic Poetry: The Feast of Fools and the Goliardic Strophe cum auctoritate*, in *Latin Poetry and the Classical Tradition: Essays in Medieval and Renaissance Literature*, ed. P. Godman – O. Murray, Oxford, 1990, pp. 39-55.

SCHMUCKI O., *St. Francis' Level of Education*, in GR, 10 (1996) pp. 153-170.

__________, *Francis's Devotion toward Mary*, in GR, 5 (1991) pp. 201-232.

__________, *The "Way of Life According to the Gospel" as It was Discovered by St. Francis of Assisi*, in GR, (1995) pp. 1-56.

__________, *Secretum solitudinis*, in *Collectanea Franciscana*, 39 (1969) pp. 5-58.

SCUDDER V. D., *The Franciscan Adventure: A Study of the First Hundred Years of the Order of St. Francis of Assisi*, London and Toronto, 1931.

SHAMKOVICH T. I., *Saintly Hero: Mythological, Epic and Ecclesiastical Perspectives on the Image of the Saint in Medieval Hagiography*, Ph. D. diss., New York State University, 1991.

SHARP D. E., *Franciscan Philosophy in the Thirteenth Century*, Oxford, 1930.

SORRELL R., *Saint Francis of Assisi and Nature: Tradition and Innovation in Western Christian Attitudes Toward the Environment*, New York, 1988.

SOUTHERN R. W., *Western Society and the Church in the Middle Ages*, New York, 1990.

STACEY R., *Nobles and Knights*, in *The New Cambridge Medieval History V: 1198-1300*, Cambridge, 1999, pp. 13-25.

STEVENS J., *Words and Music In the Middle Ages: Song, Narrative, Dance 1050-1350*, in *Cambridge Studies in Music*, Cambridge, 1986.

STICCA S., *Drama and Spirituality in the Middle Ages*, in *Medievalia Et Humanistica*, 4 (1973) pp. 69-87.

The Study of Chivalry: Resources and Approaches, ed. H. Chickering – T. H. Seiler, Kalamazoo, 1988.

TAYLOR H. O., *The Emergence of Christian Culture in the West: The Classical Heritage of the Middle Ages*, New York, 1958.

TEEUWEN M., *The Vocabulary of the Intellectual Life in the Middle Ages*, in *Etudes Sur Le Vocabulaire Intellectuel Du Moyen Age*, Brepols, 2003.

THOMSON J. A. K., *The Classical Background of English Literature*, London, 1962.

THOMSON W. R., *The Image of the Mendicants in the Chronicles of Matthew Paris*, in AFH, 70 (1977) pp. 3-34.

TILEMANN H., *Studein zur Individualität des Franziskus von Assisi*, Leipzig-Berlin, 1914.

TILLIETTE J. Y., *Les modèles du IXe au XIe siècle, d'après le témoignage des récits hagiographiques en vers métriques*, in *Settimane*, 36 (1988) pp. 381-406.

TOPSFIELD L.T., *Troubadours and Love*, Cambridge, 1975.

TOWNSEND D. R. - RIGG A. G., *Medieval Latin Poetic Anthologies (V): Matthew Paris' Anthology of Henry of Avranches (Cambridge,*

University Library MS. Dd. 11.78), in MS, 49 (1987) pp. 352-390.

Uribe F., *Introduzione alle fonti agiografiche di san Francesco e santa Chiara d'Assisi*, Assisi, 2002.

Vaiani C., *La via di Francesco*, Milano, 2001.

van Doornik N. G. M., *Francis of Assisi: A Prophet For Our Time*, trans. B. P. Fasting, USA, 1979.

Vauchez A., *The Saint, in Medieval Callings*, ed. J. Le Goff, trans. L. G. Cochrane, Chicago, 1987, pp. 313-345.

Verger J., *The Universities and Scholasticism*, in *The New Cambridge Medieval History V: 1198-1300*, Cambridge, 1999, pp. 256-276.

Vettori A., *Poets of God: The Rhetoric of Franciscan Prayerful Texts in the Middle Ages*, Ph. D. diss., University of Yale, 1995.

Vitz E. B., *From the Oral to the Written in Medieval and Renaissance Saints Lives*, in *Images of Sainthood in Medieval Europe*, ed. R. Blumenfeld-Kosinski – T. Szell, Ithaca, New York, 1991.

von Galli M., *Living our Future: Francis of Assisi and the Church Tomorrow*, trans. M. Sullivan – J. Drury, Chicago, 1972.

Vorreux D., "Tau," in *Dizionario Franciscano*, a cura di E. Caroli, Padova, 1995, pp. 2003-2012.

__________, *A Franciscan Symbol: The Tau*, trans. M. Archer – P. Lachance, Chicago, 1979.

Walsh M., *Saint Francis and the Virtue of Reverence*, in *The Cord*, 31 (1981) pp. 17-27.

Wasserman J., *The Templars and the Assassins: The Militia of Heaven*, Rochester, 2001.

Wolf A., *Medieval Heroic Traditions and Their Transitions from Orality to Literacy*, in *Vox Intera: Orality and Textuality in the Middle Ages*, ed. A. N. Doane – C. B. Pasternack, Madison, 1991, pp. 67-88.

Wolf K. B., *The Poverty of Riches*, Oxford, 2003.

Wollmering B., *Dreams and Spirituality: An Historical Perspective*, in *Dream Time*, 14 (1997) pp. 6-7.

Zavalloni R., *La Personalità di Francesco D'Assisi: Studio psicologico*, Padova, 1991.

Zen T. G., *I sogni di S. Francesco d'Assisi*, Ph. D. diss., Antonianum, Roma, 1975.

Zweerman T. - van den Goorbergh E., *Respectfully Yours: Signed and Sealed, Francis of Assisi. Aspects of His Authorship and Focuses of His Spirituality*, New York, 2001.

Internet Sources

A. H. Hooker, The Knights Templar: Fact and Fantasy, Internet (06.12.04): http://www.hrshadows.com/library/misck-o/knightstemplar-factandfantasy.php.

Alain de Lille, Internet (22.02.05): http://historymedren.about.com/od/aentries/ a/11_alaindelille.htm.

Aristotle, Nicomachean Ethics, Internet, (05.05.04): http://classics.mit.edu/Aristotle/nicomachaen.html.

Brother Angelo Tancredi from Rieti, Internet (05.05.04): http://www. sanfrancescoassisi. org/index.php?dir=storia&subdir=compagni&lang= eng&url= angelo.htm.

Essays in Medieval Studies, Internet (22.02.05): http://www.illinoismedieval org/ems/VOL4/sweeney.html.

"Goliard." Encyclopædia Britannica. 2004. Encyclopædia Britannica Premium Service, Internet (20.03.04): http://www.britannica.com/eb/article?eu=38041.

Horace, *Art of Poetry,* Internet (05.05.04): http://classicpersuasion.org/pw/horace/ horacepo.htm 99-104.

LoveToKnowFreeOnlineEncyclopedia, Internet (20.03.04): http://90.1911 encyclopedia.org/G/ GO/ GOLIARD.htm.

Medieval Sourcebook: Robert de Courçon: Statutes for the University of Paris, 1215, Internet (14.02.05):http://www.fordham.edu/halsall/source/courcon1.html.

Medieval Sourcebook: Statutes of Gregory IX for the University of Paris 1231, Internet (14.02.05): http://www.fordham.edu/halsall/source/UParis-stats1231.html.

MythologyGuide: Internet (25.1.05):http://www.online-mythology.com/castor_pollux/

New Advent. Internet (24.03.02): http://www.newadvent.org/cathen/08717c.htm.

Ovid Illustrated: The Renaissance Reception of Ovid in Image and Text, Internet (22.05.05): http://etext.lib.virginia.edu/latin/ovid/notes.html.

Prundenti Carmina, Internet (05.05.04): http://www.thelatinlibrary.com/prud.html.

Appendix

The "Vision of Arms" from 1 Celano 2:5

And so, on a certain night, after Francis had devoted himself with all of his deliberation to accomplish these things and was very much eager, even seething with desire, to make the journey, the One who had struck him with the rod of justice visited him through a nocturnal vision in the sweetness of grace. And because Francis was eager for glory, He exalted and enticed him with the pinnacle of glory. For it seemed to Francis that his whole house was filled with military weaponry: saddles, shields, spears, and other equipment. And though delighting for the most part, he silently wondered to himself what the meaning of this was. For he was not accustomed to see such things in his house, but rather stacks of cloth to be sold. And when he was greatly bewildered at the sudden turn of events, the response was given to him that all these things were to be his and his soldier's weapons. Awakening he rose in the morning at his spirit at first rejoicing, and then reflecting upon his vision as a portend of great success he felt sure that his journey to Apulia would be successful. In fact he did not know what he was saying, and as yet he by no means understood the gift sent to himself from heaven. Nonetheless, he was in a position to judge rightly that his vision was not true, since, despite the fact that the vision contained a reasonable likeness of the things Francis had been doing in preparation for his journey to Apulia, Francis' spirit did not continue to rejoice over the things portended in the vision in the customary manner. In fact, he had to create a certain mental strength in himself to carry on with his plans and to bring to accomplishment the journey to which he aspired. And indeed it is quite honorable that mention was made of weapons in the beginning and very fitting that weapons be handed over to a soldier about to give battle against one strong and fully armed, so that like a second David in the name of the Lord God of Hosts he might free Israel from the long standing abuse by its enemies.